From the corner of her eye, Lenora saw a shadow swoop down on her.

A huge mail-covered hand appeared out of nowhere, yanking her from her horse, and her back hit against a hard wall of metal. Stunned, she found herself breathless and dumped into the lap of an armor-clad knight.

"Let go of me!" She kicked and thrashed her legs, trying to free herself. "Who are you?" She twisted in her captor's grasp and her eyes traveled up to the knight's face.

A wide nosepiece on his helmet obscured his face. Only his eyes were visible. The hard-fought air she had strived for escaped her lungs in a low, desperate sigh. "Nay, it cannot be!" The knight's dark gray eyes glowered at her, and a current of fear whorled through her.

"I've come to settle our bet, Lady Lenora."
Roen de Galliard removed his helmet, tucked it under his arm and shook his head like a mighty golden lion. "Among other things." He wrapped his viselike arm around her waist and pulled her tightly toward him....

D0043491

Dear Reader,

When we ran our first March Madness promotion in 1992, we had no idea that we would get such a wonderful response. Our springtime showcase of brand-new authors has been so successful that we've continued to seek out talented new writers and introduce them into the field of historical romance. During our yearly search, my editors and I have the unique opportunity of reading hundreds of manuscripts from unpublished authors, and we'd like to take this time to thank all of you who have given us the chance to review your work.

In *Warrior's Deception*, Diana Hall's powerful first book, a young woman suddenly finds herself married to a forbidding knight who has been ordered to protect her from the intrigue and danger that threaten her family.

And be sure to keep an eye out for our other three March titles. *Western Rose* by Lynna Banning, the story of a rancher and a schoolteacher who must work out their differences before they accept their love. *Fool's Paradise* by Tori Phillips, the charming tale of a noblewoman and the jester who becomes her protector. And *The Pearl Stallion*, the story of an adventurous voyage by Rae Muir.

Four new talents, four great stories from Harlequin Historicals. Don't miss a single one!

Sincerely,

Tracy Farrell
Senior Editor

Please address questions and book requests to:
Harlequin Reader Service
U.S.: 3010 Walden Ave., P.O. Box 1325, Buffalo, NY 14269
Canadian: P.O. Box 609, Fort Erie, Ont. L2A 5X3

DIANA HALL

Warrior's Deception

Harlequin Books

TORONTO • NEW YORK • LONDON
AMSTERDAM • PARIS • SYDNEY • HAMBURG
STOCKHOLM • ATHENS • TOKYO • MILAN
MADRID • WARSAW • BUDAPEST • AUCKLAND

ISBN 0-373-28909-X

WARRIOR'S DECEPTION

Books by Diana Hall

Harlequin Historicals

Warrior's Deception #309

DIANA HALL

If experience feeds a writer's soul, then I must be stuffed.

I've worked as a pickle packer, a ticket taker at a drive-in movie, a waitress, a bartender, a factory worker, a truck driver cementing oil wells in south Texas, a geological technician with oil companies, a teacher, a part-time ecological travel agent and now an author. The only job I've kept longer than five years is wife and mother.

A geographical accident, I was meant to live in the South. After high school I left rural Ohio and attended college in Mobile, Alabama. There I fell in love with balmy nights and the beaches of the Gulf. I now live in a suburb of Houston, Texas, with my understanding husband, a beautiful daughter, a sedate, overweight collie and a hyperactive dalmatian.

To Rick for all his love and support.
To Jessica for her wonderful character names.
To Debbie, Michele, and Merydith for all their help.
To Jean, Dee, and Margaret for their energy
and belief.

Thanks

Chapter One

ENGLAND—1154

"I shan't go." Lenora's auburn braid whipped from side to side as she clipped each word.

Her aunt's icy blue eyes narrowed and her thin lips drew up into a tight pucker. Her cousin, Beatrice, cowered behind her mother's outraged body.

"You must go." The woman's voice changed from insistent to pleading. "Think of Beatrice. This may be my only chance, *our* only chance, to regain some dignity." She shoved her frightened daughter forward. "The girl's sixteen and well in need of a husband. This is the perfect opportunity to make a suitable match."

Lenora did not miss the terror-filled look that entered Beatrice's warm blue eyes. Her small frame trembled, tears glistened in her eyes.

"'Tis not to be, Aunt Matilda." Her voice carried across the great hall of Woodshadow. Her tone trumpeted defiance and she gave her timid cousin a reassuring smile. No matter the consequences, she would protect her, even against Beatrice's own mother.

The servants stopped in their preparation for the noon meal. Even the hounds paused in their hunt for scraps among the floor rushes.

The older woman's glare encompassed the room. The serfs resumed their duties. Behind her aunt's back, a young boy gave

Lenora an exaggerated wink and clutched his throat in a comic mime. She bit the inside of her cheek to contain her laughter.

"What reason could you possibly have for not going?" Matilda pressed her argument. "King Henry will expect you there. You do not turn down a request from the king." Her shrill voice rang out in an indignant huff.

"My father is too ill for me to be away. I cannot leave the keep now. Woodshadow needs me." How could she tell them her real fear? Her home and security, even those she held most dear, were slipping from her. Beatrice would not be added to that list. After three years away from her home, she had returned to find emptiness.

She felt as if all that she loved and cared for were in a grain bag with a hole in the bottom. The loss became more and more visible, but for some reason, no matter what she tried, she was unable to stop it.

"Excuse me, Aunt Matilda, I want to go to the stable to check on my mare." Lenora disregarded the summoning cry of her aunt and headed for the kitchen. She ducked down the well-worn stairs, two at a time, jumping the final steps to the ground-floor kitchen and storage room. The lad she had seen above tossed her a carrot from the basket he carried.

"Tyrus, you have my thanks and Silver's." She waved the green top of the vegetable at him.

"Give 'er a pat from me, Lady Lenora. Do ye think 'er time is soon?"

Her stride slowed and she puckered her lips into a worried frown. "Nay, 'tis still a month or more, though I wish it were not. She gets weaker by the day."

The servant boy gave his lady a bright smile, a large gap showing where his two front teeth should be. "Ye be a good'n for the healin' and all. That mare'll pull through. Ye done it afore."

Beatrice scurried down the stairs. "Hurry, Lenora, Mother's in a fury. She's out to find you and convince you to go to Tintagel."

Lenora needed no further warning and grabbed her cousin's hand. Rushing past the kitchen scullery maids, she pushed Beatrice out the lower door and into warm spring air.

Laughter came easily as she half dragged her cousin across the stone-walled inner bailey of the castle. She didn't slow down until she passed the fortified bridge and blended into the bustle of the outer bailey.

Numerous puddles and cart tracks muddied the way to the whitewashed stables. Lenora lifted the hem of her dress and tried to navigate between the mud and the busy villeins. A herd of cattle, led by a serf, took control of the lane. She tried to dodge them and ended up ankle-deep in a mud hole. Slime oozed into her leather shoe and coated her toes.

Sounds of children at play and the chatter of their parents floated on the spring air. The dreary days of winter had finally ended and she was home. Every smell and sight gave her delight. Her time with the queen had opened her mind and taught her much but her return to Woodshadow had taught her something, also. She loved this place and these people.

Splattered with mud and grime, she looked back at her cousin and marveled that Beatrice had kept her deep blue kirtle and white apron spotless. The difference between her and her cousin was like comparing a palfrey to a workhorse.

After eighteen years, Lenora accepted the fact that her height and angular features gave her a gawky, coltish appearance. Unlike the famed foals of Woodshadow, she entertained no hopes of her appearance changing as she matured. Thoughts of herself vanished when she entered the cool darkness of the stable.

She balanced herself on the stall gate and laced her feet through the rails for support. Her heart lurched at the sight of the mare standing listless by the grain bin, head low, eyes glazed. Fresh-smelling hay and the odor of well-oiled tack, usually a comfort, did not settle the uneasiness she felt in her heart.

Hopping down, she held out the carrot and tried to entice the mare. "Here, Silver, try just a bite." The horse nibbled her palm and let the treat fall to the ground. Rattled breaths sounded from the mare and echoed in the filtered light of the barn. A desire to cry sprouted in Lenora but the streak of stubbornness inherited from her father prevented it. She would see Silver through this; she wouldn't allow her mount to die.

A light sprinkle of dust coated the mare's rump. Lenora searched through the tack box in the stall for a curry comb. The slow rhythmic sweeps of the brush helped to calm her nerves.

Over Silver's back, she saw Beatrice approach the stall gate. Her cousin halted when the horse tossed her mane in annoyance. Sincerity mixed with the fear in her voice. "How does the animal fare? I know she is dear to you."

"She does not look well, my friend. She's too old to have another foal." A masculine voice came from the shadows of the back wall. The young man, wrapped in a black woolen mantle despite the warm spring day, emerged from the darkness, and Beatrice stepped away.

Lenora held fast to the halter of the startled mare. "Geoffrey, could you give some warning?" She patted the velvet softness of Silver's nose.

He removed his hood, his brown hair curled over walnut-colored eyes. "You knew I was here."

"Aye, but Beatrice and Silver did not," Lenora reprimanded her friend.

Geoffrey placed his hand over his heart and gave a half bow. "Pardon, Lady Lenora. To yourself and your mount." His eyes turned to Beatrice. His voice warmed. "And you, Lady Beatrice, do I need beg your pardon, also?"

Lenora smiled because the scarlet tint of her cousin's cheeks gave away her response. As always, the color enhanced the young woman's fair looks.

Beatrice placed her hand to her throat and whispered her reply. "Nay, Sir Geoffrey. I take no offense. 'Tis glad I am to see your face after these many days." Her eyes lowered and she fidgeted with her hands.

Lenora laughed. "Come now, Beatrice, do not be shy. Did I not hear you moon on and on about Sir Geoffrey's fair face, his prose, his voice?"

"*Lenora,*" Beatrice complained, her face a deeper crimson than before.

With a soft pat on Silver's nose, Lenora pulled herself from the sanctuary of the stall to join her friends. She lowered herself to sit cross-legged on a pillow of hay and watched Geoffrey lean against a pillar. Beatrice sat on a three-legged stool near her. Her cousin held her back straight, her hands folded in her lap.

Lenora's gaze settled on the reed-thin knight. "What do you know of this tourney?" She spread her grass-stained apron and undertunic over her knees. "Why is Matilda so intent on going?"

"'Tis as we feared. King Henry wishes to reward his siege commanders with some festivities. There are a few to whom he owes much gold. In particular, the knight Roen de Galliard." She saw Beatrice stiffen her back even more and begin to fold and unfold the hem of her apron. 'Twas easy to see the girl's nervousness at just the mention of the knight's name.

Lenora took a quick breath. "Gold the king does not have or wish to part with. Henry will pay off his commanders with a rich wife." The knight's reputation had made its way even to Aquitaine. Though she had never seen him, she knew well the type, crude and self-centered. Roen de Galliard did not sound like a man with patience for Beatrice's fears. The knight would devour her gentle cousin and leave behind only a shell of the woman.

Geoffrey gazed at Beatrice's quiet suffering. At last, her cousin spoke, her voice colored with hope. "Rich...then it cannot be me they'll seek. King Henry already owns all my lands. Mother and I are penniless."

"Aye, Cousin, but Father set aside a small manor as your dowry." Lenora did not wish to dash the young woman's hopes but 'twas best to tell the truth. "A knight desperate to have a keep of his own might not be averse to it. Besides, now that Louis is dead, if I do not marry, Woodshadow would be yours."

With inborn grace, Beatrice rose from her seat to kneel at Lenora's side. Her eyes clouded with sadness as she stared past her cousin. Old nightmares showed on her face. "Stephen and Henry's war cost us much. You, your brother, my mother, her husband and wealth. And I, my courage."

"Courage, Beatrice? 'Tis a brave girl you are. You survived the pillage of your home and the death of your father. You meet your true love in secret, unknown to your mother. 'Tis uncommon courage, that alone. Your mother is no small obstacle, despite her size."

"With much help from you," Geoffrey said, chuckling in agreement. He went to Beatrice's side and waited until she placed her fingertips in the palm of his hand before helping her to rise. When she reached her feet, she stepped back and stood apart from him. The struggle between love and fear ravaged her face.

Too many memories of the night her father died kept Beatrice from Geoffrey's arms. From hearing her cousin's nightmares, Lenora knew that the sights and sounds of the carnage and rapes still haunted the young woman's feelings for the young knight. She prayed that her childhood friend Geoffrey would have the patience and understanding to mend Beatrice's tattered emotions.

"Help you?" Lenora arched an eyebrow. "Aye, I suppose I've smuggled in a love poem or two. Guided you through the secret passages and tunnels so that you could meet. Most important, I've kept Aunt Matilda at bay so she'd not know what's going on." She winked at Geoffrey to show her words were meant to tease.

"I wish you could help us now." Dejection rimmed Beatrice's words. Geoffrey carefully placed his arm around her shoulder. She stiffened but did not pull away.

A suggestion came to Lenora. "Geoffrey, you could come forth. Declare yourself to my father and Matilda."

"Your aunt would not appreciate her only daughter considering the attentions of a poor younger son and a Champlain at that." Geoffrey spit out his family name in disgust. "Matilda is seeking wealth and the ear of the throne. She'd not get that with me as a son-in-law. I won't marry Beatrice until I can support her." His voice dropped to a low whisper. "I'm working on a plan. Soon, I'll have enough money and prestige to impress her mother, regardless of my name."

"How?" Lenora noticed the light that came to her friend's face. Perhaps he really did have a workable plan.

Geoffrey flipped his cloak over his arm and held it just below his eyes. "'Tis a secret." Like a night phantom, he drew the cloak away from his face.

Always dreaming, always telling stories to amuse and make them laugh. Geoffrey would never change. Beatrice placed her hand softly on his arm. Devotion to her knight shone in her sparkling azure eyes.

Lenora pursed her lips while she studied the couple and pondered the situation. "'Tis true, Beatrice. Your mother would be ecstatic to regain ties to the throne and restore her wealth. Unfortunately, as Geoffrey said, marriage to him would not accomplish that."

"If only Father had backed Henry instead of Stephen." Beatrice released a wistful sigh.

"So say all the adulterine lords," Lenora answered sagely. "Their lands have been taken at siege and their castles dismantled. 'Twas a bloody end to a bloody time."

"Aye, that is true enough. Stephen's reign was anarchy," Geoffrey concurred with her. "Your father did well to send you these past few years to live in Aquitaine with Henry's Queen Eleanor. With Louis in battle and Woodshadow under attack every few months, I'm sure it eased your father's mind to have you safe."

He gave Beatrice a worried look. "At least your fathers both took a side. My own is nothing but a conniver who played both sides against each other. Henry would have his head if he could find the proof."

"The war has changed us all." Lenora smiled at her cousin. "Queen Eleanor taught me a great deal while I was with her. She's a woman of remarkable power and intelligence."

"Have you decided yet if you will return to the queen?" Geoffrey pressed her for an answer. "Or have you found a nice quiet abbey to continue your studies?" His eyes searched her face. The intensity of the look made her uncomfortable.

She shook her head. "I've made no decision as yet. There is too much here to consume my time. My future will wait until the problems at Woodshadow are solved."

"Of which I am one," Beatrice berated herself.

Geoffrey took her small hand in his own. "I suffer your loss, yet I'm glad you and your mother had to come here. Without that tragedy, I might never have met you, and had my empty life filled with the pure love of your smile." The young knight gazed into Beatrice's sorrowful eyes, and his hand caressed the worry lines from her brow.

"And, of course, Aunt Matilda would never have so apt a student as myself anywhere else," Lenora quipped with sarcasm. The couple laughed, the pensive mood broken.

"'Lenora, a lady of your background should not smell of a stable!'" She mimicked her aunt's voice. "'Lenora, 'tis not proper behavior to disagree with Lord Ranulf on correct agricultural methods.'"

Her cousin joined in the laughter, then grew somber. "Mother can be overbearing at times, but she just wants to repay your father. Since your mother is dead, she feared he wouldn't take us in."

"So teaching her motherless niece to be an acceptable young lady helps to keep her from feeling like she's charity." Lenora scratched her temple. "I'm sorry, Beatrice. I'll try to be more..." A word that would express her emotions politely but spare her delicate cousin's feelings just wouldn't pop into her mouth.

"Nay," Beatrice admonished. "Do not be anything but what you are. If I were as clever as you, I'd be able to avoid Mother's plans for me. My only prayer is that the lands your father set aside for me will not interest a knight."

Though said, Lenora could tell Beatrice gave the prospect little hope.

"Perhaps, if you went with her to Tintagel, you could think of some diversion to keep Beatrice away from any prospective grooms. I will be there, also, and between the both of us we should be able to protect her." Geoffrey paused as a portly servant woman lumbered toward the stable.

"Lady Lenora, Lady Beatrice." The woman waddled into view as Geoffrey ducked behind a haystack. "By the saints!" She stopped in front of the two girls and paused, taking deep gulps of air. Her huge chest rose up and down like a blacksmith's forge. "Lady Matilda sent out the word the two of ye is to go to the great hall straight away."

"Thank you, Alyse. We will be right there." Lenora braced her arm at the doorway and blocked the view to the interior of the stable.

"See that you hurry, Lady Lenora. That woman is on a rampage, giving commands to everyone. She's got poor Sir Hywel running circles to get everything done." The woman mopped her forehead with the edge of her soiled apron. "'Tis too hot for a woman of my size to be running around like a youngster." Alyse turned and plodded back across the bailey to the kitchen, muttering to herself as she fanned her red face.

"I must leave, my love."

Lenora peeked under her arm and saw Geoffrey emerge from his hiding place. He gave Beatrice a chaste kiss on the forehead. "I will see you at Tintagel in a fortnight. With Lenora's help, we will keep your mother from executing her plan."

He winked conspiratorially at Lenora. "You two go on. I'll slip out the back." He lifted a loose board on the back wall and disappeared into the dark alley between the outer castle wall and stable.

"Don't worry, Beatrice. He'll be fine. No one has caught him yet," Lenora reassured her cousin. "'Tis time now to worry about ourselves. I imagine your mother is not in good temper."

Lenora's long legs outdistanced her cousin's much shorter ones. Beatrice had only crossed half of the inner bailey green when she skipped up the steps and threw open the door to enter the great hall. At the carved lion laver, she washed her hands and inhaled the tempting aromas of the noonday meal. Warm, rich smells of roasting meats and fresh baked breads thickened the air and caused her stomach to rumble.

"She's a-lookin' for ye," warned a servant. He bustled past Lenora on his way to prepare the high table for the noonday meal.

"I know," she mouthed back.

Beatrice slid in behind her to escape the attention of several hounds. "Go on now." Lenora waved them off after she patted each massive head. Noses to the floor, the giant beasts sniffed among the new floor rushes searching for scraps. The central fireplace smoldered. Lenora watched the smoky trail rise up the new chimney.

The pantier entered the great hall from the passage leading to the downstairs pantry. His arms filled with crocks of wine, he was followed by her father's steward, Sir Hywel.

The steward looked up and smiled at the two girls. She saw his smile fade and he ducked down a passage leading to the buttery.

"Lenora, where have you been?" a familiar voice shrieked from behind her.

She turned to see her aunt striding toward her. Biting her lower lip, Lenora arranged an innocent look on her face. "Have you been looking for me?"

"Come here, Beatrice." Matilda's jet black eyes darted from one girl to the other. Although petite in size, she propelled her two captives toward a less active area of the great hall. With a firm push, she sat Lenora at one end of a massive carved pew and her daughter at the other. Her eyes traveled up and down her niece's stained clothing and tangled hair.

Her teeth close together, Matilda launched into a lecture. "I must speak to you about this ridiculous notion that you are not attending the king's tourney. Such behavior would not be tolerated at King Stephen's court." The dignified voice became more elitist. "When I was at court, a woman knew her place. She obeyed her elders without question."

Lenora schooled her features to look attentive and copied her cousin's repentant posture.

"Aunt Matilda, thank you so much. You are truly wonderful to show such interest in the day-to-day chores here." Lenora grinned; she had learned quickly that flattery was her aunt's weakness.

"I'm glad you are finally realizing that. Three years with that woman has filled your head with all kinds of nonsense. Imagine, adultery with her own uncle, divorcing the King of France, and scarcely a month passes before Eleanor manages to ensnare Henry II. Why, the man is nine years younger than her." Matilda sniffed her nose in disdain. "Someday you must fulfill your position as Lady of Woodshadow. Your father allows you to shirk your duties. You must begin to oversee the servants, the replacing of the rushes, the soap and candle making. A keep this size must be supervised vigilantly. 'Tis my deep sense of loyalty to your father that forces me to assume the role of Woodshadow's mistress."

"I understand that, Aunt Matilda." Letting her Aunt Matilda relive her glory days as a chatelaine served both Lenora's and her father's interests. The action kept Matilda busy in the keep and unaware of Lenora's actions on behalf of her father. Actions that would earn Lenora several lectures from her aunt on proper decorum and would herald the seriousness of Sir Hywel's illness.

"Good. Enough of this foolishness. You will enjoy yourself, both of you." Matilda tucked an imaginary strand of hair into her wimple. "The king will be at Tintagel for less than a fortnight. He will preside over a tourney and hear grievances from nearby lords. That evening there will be dancing and entertainment."

Lenora released a slow breath of air when her aunt turned her attention away from her. Beatrice became the new target.

"You will wear the lapis necklace your father gave me at our wedding. We must make sure that you are the loveliest young woman there. I'm sure you will catch the eye of a suitable partner." Her aunt began to rattle off a list of elaborate gowns for Beatrice to pack for the coming trip. Meekly, she nodded at each of her mother's suggestions.

Bored with details of gowns and matching slippers, Lenora decided now would be a perfect time to escape. She jumped up from the massive carved pew.

"Wait." Her aunt motioned for her to remain seated. "You can't leave yet, we must also plan your wardrobe. The maids need to be directed as to which gowns you will be taking and—"

"My position hasn't changed." Lenora's calm voice caused her relatives to gasp in surprise. She took leave of her vexed aunt and escaped up the narrow curved stone stair that led to her father's chambers. On purpose, she climbed the stairs two at a time, knowing it would infuriate her aunt.

A step sagged beneath the weight of Lenora's foot. She made a mental note of the slight wood rot in the wooden section of the defense stairs as she sped to her father's third-story chamber. Tomorrow, she must maneuver Sir Hywel to notice the decay. Right now, she wanted to talk with her father.

Without knocking, she barreled into her father's private chambers and announced, "She's at it again." Lenora bounced up onto the red velvet coverlet, tucked her long legs under her and wrinkled her nose.

Her father, Sir Edmund, smiled from his bed, the curtains pulled back to let in the welcomed cool spring air. "So, you're having a spat with your Aunt Matilda, are you? And why are you so determined not to attend the king's festivities at Tintagel? The occasion should be quite merry."

"How do you know that's what the argument was about?"

"You forget about the squints. I keep well informed of what goes on with those to help me." Her father pointed toward the floor. Lenora was just able to make out the small peephole concealed in a knot in the lumber floor. She slid off the bed and peered down through the squint.

The old Norman device enabled her to spy on the activity of the great hall below. She stifled a laugh when she spotted the bald head of her father's seneschal, Sir Hywel, pass below her. Light whispers of his instructions to a passing servant floated upward. The high-pitched voice of her aunt drifted up as she continued to discuss the upcoming trip to Tintagel.

"You, sir, are an unscrupulous spy." Her voice sounded with false indignation. She stood and shook the wrinkles from her tunic and rearranged the simple rope girdle at her waist. "You promised you would remain abed."

"You, daughter, are a mischievous wench who needs her backside warmed for talking to her father in such a manner! It wasn't I who peeked, but Tom." Sir Edmund's smile abated his threat.

"With your direction, I'm sure."

"Of course," he agreed readily.

Laughing, Lenora wished she could transform into a little girl and once more cuddle up next to her tall, strong father. She could listen to his stories of battles and the courtship of her mother over and over again.

Although bedridden for more than a month, Sir Edmund still possessed a commanding figure. His lanky form stretched the length of the six-foot bed. Red gold hair showed no signs of gray. Clean shaven, he reflected the rugged, handsome features of his youth.

"So, tell me what you have accomplished today." Her father punched his silken pillows and snuggled back to rest against them.

"I managed to have Sir Hywel notice that the east bailey wall needs to be fortified, and I saw the smithy as you asked. His proposal to enlarge the blacksmith shed has merit. Oh, and as

I climbed the stairs I noticed there is some rot in the wooden steps."

Sir Edmund knit his fingers together and placed them behind his head. "I'll talk to Sir Hywel about the blacksmith. I'll also mention those damn steps. Those wooden Norman steps are a great defense in case we are invaded, but they are in constant need of repair." He cast her a concerned look. "It's not been easy on you, Lenora. You are my eyes and ears while I'm stuck in here."

"Father, I don't mind. 'Tis rather entertaining to invent ways for your steward to discover things."

"Aye, I can imagine it would. Hywel is a good man. He warned me his father suffered from senility at an early age. He had to be watched for fear he would leave the keep and lose his way. Toward the end, the man didn't even know his own name. I fear our good friend suffers from the same ailment." Her father defended his seneschal. "Sir Hywel is as loyal as a hound and as fierce as a boar. I should replace him, but would do so when I have someone I can trust to take over. For now, I must lay this boon at your feet and trust you to do my steward's thinking for him."

"Aunt Matilda is doing his thinking for him now." Lenora giggled and rotated her index finger around in the air. "She has him running circles downstairs in preparation for the King's tourney."

"Daughter, I believe you should go to this tourney." Her father's voice interrupted her musing.

"Father, I don't want to go. I have too much to do here. Mother's mare, Silver Maple, will foal soon. I need to be here to help. Then there are the new spring herbs to tend. I have several new ones given to me by knights from the Crusades. And of course there's you...." Lenora stopped, bit her tongue, and wished once again she would think before opening her mouth. Her father's eyes blazed liquid gold. Another inherited trait from her father, she recognized this sure sign of anger. She prayed the blast would be short.

"The only thing wrong with me is that I have too many women trying to tell me what to do! A few days without female company will do me good. You women are always seeing disaster. I've a tiny cough, a little weakness in the legs. This will pass if I'm not coddled up like a nursing babe. I'm still lord of this keep, and I can manage quite well with my seneschal. Sir Hywel may not worry about your precious plants but he and I can manage for a fortnight on our own. If 'tis proof you need, I'll be up out of this today." Edmund jerked backed the ermine-trimmed coverlet and twisted his long legs toward the wooden floor.

"Nay!" She rushed to her father's side and replaced the coverlet. "Please, Father, the physicians ordered you to rest."

"And rest I will, but only if you attend the tourney," Sir Edmund countered. "King Henry needs me to fulfill my vassal obligation of counsel. He intends to use the tourney as an opportunity to plan alliances and settle a dispute between Sir Champlain and Sir Ranulf. Since their claims are on land that borders ours, I want to have input into the outcome."

"But, Father," she protested, "surely the king will understand that you are ill. Besides, I could not speak at counsel."

"I do not expect you to. Just keep those quick eyes and ears open and deliver a message to the king on the land dispute. I have a fear that whatever the outcome, the conflict will spill over onto Woodshadow."

"Aunt Matilda would not approve!" Lenora cautioned.

Edmund gave her a wary look. "Then perhaps 'twould be best for you not to mention the letter to her. Just as you neglect to mention those messages your cousin receives from her suitor."

She wagged her finger at her father. "Nothing escapes you. You know everything that goes on in your demesne. Very well, I'm not eager to hear another lecture on how I am not in the reins of propriety. We will keep the true nature of my visit a secret."

"Beatrice will be glad you are going, and I think 'twill do her some good. She can't overcome her fears if she's never given the chance to face them," Edmund reasoned.

Lenora's chin lowered. "She was counting on me to help her escape Matilda's matrimonial plans."

"Do you really think Geoffrey is the man for her?"

She sighed and leaned her head against the canopy bedpost. "I fear he is the *only* man for her. Never have I seen him take the smallest liberty with her. He treats her more like a brother than a suitor. But he is the only man I have ever seen her with that does not drive her to fits of terror. How can Matilda offer her up to the highest bidder knowing how Beatrice feels about men?"

"The girl is Matilda's only asset and daughters are married off to improve or protect the demesne. I blame your attitude toward marriage on myself. I've filled your head with stories of your mother and me. Ours was a love as well as a political union. 'Twould do you well, my daughter, to use this opportunity to search for a husband for yourself." He raised his hand to silence her expected protests. "You have enjoyed your books, gardening and your time galloping wildly around the countryside. Before Louis died, I obliged your wishes, I paid the king's fee so you could remain unmarried. Now you are my only heir, and Woodshadow's future. Rest would come easier if I knew that your inheritance could not be taken from you."

"Beatrice could inherit." She searched for excuses to ease her father's worry and still keep her freedom. "Aunt Matilda has mentioned many times the abbey she and Beatrice stayed at. The enormous library there, the peaceful gardens. I had thought to perhaps spend time—"

"Beatrice is not a Marchavel. I inherited most of these lands from your mother, but they were poor and ill-kept. 'Twas I that built up these properties for my descendants. I have fought with sword and words to keep Woodshadow for my heirs, for you. I do not want all of your mother's and my sacrifices to be handed over for another's prosperity. This was not our dream." Sir Edmund struck his chest with a clenched fist.

Lenora bit her lower lip. She rose from the bed and moved slowly to the window. Her gaze followed the ramblings of a small boy as he chased a multicolored butterfly through new spring grass in the bailey. The steady beat of the blacksmith's bellows blended with the *clip-clop* of a passing draft horse and cart. The soft sound of the grooms sweeping out the stables, the reassuring neighs of her treasured white mares whispered to her. Everyone in the demesne carried on about their business, happy to be outside after the long confining winter.

Lenora thought, *If my brother had not died, I would be out there, reading or tending to Silver, or working on the new herbs.*

Louis would be the one with a duty to provide an heir. She had a duty to her father and to her home.

"I'll go, Father, and deliver your letter. My eyes and ears will be open." Lenora breathed deeply. "And I will consider what you said. But please, Father, let me choose."

Sir Edmund relaxed his tense muscles. He opened his arms, which were quickly filled by his dearly loved only child.

Chapter Two

Roen slammed his fist against the trestle table. The crash of the waves outside the castle added to the thunder of the sound. King Henry had laid a trap for him under the guise of a tourney. His victory at Tintagel became bittersweet.

The young man with his feet propped up against the table scrambled to elude the crimson wine sloshed from the goblets on the table. "Take care, Roen! You'll stain my tunic!" he admonished his friend. "I plan on stunning some young heiress tonight."

"Take care? I am being cheated of my due, Hamlin, and you ask me to take care." Once again his giant fist crashed onto the table. The wine goblet rocked, nearly toppling over. Hamlin dived across the table and successfully righted the containers before the precious liquid stained his finery.

Roen crushed the letter under his friend's nose. "I have fought his wars, defended his castles and captured his robber barons. And this is how he repays me. Henry owes me gold, not a wife!" He stared at the wilted piece of paper. "I curse the day I learned to read."

"Your mother did you a service. The ability to read—"

"My mother never did me service. 'Twas not a kindness she sought, but a mark. A mark to show my father and brothers I did not belong." Roen roared his outrage. "Henry would wish on me a conniving bitch instead of relinquishing the gold he owes me."

"Stars! Roen, he offers you not *a* wife, King Henry offers you *any* wife you want. You can have your pick of beautiful heiress maidens." Hamlin winked at his outraged friend. "Or lusty landed widows. I wish I could be so rewarded, but alas, I am to always be covered by your exceeding large shadow." Hamlin's chestnut eyes took on a resigned expression.

Roen de Galliard raised his clenched hands in the air like the talons of a hawk. Cast a large shadow, indeed he did. Both in size and reputation. At well over six feet, he dwarfed most men in England and in his homeland of Normandy. His reputation as a warrior was well-known throughout King Henry's realm.

"And what good has that shadow done me?" Roen demanded. He didn't wait for his friend to answer. "I'm one of Henry's elite siege commanders. The sound of my name causes any of the adulterine lords to quake in his shoes. And do you know why?"

Hamlin pointed his finger at him and opened his mouth.

Roen didn't give his friend the opportunity to interrupt him. "Because I never give up. They know I'll bide my time. I'll find their weakness, no matter how formidable their stronghold."

How many attacks had he survived? It seemed endless. He always made short work of his enemy. Fast and brutal attacks, over and over again until the besieged lord surrendered or died in battle. Study, calculate, attack. An anthem for battle, his philosophy of life.

Hamlin jumped into his friend's one-sided conversation. "I can think of no other man who needs a wife worse than you!" He held up a hand to check Roen's outburst. "You are happiest when planning and executing a battle. Do you wish to give up such challenge when you are landed?"

"Do not be foolish! Of course not!" Roen thundered.

"Then will you remain landless? Never to be a *senior,* always a landless *juvenis,*" Hamlin countered.

"You know I wish a keep of my own. There will be no inheritance from Normandy, my mother saw to that. You have known me since we were pages. Why ask questions you already know the answers to?"

"To make you see that a wife is the answer to your needs. I see it and the king sees it. You're too stubborn to see the practicality of a wife. Who will oversee the needs of your villeins and keep the servants in line when you are gone on one of your battles for the king? Who will keep an accurate account of spending and entertain your guests while you plan a siege or serve your aid and knight's fee to Henry?'' Hamlin asked the questions, then took a deep gulp of his wine.

Roen pondered his friend's words but refused to concede defeat. Self-justified anger seeped from the pores of his skin.

His second in command pushed the point further. ''A wife will bring you land *and* make sure your castellan does not rob you blind. She is trained to be her husband's helpmate, to take charge when her lord is away on the king's affairs. A wife is the answer to your needs, unless of course you wish to personally oversee the making of candles, the changing of the rushes, the weaving, the—''

''Enough! I see your point. The prospect doesn't thrill me any more than before. Women are nothing more than vessels for tricks and tears to get their way. They're not to be trusted. My own mother . . .'' Roen clamped his jaws tightly. The veins in his neck pulsated with hot blood.

''My friend, I know the way your family has treated you. Through no fault of your own, you have born the brunt of your father's suspicions. But do not mark all women by your mother.''

''I have not seen any who are different.'' Lowering himself to a three-legged chair, he rested his elbows on his knees. The rickety chair groaned in protest at Roen's weight. He raised his wine goblet from the table to his lips. All those years fighting and sacrificing for the chance to own land . . . Whatever Hamlin and the king thought, he knew the truth. He was being cheated.

His too-cheerful friend gave him a broad smile and slapped him on the back. ''And what women have you associated with these past ten years? Camp followers, a lord's cast-off mistress, tavern wenches? We will find you a comely woman tonight with an impressive dowry and sizable inheritance. One who is properly trained to be a lady and servant to her lord husband.''

''We?'' Roen arched his brow as he brought the wine goblet from his mouth.

''I do have an interest in the outcome. As your second in command and boyhood friend, I know that you will always want me near. So I want to make sure that I, um, you get the best possible arrangement.''

"By the blessed saints!" Roen finished off his wine in one huge gulp. "How do you always end up missing the manure pile, my friend? I am to be stuck with a wife and the duties of a lord, while you enjoy a home, your freedom, and serve only light duty."

A sly smile played across Hamlin's face. "I resent that. 'Tis extremely hard work being your friend. See how diligently I have had to work to show you the king's wisdom? Light duty, indeed. Come, Roen, 'tis time to…evaluate…your choices for a bride."

Roen followed his friend reluctantly from the chamber down the narrow steps to the great hall of Tintagel. The sound of the crashing ocean waves synchronized with the throb in his head. He did not relish the idea of sharing a trencher with a lady or the necessary polite conversation he would have to make with prospective brides to "evaluate" their identity and wealth.

An ember of hope began to flame in his chest. "Henry cannot force a woman to marry."

"But what lord would deny the king's request. Especially those who did not openly defend Henry against Stephen. The king's vassals are all eager to prove their loyalty to him now that he has the throne. Do not worry, Roen. Anyone you pick will surely agree," Hamlin reassured his friend.

"Very well." He sighed deeply. "I will attend this function with an open mind. But remember, Hamlin, I want obedience in a wife. I will not suffer as my father did." Closing the door, he took a deep, cleansing breath as he always did before engaging in a battle, and headed toward the enemy—the single women of King Henry's realm.

Lenora slipped through the rough planks of the stall gate. The magnificent animal inside tossed his head to warn her off. She paid no attention to the gesture; she had itched to examine the horse since reaching Tintagel late yesterday.

"Easy, I'll not harm you." She crooned while the ivory-colored war-horse stomped his hooves. Convinced she could win the steed's trust, she reached out and placed her fingertips on the velvety nose. The stallion didn't nip or bite so she drew closer. On tiptoe, she brushed aside the mane and scratched the horse's ears.

"Not one flaw," Lenora marveled. "'Tis a model you are for every knight's destrier." A toss of the horse's white blond mane signaled agreement. "I have some mares at home I would love to breed with you. 'Twould be a handsome sum I could call for those foals."

"Lenora, are you in here?"

She turned to see her cousin enter the shaded stable. After the bright light of the noonday sun, it took a moment for Beatrice to spy her in the stall. Her cousin's face drew up in mock surprise. "The stable is the last place I would think to look for you."

Lenora squeezed through the slats of wood and the hem of her dress snagged on a splinter. The gown tugged her back and she reached to yank it free.

"That is your best kirtle." Beatrice threw up her arms in annoyance. "Mother will have your hide if you show up at the meal with another ripped hem." Her patient fingers extricated the cloth from the jagged piece of wood.

"See. No damage." Lenora pushed the edge of her dress under the younger woman's nose. "Your mother will have nothing to complain of, though 'tis little reason she needs to complain."

"She needs not little reasons when you are so adept at providing big ones." Her cousin shook her head and her blond curls bobbed.

Lenora drew a piece of straw from the fresh bale and chewed on the end. After a moment of reflective munching, she announced the result of her contemplation. "Life is not fair, Beatrice. I work long hours to train and plan the breeding of Woodshadow horses, yet I cannot take credit for my work."

Her cousin gave her a sympathetic nod. "'Twould be a surprise indeed for all the mighty lords who clamor for a Woodshadow mount to discover their perfect animal was bred and trained by a woman."

"Aye, but I do not fear that day will ever come. Nor is it likely those men will discover 'twas I that divided our fields into threes and planted the fallow field with grain. 'Twill not happen because no man would believe it. Every success is attributed to my father. 'Tis not fair."

No offer of solution came from the petite young woman. "'Tis a woman's lot, cousin. There is naught we can do." Beatrice shrugged her shoulders.

"The queen would not say so."

"The queen has land to back her up and a husband who awaits us now," her cousin reasoned.

"Aye, yet I will seek out the owner of this destrier. Perhaps, in Father's name, I can contract his loan as a stud. The horse will suffer none for it." She gave the animal one last perusal. "Come, we must find Geoffrey and lay out a plan."

The idea caused Beatrice's eyes to sparkle. Lenora surveyed the deep azure tunic and kirtle that matched the wide blue eyes. A delicate gold-link girdle accentuated her cousin's tiny waist. "He's sure to fall in love with you all over again."

"Enough to speak to my mother and your father?" She lowered her head and spoke in a tight voice. "I don't care if I'm a lady of a great castle. All I want is to be safe."

The statement made Lenora uneasy. Too often when her cousin spoke of her feelings for her suitor she expressed them in terms of safety instead of love. But she had informed Geoffrey of the deep-seated fears the girl suffered. He accepted them as part of loving Beatrice.

She started to speak but a page barreled past her. He ran to the war-horse's stall and began to scoop grain into the empty food bag. "Boy, to whom does this animal belong?"

"Why, milady? Is he ill?" The boy's voice cracked with worry. "I forgot to feed him this morn but rushed here as soon as I remembered. The knight will beat me sure if he finds I've not taken good care of him."

"Nay, he is fine."

The lad gave her a doubtful look.

"Believe me, I know the beasts. He is none the worse for a late meal, though do not make a habit of it," Lenora reassured the page.

His eyes showed the first signs of tears and his young body trembled. A flare of hot temper blazed through her. What knight would so threaten the lad? He could only be eight or nine.

"Are you sure, my lady? Sir Roen de Galliard is not a knight I wish to cross." The boy looked hopeful. "I think I will check on the animal myself.'' He ducked into the stall and began to inspect the horse.

Lenora shook her head in disapproval. So the great warrior scared children as well as barons. The code of chivalry demanded a knight protect women and children, not frighten innocent boys. In her eyes, Galliard fell far short of that code.

''Lenora?'' Beatrice's voice intruded into her thoughts. ''What will we do about him?'' Her cousin dropped her shoulders in defeat.

''You're not to worry about Galliard. Geoffrey and I will think of a way to keep you from him.'' She gave her cousin a confident wink. ''Come, we need to return to the hall for the midday meal.''

During the short trip back, Lenora racked her brains for some plan to help her cousin. She entered Tintagel's great hall and joined the assembly of people. Entertainers, nobility and servants wove through the hall. Voices chattered and dogs barked. The melodic sounds of the musicians could barely be heard above the din.

Beatrice poked her in the back. ''There's Mother.''

Across the hall, Matilda maneuvered between the gaily dressed aristocrats. The elder woman's gaze swept from side to side, searching. Lenora pulled her cousin back. A hand settled on her shoulder, and Geoffrey squeezed his body between two heavy-set warriors.

''Come with me.'' He motioned toward the wall. The noise in the hall drowned out most of his words. Lenora followed with Beatrice in tow. He led them to an indentation in the thick castle wall. An arched window allowed in midday light.

''We must plan.'' Geoffrey's sienna gaze darted about the room. ''Our fears are more than warranted. The rumor is the king intends to repay Galliard with a wife.''

Beatrice's back stiffened, color drained from her face. Her voice wooden, she stated, ''If you know this, my mother is sure to, also.''

''Aye,'' Lenora theorized, ''but from what I hear, Galliard strikes me as a man who would want more than Father has set aside for you. Pray the man is as greedy as I believe him to be.''

"Can we take that risk?" Geoffrey held up a hand to silence her protest. His voice sounded bleak. "There is always the chance Galliard could be turned by Beatrice's face."

Lenora crossed her arms and began to pace back and forth in the small area. Three steps forward, a sharp pivot and then three steps back. The answer came to her on the fourth trip.

"We must make sure he does not see her." She pointed her finger at the young couple. "There is naught we can do till after the meal. When the trenchers are cleared for the poor, that will be the time Matilda will try to introduce Beatrice to Galliard. Geoffrey, you must see that your lady removes herself from the hall." Lenora squeezed her alarmed cousin. "The gardens will be populated but do not strike me as a site where Galliard is likely to spend time."

"What of Matilda?" There was a critical tone to Geoffrey's voice.

"Ah, my dear aunt." She snapped her fingers. "Lady Marguerite is here. Matilda will jump at the chance to be introduced to one of Queen Eleanor's ladies-in-waiting."

"Will that delay her long enough for me to spirit Beatrice away?"

"Lady Marguerite was one of the castle's biggest gossips. I trust she has not changed. She will hold my aunt's interest."

Geoffrey patted Beatrice's hand and gave her a wink. "Do not worry, my love. We need only hide you till Galliard chooses a bride. He is sure to arrange a betrothal soon."

And I will hasten that along, Lenora vowed to herself. *Before this night is over, Galliard will be betrothed to some unlucky girl.* A trumpet blast intruded into her promise.

"The meal begins. When the trenchers are distributed to the poor, look for me." The young man blended into the crowd.

"Always I am looking for you two. Have you no thought to proper etiquette?" Matilda swooped down on the girls from behind.

Lenora smothered a groan and turned to face her aunt. Her hand moved in a tiny sign of the cross in hopes her aunt had not seen Geoffrey speaking with them.

"Aunt Matilda, we were just..." She hesitated and explored the recesses of her brain for a believable excuse.

"I don't have time for your stories now. Come, I have us seated at the far table." Matilda gripped her daughter's hand firmly. "Lenora, your father's friend requested you to sit with him. Lord Ranulf is on *this* side of the hall." Beatrice gave Lenora a helpless look while Matilda dragged her to the opposite side of the room.

Lenora scooted to her seat just as the royal party entered. She dutifully rose with the rest of the hall, lowered her eyes and folded her hands. The crackle of paper in her pocket reminded her of the letter she had been entrusted to deliver.

As she curtsied, Lenora ventured a peek at England's sovereign. She met Henry's curious eyes, alight with good humor. He gave her an impish wink when he passed. The cleric at the king's side cleared his throat and pretended not to notice the lack of decorum. She returned the devilish wink. Servants directly behind the party almost tripped with their heavy loads. Henry's laugh boomed out across the great hall. He took his seat at the raised table and commanded, "Food and drink."

Great platters of artfully displayed food were presented to the guests. Four men strained to support pallets with two golden brown suckling pigs. The glistening skins made Lenora's mouth water. Two porters carried a mountain of sweet cakes and honeyed nuts. They managed to genuflect before the king with their delicious load. Servants ladled bite-sized pieces of meat into the guests' trenchers. Bells tinkled from the juggler's hat. A minstrel rehearsed a ballad while he strummed a lyre.

Seated at her right, Lord Ranulf stabbed a piece of spiced meat from the trencher and offered it to her. "How is your father? When you were delayed, I feared 'twas due to my old comrade's health."

"He's much better, thank you, Lord Ranulf." She chewed the tender morsel. One of the many pages scampered over to fill the agate wine cup. The tip of his tongue showed while he poured the red liquid into the heavy cup.

Lord Ranulf waited with patience for the lad to finish his task. "I suppose 'twas the heavy rains that delayed you. 'Tis a shame you missed what competition there was. The rains canceled much of the tourney, also."

"The roads were nearly impassable, but my aunt was determined to come." She watched the page and felt the lad's nervousness.

With trained grace, the page returned the goblet without a spot on the white linen tablecloth. He let out a loud sigh of relief. She gave the boy an understanding smile. 'Twas not easy to be at everyone's beck and call. An opportunity to gain information on her adversary came to her. "I have heard that much of what victories there were belong to Sir Roen de Galliard. Is he here?" She flashed the elderly knight a brilliant smile.

"I'm sure he is." The gray-haired man scanned the crowd, then smiled. "The knight approaches Henry now. He's a hard man to miss."

She turned toward the high table and knew instantly who Lord Ranulf spoke of. Roen de Galliard towered over the king and the rest of the men in the room. The modest cut of his tunic did nothing to hide the man's brutal strength and power. Lenora wondered at the aura of self-assurance the man radiated.

Broad shoulders filled the back of the chair he sat in while he conversed with the king. Worn long and in the old Saxon style, his mane of hair flowed to just past his shoulders. The flaxen hair hid much of the man's face.

She concentrated on deciphering what she could from his half-hidden features. His sharp profile showed rugged lines and dark color. Battle scars, white with age, gave him a fierce look but did not mar him in disfigurement. No emotion humanized his face. Like a marble statue, he sat on the dais. He seemed to dismiss the crowd of people with a bored disregard, as though they were not important enough to consider.

A sudden movement and he turned to face her intruding gaze. Eyes the color of thunderclouds pierced her own. Humiliated, Lenora broke contact, not sure if he had truly seen her or if her guilt made her self-conscious. Unwelcomed warmth burned her cheeks.

"Lady Lenora?" Lord Ranulf wrinkled his brow in concern. "You look ill."

"Nay, I am fine." A quick gulp of wine calmed her. She prodded the man to speak to give her a chance to recover from her embarrassment. "Pray, tell me of your daughter. I have not seen her here."

"Expecting again. The girl has given me three strapping grandsons. I think this time she and her husband wish for a daughter to spoil."

The gregarious elder recited story after story of his eldest grandson's strengths and wits throughout the meal. She nodded at the right moments and made the correct oohs and aahs but listened only halfheartedly. Every long tale gave her the opportunity to reconstruct her composure.

Fortified at last, Lenora hid behind heavy lidded eyes and spied on the dais table. The king sat with his advisers and the Lord of Tintagel, but the knight had disappeared. She probed the hall for his whereabouts and spotted him with no trouble. He stood near the back of the hall with a dark-haired man. At first she thought 'twas Geoffrey he spoke to, but the smaller man carried himself differently, his stance more lighthearted than her friend's serious one.

Lord Ranulf's tales continued to roll from his tongue. The abundance of wine the man had drunk probably explained his exceptionally good memory. A horn blasted from the balcony above. At last, the end of the meal; time to break away from her talkative companion. "Lord Ranulf, thank you so much for the delightful entertainment. You must come and see us soon."

"Oh, aye, I will." The man reached for the wine cup and slurped the last few drops. "But let me finish my story. Charles, that's the oldest boy, he grabbed the horse's tail and—"

Lenora shot to her feet; friendship could demand only so much. "As much as I would love to hear the tale of the tail, I must speak to King Henry. Father wishes me to extend his sorrow at not being able to attend."

"Of course, of course. I will see you later and finish the story. That boy is a rascal." Lord Ranulf raised his hand in salute and turned to the man seated across the table from him. "Darius, my friend. Come let us share a cup of wine. Have you heard of the prank my grandson pulled?"

Lenora whistled under her breath at her escape and took off to scan for her relatives. Luck came her way; they stood not far from her. A woman in a garish blob of color flittered near them. Lady Marguerite. Thank heaven for such a stroke of luck.

Rushing to her aunt's side, she whipped her arm through Matilda's and swung her around. "Aunt Matilda, may I introduce you to one of Queen Eleanor's favorite ladies-in-waiting. Lady Marguerite, this is my aunt, Lady Matilda."

With a slingshot motion, she propelled her aunt forward and pushed the two ladies together. "I know you have much to discuss. Lady Matilda was at Stephen's court, you know."

The two dowagers sized each other up. Curiosity won. Each dropped a snippet of gossip, then their heads drew together and the real news began. Her plan was working.

She backed away with Beatrice behind her. After she cleared the eagle eyes of Matilda, a giggle burst from her lips. "Step one, accomplished. Hurry and find Geoffrey. I'll take care of Galliard."

For the first time all day, her cousin's face glowed with hope. "Perhaps this will work."

"You had doubts?"

"Your plans don't always work. Remember when you tried to—"

"Don't think failure, think victory." A gentle push toward the window displayed her urgency. "Now hurry off. Stay in the garden as long as you can and watch for your mother."

Beatrice merged with the crowd and met Geoffrey near the window. He leaned to whisper in her cousin's ear, his brown curls merging with the blond ones.

"Step two, taken care of." The blond giant of a knight came into view and she slapped her thighs. The crunch of paper reminded her of another mission. She struck her forehead with the palm of her hand. "I've got to deliver Father's letter."

King Henry rose from the high table when she scurried to his side. Breathless, she pulled the wrinkled sealed missive from her pocket. "Your Majesty, my father wishes me to extend his regrets at not being able to fulfill his obligation of counsel due to his health. He hopes this will aid you in your decision on the property dispute between Sir Ranulf and Sir Champlain."

" 'Tis with sorrow I heard of my hunting companion's malaise. He will improve, I'm sure," Henry stated good-naturedly. "We've planned a hunting adventure this spring. I want to try out my new falcon against your father's Swiftkill." Henry's bright eyes shone with warmth.

He opened the letter and browsed its contents. The king's brows knit together. "When did your father give you this?"

"Shortly after your invitation reached us."

"Did anyone else see this message or know you were to deliver it to me?"

"Nay, Your Majesty. We, uh, Father felt 'twould be less of a commotion if my aunt knew nothing of it. Is something wrong?" Lenora queried.

"Your father has given me something to ponder. Don't worry, dear, nothing to concern yourself with. Go, enjoy the entertainment." He brushed her off and retreated from the room, the letter still in his beefy hands.

Step three, accomplished.

Now for Galliard. She surveyed the crowd for the knight. Young girls in brilliant gowns glided about, casting flirtatious glances at wealthy lords. Laughter boomed from a group of war-hardened knights as they recounted old battles. Lenora took a deep breath and began her search for Roen de Galliard, not quite certain of her battle plan but determined to protect her cousin's happiness.

Chapter Three

"Hamlin, take your pick. They are all the same to me." Roen turned his back on the assembly of possible brides. "Only make sure you choose one with a prosperous demesne and a proper attitude."

"How am I to know that? 'Tis battle we've spent our time in, not tallying up what riches belong to what lord," Hamlin replied, irritated. "I'm afraid this is going to be more difficult than I thought." He stroked his chin while Roen gave him a cynical smile.

The great hall of Tintagel blossomed with the beauty of English ladies. Overadorned children, displayed like trinkets by their mothers, danced by him. The sight nauseated him. Roen would rather have his fee paid in gold, but the chance to own land compelled him. A lord with no other feudal obligation except to the king was a prize few obtained. However distasteful, marriage enabled him to become landed.

"I suppose we could ask someone," Hamlin ventured.

"If a decent heiress is in the room, a man with good sense would not proclaim it to us but use the information to better his own lot," Roen said, rebuffing his friend. The two men simultaneously dropped down onto a half-log bench.

"I'm better prepared for battle than I am to search for you a wife. I say let's just look for a pretty one," Hamlin suggested with a shrug.

"Perhaps I can help you with this dilemma." A feminine voice intruded on their conversation.

Roen did not stand but turned his head to view the speaker. His tone sarcastic, he asked, "In what way could you be of any help to me?'' He purposely conveyed his contempt and gave the wench a look meant to dissolve her audacity.

She almost turned away, but didn't. Her eyes changed to a shade of brown that tantalized him. They reminded him of something familiar, yet it eluded him. His inability to stamp a name on their color needled him. It did nothing to improve his impression of her.

The woman did not lower her eyes from his scrutiny. He saw her back pull up straighter. The pointed chin tilted up like a defiant child. Her eyes blazed, her voice strained to rein in her anger. ''I know most, if not all, of the women present and the worth of their landholdings. I'll give you information on any women you choose.''

Roen snorted with indignation. ''I should trust you? How do I know you won't lie to further your own cause?''

''How would being untruthful aid me in acquiring your warhorse?'' The woman scrunched her brows together, perplexed.

''You want Destrier!'' Roen felt an almost uncontrollable urge to shake the wench senseless. ''No woman is worth that horse.''

''Destrier? You named that magnificent animal Destrier? I suppose your dog is called Dog.'' The woman's voice held back none of her scorn.

Roen opened his mouth to speak, but the truth of her words muted him. What did it matter what he called his hound?

''I don't want to keep the animal, just use him for stud service on some of my father's mares at Woodshadow.''

At the mention of the keep, Roen's interest peaked. ''Woodshadow, you say. Does not the king have a palfrey from your stable?''

''Aye, that he does, a gift from my father.'' Pride marked her words. ''A steed from Woodshadow is much desired. Your mount, Destrier—'' the woman rolled her eyes ''—would be no worse from the wear.''

''Perhaps she could help us at that,'' Hamlin noted.

Not willing to concede yet, Roen sneered. ''An idiot could tell that Destrier is an unsurpassable mount. That she recognizes the fact hardly merits us trusting her judgment. How do we know she doesn't wish to marry me herself?''

The words were no sooner uttered than Roen knew exactly what her eyes reminded him of—molten gold. He had seen a man in the Holy Lands melt down the precious metal to form items for the church. The woman's eyes reminded him of hot gold, rich in color, scalding in temperature. Her eyes seared his with their intensity.

"I can think of no greater purgatory than to be your wife. For a number of reasons, most of them dealing with you." She blasted out her words in a fiery voice. Nearby, heads turned toward them. The woman lowered her voice and gritted her teeth. She turned from him to face Hamlin, who looked both shocked and amused.

"Pray, knight, you seem to have a sensible nature," she began placatingly. "Kindly tell your friend that not all women seek the confinement of marriage. Some wish time to study and learn. I am one such woman. Marriage is not what I seek for myself." She smiled, and the embers of anger in her eyes began to fade. "Besides, I'll be honest." Her smile twisted into a mischievous grin. "I am cursed with three faults which make marriage not an option for me."

Cursed! Her smile kindled a twinge of arousal but he quickly doused it. She seemed too intelligent to believe in superstition. Roen started to terminate the conversation with her but her eyes held him. They no longer burned, but had mellowed to the shade of warm cider. A half-hidden smile twitched at her full lips. She dared to tease him!

"Only three? You do yourself service, woman." Roen arched his brow cynically.

The smile became more animated. "Aye, only three, but as far as men are concerned, major ones. The first is plain to see, I am no beauty."

His gaze raked down the length of her body. She stood almost to his shoulder, and he savored the length of time it took to explore her body. With caged patience, she waited while he noted her generous mouth and elflike chin. He let his gaze linger on the mature breasts. The unpretentious gown hugged at the gentle swell of her hips. Dark braids hung between the valley of her breasts. Wisps of curls escaped the confines of the butter-colored ribbons of her plaits.

Roen studied the wavy mass of hair. At first it appeared dark brown, but as the sunlight filtered through the window, it highlighted the copper tresses. He smiled despite himself when, once more, the maverick lock of hair escaped from behind her ear and she replaced it yet again.

Aye, no English beauty: she was too dark and her features too irregular. Yet, she intrigued him, especially her eyes. Never had he seen eyes the color of gold, or ones that expressed so much of the person's inner self. Now those eyes stayed on him. Surprised, Roen realized she was evaluating him.

Humph! Roen admitted to himself. *The chit has backbone. A mere look does not send her off in tears.* Finally, when he saw she would stand her ground, he answered, "I concede, and the other faults?"

The wench relaxed: he could see the tension leave her body. A grudging look of admiration tinted her eyes. "I'm afraid you've already had a taste of the other two. I'm exceptionally intelligent, and not afraid to let others know it. Lastly, I have a bit of a temper." She held her fingers apart slightly to demonstrate how small a "bit."

Hamlin bubbled with laughter, while Roen quirked his mouth into a reluctant smile. "I can readily see how those three particular faults might make it hard to find a husband, Lady..." Hamlin paused. "You know our names but yours remains a mystery."

"I am Lenora de Marchavel of Woodshadow. My father is Sir Edmund. Now, do we have a bargain?"

Roen racked his memory for information on Sir Edmund. The king spoke of him often and considered the man a loyal friend. From what he had heard, the girl's father was a man of honor and integrity. Would the same hold true for the daughter? Still reluctant to enter an agreement with a woman, Roen assessed his alternatives.

"You drive a hard bargain." Lenora's eyes gleamed. "I will give you the choice of one foal your animal sires. The foal will be worth a hefty bag of gold, not to mention the prestige of owning a Woodshadow mount."

"Agreed. You will tell me truthfully of any woman I choose. In return, Destrier is yours for a month." Roen knew he had the better deal, yet Lenora's eyes troubled him. Instead of defeat, her warm spice-colored eyes shone with victory. Roen nodded toward the ladies milling about in the great chamber. "Pick one and tell me what you can."

"Roen, there is no use wasting Lady Lenora's time on all of these women." Hamlin gave Lenora a crooked smile and pointed toward the crowd. "How about that one in the yellow gown? The one seated at the feet of the rather large dowager."

"Lady Daphne. She is two years my junior. Her father is Sir George Champlain. He lays claim to much land, though 'tis spread widely and difficult to oversee."

"The condition of her inheritance?" Roen asked impatiently. He barely registered the presence of the flaxen-haired young girl.

"Well, she stands to inherit a sizable fief on the birth of her first child. In fact, that property is the major income for Sir Champlain." Lenora bit her upper lip, the edges of her mouth upturned in an engaging grin.

Roen eyed his informant carefully. A faint light danced through her eyes. She held something back. "The rest," he demanded.

An impish smile slid across her lips. "The only thing I could add is the fact that she is thrice widowed."

"Three husbands!" Hamlin jumped up and peered at the innocent-looking beauty across the room. Daphne, her eyes downcast, continued to listen to the never-ending complaints of the older woman. "What happened to them?" Hamlin asked in a hushed voice.

"The usual—hunting accident, illness, thrown from a horse—things like that," Lenora replied matter-of-factly.

"Why so many husbands lost to accidents?" Roen queried. He noted the intelligent sparkle in Lenora's eyes. A ripple of admiration intrigued him, but he brushed the emotion aside.

" 'Tis no secret, Daphne's father does not wish to part with her dowry land. By allowing his daughter to marry but not to conceive, he keeps control of his best property and gains from Daphne's inheritance as a widow."

Roen slammed his fist into the palm of his hand. "He should be hanged. Why have you not taken this matter before King Henry?"

"Because I have no evidence. Though I nursed the poor girl through two miscarriages, I've no proof her father caused them or the demise of her husbands. A village woman who came to me to speak of the tea Sir Champlain forced upon his daughter prior to her miscarriages died on her return home. Daphne knows what her father and brothers are capable of, as do I. She would never live to testify against them."

Lenora drew back and leaned against the cold stone wall. Misery dulled the glow in her eyes and face. "Someday that man will pay for the way he treats his daughter."

Brittle agate eyes displayed anger, sadness and fear. Roen knew Lenora did not lack spirit, for few men stood up to him as she had. Lord Champlain must be a monster to cause her such dread.

"Your counsel is well taken, go on to the next." Roen waved his hand dismissively toward the great hall. For the next hour he listened to Lenora recite all she knew on each woman Hamlin pointed out. She informed them of gambling debts, land disputes, how complex their obligations to area lords and the disposition of each woman. Roen sat on the pew with his long powerful legs stretched out, ankles crossed, disinterested. If he bothered to ask a question, it dealt with the woman's holdings or family reputation. Finally, he rose, his frustration and disdain erupting.

"I have had enough. Every woman here has either a poor dowry, a plain face or some other shortcoming." Roen paced in front of his two confidants. He stopped and turned to face Lenora. "Are there no women here capable of meeting the most basic of standards?"

"What do you expect?" Lenora could hold her anger no longer. "You look over a possible wife with the same enthusiasm as purchasing a...a cow for pasture. Do you feel that you are so great a prize? Think what the woman gets in return from a marriage to you. Nothing, since you bring no land and she becomes the brood mare for an overbearing oaf. A dullard who can't even think up a proper name for his own horse." Lenora took a breath, ready to continue her tirade.

"Who is that?" Hamlin interrupted the tongue-lashing and pointed to the opposite side of the room. Lenora swiveled, looked at the young woman Hamlin pointed at and groaned.

She swallowed hard and cursed Beatrice's timing. Why couldn't she have remained hidden for just a while longer? By Hamlin's dropped jaw, she could tell Beatrice had made an impression, the wrong impression. Lenora stepped back and stumbled into the wall-like chest of Roen de Galliard. His strong arms wrapped around her and pulled her tight against him.

"Steady, Lady Lenora," Roen whispered in her ear. His breath caused gooseflesh to race down her neck. She closed her eyes to regain her composure. Instead, it fortified the sounds and sensations about her. She heard the pounding of his heart, felt the rise and fall of each breath he took. Suddenly, the sensations stopped. Roen released her as if she were a cocklebur bush. He stepped away from her and moved toward Hamlin. The siege commander took a deep breath and surveyed the room. His eyes settled on her cousin. Lenora knew his thoughts, what size dowry did Beatrice possess and would she act the docile servant of her husband.

"Who is she?" Hamlin did not drag his gaze away from Beatrice. Lenora hesitated. When she did not answer, Hamlin looked over his shoulder, misery evident on his boyish face. "She's married to someone already, isn't she. A beauty like that could not remain unclaimed for long." He sighed and shook his head sadly. His ashen locks swayed with the movement.

"Tell him," Roen ordered.

Lenora thought fast. If she told them Beatrice was married it might work for a time, but Aunt Matilda would find a way to introduce Beatrice to Roen and eventually her lie would be discovered. The greedy lout might marry her cousin just to get even with her; he was mean enough. The knight had more pride in himself than any man she had ever met. Pride! The answer to her problem unfolded. She could save Beatrice.

Lenora straightened up to her full height and crossed her arms. She looked the knight in the eyes and stated, "That is my cousin, Beatrice de Greyere. She is unmarried, but unavailable."

"Why is that?"

"Because she is in love with someone."

Roen stared at her, incredulous. "And why should that deter me? Women are always falling in and out of love. It means nothing as long as she has an acceptable dowry and is obedient to her vows." He laughed like a satyr and turned to his friend. "Come, we will introduce ourselves to this beauty that has so bewitched you." Roen pretended to close Hamlin's gaping mouth and lead him toward Beatrice.

"Very well, then." Lenora took one more chance, a dangerous one, but calculated to prey on the man's overbearing pride. "I'll introduce you, but you do not strike me as the type of man who could make love to his wife knowing she wished he were someone else."

The sound of his quick intake of breath warned her to brace herself for the storm of his anger. She contemplated running, but where could she go that he could not find her? Roen advanced, his square jaw clenched, neck veins visible. His huge hands were balled up into fists at his sides. Lenora had a momentary vision of those two clubs pummeling the life from her body. She steeled herself to meet his gaze. His eyes were no longer the color of thunderclouds. Now they reminded her of a full-blown gale, one that would wreak havoc for days.

"By God's Wounds, woman, you go too far," Roen snarled. "Do you doubt I can command obedience from my wife? I will not tolerate a whore for a wife."

"I've no doubt you would try to command your wife's very thoughts. You can use those powerful hands to control a body, but not a mind, and never a heart." Lenora stood firm, anger overruling her fear as usual.

"Sir Roen," the young page from the stable interrupted. He smiled at Lenora and handed Roen a message. He turned with a smart bow to the lady and started to leave.

"Hold, boy." Roen's voice stopped the page in a dead halt. "When you deliver a message, you wait on a reply." His gaze dropped from Lenora and spotted the insignia of King Henry scrawled across the bottom of the missive. Damn! He would have to attend to the business of royalty before the woman's punishment. Lenora's jabs had hit close to home. His father's attempt to control his mother's heart with fists and cruel punishments had been to no avail. His mother still had betrayed him and left Roen to suffer the painful taunts of his brothers and the mental and physical blows of his father. How many times had his father told him not to trust the heart of a woman?

No woman would ever hurt him again, least of all a mouthy shrew.

"This is not over." Roen glanced up from the message, but the woman had vanished. There were many dark recesses and support beams in the great hall, too many places that could cast shadows even in daylight. He could not keep Henry waiting. Cursing under his breath, he barked at the page, "Where is the king?" Roen did not wait on a reply but marched ahead. The boy scurried to catch up with the knight's long strides. Hamlin followed behind, craning his neck to watch Beatrice.

When she saw the two men leave, Lenora stepped out of the shadows, shaking her head in disbelief. What a bore, an unimaginative mass of brutality. No matter what the cost, she would not let this brute have gentle Beatrice. He would have her cowering in some corner at his first angry glare. Lenora picked up the edge of her gown and raced across the hall to her cousin. Beatrice must be warned; they must leave immediately. For Beatrice's sake and, as she thought of the knight's fury, her own.

Roen climbed the stairs to the king's bedchamber and wondered why the need for such privacy. In the close confines of the castle, the king's chamber was the most secure place. After instructing his second in command to patrol outside the room, he entered and greeted his king.

"Your Majesty." He approached the red-haired man seated near a table. Henry stood and grasped his extended hand in a bone-crushing handshake. Not as tall as Roen, the king was still an impressive man. His love of hunting and riding kept him trim and washed his freckled face with healthy color. Faint laugh lines creased his mouth and eyes.

"Roen, my dear friend, so how goes the hunt?" The king gave him a wicked grin. Roen knew to which "hunt" the king referred. Henry had followed the same hunt several times. With his wife, Eleanor, living in Aquitaine, the king consoled his loss with several mistresses, the Lady Rosmund in particular. Roen wondered how wise it was of Henry to parade his lovers at court so openly. Queen Eleanor was a shrewd and jealous woman. Henry could not afford an arranged annulment and lose his wife's overseas holdings.

"I prefer to speak of more pleasant subjects," Roen answered dryly. There was more on the king's mind than just teasing him.

Henry crossed to the table and retrieved a letter. "Read this. Tell me what you think." The king sat down, arms folded across his barrellike chest.

Roen browsed through the letter to the king. The sender stated his opinion on a nearby land dispute. Odd choices of words made the letter somewhat convoluted but the gist could be easily understood. He stroked his chin and looked at the missive again. From the corner of his eye, he spied King Henry watching him for a reaction. There must be something he had missed. He restudied the letter.

"'Tis in code!" A familiar pattern emerged from the confusing phrases. "We used this code during the war with Stephen!"

King Henry nodded and reached for the paper. "It took me some time to discover it. If I did not know the sender so well, I might have missed it. He has purposely mentioned battles where the code was used."

Roen glanced through the letter again, using the code to glean the true message. "He asks for help to protect his family and his land. A traitor is in his midst." He turned toward the king. "What will you do?"

"This—" Henry took the letter from his hands "—could simply be a letter on a land case and the code a coincidence. Or a good and loyal friend could be in need. Sir Edmund has aided me countless times. I shan't abandon him now. That is why I need you to help him. First, because he is a loyal compatriot. Secondly, there are still those who secretly oppose me as king. I cannot afford to let his keep fall into a traitor's hands."

The dull ache in the back of his head turned into a crashing storm of pain. Sir Edmund! Heaven would not punish him like this. He searched his memory for every knight named Edmund he had served with. Unconsciously, he massaged his left temple. Sharp daggers of pain lanced through his head. Roen asked, "Is the man Sir Edmund de Marchavel?"

"Aye. I'm surprised you could tell that from his letter. I want you to think of some excuse and investigate this matter. His daughter—"

"I've met!" Distaste flavored his voice. "Why hasn't Sir Edmund married the shrew off to some poor fool?"

Henry threw back his head, and his laugh boomed across the room. "So you've met the sharp-tongued Lenora. I see no blood. Her wounds could not have been too deep." The king chuckled while he poured a tankard of ale for himself and Roen. "Ah, Lenora, she's a favorite of mine. Always asking questions and demanding answers. She must be what Eleanor was like in her younger days. Before life made her hard." The king paused thoughtfully and sipped his drink.

"The girl has a tongue as hideous as Medusa's hair." Roen took a long gulp of ale and wiped his mouth with the back of his hand. "I'll warrant 'tis just as deadly to a weaker man."

The king slapped his knee and gave a belly laugh. Then he pointed his finger at Roen and warned, "Don't let the girl fool you into thinking she's had no suitors. There have been several, but she spurned them all. Books and horses hold her interest more than marriage. Since her older brother stood to inherit, Sir Edmund paid the fee to keep her unmarried. Allowed her to follow her fancies at home. There was some discussion of her entering a convent to further her education."

"I pity the abbess who receives her as a novitiate." Roen could not picture the fiery girl in drab gowns and the bleak surroundings of an abbey. Nor could he see her taking vows of silence and obedience.

"Things have changed recently, perhaps the reason Edmund is in danger. Her brother died last year in battle against one of Stephen's men, which leaves Lenora as Edmund's only heir to Woodshadow. The girl must marry and have a child in order for the keep to stay in the family." The king shook his head and muttered under his breath. "So many good men lost their lives for me. I owe England much in restitution."

"Who inherits if Lenora remains childless or—" Roen hesitated "—dies?" Although the woman vexed him sorely, the thought of the spirited girl dead did not sit well with him.

"The property is held through Lenora's mother. If she dies or is without an heir, then Woodshadow will revert to her aunt, the Lady Matilda and her daughter, Lady Beatrice. Both have motive. They are landless and living on Edmund's good graces at Woodshadow."

"They should be easily dealt with. Bring the women in and let them view the rats and roaches of the dungeon. A few threats and they will break quickly." Roen took a gulp of his drink and considered the matter settled.

"And what if 'tis not them? Then the traitor will know we are on to him. We may push the treacherous party too far and forfeit the lives of both Sir Edmund and his daughter. We must go carefully and gain the proof we need."

Roen gave him a resigned nod. "What is it you want me to do?"

The king stood and continued, "So far, Lenora has not been harmed and is unaware of the danger. The traitor may hope she will still enter the convent and thus give up her inheritance. But if she had plans to marry, it might flush our prey out." King Henry gave him a speculative look.

"Nay!" Roen roared his refusal. "I would never consider marrying that sharp-tongued hellcat. Nay, Henry, you are my liege lord, but do not ask this of me."

"'Twas—" the king spread his hands out eloquently "—a suggestion. A possible solution to two problems. But if 'tis unacceptable..."

"Unacceptable? Your Majesty, can you imagine a lifetime with that woman? She'd drive a man insane." Roen didn't think Henry understood the depths of his strenuous protest. "'Tis obvious her father has not kept a strong rein on the girl. I doubt she even knows how to run a household." A groan erupted when he saw the king fold his hands across his chest and give him a steely look. "Your Majesty, the Lady Lenora is definitely not what I want in a wife...."

Henry leaned back in his chair, pursed his lips and contemplated the strong ale in his goblet. He knew Roen well, and the knight's protest intrigued him. The man was more interested in Lady Lenora than he cared to admit, or he would not still be cursing the girl. Perhaps marriage was a viable solution to his problem. His siege commander would be repaid for his military aid with a wealthy keep, Woodshadow would be secure with a vassal loyal to the throne, and his old friend's daughter would be protected. He just had to deliver the solution to Roen in a more digestible form.

"Perhaps you are right," King Henry agreed. "After all, since the fee has been paid, she would have to agree to marry you. I could not command it or even request it. She may refuse you."

"She wouldn't dare!" Roen could not believe that any woman would not be eager to jump into the marriage bed with him. "I may be landless, but I don't enter the contract with nothing. I've enough in booty and ransom money to impress even the likes of the Lady Lenora."

"Nevertheless, we must think of a ruse for you to visit Woodshadow for a time. Long enough for you to discover if there is a threat, and if there is, the source."

"I already have one," Roen admitted with reluctance. His mood did not improve when the king raised his brows in mock surprise. Above all things he respected loyalty; he would help his liege's friend. "I need a few days to collect my winnings from the tourney. I'll be in Woodshadow before the next fortnight." He took leave of the king and met Hamlin at the end of the hall.

"What happened?" Hamlin asked. "I heard you bellowing from here."

"Come with me." He strode out of the hall, leaving his friend behind. Unmindful of Hamlin's pleas to slow down, he strode toward the stables. Reaching Destrier's stall, he checked the horse's feed and well-being.

"Well, my friend," Roen said, patting the horse's neck. "At least one of us will be enjoying himself at Woodshadow. You'll be busy with the mares and I'll be..." His mouth grew dry and his voice died out. Like a bit of fog, a dream of Lady Lenora enticed him. An image of her long, slender white legs wrapped around his waist seized his imagination. Her hair, like copper bracelets, tangled in his fingers. The ragged sound of his breath shook him from the spell. He ran his hand across his forehead and down the back of his head. His body's reaction to this woman did not make sense.

A quiet, demure, obedient wife was what he sought. He would go to Woodshadow and protect the girl and her father because the king had asked him. But he would use the opportunity to exact his revenge against the woman's dagger-sharp words. As with any battle, Roen intended his revenge to be costly to his opponent, Lenora.

Chapter Four

"By the blessed saints!" The gnarled old man threw down the twig broom in disgust. "Lady Lenora, I'll never be gettin' my morning work done with ye tramping back and forth."

Lenora halted her relentless pacing and looked down at her feet. The stableman's neat piles of dirt lay scattered, her footprints visible in each.

"I'm sorry, Tom. I was so worried about Silver I didn't look where I was walking. I promise to be more careful."

"Aye, ye promise to look out. Just like ye promised to not be worrying yeself sick over this mare...and Gladymer...and ye father...and..." Tom poked an arthritic finger at her. "And about whatever happened over at that tourney."

The desire to deny the charges stuck in her throat. Tom's one-eyed stare silenced all her rebuttals. He pointed to the black patch that covered his left eye and added, "I may 'ave lost an eye in battle, but the one I still got works good enough for me to know somethin's amiss. What was it that made ye have to leave Tintagel so quick ye barely had time to brush the sweat marks off your horses?"

"I was homesick. I wanted to be at Woodshadow with Father and Silver Maple." Lenora smiled. "And you."

"Humph! There's no need to be trying to grease me. It won't work like it does on your aunt. So ye don't want to talk to me. A loyal servant all my life. Served with your father, saved his life countless times, taught some pesky little miss to ride." Tom began to number off on his fingers all of his numerous sacrifices.

"Believe me, nothing out of the ordinary happened." She fixed a bright smile on her face to reassure her father's retired infantryman. To escape from Tom's prodding questions, she moved to her mare's stall. Leaning her elbows on the gate, she rested her chin on her hands.

How could she tell her father's man about her confrontation with Roen de Galliard? Anything she told the old man would be channeled to her father's ear. She wanted desperately to talk to someone about her fears and confused emotions concerning Galliard. Beatrice had her own concerns, Aunt Matilda was out of the question and she didn't dare tell her father. Lenora knew she had pushed the golden giant beyond the safety point. 'Twas only luck that had spared her from the man's bad temper.

Closing her eyes, she sought the comfort the stable always offered. Images of thunder gray-blue eyes and wide shoulders splintered the stable's calming aura, leaving her tense and full of nervous energy.

Tom scrutinized the young girl he had watched grow up and mature into a spirited young woman. *So, something happened at the tourney you don't want me or your father to know,* he deduced to himself. He winced when his troubled mistress, lost in thought, once more paced through the dirt, destroying his morning's work.

"There's only one answer for this, your ladyship," Tom announced in a loud voice. Her worried eyes broke from their trance. He shuffled toward the back of the stable. Hoof stomps and angry snorts cracked the silence.

Lenora heard several grunted curses before Tom reappeared moments later with a prancing dapple-gray stallion, tacked with her father's saddle. Shoving the reins into her hands, he commanded, "Ride him."

"You want me to ride Father's stallion, Jupiter? Astride?" The horse pawed the smooth dirt floor of the stable, irritated with Tom's restraining hands. The stallion jerked his head, almost dislodging the reins from her hands.

"Aye, lass. I know ye can handle him and he needs the workout. With the lord ailin', Jupiter here is sorely in need of his daily gallop."

"But Father has always been with me when I rode him. I don't know if I should."

Tom's twinkling eye squinted and studied her. "You're needin' to ride your worries away, a ride that'll make ye one with the wind. Ye can't do that perched on a saddle like a pet bird. Ye gotta dig your talons into the saddle, hold on and outride the devils that are a-plaguing ye so. Jupiter is the horse that can outride any demon ye've got tagging after ye."

The truth of his words hit home. She paused a moment, then lifted the back of her grass-stained work dress and tucked it into the front of her girdle. Tom tossed her a coarse woolen hood from a peg. She stuffed her thick auburn braid into the loose hat. In her makeshift braes, she mounted Jupiter. The long, well-oiled reins cut into her hands as the stallion strained to break free. A quick nod of her head to her old friend and she clicked her tongue against her teeth.

Tom dropped his hand from the bridle and watched the girl he loved like a daughter—and the horse he cursed like the devil—walk out of the stable toward the outer bailey and the open fields beyond the castle gate. "Don't worry, Lady Lenora, there are those of us here a-watchin', out for ye," he whispered to himself, and then retrieved his twig broom.

Lenora's fingers curled tight around the reins to keep the powerful stallion at a bouncy walk. She maneuvered her impatient mount among the working villeins and freemen of Woodshadow. Once past the smithy, she entered the more open space of the outer bailey courtyard.

Her attention gravitated toward managing her excited horse. Jupiter's muscles contracted and he arched his neck, impatient for the signal from his rider to break into a more taxing gait. When she reached the marshal's tower at the castle gate, the dewy rolling hills of the meadow became visible. New spring grass sprinkled with just-opened multicolored wildflowers swayed in the still-cool air, beckoning horse and rider.

She leaned forward and whispered into the stallion's ear, "Let's see if we can outrun that nagging Roen de Galliard." The horse sprang forward, almost unseating her. Her fingers wove into the gray black mane, and a breeze of refreshing air blew the hair from her eyes. The rhythmic beat of Jupiter's hooves on the dirt road became hypnotic.

Tender shoots of grass blurred with the darker green of hedges and trees. She swept past peasants toiling in the black soil of recently furrowed fields, past huddled flocks of woolly, bleating sheep and grazing cattle. The tension pulled away, left behind in the dust of the stallion's thundering hoofbeats. Her anxiety tumbled away from the force of the wind. She smiled, then laughed. To her right, she spied a low hedge. A quick move of the reins guided the galloping horse toward the emerald hedges.

"Come on! Let's do it!" Horse and rider concentrated on the obstacle ahead. The hedge seemed to grow in height as they approached it. 'Twas not a low-lying wild brush but a natural fence, grown to keep out deer and roving cattle. Jupiter sensed the challenge ahead of him, and she felt the horse's hard muscles contract as he prepared for the jump. The hedge loomed before them.

Her heart pounded against her chest. Even to her own ears, her breath sounded ragged. Her conscience berated this latest folly but 'twas too late to change course now.

Two strides from the hedge, Lenora laced her fingers into the flying mane, leaned forward in the saddle and gave the stallion his head. She felt the surge of strength course through Jupiter's body, a lurch, then she was airborne. Her body transcended the confines of the earth and she became weightless, suspended in midair. Air whipped around her and tore the hood from her head. Her waist-length braid came unbound and streamed about her. Pleasure, excitement, complete freedom sprouted within her. Too soon, she saw Jupiter's long legs reach the fast-approaching ground. The hard impact jarred her backbone and jerked her back in the saddle.

Exhilaration made her giddy. Another hedge lay a short distance away. Laughter bubbled from her. Lenora pushed her long tresses from her face and pivoted Jupiter toward the next jump. Thoughts of the bad-tempered knight cleared from her mind.

She dug her heels into Jupiter's flanks, and the pounding of horse's hooves drummed in her ears. She prepared for the jump, mentally picturing when she would need to ease off the bit to give the stallion his head. Just a few more strides, five more, three more, "Now!" She loosened her hold on the reins, grabbed the flying mane, and leaned forward in the saddle. From the corner of her eye, a shadow swooped down on her. A huge mail-covered hand appeared out of nowhere, yanking her from Jupiter's back just as the horse sprang. Jupiter cleared the hedge as her back hit against a hard wall of metal. The blow knocked the air from her lungs. Stunned, she found herself breathless and dumped into the lap of an armor-clad knight.

"Let...go...of...me." The words came in several wheezes while she attempted to fill her empty lungs with air. She kicked and thrashed her legs, trying to free herself. "Who are you?" She twisted in her captor's grasp and her eyes traveled up to the knight's face.

A wide nosepiece on his helmet obscured his face. Only his eyes were visible. The hard-won air she had strived for escaped her lungs in a low, desperate sigh. "Nay, it cannot be!" The knight's dark blue gray eyes glowered at her, and a current of fear whorled through her.

"I've come to settle our bet, Lady Lenora." Roen de Galliard removed his helmet, tucked it under his arm and shook his head like a mighty golden lion. "Among other things." He wrapped his viselike arm around her waist and pulled her tightly toward him. His deep musky smell filled her nostrils. The hard steel links of his chain hauberk bit like metal teeth into her back. Pain shot through her shoulders and festered her outrage.

"I had no need of rescue, Galliard. I was in control of my mount. I demand you release me immediately!" Hot blood rushed to her face. The heat of her ire changed to humiliation when Roen moved his mount toward a group of knights and squires. The wind carried hoots and cackles from the men.

"'Tis not you I'm worried about," Roen retorted calmly. "My concern is for the horse. I don't want your stupidity to risk hurting a good mount."

"Oh!" Lenora floundered for a sarcastic reply, but her mind was frozen, like a pond in midwinter. Instead, she shot him an icy look, crossed her arms and retreated into an angry silence. She was forced to look either ahead at the jeering men or down at Roen's thick muscular arm, imprisoning her. The tension of the past few days returned and her will weakened. She chose to look down, centering all her fury on the ironlike arm that held her captive.

Roen rejoined his men at a leisurely gait and savored the feel of the woman against his chest. He chuckled to himself, amused by her silence and angry indignation. The faint hint of lavender mixed with the familiar scent of hay wafted from her windswept coppery locks.

When his men pointed out the young lad on the horse, he had admired the boy's horsemanship. 'Twas obvious the vigorous stallion was well under control. Admiration had changed mid-jump when the boy's hood blew off. The "lad" transformed into a tall, copper-haired lass. He had held his breath until horse and rider came down to earth. Heaven's grace had spared the girl once. Why had she tried to push her luck by trying again? She could have broken her neck. His arm tightened instinctively around her.

"That hurts!" Lenora gasped. "I'm not fool enough to jump from horseback."

He forced his arm to relax and stared down into her upturned face. Auburn tresses lay in disarray around her face and gave her a Gypsy look. Faint golden brown freckles were sprinkled lightly across her straight nose and high cheeks. Her eyes no longer burned from the fire of her anger, but he could still see smoldering embers of gold in the earthen-colored orbs. His fingers played with her unbound waist-length hair. They wove into the thick strands and took a light but possessive hold.

"Really?" he questioned. "You jump a hedge that is waist-high to me, you barely regain control of an animal that is clearly too much for you to handle, and then you try to jump a hedge even higher than the first. Aye, you have need to warn me you're no fool. Your actions do not show it!"

Lenora wanted to smack the smug smile from his face and scream at him that it was all his fault. If not for him, she wouldn't have been riding in such an outlandish fashion in the first place.

Determined not to let him see how upset she was, Lenora arranged her features into a mask of calm and serenity. "Galliard, I suppose that in your own misguided way you were trying to be chivalrous, although there was no need. So why don't you stop, let me down to catch my horse, and each of us may travel our own way?''

His smile turned to an irritating smirk. "But, Lady Lenora, my way is your way. Remember our bargain?''

"Let us say that your... aid to me just now more than fulfills your obligation.''

"That would be true, if the aid had been needed. Since you have mentioned several times that it was not, I cannot feel justified in letting this small act be your...reward for all you have done for me.''

She bit her upper lip to help keep her tongue in check. Mentally, she questioned the possible double meaning of his words. Her thoughts were interrupted by the loud laughter from the men ahead.

"Roen! You've caught your prize, but poor Landrick is still chasing his.''

Lenora recognized Hamlin, sitting astride a sturdy chestnut stallion. She followed his gaze toward the rolling hills and saw a mounted young man, armorless, trying to outmaneuver the still-galloping Jupiter.

"He'll get him. If Roen gives an order, Landrick won't give up till it's completed," a young squire declared.

"I'll clean your tack and that of your knight for a week if he does.'' Another young knight gave her a wink and wagered with the squire.

Her elbow jabbed into Roen's side as he moved to join his men. He paid no attention. The move only caused her to yelp in pain when the sharp metal of his haubrek pinched her skin.

Lenora bridled. The knave's quiet chuckles proclaimed his amusement with her predicament. Her mask of composure cracked. She was not about to let Galliard's men think she needed rescuing. "I'll take that bet, to get Jupiter, if you'll include all my knights.'' She gave the wagering knight an innocent smile.

"Forget the bet, Roderick,'' Roen warned. "She's not leaving me until she is safely dumped at the gates of Woodshadow.''

"I have no need to leave your side to capture Jupiter.'' She broadened her smile. "And I do believe the squire is quite tired by now.''

The group watched as once again Landrick tried to steer the running horse toward the waiting men. At first, the young squire appeared successful, then Jupiter broke. With a sharp turn the stallion evaded Landrick's rope and the strange men ahead. The action diverted her captor's attention.

Lenora saw her chance. She slid out from between Roen's arms and dropped to the ground. Her feet hit the earth hard and she stumbled a few steps away to escape the knight's reach. "This is as far as I need to be. Is it a wager, Sir Roderick?"

Roderick took one peek at the black look of his commander's face and shook his head. "Nay, Lady Lenora, I do not doubt your skill with the animal. If you can bring him in, pray do so, and save our friend further loss of pride."

A warmth of satisfaction cloaked her. She had escaped the moody knight and his man admitted her horsemanship. A challenging neigh caused her to turn. Jupiter feigned surrender, then just as the sweat-soaked squire drew close, the horse pivoted and raced away. When her stallion paused, she pursed her lips together and emitted three sharp, shrill tones. The animal's ears twitched toward the sound. Once again, she whistled three sharp blasts.

Hearing the call, Jupiter reeled and galloped toward her. Sides heaving and sweat-stained, the horse skidded to a stop at her side. She captured the loose reins and swung up into the saddle. Relaxed from his workout, the charger stood docile, waiting for his rider's command.

Roen gave his horse a slight squeeze, nodded to his second and moved nonchalantly toward her. The set of his rocklike chin mirrored his granite-colored eyes. She did not doubt that he felt he had one more score to settle with her.

Gathering the reins tightly, Lenora pumped a cheerful tone into her speech. "I would like to extend the hospitality of Woodshadow to you all. I hope you will join me for the nooning." Secretly, she prayed they would all ride away and she would never see Roen de Galliard again.

She kept her eyes on the leader of the group of men. The hard line of his jaw, the bulging neck veins and the scowl announced his emotions. His eyes narrowed as he moved his mount next to hers. The brush of his leg against her own sent currents of excitement speeding up her thigh, settling in the pit of her stomach.

"Drop your reins!" Roen commanded. "Return to my horse."

"I'll do no such thing. I'll ride into Woodshadow on my own mount." She squeezed Jupiter with her knees, but the horse did not move. Glancing from Roen, she saw Hamlin firmly holding on to her horse's bridle. He gave her a dimpled smile of apology.

"The horse needs to be cooled down or he'll colic. Give the reins to Landrick. He also needs to cool his mount." At the mention of his name, the boyishly lean squire held on to his saddle and slid his feet to the ground. He grasped the girth until his feet would support him. Sweat streaked his red face.

"My grooms will see to my horse. You have no need to be concerned, Galliard." She tried to wrench control from Hamlin but the knight's hold persisted. Roen lifted her from her saddle and plopped her down onto his lap.

"But it is my concern, Lady Lenora. 'Twas my man that ran the horse. 'Tis his responsibility to care for it now. He will return to your home when the horses have been walked and cooled down. I will be glad to offer you a ride back to your home."

She opened her mouth to utter several of Tom's more colorful curses but she was slammed back against Roen when his charger cantered toward the castle. Her back kept colliding with Roen's powerful chest from the horse's rocking movement. Each time she banged into the knight's massive torso, she winced. He made no move to prevent her discomfort.

Exasperated, Lenora finally grabbed Roen's arm, pulled it tight around her and leaned against him. "'Tis this or bruises," she muttered under her breath, and shot him a murderous glance when she felt the deep rumble of laughter reverberate in his chest.

The rumble stopped, as did the horse. Only her tight hold on Roen's arm kept her from being thrown forward. The contingent of men drew close to form a barricade between her and the road ahead.

"Release Lady Lenora!" a voice ordered.

"Sir Hywel." She craned her neck to see a group of her father's men blocking the road. Roen's men waited, their hands resting on the hilts of their undrawn swords.

"Release her now!" In unison the knights of Woodshadow drew their swords, their upheld blades casting a blinding reflection of the sun.

Roen moved forward, his men parting for him. He stopped his horse a few paces from her father's seneschal. "Greetings, Sir Hywel. I and my men aided her when she lost control of her mount. See, yonder is my squire bringing the horse back."

Sir Hywel glanced over Roen's shoulder at Landrick, who was walking the two horses back. "Lady Lenora?"

She gritted her teeth and seethed with inner frustration. Galliard gave her a benign smile that only served to stoke her anger. If she contradicted Roen's story, the two groups would come to blows. To admit, in front of her men and his, that she needed his help galled her.

"'Tis as Galliard says," she managed to get out through clenched teeth, "I was riding Jupiter and—"

"Jupiter! Girl, are you daft? That horse is more than most men can handle." The steward raised his hand and signalled her protectors to resheath their swords. The knights surrounding her relaxed.

"I thank you for your aid to our lady. She is at times a trifle foolhardy." Sir Hywel approached Roen and Lenora. "I will take her back to Woodshadow. I am sure her father would like to extend his thanks, also."

Roen did not remove his arm from around her waist. "Lady Lenora has graciously extended the hospitality of her home to my men and me. Since we travel the same way, I will be glad to take the lady home." Spurring his horse, he led the group of knights through the gates of Woodshadow and into the inner bailey of her home.

Damn Roen de Galliard! Lenora swore to herself. The man had caused her nothing but trouble and embarrassment since she met him. Gawking villagers lined the hard-packed road to the castle entrance. The sight of her aunt and cousin on forebuilding steps caused her to cringe with mortification. Roen swung her down and deposited her at Matilda's feet. Dust, from the horses, stirred whirlwinds of dirt around her. She coughed as grime coated her hair, face and clothes.

Roen gave her aunt a polite smile. "Your niece was in need of help, Lady Matilda. I was more than happy to assist her."

"Sir Roen!" her aunt gushed, as she brushed past Lenora, pulling her skirts close to avoid soiling them on her filthy niece. "I recognize you from the tourney. We are honored to have a knight of your reputation as our guest."

A stableboy took hold of his horse. Destrier tossed his mane and twisted his head to take a bite from the lad's arm. One of Roen's squires scrambled from his saddle and took a tentative hold of the animal. A one-word command from his master and the horse settled. Roen dismounted and Matilda latched onto his arm. She waved to her daughter and steered the knight in the direction of the steps. Eagerness and hope rushed through the older woman's voice. "I would like to introduce you to my daughter, Lady Beatrice."

"Galliard! I want a word with you."

Roen turned casually toward Lenora. She stood covered in dust, her skirt partially tucked into her belt. Her hair formed a red gold mantle; her anger caused it to sizzle around her shoulders like tongues of flame.

"Lenora, you should not delay Sir Roen," Matilda scolded, and tried to tug Roen up the forebuilding steps.

"I don't mind. I am sure Lady Lenora wishes to give me her thanks in private. Pray, continue on with my men. We will follow shortly."

Lenora held her tongue until her aunt and cousin disappeared into the keep. "Things have not changed. My cousin remains off limits to you."

Roen shook his head in amazement. Regardless of how she looked, she sounded like the mistress of the keep. He had bested the girl in front of everyone and she still dared to oppose him. Her use of his family name needled him. She remembered Hamlin or Landrick's title with no problem. His should not be any harder to recall.

"I am Sir Roen de Galliard of Normandy. You may address me as Sir Roen or Sir Galliard."

"The way that I address you is not what I wish to discuss."

" 'Tis what I wish to discuss."

Lenora shook her dust-caked apron, a delighted look on her face when a light cloud of dirt hovered over Roen. Her full lips curled into a sarcastic smile. "I do not wish to keep you from your admirers, Galliard." He heard the relish in her voice at the insult. She spun around and trudged up the step to the keep.

Left in another cloud of her dust, he started after her. "And I do not wish to keep you from your much needed bath, Nora."

Lenora stopped, her mouth moving like a fish gasping on dry land. "My name is *Le*-nora."

Roen skipped up the stair past her. "I don't wish to discuss that right now. My admirers await." His laugh rang triumphant as he entered the great hall.

Lenora fumed. If today was Galliard's payment for her loose tongue, then they were even.

"Lady Lenora." Sir Hywel stood on the top step. "Your father wants to see you. Now!"

Her chin sank to her chest. The scales had just tipped. She owed Galliard now and she intended her payment to be a painful one to the arrogant lout.

Chapter Five

"Sir Roen, I'm so glad you came along when you did," her aunt cooed. "Poor Lenora could have been killed trying such an outlandish stunt." She took a sip from the wine goblet she shared with Roen. The rest of the meal participants listened with rapt attention to the knight's exaggerated account of the rescue.

Lenora felt a needlelike jab in her head and tried to fix her concentration on her meal. Under the table, her foot tapped the floor in a staccato beat. She wished it was Galliard under her foot instead of the rushes.

"You were so brave to attempt such a rescue." Matilda continued to heap praise on Roen. Every word of gratitude triggered another pain. Lenora's head felt like a pincushion.

"Lady Lenora, you have a fine cook. The meal is..." Her dinner partner, Sir Alric, stopped his polite conversation at her icy look.

Alric retreated into a quelled silence. Lenora grabbed their shared wine goblet without asking for help from the knight seated next to her. She dared him to comment on her breach of proper etiquette, which demanded the knight hold the goblet. The last thing she wanted was help from any of Roen de Galliard's men.

Just as she took a huge gulp of wine, she heard Roen say, " 'Twas pure luck that she stayed on the beast's back after the first jump. Then to see her barreling down toward a second! Well, dear lady, I knew I had to intervene or a terrible accident would occur."

Her wine almost spewed across the table. She forced the liquid down her constricted throat and was seized by a fit of coughing. All eyes at the head table turned toward her.

"It seems the lady needs my assistance once again." Roen smiled ruefully at Matilda. He started to rise from his seat of honor next to the saltcellar.

"Nay. Nay." Lenora waved him back to his seat. "I am fine. The wine was sour."

"Really!" He took a long swill from his cup. "Mine is deliciously sweet." Roen gave her a crooked smile. Mischief brought out the blue in his eyes. "Perhaps, 'tis not the wine that's sour."

He turned to Hamlin, seated next to Beatrice on his right. "I have heard, my friend, that the flavor of the meal is enhanced by one's disposition. I myself feel extremely well satisfied, and my meal was extremely savory. Perhaps 'tis the lady's disposition that soured her meal." The high table exploded with laughter.

Beatrice opened her mouth to defend her dear cousin. Hamlin lightly placed his callused hand over her delicate one. "Nay, Lady Beatrice, this battle is not for one as gentle as yourself. Besides," he whispered, "I do not think the Lady Lenora is ready to admit defeat just yet."

As if in response to Hamlin's statement, Lenora, her eyes aflame, parried back. "Nay, Galliard. My disposition is wonderfully content after my refreshing bath. How could one help to be otherwise when the water was so soothingly warm and scented with mint. I trust yours was the same."

Roen tapped his index finger on his wide, generous lips, forcing his smile to remain. When he had seen the scrawny, toothless old woman sent to assist him at his bath, he suspected Lenora had arranged it. His men relaxed in hot tubs while he nearly froze in a bucket of tepid water. Not to mention he had had to bear the tale of the hag's many ailments. Roen nodded appreciatively toward his adversary. Lenora was not a woman to give up any battle easily.

"My bath was exactly as you would expect it to be." Roen turned toward his dining partner. "Lady Matilda, your niece sent the . . ."

Matilda giggled like a young girl. "Lenora is too interested in her horses and plants to be concerned with taking proper care of her guests. I am afraid the stress of managing this keep falls on my shoulders and those of my daughter."

"Then I have you to thank for my bath and the care I received?" Roen questioned.

He was surprised to see Matilda accept the statement as a compliment when he knew Lenora was responsible for his inhospitable treatment. He turned toward the young woman, her face radiant with triumph.

"Sir Roen, my lord will see you now," the castle seneschal announced. Roen tore his gaze from Lenora. Sir Hywel continued, "Sir Edmund apologizes for the delay in addressing you, but his illness forces him to rest at midday. If you are finished with your meal, I will lead you to his chambers."

Roen stood and turned to face Lenora, a mocking grin unsuppressed on his lips. It vanished when he found her seat empty.

"Sir Hywel..." Roen was surprised to find Lenora at his side as she spoke to her father's steward. "Since 'twas I the knight assisted, I feel that I should present the man to my father." Turning to her aunt, the vixen transformed her waspish tongue with a demure guise. "'Tis only the proper thing to do."

Before her aunt could reply, Lenora grabbed his arm and led him across the room to the stairs. He lengthened his stride to keep up with the girl.

Roen's battle senses noted with approval the construction of the stairs. As the stone steps reached the upper stories they narrowed and curved. Forced to climb single file, an invading army was blind to what lay ahead. A snatch of Lenora's dress was all he could see of her as she disappeared around the curve of the step.

The creak of wood contrasted with the cold echo of the stone. Roen quickly identified the sound, wooden defense steps. The structures could be burned or demolished if invaders entered.

"Hold, Galliard!"

Roen pulled himself up short. Lenora blocked his passage. She stood on the upper step, her eyes level with his own. Her chin tilted at a defiant angle and she crossed her arms over her chest. The golden shade of her eyes signaled her state of mind. The docile lamb had reverted back into a bad-tempered lion.

Lenora held her ground. The narrow steps prevented Galliard from brushing past her and the curve of the stair hid them from people below, in the great hall, and above, in her father's room.

"We will talk before you see my father," Lenora commanded.

"Orders! You give far too many orders for a woman!" Roen sighed, exasperated.

Her voice dripped with false sincerity. "And would the words sound sweeter coming from the mouth of a man? Do you want me to look humbly at the ground and ask requests of you in my own home, in my own hall, after you have eaten my food and drunk my wine?

"This battle we have—" Lenora saw Roen's startled expression. "Aye, 'tis a battle, Galliard. But this is between you and me. You will not involve my father. The story I told him is the same we told his steward." Lenora clenched her fists and fought to control the timbre of her voice. "My father is ill. He must not be unsettled."

Afraid to show her tears, she lowered her head. A hand on her chin forced her face upward. She searched his face through blurry eyes for a sign that he understood her pain. His eyes, no longer the color of cold granite, warmed to mist gray. They reminded her of a stubborn fog that lingered in the morning sun. Could he really have a heart after all?

He cupped her upturned face in his large rough hand. His fingers massaged the knotted muscles at her scalp. A solitary tear escaped one eye and meandered down her cheek. Roen tenderly wiped it away with his thumb.

"Ah, Nora, if only Henry had a dozen warriors like yourself, he would have England back to rights in no time." Roen dropped his hand from her face. He stared at it and the evaporating remains of Lenora's tear.

"I do what I must to protect my father," she explained hesitantly.

"I see that now," Roen whispered. "Which is the crux of the problem." He fought the desire to wrap Lenora in his arms, to reassure her with brave words.

The tender feelings he felt toward her must be killed. Love was an emotion for bards and women, not warriors. He stepped away and jeered at the tender emotions he accidentally felt. To push away the sentiments, he gave a brisk wave with his arm. "Come, Nora, I see your point. I'll do nothing to upset Sir Edmund."

Confused and surprised that the battle had been won so easily, she led him to her father's chambers. She knocked on the heavy oak door and whispered, "One more thing."

Her father's reply to her knock corresponded with Roen's disgruntled, "What else?"

"Don't call me Nora!"

Lenora opened the door and flounced across the chamber to stand next to her bedridden father. Tall and proud, she placed her hand lovingly on his shoulder. "Father, this is the knight that assisted me today, Sir Roen de Galliard of Normandy."

Roen's attention moved from her to the gaunt man lying on the massive bed. Sir Edmund lay atop the ermine-trimmed coverlet, propped up by several overstuffed pillows. His long legs filled the length of the bed. His feet were bare, his torso covered by a calf-length robe of rich blue, trimmed in dark sable fur. The shadows from the one window accentuated the darkness beneath his still-lively eyes.

"Sir Roen, I wish to express my deepest gratitude for your rescue today. Pray, avail yourself of my hospitality for as long as you wish." Sir Edmund's voice barely carried across the room. "Draw up the chair so that we may talk."

Lenora ran to snatch the heavy oak chair from the table on the far side of the room. She struggled to drag it to her father's side. Roen lifted the chair from her easily and placed it near the bed. She scurried to return to her father's side.

Seated, Roen saw two sets of earth brown eyes assessing him intently. *There's no doubt she's a Marchavel. She has the look of the old man, only softened,* he thought bitterly. The strong family resemblance between father and daughter rekindled old childhood scars. Roen's heart retreated into the emotional armor he had devised in childhood. He concentrated on the muted colors of the floral depictions on the whitewashed castle walls.

"Lenora, you may leave us now. I wish to hear news from London and swap battle tales." Sir Edmund patted his child's arm. "You have already heard the news and my old stories. 'Twould only bore you."

"Father, I don't mind staying." Lenora moved closer to her father, as though to shield him from Roen.

Edmund laughed and gave Roen a leering wink. "But, my dear, a father tells his daughter a story one way, and tells another warrior the same story in an entirely different manner. Certain details that he neglected to tell his wife or daughter are sometimes remembered with a fellow knight."

Lenora pushed back a lock of her hair and tapped her foot against the wooden floor. She had hoped to remain and see that Roen kept his word. Her father's dismissal left her no choice. To tarry longer would only make him suspicious.

She shot Roen a murderous glance, then moved to the exit. His back to the door, he heard the loud slam echo in the room and down the hall.

Edmund licked his lips and pointed toward a wardrobe near the window. "Those women seek to keep me on weak tea and watered-down wine. A man can't regain his strength from such as that. Friend, look on the upper shelf of that closet and see if a bottle of ale can't be found."

Roen's smile and mood brightened. He crossed the room in three strides and threw open the doors of the huge oak wardrobe. The piece held little, a fur-lined cloak, a green embroidered tunic and a leather jerkin. Several boots lay on the bottom. The wardrobe was so huge, Roen had to climb into it to reach the top shelf. He pushed aside the soft woolen braes and shirts folded neatly on the shelf. His hand found the smooth handle of a clay jug. Roen turned and displayed his prize.

"Well-done, man!" Sir Edmund smiled gleefully. "Grab that bowl and tea mug and we will toast each other's good fortune."

Relaxed, Roen retrieved the articles and returned to Sir Edmund. He drew his chair closer as he poured the strong ale into the mug and offered it to the ill man. After pouring his drink into the soup bowl, he placed the jug of ale on the floor be-

tween them. Edmund tilted his mug in salute. Forced to hold
the bowl with two hands, Roen brought the drink to his lips.

"I hope 'tis fine ale ye be drinkin', 'cause if'n ye don't be
tellin' milord the truth, 'twill be ye last."

Roen felt the pressure of a dagger against the base of his
neck. He drained the bowl and with slow movements set it next
to the jug.

The older knight swirled his ale in his mouth, obviously enjoying the flavor of the strong drink. "Tom, we don't know for
sure he is a liar." Edmund quirked a smile at the motionless
Roen. "So tell me, Sir Roen de Galliard of Normandy, why are
you here? Why the fairy story about saving my daughter?
Lenora needs to be delivered from her sharp tongue and hot
temper, but never from the back of a horse."

"I come from King Henry." Roen spoke quietly. He could
feel the hot breath of his assailant and the prick of a dagger
point on the back of his neck.

"'E could be lyin', Sir Edmund." The sharp point pressed a
trifle more.

Roen willed his heart to beat normally, his chest to rise and
fall naturally. His huge hands gripped his knees, his knuckles
white with indignation. As he spoke, his outrage spilled over.
"You wrote a letter to the king using the code from the battle
at Hastings. You asked for help, Henry sent me."

His words caused Sir Edmund to pull back and the blade
moved just a hair away from his neck. Now was the time to act.
Roen dived forward and kicked the chair hard. It thumped into
the midsection of the man with the knife. Roen scrambled to his
feet. Grabbing the overturned chair, he prepared to break it
over the head of his assailant.

"Wait!" Sir Edmund shouted.

Roen held the sturdy chair high over his head, his breath
ragged. It took only a few seconds for him to realize the dazed
man was unable to rise and was blind in one eye.

"Well, ain't ye goin' to help me up?" The old man wheezed
and held up his hand.

"You must be daft, both of you." Roen swung the chair to
the floor. He grabbed the old man's arm and plopped him into
the chair Roen had nearly crushed his skull with.

"Tom?" Edmund examined his coconspirator with a critical eye. Tom nodded while he tried to regain his breath. "Sir Roen, I apologize for the subterfuge. In a case like this, I can trust very few."

"And you trust me now?" Roen towered over the men.

"Aye. One, you held your blow when you saw the condition of your attacker, and second—" Edmund arched his brows "—I have no choice. I need help to protect my family."

Roen paced the room before hitching a leg onto an iron-banded chest near the window. "What makes you think you are in any danger, other than from your own harebrained schemes?"

Tom stopped wheezing and started to sputter, "What—why, you... I don't care if'n you are a lord, ye don't go talkin' to Sir Edmund like that."

Sir Edmund silenced his man with an annoyed frown. "'Tis little proof I have, more of a hunch. My illness for one." He released a long, anguished breath and eased himself back against the pillows. The stress of the recent events shone on his face.

"Aye, 'tis a strange illness." Tom's muscles creaked, his bad knee popped. He used the back of the chair to pull himself up. "My lord grows weak, then grows strong, then weak again."

"He's old. It happens," Roen replied nonchalantly.

"Then why is it when I bring his food myself, not from the kitchen, he gets stronger? Why is it that when I fed his kitchen food to the rats in the stable, they died?" Tom gave Roen a nearly toothless grin. "Someone's a-tryin' to poison 'im."

"Rats die, they eat spoiled food. You doped the stable with poison, they got hold of it." Roen scrutinized the ill man, noted the paleness of his face.

"Aye, it could be so, I wish it were so," Edmund replied wearily. "I do not wish to think someone of my house would poison me. But 'tis true. Tom smuggles me food through a secret chamber into this room. Yet, I still suffer from bouts of illness. I know not if this is a permanent result of the poisoning, or if the traitor still reaches me, despite our precautions."

"There's other things. Before the lord got sick." Tom held his back as he shuffled over to Roen. "Accidents! The lord 'ere was nearly trampled to death when the girth broke on his saddle. Then his lance broke during a hunt. The whole castle was a-talkin' about the lord's run of bad luck.''

The one-eyed man gave Roen a calculated look. "All the talk scared the coward. Not too much longer, Sir Edmund starts to feelin' poorly.''

Roen scratched his chin. "All you really have is supposition. No real proof.''

Tom snorted in disgust. "And what about Lady Lenora?''

Roen jumped off the chest. "What's happened to Lenora?'' he demanded. "Sir Edmund, your letter did not mention any harm to her.''

There was silence as Tom and his lord exchanged appraising glances. Edmund's voice wavered. "No harm—yet. Just things that make one wonder. I never received an answer before—why did Lenora lie for you? I'm surprised she didn't strip you to the bone with one of her tongue-lashings.''

Roen wandered about the room to collect and organize his thoughts. "Your daughter did not wish to upset you. Believe me, I have heard enough of her bad manners. What do you want from me?'' Roen asked tentatively. He suspected the answer would not be to his liking.

Edmund reached out his hand. Tom slipped two brown leather-wrapped missives from under his worn jerkin. He placed them in his lord's hand. The elder knight opened each, read each briefly.

"I believe this will draw the culprit out." He held one out to Roen.

"This is a marriage contract!'' Roen stared at Sir Edmund as the man's plan dawned on him. "Nay, I'll not marry that hellcat daughter of yours.''

"Then don't. Read the contract, man. All you have to do is announce your engagement," Sir Edmund replied briskly.

Roen reviewed the document. "This contract is quite generous to me. I become Lord of Woodshadow the day I marry Lenora.''

"Aye, to be passed on to your and Lenora's children at your death.''

"This cannot be! If Lenora has no children I'm to be given a settlement of three hundred gold coins. You are that rich?''

Roen asked, thunderstruck. Not even the king had that much hard coin.

Edmund chuckled slyly. "Nay. The holdings would have to be sold to pay you off. I can't deed you Woodshadow itself. 'Tis held through my wife's family. But I can gift you with enough gold that whoever inherits will have nothing if Lenora dies."

Roen slung the document onto Edmund's chest. "You dare propose this plan. If someone is trying to kill you, Lenora's life will be forfeit. What will prevent the cad from killing her to prevent the marriage?"

"You will." Edmund's eyes pinned his with their sharp gaze. "You say I have no proof, this will get it for me." The older man lifted the contract.

"You risk the life of your daughter so easily?" Roen challenged.

"This is the most difficult thing I have ever done," Edmund admitted. "I have fought battles with less fear than I feel now. But this is the only way I can guarantee her safety in the future. I cannot rest until this is settled."

Roen shook his head. He crossed to the window, placed his arm against the cool wall and rested his head on his wrist. Finally, he turned to face the two elderly men.

"What's to keep me from marrying the girl and killing her myself? That's a handsome amount of money you offer."

Tom stepped forward, his one eye glaring at Roen. He gave Roen the remaining leather-wrapped parcel. Edmund explained, "This is the true marriage contract. It gives the property to Lenora and her offspring. If she dies childless, the land reverts to her mother's family. You will receive a small settlement. This is the document that will be sent to King Henry to be recorded."

Edmund added reluctantly, "I could be frank with Lenora, tell her what I suspect."

Roen massaged his temple as he answered, "Then she really would be in danger. She'd stop at nothing to ferret any would-be assassin. We will delay any decision until I am sure there is some danger. If—" Roen stressed the word "—I sense any real danger, I will participate in your deception. But understand this, I have no intention of carrying through with this. How will she react when she discovers the truth?"

"Better a bit of dented pride than death," Edmund answered bluntly. "There is one more thing."

Roen spread his mouth into a thin-lipped frown. Edmund ignored his expression and spoke quickly. "I gave Lenora a promise, that she could choose her husband. I even paid the king a fee to keep her unmarried for the remainder of the year. I cannot mandate she marry you. You must persuade her to make this match."

"God's blood, man!" Roen's patience stretched beyond his tolerance. "I will do what I can to discover the culprit and protect you and your family because the king wishes it. But I am a fighting man. I will not go around at her heels like a lap dog. If I decide to marry the girl, by God, she will marry me."

Roen turned on his heel and marched to the door. As he opened it, he pierced each man with a baleful stare. He exited, allowing the slam of the door to demonstrate his ire.

Tom sat down gingerly in the chair. He let out a long whistle of air. "What do ye think, Lord Edmund? Will your plan work?"

Edmund, the slam of the door still ringing in his ears, remained quiet for a time before he answered his trusted friend and servant. "All we can do is pray Henry sent the right man."

"And if'n he is?" Tom asked as he returned the clay jug to its hiding place.

"Then we execute our own deception, Tom, and pray 'tis the right decision. Lenora's life depends on it."

Chapter Six

"I thought I told you that Beatrice was not for you." Lenora placed her fists on her hips and glowered at the two knights. For two days the siege commander and his men had taken her hospitality; 'twas time he left, without her cousin. The hot afternoon sun beat against her back and she purposely moved to let the sun blind the men when they looked up. Roen and Hamlin sat on a crudely fashioned bench. In the cool shade of the sprawling oak, the two men labored on their tack. Soap, oil and parts of their saddles lay about them.

Roen looked up from his task, but his tanned face showed no emotion. He continued to work lubricant into his saddle girth, his strong fingers massaging the leather. A leather thong held back his flaxen hair at the base of his neck. He looked all the more like a barbarian invader. *He is an invader,* Lenora thought, *an invader to my home and peace of mind.*

"Galliard, did you hear me?"

With a careless wave of his hand, Roen signaled Hamlin to leave. His friend threw his work rag on the pommel of his saddle and caught sight of Beatrice as she rushed toward the keep. She carried an overloaded basket of vegetables. He quickened his step to intercept the girl.

Once alone, Roen gave Lenora his full attention. His granite eyes captured hers with their intensity. "Again with orders, Nora. I thought we had already settled that."

"There is nothing settled between us," she declared.

He shook his head, and a wry smile softened his face. Slight laugh wrinkles creased the corners of his eyes, and a shallow dimple formed in his left cheek. Lenora felt her heart leap. The afternoon sun became extremely warm, too warm. She moved into the shade but kept her distance from the knight.

"Aye, Nora, that's true enough. There is much that needs to be settled between us," Roen answered.

Lenora's eyes narrowed. "My cousin's future is settled. You are not a part of it." She enunciated each word.

"Why do you think I want your cousin?" he asked, his smile deepening just a notch.

Her anger boiled over. "Don't talk to me like I'm a simpleton. Your men have been bellowing across the countryside that you are here to claim a bride."

"My men are discreet. They do not bellow." A grin overtook his features. The impact stunned her. His smile displayed white, even teeth against the darkness of his tanned skin. The hint of a dimple on his left cheek ripened into a deep indentation. This dimpled smile unlocked an intense flare of emotion in her.

Her knees quivered. The palms of her hands grew damp and tiny spasms contracted in her stomach. The day was too hot, she had eaten too fast. She tried to lay the blame for the way she felt on anything besides the tantalizing smile of the man near her. Slowly, she slid down the rough bark of the old oak, curled her legs under her and leaned her back against the strong trunk for support.

Roen's smile evaporated and he leapt from the bench. Kneeling beside her, he laid his palm against her forehead and forced her head to bump against the trunk.

"Ouch!" She tried to slip from his hold but he captured her with his other hand on her shoulder. The touch sent a prickle of gooseflesh across her chest and breasts.

"Nora, you're flushed. Are you well?"

Her cheeks burned. His large hands gripped her shoulders hard, his eyes searched her face.

"When you were with your father, did you eat anything from his plate?"

"Nay. I . . . I was only able to get him to eat a few bites. Tom took the plate away as soon as he finished. I—I'm fine," Lenora stuttered, perplexed at Roen's question.

The painful grip on her shoulder eased. The muscles in his neck and shoulders relaxed. He sat back against the tree with his shoulders just a breath away from her own. Color drained from his face and he closed his eyes.

"Roen?" Her voice was a whisper. She reached out to touch his hand. His eyes shot open. The man of a few moments ago was gone, replaced by the granite stare of the cold knight from Tintagel.

"Woman, you try my patience." He scrambled to his feet. With one swift movement of his arm, he reached out and yanked her upright. For a moment, he held her. Lenora felt the gentle caress of his breath on her face. A masculine perfume of leather, horses and sweat wafted in the air. She inhaled his intoxicating smell.

Hiding behind lowered lids, she watched him turn his back to her. He muttered curses under his breath and began to gather up his equipment.

"I try your patience." Her queasiness vanished. How could she have imagined the man had any gentleness about him? Lenora pushed herself in front of him and stabbed him with her index finger.

"You are the most insufferable person I have ever had the misfortune to meet. Your wife will have much to put up with."

His response was to double over in loud, baritone laughter. "I have no doubt at all about that. She'll have a time of it, but no more than I."

She snorted with disgust. "Oh! You and Beatrice are not suited for one another. Can't you see she is not the woman to be your wife?"

The laughter ebbed, but the humor lingered in his eyes. "Oh, but I can see. Perhaps 'tis not the Lady Beatrice I intend to marry."

His statement threw her off guard. She stared at him, her mind racing. If it wasn't Beatrice he intended to marry, who was it? She saw Roen stoop down to pick up his tack when the realization hit her.

The small reservoir of composure she possessed evaporated. She took both hands and pushed Roen as hard as she could. Caught off balance, he toppled over on his back.

"If you think for one minute I believe you intend to marry my Aunt Matilda, you have less of a brain than—" no adequate comparison came to her "—than that tree trunk." Her frustration begged for satisfaction. It didn't help that he was still laughing.

"You're impossible." Lenora stalked off. The sound of Roen's undiluted laughter echoed in her ears.

She forced herself not to run from the irritating sound. An old discarded basket lay at the entrance of the outer bailey wall. She swept it up in her arms and headed toward the main fortress gate. Once past the outer bailey wall, hidden from all eyes except the watchmen, she raced across the meadow and into the wood.

The cool darkness of the forest felt refreshing after the hot sun. She plunged into the shadows and dropped her basket on the moss- and fern-covered floor. Her mind jumbled and, confused, Lenora tried to search the wood for any new spring herbs.

"This is useless." Frazzled, she turned in a slow circle. "I can't help Mother's mare, or Beatrice, or my father." A desire to give in, quit fighting, took root. A good cry would be a wonderful luxury.

"Lenora!"

She turned toward the voice. Geoffrey Champlain emerged from the gloom of the wood. God preserve. A friend when she most needed one. "I'm so glad you're here."

Geoffrey pulled his dark woolen mantle from his shoulders and gallantly spread it on the ground. "I didn't expect to see you. I thought perhaps to get a glimpse of Beatrice as she walked in the meadow. What has happened? You look distraught."

"Geoffrey, I don't know what to do. Galliard is at Woodshadow." She knelt on the edge of the cloak and tucked her dress underneath her for more padding. The loose weave of the cloak allowed sticks and stems to poke through.

The slender knight sat on his heels beside her. "I know. The whole area is buzzing with the gossip. Does he plan to marry Beatrice?" He rushed the last sentence and stared into the dark shadows of the deep wood.

"I'm not sure." She was so tired her eyelids throbbed.

Geoffrey clenched her wrist painfully. "You're not sure. Have you heard something? What is it?"

Her gasp made him conscious of his behavior, and he released her wrist. "I'm sorry, Lenora. I'm so overwrought with fear."

She placed a forgiving hand on his shoulder. "'Tis forgotten. I know how much Beatrice means to you, and you to her."

Looking to the heavens for guidance, Lenora pondered out loud. "I don't know what to think. Earlier, Galliard had me thinking he means to marry Aunt Matilda."

"Nay." Geoffrey shook his head in bewilderment. "I didn't think about that possibility."

"He must have been jesting when he said 'twas not Beatrice he intends to marry." She couldn't seem to fathom Galliard's plan.

"He could marry you and get Woodshadow through your children." Geoffrey's voice was full of accusation. "Has he said anything to you about marriage."

"Nay. Geoffrey, I can assure you the man has no intention of marrying me. We can barely say a civil word between us. It must be Beatrice," Lenora assured him.

"Still, 'tis an idea I hadn't thought of. Your father has agreed to let you remain unmarried this year?"

She hesitated then moved her hand back and forth. "He's agreed for this year, but he insists I marry soon. Since his illness, he's worried about my future and Woodshadow."

"Then he could marry you off to Galliard." Geoffrey's voice expressed his displeasure.

"But he wouldn't." Her friend's concern warmed her heart. "Father promised that he would let me choose."

Geoffrey condemned her with his eyes. "Two years ago when you returned from Aquitaine, you fought your brother and father with such passion each time they suggested marriage. Queen Eleanor had filled your head with lofty ideas about a woman's place and power. You spoke so forcefully. I didn't think you would ever change your mind. I tried to tell you to leave before your father changed his mind. You should have listened to me."

"Two years ago I had a brother to inherit. When he died it changed everything." Her voice echoed with loss.

"Aye, it did," Geoffrey concurred. "Now we must look to your problem. I've concentrated on Beatrice. I didn't take your situation into account."

"Don't worry about me. I'll figure something out." She rose from her seat.

Geoffrey picked up his cloak and swirled it to his shoulders. He gave her a wily smile. "Aye, I'm sure you will. You are intelligent enough to figure out anything, eventually." He retrieved Lenora's abandoned basket. "I saw some sorrel herbs and parsley in a clearing just beyond these trees. There should be enough to fill your basket and explain your absence to Matilda." His hand squeezed hers in friendly support. "Promise you'll keep me informed."

Lenora returned the affectionate gesture. "Of course, Geoffrey. I know how much this all means to you."

He moved into the shadows of the wood. Lenora pulled her eyes from the disappearing shape and headed off toward the herbs Geoffrey had told her about. She felt more serene since sharing her worries. When she entered the clearing and saw the dainty leaves of the tasty herbs, she counted herself lucky to have such a trustworthy friend.

After several hours, her basket could hold no more. She wandered home not eager to rekindle her battle with Roen. The watchman in the marshal's tower waved to her and she returned the greeting.

She spotted her nemesis after she crossed the fortified bridge to the inner yard. Roen and his second were deep in conversation, watching Destrier running free in the pasture. A herd of Woodshadow's best mares followed behind. Galliard must be calculating the price he could call for his foal. Not willing to confront the man and lose her newfound peace, Lenora headed in the opposite direction of the two men.

The scaffolding along the east wall caught her attention. Several sturdy poles reinforced the crumbling stone wall. Heavy boulders, removed from the upper section, rested on planks suspended on the support poles.

"That man makes me want to scream," she complained to the thick support pole. "He's as dense as the tree you came from." A rain of stone and dust cascaded down the scaffold and peppered Lenora's hair. She dropped the basket of herbs and brushed the rubble from her hair.

Like a dancer around the Maypole, she moved in a sinuous path between the supports of the scaffold. A wrist-thick scrap of wood rested on the ground. A way to vent her frustration materialized.

"Roen de Galliard, you are a despicable, lack-witted, ill-bred tyrant." Hefting the scrap like a club, she pulled back and whacked the support pole with all her might. The pole shuddered. Her hands vibrated from the force. She dropped the pole and dusted her hands off. A prayer of thanks on her lips, she looked heavenward. Then she screamed.

Roen and Hamlin walked among the crofters' cottages inside the inner bailey walls. Roen's nerves tingled, a sense of forboding haunted him. If he were in battle, he would be guarding his back. He looked over his shoulder. No unseen foe appeared.

The bailey showed no reason for his uneasiness. The crofters tended their small private plots of land. Chickens pecked the ground for insects. A swaybacked pony drowsily plodded along the worn path to his lean-to manger. His master, a young boy, directed the pony and cart around Roen, giving the two knights a wide berth.

"Roen?" Hamlin nudged his friend with his shoulder. "You keep looking over your shoulder. Do you think we're being followed?"

"Nay, I'm restless. 'Tis this place. This situation. That woman." At the small fish pond he halted and picked up a round smooth pebble. He tossed it into the middle of the pond and watched the concentric circles ripple across the water.

"I have never seen you so agitated, my friend. Especially over a woman," Hamlin teased.

"Ha," Roen continued. "The wench is undeniably the most stubborn woman I have ever met. She has one discourse, my nonmarriage to her cousin."

Hamlin picked up a stone and skipped it across the pond. His ripples spread across the water, erasing the previous ones. "And what of that? Do you intend to marry Lady Beatrice?" Hamlin's usually jovial eyes grew somber. His lithe body stiffened.

"I haven't really given it much thought," Roen admitted. He tried to picture the girl in his mind but the blond hair and blue eyes melted into fiery auburn hair and earth-colored eyes.

Hamlin opened his mouth to speak when a scream pierced the air.

"Nora!" Roen shouted, and raced toward the sound. His long legs outdistanced Hamlin. His heart hammered as he sped across the bailey to the east wall. A crowd gathered near the scaffolding and he pushed his way through. The villeins shuffled aside for him.

Roen entered the core of the crowd and gasped. Lenora lay crumpled on her side. A weighty block of stone pinned her against the poles. Dirt and gravel whitewashed her hair and kirtle.

He rushed to her side. Terror circulated through his body. With trembling fingers, he placed his hand on her chest for signs of life. The shallow lift of her chest calmed his rampaging heart.

"Lady Lenora!" Hamlin broke through the circle.

"Quick, Hamlin, help me move this boulder. She's trapped against the scaffold." The two men strained. The stone begrudged each small advance. With a final, heroic push, the stone rolled away.

Roen scooped Lenora up in his arms. He cradled her against his chest. Joy and relief engulfed his senses when he saw her dark, thick fringe of lashes flutter. Her eyelids strained to open.

She took a ragged breath. "Put me down."

Stunned, Roen dropped his hold on her legs. Lenora seized his tunic for support as her feet thudded to the ground. A groan of pain shot from her and she rubbed her left ankle.

When she felt steady, she released her hold on Roen and tried to step away. He pulled her back with his arm around her waist.

"I'm fine. Really. Pray let me go." A hoarse whisper was all she could manage.

"What happened? Did you see who did this?" Roen demanded.

"A stone fell. 'Twas an accident." She twisted in his arms and refused to meet his gaze.

"Are you sure? Hamlin, search the top," he directed.

"There is no need." She pushed the hair from her face. "I did it."

Roen's face mirrored puzzlement.

"I hit the pole with a big piece of wood. Hard." Lenora squirmed out of his grasp. "It must have toppled the stone over."

"Why would you attack a scaffold?" He stared at her. Was the wench daft?

"Because I wanted to. It reminded me of someone," Lenora admitted through clenched teeth. The cluster of villeins began to disperse. The excitement over, they returned to the daily chores. Whatever else transpired was between the nobles.

Roen gazed at the thick pole. "Who could it remind you of? It looks exactly what it is, a piece of wood."

"It wasn't its looks that reminded me of someone. 'Twas its intelligence," Lenora snapped. She limped from him, holding her left side.

Roen watched her go and tried to understand her statement. A gentle smile creased his lips as he remembered Lenora's comparison between him and the tree. He started after her.

"Roen!" Hamlin's call from atop the scaffold stopped him. "Come up here. I have something to show you."

He clambered up the platform to his friend. Hamlin held a bit of cloth in his hand. He gave it to Roen and pointed to the footprints in the dust.

Roen felt the soft wool between his fingers. Worn but well made, the material was an expensive weave. Not the type of material a workman would wear. He knelt on one knee and considered the boot prints in the dirt.

"Why would a nobleman be up here?" Roen queried. "See, the prints of his hard soles obliterate all the workmen's."

"Aye," Hamlin added. "I remember seeing workers here till right before the evening meal. Whoever it was came after they left."

Roen traced the outline of the boot print with his finger. Smaller than his own, but too large to be a woman's. He estimated the man was of average height. Nothing that would distinguish him from any of the many nobles at Woodshadow. Roen followed the prints to the edge of the scaffold.

"Where did you find this bit of cloth?"

"Here." Hamlin pointed to the heavy stones. "'Twas lodged between the two. He must have tried to move one and trapped his cloak."

"Perhaps. Or his victim moved. Look." Roen pointed below. Lenora's basket of herbs lay on the ground directly below them. The two men followed the boot prints to the opposite side of the platform. The prints stopped. Directly below, the boulder and rubble that had almost ended Lenora's life lay on the ground.

Roen watched Lenora's retreating shape as she limped toward the inner sanctuary of her home. Her hips swayed to and fro, the long material of her kirtle moved in harmony.

"The men have done as I asked? They have spread the word to the neighboring keeps that I plan to claim a bride at Woodshadow?" He kept his eyes on Lenora.

Hamlin nodded. "Aye, people for miles around should know the news. It seems as though your plan to draw out the phantom assassin worked. Sir Edmund is right—Woodshadow is in danger."

Roen clenched the woolen material in his hand. He stared at the crushed cloth and whispered, "And because of me, so is Lenora."

Chapter Seven

"'Tis done." Roen blew faintly on the wet ink. A wrinkled hand snatched the contract from the table and carried it to the pale man in the bed.

"Let me see." Sir Edmund's hand trembled as he took the paper from his servant. Satisfied that all was as it should be, the ill man closed his eyes. His lips moving in silent prayer, Sir Edmund held the paper to his chest, his hand over his heart. His voice slow and ragged, he asked, "When will you tell her?"

Roen reached across the table and took a fold of papers in his hand. He placed it safely inside the rucks of his embroidered overtunic. With the palm of his hand, he patted the hiding place.

"I'll show her the false contract today. The sooner this business is concluded, the happier I will be." Roen grimaced. 'Twould not be a pleasant encounter.

"How will you get her to agree?" A father's affection for his only child showed in Sir Edmund's voice.

"'Twill be done. She'll not naysay me," Roen guaranteed, then pointed to the contract on the older man's chest. "What of that? Where will the real contract be?"

"'Ere with me." Tom took the contract from his lord's chest and folded it carefully into a leather pouch. He challenged Roen with a baleful one-eyed look then placed the contract inside his rough leather jerkin, mimicking Roen's stance and gesture.

"I assume 'twill be guarded well. If 'tis discovered, our plan will unravel." Roen addressed his remark to Sir Edmund but he kept his granite stare on the servant.

"Tom can be trusted." Sir Edmund drew himself up. "If the need arises, Henry will receive it." Roen did not miss the man's thinly veiled threat.

"Rest easy, man. 'Tis but a deception on my part. No marriage will take place." Roen took his leave of Lenora's father. Hamlin waited outside the door.

"Have you seen the wench?" Roen asked while they descended the stairs.

"Not since last eventide. The lady has made herself scarce in the keep. From what I understand from Bea—Lady Beatrice, 'tis her norm to wander outdoors during the day," Hamlin informed his comrade.

"I've seen that, also. The aunt is the power here." Roen and Hamlin entered the great hall. Servants brushed by with platters of roasted meat. "Thank the saints I don't really have to marry her."

Roen heard the distinct ring of a familiar voice. Lenora stood just to his left, her back to him, deep in conversation with a stout kitchen woman. He let his eyes linger lazily down Lenora's backside, his imagination filling in the image underneath her simple blue woolen gown. It was hemmed too short, or had been worn for too many years, he noticed. The edge of her ecru chemise showed at her feet. Lenora's soft leather slippers were dark from the morning dew.

She wore no jewelry, she needed none. No gem could outshine Lenora's hair. Tendrils danced around her face and down her long, graceful neck. The bulk of her hair was pulled back into a loose braid.

The servant woman tilted her head in his direction. Lenora did not turn to look his way. She walked off, disdaining to acknowledge him. Roen's watchful eyes kept her in sight. He noticed an improvement in her limp.

"I think you are in for a long siege, Roen," Hamlin observed.

"Aye, and the first skirmish lies just ahead." Roen nodded his head toward the great hall. The room resounded with noise from knights, ladies, dogs and attendants.

"Nay, Roen, I was but jesting." Hamlin did not like the battle look in Roen's eye. "You needs must woo the girl. Have her agog with your charm and gallantry."

"I've neither the time nor the inclination for such foolishness. I need the girl's obedience. She must have a weakness. I will fish it out and use it to my advantage." Roen pursed his lips as battle plans formed in his head.

"God's blood, man!" Hamlin pulled his liege lord up short. "She's a woman, not a fortress." He paused before he accused, "You are enjoying this."

"'Tis a service I do for my king," Roen replied, defending himself against Hamlin's outrageous charge. But if he could pull the arrogant wench down a peg, 'twould make the job more acceptable.

Knights milled about the side tables, conversing in small cliques. Several young girls, fostered at Woodshadow, giggled as Roen and Hamlin passed. Hamlin gave a flirtatious wink. The girls scurried off, blushing and laughing.

"See, 'tis easy," Hamlin instructed.

"Sir Roen," Matilda greeted, and went to Roen's side. Her daughter followed quietly behind. "Would you be kind enough to escort us to dinner?"

Roen hated the pomp that Matilda demanded with each meal. Since his first night at Woodshadow, the woman had ordered every status ceremony performed. He might as well be at court. 'Twas just one more reason to finish his business here as quickly as possible.

He scowled, his distaste for the charade showing plainly on his face. He muttered, "Very well. Let's get on with it."

A glance at Beatrice's face stopped him. Her white blond hair accentuated the ashen color of her face. Two terror-filled blue eyes gazed intently at the embroidered neck of his tunic. The girl could not meet his direct stare.

She looked like a frightened animal. Her mother's fanatical expression reminded Roen of a pagan priestess offering a live sacrifice to a bloodthirsty deity.

It pricked his conscience to have to admit Lenora was right. Beatrice was terrified of him. Any thoughts concerning a marriage to the frightened girl fled. Too many innocents like her, terrified of what goes on between a man and woman, ended up killing themselves on their wedding night. He did not wish Beatrice's death on his conscience.

"Lady Beatrice." Roen kept his voice calm and polite. The girl startled like a petrified fawn. He forced the gruffness from his words. "I would be honored to escort you, but I believe the true lady of Woodshadow should enter her hall first." He glanced about the stone walls for his quarry. Lenora was nowhere in sight.

"Lenora is not here, as usual." Matilda pushed the wooden body of her daughter closer. The crimson folds of Beatrice's kirtle swirled against him. The frightened girl grabbed her dress, afraid even to let that much of her touch him.

"I was speaking of yourself, Lady Matilda." Roen fought down a wave of revulsion for the older woman. He knew exactly what kind of woman she was, exactly the kind of mother. He had lived his childhood with a woman who could instruct even Lady Matilda on trickery.

Taking the woman's arm, Roen led the procession toward the raised dais to the high table of the keep. Hamlin followed with Beatrice, her body still numb from fear of the man ahead of her. Woodshadow's steward and cleric followed.

Sir Hywel abruptly hailed Roen. The seneschal cocked an eyebrow and asked, "Are you the rascal who stole my shoes?" The cleric hastily hushed the bewildered older man and positioned him back in line.

"This is a madhouse." Roen gritted his teeth and entered the great hall.

The room grew silent as the entourage approached. Each knight and lady stood at the side tables. The women curtsied, the men bowed. Roen sensed the reserve. Woodshadow's nobles executed the correct decorum, but without a sense of loyalty. Matilda served as chatelaine, but no love existed between her and the people of the keep.

When the group reached the high table, Roen took Sir Edmund's seat, directly behind the elaborate nef full of salt. Matilda sat regally to his left. Beatrice stopped when she realized she would sit next to Roen. Hamlin moved ahead, despite Matilda's scowl, and took the seat on Roen's right. Now that there was a buffer between her and Roen, Beatrice took her place next to Hamlin. She rewarded the gallant knight with a shy, grateful smile. Sir Hywel and the friar filled in the remaining seats. One chair remained vacant.

Lenora watched the procession from an alcove. With no regrets, she gave up her seat at the high table. Too many splendid meals had soured in her stomach due to Galliard's snide remarks. She waited until the group was seated and the servants began to ladle out the food. When the hall resumed conversation, Lenora maneuvered to a side table, one with none of Galliard's men.

From her vantage point, she studied the high table. Beatrice's panic was evident. Lenora saw Hamlin offer her cousin a bite of roasted lamb. Beatrice shook her head, too alarmed to eat.

A surprising stab of jealousy hit her when she saw Matilda seated as the lady of the keep, where, by all rights, she should be. It had never bothered her before, but then her aunt had never so dramatized the role. Her black hair was parted in the center and wound into two plaits on either side. A translucent oblong veil covered her head and matched the cream-colored wimple that framed her face. A gold coronet, set with unfaceted diamonds and amethyst, held her veil like a crown. Her long purple silk overtunic shimmered in the candlelight of the great hall.

Lenora smoothed the long sleeves of her kirtle. Dismayed, she noticed where a long stretch of seam had come undone. Hastily, she pushed the sleeves back up to her elbow. She knew without looking that the hem of her gown was mud-spattered and stained from her morning inspection of the spring-planted fields.

The older woman clung to the knight's every word. She leaned her dark head closer to Roen's fair one. Refined laughter fell from Matilda's lips and she placed her hand on Roen's when the knight lifted his wine goblet. Lenora felt another meal begin to sour as her aunt artfully guided the silver cup to her thin lips.

Lenora caught her aunt's eyes. They glittered, sharp and brittle. She sat back, stunned at the victorious look her aunt shot her way. Matilda spoke, her voice carrying across the boisterous hall. "Sir Roen, pray tell me if the rumors I have heard are true. Do you plan to marry a woman of Woodshadow?" The room quieted. All eyes were on the high table.

Roen raised his goblet to Matilda. "I *am* here to claim a bride." He pulled the contract from his tunic. "I am to be the new lord of Woodshadow. The woman I *wed* will be the lady of this keep, in action as well as station." His gaze sought out Lenora. He evaluated her reaction to the news. 'Twas what he anticipated.

Matilda clasped her hands together. A satisfied smile slanted across her lips. She jumped from her chair and gave her daughter a hard squeeze. "At last. After all these months of holding this keep together, I will finally be rewarded. Beatrice, I'm so happy for us." Triumph resounded in her voice. There could be no doubt in the woman's mind who the intended bride was. At her wedding, Beatrice would become the Lady of Woodshadow, regardless of her station now.

Her face drained of color, Beatrice sat stunned. Matilda drew her daughter to her feet. She stood stiff, frozen by the horror of the news. Lenora saw her cousin's white face and the petrified stare in her eyes. Blessed Virgin, Lenora thought, she's going to swoon.

Beatrice's knees buckled. Hamlin was at her side like a guardian angel. He circled her waist with his arm, offering support. Confused and frightened, Beatrice tilted her head to rest on his shoulder. The young knight guided her away from the commotion of the head table.

Matilda fluttered back to Roen, aghast at her daughter's reaction. Her deliberate stare silenced the murmuring. "Please excuse her, my lord, she was taken aback by the news. A betrothal is a heady thing for a young girl."

A sardonic smile twisted Roen's lips. He pierced Lenora's gaze with his own as he asked loudly, "Then tell me, Lady Lenora, is that how you feel?"

Unmasked hatred for the golden lion of a man who was determined to ruin her gentle cousin's life flamed in Lenora's soul. She bolted from her seat to stand in front of the arrogant lout. Her anger overrode the pain in her ankle and side.

Lenora held herself majestically, defiance an aegis around her. Uncontrolled rage fired her voice. "Nay, Galliard. 'Tis not a swoon I would do now. If I had but a weapon to do me justice, you would feel its point. Do not pretend ignorance of my feelings. I have told you time and time again how I feel about this union."

The sarcastic smile did not leave Roen's handsome face. He scraped his chair back along the floor and stood. "And I have listened . . . time and time again." He opened the contract and turned it toward her. "That is why I am betrothed to you. When you are Lenora de Galliard, perhaps then you will give the name the respect it deserves."

Her tawny eyes widened. She gasped when she saw her name and the unmistakable flourish of her father's signature. Lenora snatched the contract from his hands. Oblivious to the murmuring room of people, she sank into the abandoned head chair.

Matilda pushed her way forward and leaned over Lenora's chair. Decorum forgotten, she rudely read the private document and tried to discredit the written words. "This cannot be!" She turned to Roen, dazed. "Edmund gives you everything. Woodshadow is lost."

"Lost?" Roen quirked his eyebrow. "'Tis an interesting choice of words, Lady Matilda." The older woman's response gave validity to Roen's reasons for displaying the document to all during the meal. Judging from the rest of the keep's reaction, none but Matilda bore a grievance. He pushed the matron further. "Woodshadow will go to Lenora as it should. From her to her heirs. Lenora's and mine."

"And if no heirs, you will still get this keep. 'Twould be the only way to pay your settlement," Matilda denounced. "This is my family land. Edmund does not have the right."

"Are not your niece and brother-in-law family?" Roen questioned. "Did your sister's husband do nothing to make this land prosper, to protect it from those who would take it by force?"

Matilda stamped her foot. "Edmund cannot do this to me."

"He would not do this." Lenora's quiet voice sounded deceptively calm. She thrust the contract back at Roen. Her eyes, the color of liquid gold, were clear and confident. "I do not know how you tricked my father into this travesty. I've suspected his illness was more severe than he showed. This proves it. If he were able, he would never have signed such a lie as this."

Lenora released the offending document. The paper glided to the floor. She placed the heel of her slipper on the offending document and ground it into the wooden floor. "But your trickery is for naught. You did not know that Father has paid the king's fee for me to remain unmarried for the rest of the year. I cannot be forced. You lose this battle, Galliard."

"But not the war, Nora. The year will pass. Why postpone the inevitable?" Roen's smile softened. Lenora was beautiful in her outrage. She held herself to her full height, taking advantage of every asset. The set of her shoulders pulled her bodice across her full breasts. One copper-colored ringlet escaped the confines of her braid. He met her indignant eyes, undaunted.

"A year is a long time to wait. My father will get well. He will petition the king. There are few closer to Henry than my father. King Henry will deal with you harshly. 'Twould serve you better to leave this demesne now." Lenora delivered the order with authority.

"Aye, to leave this place has ofttimes crossed my mind of late. But that was before 'twas the home of my betrothed. My future home. Nay, I will stay. We will marry. Soon." Roen's declaration of intent sounded more like a threat, even to his ears.

He tried to defuse the tension. "Come, Nora, 'tis for the best. You could do much worse than me for a husband. We will talk of it later, after you have had time to accept the idea."

"I have no intention of speaking with you later today, tomorrow, next year or anytime." She was livid. The knave dismissed her like a child. Did he think that marriage to him was such a prize? She'd not swoon away in his presence. Nay, she would fight and win.

Roen patted her head like an indulged child. "Really? What a truly heavenly gift for your husband. Alas, I must leave you now, my dearling." His lips twitched when he heard her angry gasp at the term of endearment. "I must have words with my men. Messengers must be sent to your vassals on the upcoming nuptials."

'Twas a joy to tease her. She was so quick to rise to the bait. He intended to leave her to wallow in her anger but a devilish vision made him stop.

"But before I leave, a token of my affection." He drew her close, trapping her hands on his chest. One muscular arm at her slender waist pulled her to him. The other grabbed a handful of fiery locks. He tugged at her hair, coercing her to tilt her chin up. His lips paused a thread's distance from hers. He inhaled the sweet aroma of her breath. Roen looked into Lenora's golden eyes, a conqueror's smile on his face.

"You are mine," he whispered for her ears only.

"Never." She issued a challenge for all to hear.

In answer, he closed the distance to her lips and captured the red fullness. Roen thought to tease her, perhaps to frighten some sense into her. He plundered the ripeness of her mouth and drank in the fresh nectar. The taste quenched a deep thirst in his soul but made him thirst for more of the elixir.

The sweet smell of her fragrance ensnared him. Roen became engulfed in the intoxicating lavender scent of Lenora's skin. It compelled him to pull her even nearer to him. She fought him, arching her back to escape his mouth. Her hips pushed against him. The response in his braes was immediate. His manhood quickened. He could feel his hardness push against the softness of her abdomen.

Roen realized that his plan had somehow gone awry. Instead of him capturing Lenora, she had captivated him. Still, he could not release her. His hand moved from her braid to the back of her neck. He forced her to him and felt the exciting heaviness of her breasts against his chest. His tongue pushed against the restraint of her closed teeth.

Lenora struggled for breath and Roen seized the opportunity. When she opened her mouth for air, his tongue gained entry and explored the intimate reaches of her mouth, her movements stopped. He reveled in consuming her lips without wasting energy on her futile attempts to escape him. The moment was short-lived.

The pain in his leg chilled his ardor. "God's blood." Roen released her and grabbed his shin.

Lenora, her face flushed, her lips seductively swollen, drew back her slender foot and kicked him again in the other shin. She gave him an unmistakably contemptuous look before leaving the hall. Roen was glad to see her limp become more pronounced.

"I believe that is two battles won by the Lady Lenora," Hamlin said dryly. He leaned against the wall, his arms crossed nonchalantly at his chest.

Roen returned to the head chair, glad to see Matilda had vacated the room. The rest of the hall remained mute. Knights stood, unsure of the correct move. They looked to Sir Edmund's steward to guide them. Sir Hywel continued to eat, unaware of the commotion around him. The men and women gave Roen furtive looks as they gossiped behind their cups of wine. He watched Lenora climb the stairs.

" 'Tis true I've lost a few battles in my time, Hamlin." Roen kneaded his shin. "But I always win the war, eventually."

Obviously, the kiss had not affected her as it had him. That unnerved him. He had felt the brunt of too many of her tantrums to believe Lenora was passionless. Nay, the wench was ruled by her passion. He directed his remark to Hamlin, but his eyes never left Lenora's body. "Especially this war, Hamlin. This is one I intend to win, at all costs."

Chapter Eight

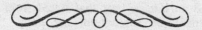

Lenora slammed the oak door behind her and fled into the poorly lighted women's dormitory. She threw herself face-down onto the rope bed she shared with her cousin. Strangled sobs tore from her in heartbreaking spasms. "'Tis a lie—a lie," Lenora chanted in hopelessness. "Father would not do this."

Time you married, Sir Edmund's voice reverberated in her head. *An heir. Woodshadow needs an heir.*

An embroidered pillow from the bed caught her eye and her anger. She hurled it across the room and shouted, "Damn you, Galliard." The pillow hit the door and hung in midair, its threads caught on the iron braces of the heavy door. She cringed as she saw her delicate stitches pulled, her work destroyed.

Lenora sprang from the bed. Eyes blurred by tears, she tried to untangle the hairlike threads from their confinement. Each strand she tugged caused a pucker or a broken thread. Finally, she freed the last string and stared at her meticulous work, ruined beyond repair. Clutching the pillow to her chest, she rocked back and forth. Late afternoon shadows crept into the recesses of the room as despair engulfed her. All of the intricate strands of her life were being pulled apart.

Sinking to the rushes on the floor, Lenora laid her cheek against the ruined pillow. She had caused the destruction of her artwork in a moment of anger. Galliard's destruction of her life was by design. His greed threatened to rob her of her freedom.

"I'll never marry him," Lenora vowed. The words left her lips with little conviction. Heady waves of emotion rekindled in her breasts as she remembered the hardness of Galliard's

warm body against hers. Currents of passion bit at her lips
from his kiss. Lenora closed her eyes tightly. It was difficult to
breathe, as if an iron belt encircled her chest, or was it memories of strong arms holding her, caressing her. Gooseflesh
prickled along her arms and up her neck just as it had when
Roen's lips had invaded her mouth.

His breath had smelled sweet from the wine, his lips had
teased, enticed. Flashes of Roen, his shirt loose, his chest exposed, created an intense heat that flared from the core of
Lenora's womanhood throughout her body. "Nay." She
pounded her head with her fist. "He disgusts me." Her voice
echoed in the empty room and begged her body to listen.

"Lady Lenora, are ye in there?" an urgent young voice called
from beyond the door. A knock banged on the thick wood.
"Tom's sent me for ye. He says to come right quick. That mare
of yours is—"

Lenora jumped to her feet and threw open the door. "What
about Silver Maple? What did Tom say? Hurry, Tyrus, exercise your tongue."

The startled stableboy stepped back from the doorjamb.
"Tom, he says the mare's goin' to foal. Tonight." The boy
opened his mouth to continue but Lenora charged past him.
Down the stairs she bolted, thoughts of her own troubles va-
porized like morning fog.

Instead of tearing across the main hall and reckoning with
her aunt or Roen, she turned down a passageway and exited
onto the high inner-bailey wall. The condition of her beloved
mare filled her with worry as she ran along the inner curtain
wall and down the staircase of the round tower to the ground
floor.

The setting sun began to paint the English sky in bright pinks
and blues when Lenora made her way to the stable. She pulled
up short. The terrified anguish of Silver Maple's neighs
knocked the air from her lungs. "Sweet Jesus," Lenora cried,
and pushed aside the stable gate.

The mare lay on her side. Her glazed eyes rolled back into her
head. Tom stretched across the dark, sweat-stained horse's
middle and tried to keep the pain-crazed animal down. A spasm
shuddered across the mare's bulging stomach. Sharp hooves
thrashed as she tried to regain her feet.

"Silver Maple." Lenora threw herself across the mare's neck. The acrid smell of sweat and fear inhabited the stall.

"Get yourself out of here. 'Tis too dangerous for ye in here," Tom chastised Lenora. Breathing heavily, the old man poked her with his good leg. "The mare don't know ye. She's mad with the pain, girl." Tom didn't dare move for fear the mare would escape and pound both him and Lenora into the ground.

"Tom, I can't leave her." Fresh tears streamed down Lenora's face. "What's wrong?"

Too tired to fight both the man and girl, the mare lay restlessly under them. "'Tis a breech." Tom leaned against the mare and rested. "The foal's turned inside her and a-rippin' her up inside." His voice low and deliberate, he finished what Lenora already knew. "She ain't gonna make it, girl. 'Tis best we put her out of her misery."

"Nay!" Lenora sobbed her denial and knelt to stroke the velvety muzzle. The mare squealed as another labor pain contracted her body. Lenora cringed. She felt the grip of pain, also. "Nay." She choked and tasted the salt of her own tears. The flavor did not sit well on her palate. Faith and unwavering determination set the fine lines of her face. "There must be something we can do. Think, Tom. Is there any way to turn the foal?" Lenora demanded, and applied all her weight against the near mad horse.

"We can't. The mare's not gonna let anyone near her but us. It takes the both of us to hold her down. We need someone to pull the foal out." Tom searched the evening darkness for help. The stable was empty except for them. Faint strains of music drifted in on the brisk night air and clued Lenora as to the whereabouts of the stableboys.

Silver screamed out in pain and threw off her subduers. Trapped between the horse and the wall, Lenora made a desperate grab for the halter. Silver tossed her head violently and slammed Lenora against the rough boards of the stall. Splinters of pain lanced through her wrenched shoulders, but she managed to hold on to her horse. The mare's hooves lashed out in an attempt to escape. Silver's sharp hoof caught on Lenora's dress. It sliced through the coarse material of her kirtle and exposed her calf. A thin red welt puckered on her leg.

"That's it." Tom reached for the long thick knife he had sheathed on his belt. "She's gettin' wilder. 'Tis time to have done with it."

Tap. Tap. Tap. The polished chess piece in Roen's hand met the arm of the chair with methodical regularity. His eyes continually strayed toward the winding staircase at the far end of the hall. Hamlin, seated across the chessboard from his friend, could not contain his delight at Roen's displeasure. Hamlin raised his tankard of ale in mock salute. "I think 'tis time to seek other pursuits, my friend. She's not coming down."

Roen dropped the pawn on the table near the elaborately inlaid chessboard. "I'm not waiting for the chit to come downstairs." He waved his hand imperiously over the board. "I've been waiting for you to move your piece. Come on with it, man."

"For me?" Hamlin grinned. "Roen, 'tis your turn to move. I've already told you that twice." He stood and shifted his body to block Roen's view of the stairs. The soft shuffle of footsteps caused his friend to jump from his seat and push him aside. A breathless lad scampered down the stone steps. Hamlin chuckled when Roen checked his advancement.

"Friend, I leave you for my bed." Hamlin gave a retiring wave of his hand. A shapely servant girl hurried past the two men, a jug of wine in her hand. "But perhaps I won't retire alone." He executed a sharp turnaround, winked to his friend and followed the girl.

Soft giggles and gentle laughter told Roen his compatriot would not be lonely tonight. He returned to his seat and contemplated the abandoned chess game. His white queen, captured by Hamlin, lay on its side. Roen retrieved the piece and traced the queen's profile with his thumb. High forehead, straight nose, a gentle smile. The carver had done exquisite work. His thumb paused on the queen's full lips. He examined the piece. 'Twas Lenora! He could see the resemblance now. Roen threw the white queen on the table in disgust. Was there no way to escape the woman? A movement on the stairs snared his attention. "Nora?" he bellowed.

The boy seated on the bottom stair jumped to his feet. "Just Tyrus 'ere, milord. Just restin' a spell 'ere on the step. Just deliverin' a message for Lady Lenora." The boy staggered back from the knight and tried to work the door latch.

"What message?" Roen clamped his hand on the boy's slender shoulder. "When did you deliver it?"

"'Twas a message for Lady Lenora."

Roen could hear the boy's knees knocking together. He gave the youth a sneer that had brought knights to their knees.

The boy began to quake and squeaked out a reply. "'Ere, sir, ye could rightly throw me against yon wall there and break me bones. 'Tis your right and all. But I gives the message to Lady Lenora 'cause it were for Lady Lenora. If'n ye want to know what 'tis about, then ye needs to talk to her." Tyrus squinted and stiffened his small body to take the expected blow.

Roen lifted the weight of his hand from Tyrus's shoulder. He saluted the boy's courage. "I apologize. You are correct. I should discuss this with Lady Lenora."

Tyrus opened one eye, then the other. The look of awe, then boyish bravado on the young stableboy's face quirked a smile on Roen's lips.

"You think highly of your lady." Roen stroked his chin with his hand. "'Tis commendable to find a lad so loyal, considering the lady in question's behavior."

Tyrus forgave the nobleman and gave Roen an agreeing nod. "Think nothin' of it." He resumed his retreat from the hall. "There's not much any of Woodshadow wouldn't do for our lord and lady."

"Wait, boy." Roen saw him stop in midstride. "I would have you go upstairs to the ladies' quarters and give Lady Lenora a message from me."

"Can't, Sir Knight." Tyrus reached the handle and opened the door. "Lady Lenora ain't up there no more. She's surely out to the stable by now." The boy slipped through the opening and pulled the door shut.

He pondered the lad's loyalty. Why were the people of Woodshadow so devoted to a lady who neglected her duties? Roen decided to follow Tyrus out the door. He rushed down the forebuilding steps and made out the small shape near the kitchen. A couple of long strides and the distance between him and the boy became negligible.

From the kitchen, Roen heard loud, welcoming shouts greet the lad's arrival. The boy ducked into the crowded structure and grabbed a trencher. Tyrus ladled out hot rich stew and began to shovel spoonfuls into his mouth. His mouth full, he wiggled into a seat on the long bench with his friends.

Loud laughter and the smell of spiced wine spilled from the open door. A bawdy song was being mangled by several off-key singers. Roen noted the camaraderie and content of the villeins, the signs of a well-run keep.

The question remained: by whose hand was the keep run? Sir Edmund was too ill, the steward was not always in his right mind, Beatrice was too timid, and Matilda was at best tolerated. As far as Roen could deduce, Lenora did not interest herself with the duties of the keep. Roen didn't like riddles, he wanted answers, and he knew where to get them.

He sprinted across the courtyard to the stable. It lay in darkness, save for one feeble light that flickered in the open window. Roen steeled his backbone, ready to confront the shrew. Approaching the stable, he mentally rehearsed a speech. He would make her see reason.

"Nay, Tom! You can't do this! Put away the knife." Lenora's desperate cries reached Roen. The warrior unsheathed the heavy broadsword from his belt and peeked through a knot in the wood. Shadowy light illuminated Lenora lying on the ground in a stall. Sir Edmund's man, Tom, stood above her, his all-too-familiar dagger in his hand.

"'Tis time," Tom threatened while he edged closer to Lenora. Tears streamed down her face. Despair and sadness etched her face with breathtaking beauty. Roen slipped into the darkening shadows and inched closer.

"Tom, please," Lenora begged. She covered her face with her hands. "I cannot see this."

"Nor will you have to." The tip of Roen's sword rested lightly at the base of the old man's neck. "So, I discover the traitor in Woodshadow's midst, right at the lord's side." Roen emerged from the shadows. "Nora, come away from there." He was pleased to see that for once she did as she was told.

Lenora jumped up and thrust her body between him and the tired old stableman. She batted the sword away with the back of her hand. "What do you think you are doing?" Her red-rimmed eyes flashed with anger. Behind her, an animal moaned and thrashed.

Roen stared at her in disbelief. "Saving your worthless life." He sheathed his sword as he reviewed Lenora. Copper-colored locks fell in alluring disarray. Hay straws clung to her hair. The compulsion to remove each one so that he could run his fingers through the silky strands almost overcame him. He seized the pommel of his sword to ensure his fingers would obey his mind and not the raw hunger in his loins. Roen's anger flared when the swirl of Lenora's dress displayed the rent in her kirtle and a puckering red welt.

" 'S all right, Lady Lenora. No 'arm done." Tom gave Roen a knowing nod. "The man's edgy. 'Tis why he's still alive with the reputation he's got."

Lenora's attention was diverted by the mare. The animal's moans grew more insistent. Tom gripped his dagger once more and Lenora's eyes widened.

Words tumbled from her quivering lips. "The foal is turned. Pray, help us to save her. Silver can't die." She squeezed his arms tightly and pleaded, "Roen, I need your help."

Lenora's use of his name jolted his emotions unexpectedly. He sucked in his breath and felt her pleas sift into his heart, reawakening a long-dead part of it. He found he could not deny her.

The mare tried to stagger to her feet. "Old man, keep the mare down," Roen ordered. "Nora." He subdued his voice. "I can't promise you anything. If the mare needs to be put down, I'll do it. The animal shan't suffer needlessly." Lenora bit her upper lip and nodded. Silent tears streamed down her face.

Tom shuffled to Silver's side while Lenora grabbed the rope halter. Roen clutched at her kirtle to stop her. "Lenora, step away."

Deaf to Roen's command, she grasped the halter and attempted to lull her horse. "Easy, girl. Everything will be all right." With gentle words and hands, Lenora eased the horse back down onto the hay. "There's not much time. Do it now." She cradled the mare's head in her lap and whispered into the feathery softness of the animal's ear. "Don't worry, Silver. Roen will help you." Lenora was surprised to find that she really believed it.

Tom leaned against the mare's middle with his hand against her tortured belly. "Get ready, I can feel another'n coming on." Silver rattled out each labored breath.

Lenora squeezed the prickly rope halter until her knuckles turned white. The strands of the hemp rope hurt her fingers but gave her something to concentrate on instead of the pain in her heart. A silent prayer on her lips, she sneaked a look at Roen. He knelt near her mare, one leg braced against the equine. Lenora raised her gaze to find his eyes searching her face. The tremor in her voice bespoke the pent-up emotion she fought to contain. "No matter what happens, thank you, Roen."

Silver thrashed out as the contraction possessed her body. The horse's moans echoed in the tiny stall. Lenora fought to keep the mare still. Tom's holler of "Pull!" could barely be discerned from the agonized cries of the horse and the physical straining of the three of them. The rope burned deeper into her palms. She heard Roen's grunts as he reached to extract the small life from its mother's womb.

"I've got it." Roen pulled and sweat beaded across his forehead. The biceps of his arms contracted as he tugged on the foal. Another contraction shook the mare, and he renewed his tug-of-war. Silver's movements became more frantic. Roen gave one last pull. A coal black, wet foal slid out onto the hay and puffed rapid breaths of freedom. Its mother, suddenly released from her pain, moaned softly in Lenora's lap.

Through glistening, tear-filled eyes, she watched the newborn suck in life-giving air. The tiny rib cage expanded in short, jagged breaths. Tom threw Roen a rough grain sack and scooted over to Lenora. The gnarled stableman watched the tiny foal like a proud grandfather. "Look at 'im, will ya? He's a purty thing, right purty."

"He's beautiful," Lenora agreed. She reached over and gave her friend a fierce hug. Tom's face crimsoned.

"They're not out of danger yet." Roen dashed her rekindled hope as he dried his hands. He threw down the hemp sack and grabbed Silver's halter. Flint gray eyes bored into Lenora's as he yanked on the halter. "We have to get both of them up on their feet."

"Wait, let her rest," Lenora protested. "She's drained from this."

"We can't. You know we need to do this." Roen's eyes flashed a gentle warning.

New tears formed, and she nodded. As she rose from her cramped position, a painful tingle coursed through her calves. She struggled to stand, but her legs caved in. Roen caught her easily.

"Damn." His voice was a husky whisper. The tip of his tongue brushed against the outside curl of her ear. She shuddered.

Her body ached from fatigue but a yearning grew in her like a spring plant. And just as a new plant took nourishment from the sun and earth, the need inside of her desired nourishment, from Roen. Lenora leaned into the hard muscular torso next to her.

Roen felt Lenora's body fit so easily against his own. His mouth grew dry. He fought to control the desire to throw her down on the straw and ravish her. "Lenora." He pried her from his body with gentle fingers. The absence of her body next to his caused an ache of emptiness in his chest. "We have to get the horses up. I need you to help. Talk to her, yell at her, whatever it takes."

Lenora stiffened, shame washed over her. How could she so easily forget Silver and the foal? Wiping her tears away, she sniffed and grabbed the halter next to Roen's hand. "Tom, you help the colt." Lenora took a deep breath and began to urge Silver up from the dirty hay. She started in a sing-song voice. "Come on, girl. Time to get up. I know you're tired, love." The only movement the mare made was to close her eyes. Panic flourished in Lenora's heart.

"Grab her tail." Lenora gripped the halter with two hands and planted her feet firmly on the slippery stall floor. "Now!" she commanded. Roen pulled on Silver's tail while Lenora screamed and tugged at her head. "Get up, you old lazy thing. Up, I say." She kicked the horse hard under the breastbone. The mare's eyes shot open. Lenora and Roen continued to pull and tug until Silver staggered to her feet.

The mare swayed to and fro while Lenora and Roen leaned against the animal to steady her. They watched the tenacious colt take dainty steps toward them. He paused to view the two strange beings near his mother. After a long perusal, the colt's hunger overcame the fear and he began to noisily slurp nourishment. Tom raked up the old bedding and replaced it quickly with clean, fresh-smelling straw. As the mare steadied, Roen brought clean water and feed to the groggy horse.

Lenora shoulders ached, and her arms felt like leaden weights. The scratch on her leg stung and her head pounded with every step she took. The colt stepped on her toe as he maneuvered for a better angle to nurse. She gave the greedy newborn a tired smile.

"Nora, you need to sit down." Roen led her away from Silver. She was so tired she didn't have the energy to correct Galliard's pronunciation of her name. He guided her to a small bench outside the stall. Lenora sat and rested her head against the wall. Her eyes wouldn't stay open. In a dreamlike state, she concentrated on hearing the conversation between Roen and Tom.

"Ye think they'll pull through?" Tom queried.

"There could be complications. With a little good luck, there is an excellent chance both will be fine," Roen answered.

The words penetrated her sleep-draped reasoning and Lenora bolted awake. There had been too much bad luck at Woodshadow of late to leave anything to chance.

"You're right, Galliard. Silver is not out of danger yet. There could still be trouble. Tom, do you have any blankets here?"

The two men eyed her in surprise. "There's some horse blankets in the tack room but they got moth holes in 'em as big as your fist," Tom answered slowly, not yielding the information easily.

"That will do. Pray, fetch them for me."

"Why?" Roen asked the question with lethal calmness. Tom limped off, determined to avoid the confrontation between two hot tempers.

Relying on her lance of determination, Lenora met the knight's gaze. Galliard was not her master, yet. Until that time he had no right to impose sanctions against her movements. Still, she hesitated before speaking, knowing the tempest that her words would bring.

Chapter Nine

"You will do no such thing. You will return to your room now." Roen's voice boomed through the murky stable.

"Keep your voice down," Lenora hissed. "You'll disturb Silver and the colt." She wagged her finger at Roen's chest. "You don't own me, Galliard. I do what I want in my own keep." Catching sight of Tom, she instructed the stableman to drop the blankets near the pile of hay.

"Take the blankets away." Roen issued a countercommand. "Lady Lenora shan't be in need of them."

In reply, she lifted the heavy blankets from Tom's arms and began to spread them out on a pallet of hay near the mare's stall.

"What's goin' on 'ere?" Tom asked.

"Your *lady*—" Roen stressed the last word "—intends to spend the night in the stables like a common tavern wench." He stepped on the edge of the blanket Lenora knelt on. "She plans to rest out here, alone, in case the mare needs her in the night. Would that she attended her duties to the castle as intently as she does this flea-bitten animal."

"Would that you had a heart instead of stone in your chest. Silver was my mother's favorite mount. To me, the horse is more than an animal, she is a living remembrance of my mother's love. To touch her is to touch that love. Can you not remember the love of your own mother and understand my concern?"

His eyes turned cold, the color of a wind-buffeted hill devoid of life. His full mouth twisted into a scornful snarl, an animallike growl rumbled low in his throat. "My mother's love? I do not waste my time on such maudlin frivolities. 'Twas not love I learned at my mother's knee. Though I will admit the lessons she taught me have served me better than that foolish sentiment.''

Silence echoed in the velvety blackness of the stable. The glow of the candle illuminated the anguish on Roen's face. Lenora felt that to understand his pain would take more light than a thousand candles could give. "I know not the story behind your words, Galliard. But I know mine. I have known that love and will protect the 'foolish sentiment.' I will rest here this night, and every night, until I am sure Silver is out of danger." She refused to allow Roen to intimidate her.

The loose boards shook from the shout he threw at her. "Woman, why do you refuse everything I tell you to do? Your mother should have taught you duty instead of babble. Tom can spend the night here. If the mare is in distress, he can help her."

The dry tinder of her temper sparked to a flame. "What my mother taught me is no concern of yours, Galliard, now or ever." She unfolded a blanket with a loud crack. Silver neighed in the stall and Lenora brought her voice to a controlled calm. "Tom's leg will give him trouble for sure if he sleeps on the cold ground. 'Tis inconsiderate of you to even suggest such a thing. Besides, he alone could not handle her. He would still need help."

Roen fumed. He conceded her point but he wasn't finished yet. "The man will find help."

Lenora paused while she positioned the harsh woolen blanket on top of the others. She met his eyes with her own warm sienna-colored ones. "Silver knows no other hand, before tonight, save my mother's, Tom's and mine. She allowed your hands on her because of our presence and her pain. In the night, with a new colt, the mare would stomp a stranger to the ground should they enter the stall."

Determined not to be swayed from her decision, Lenora fluffed hay in between the layers of blankets. "Tom, are there not a few more covers to be found? I fear 'twill be a cool night." She prayed Galliard would not pursue the issue further. The ache in her shoulders intensified, her jittery nerves were barely controllable.

"Aye, there might be a blanket or two tucked in the loft."
Tom rose slowly; the night's exertions weighed on him. As he
turned, his damaged foot dragged the ground.

"Sit, I can get them. You stay here and watch the horses."
Lenora steered Tom toward the bench, seizing the opportunity
to escape Roen's dark scowl.

When Roen heard Lenora's steps creak on the loft above, he
plopped one foot on the bench and leaned an elbow against his
bent knee. His voice seethed as he asked, "Why do you go
against me, old man? You know as well as I her life is perilous
at best. She cannot spend the night out here alone."

Tom scratched his sparse beard. "'Cause I'm a-thinkin' there
just might be a need for a-watchin' those two horses."

"The fact that someone is here in the barn is not going to
save those horses," he blurted out impatiently.

Limping toward a neglected blanket and some wooden bowls
beneath the stairs, Tom shrugged his shoulders. "It might not,
then agin it might." The faithful servant motioned to the nest
beneath the stairs. "Lady Lenora's dog kenneled 'ere. He's
been a-missin' for a time now. Don't figure to ever see old
Gladymer agin."

"What's your point, old man?" Roen demanded.

"Well, I'll tell ya. Lady Lenora knew Silver might not live
if'n she took with a foal. I watched that girl come every night
and lock that gate. Yet that mare escaped her stall. Escaped,
mind ya, not busted, 'cause that lock weren't broken. The
morning we find Silver out in the pasture, that's the morning
Gladymer comes up missin'."

Roen did not miss Tom's innuendo. "What purpose would
be served by killing a dog and horse?"

Tom shook his head in dismay. "I got one eye and can see
better than anyone in this room. To drive Lady Lenora away.
That girl don't take to pretty baubles and things. She takes few
things into her heart, but the ones she does are there for life.
She holds her family and friends dear. There's not anything she
wouldn't do for 'em. If she lost that horse, her dog, her brother
and her father, there ain't no reason for her to want this here
keep, ye see. Chances are, she'd up and leave and go back
across the Channel to the queen. She'd give up control of
Woodshadow and live on a trust her father set up fer her."

Roen's mind analyzed the information. "If you're right, then the traitor is someone who knows Lenora well. Someone with access to the stables. The scoundrel must be one of Sir Edmund's own men. The question remains, who has bought the man's loyalty?" Lenora's steps could be heard moving toward the stairs. "We must convince her not to stay here. 'Tis a risk. If someone tries to get at the horses, Lenora could be harmed."

"When that girl gets an idea stuck in her head, there ain't no way to yank it out that I knows of." Tom shrugged his shoulders. "And she ain't too mindful where you're concerned. Both of ye got a temper so hot it would heat the entire castle for a winter and a stubborn streak that'd task the holiest saint." He stroked the stubble of his gray-and-black beard. "Sorry, Sir Galliard, you're on your own 'ere."

"On your own for what?" Lenora quirked an eyebrow as she addressed them. She held several threadbare blankets in her arms. Roen could see that, though she tried to hide it, the night had taken its toll. Dark smudges underscored the tiredness of her face. She swayed ever so slightly, fighting to remain upright. 'Twas only her stubbornness that kept her on her feet. She'd fall asleep as soon as she lay down. Asleep, and defenseless.

"On my own, on my walk back to my room," Roen answered. *A woman who does what she's told is truly worth a king's ransom,* he thought to himself while he noted Tom's and Lenora's shocked looks. "I'll send down a boy with food to break your morning fast." Roen exited the barn and headed for the dark shadow of the oak tree.

Tom struggled to catch up. The older man's leg dragged more than usual. "By all the saints above, are ye crazed? Did ye not hear a word I said? I'm tellin' ye there's a worry here," Tom lectured when they were out of earshot.

"Hush, old man. I heard you. Did you not tell me that there was no changing Nora's mind once 'twas set? Wait a few minutes, she'll be sound asleep. When she is, I'll return and stand sentry. I'll be gone before she wakes."

"Aye, sounds good. But what are ye goin' to do about the next night?"

Roen rested himself against the rough bark of the ancient oak. Stars shone overhead, brilliant light in a clear, blue-black sky. A beam of moonlight basked the quiet keep in a soft yellow glow. "I've tomorrow to think on that. Let's concentrate on this night, shall we?"

Lenora checked one last time on the horses. The colt lay on its side. Frothy bubbles of milk laced the fine whiskers around its mouth. The foal's nose quivered as it slept. Lenora turned to Silver. The mare's crazed look had been replaced with one of infinite tiredness. The horse's head hung low, her eyes closed, her breathing even. Lenora prayed that rest, extra love and care would restore Silver's health.

"I wish that my life could be restored so easily," Lenora whispered out loud. So many responsibilities fell on her shoulders of late. A deep sense of loneliness permeated the stable and infected her.

There was no one to whom she could speak of her confusion and fear. Her brother and father had always been enough for her, her protectors, friends and confidants. Wistfully, Lenora dreamed of a person with whom she could unburden herself. Someone who would help her take the reins of her life in hand and give her guidance. She returned to the straw mattress and pulled the old blankets tightly around her.

Her thoughts turned to Galliard. He was a selfish, stubborn lout driven by greed, yet he had saved something she held very precious. It galled her to owe him a boon. A long yawn escaped her. Lenora snuggled down in the blankets as the night air began to cool steadily. "Tomorrow. I'll settle all this tomorrow." She yawned, her eyelids drooped, and she surrendered to her body's call for sleep.

Roen rested on his heels and fixed his gaze on the sleeping woman. Moonlight filtered through a window and displayed her sinfully long lashes against pale skin. Her auburn hair covered part of her face. With a gesture as soft as a whisper, he wrapped the locks around his hand. Lenora's wayward curl encircled his finger like a caress. He brushed the tips of his knuckles across the plane of her cheek. The coldness startled him. He reached for her hand, nestled beneath her chin. The tips of her fingers were icy. Lenora snuggled deeper into the worn blankets, curling up into a fetal position to stay warm.

"Little fool, I should let you freeze," Roen muttered. He paused and contemplated his options: wake Lenora and face an argument, or find some way to warm her. The invitation proved too tempting. He unbuckled his sword, leaned it against the loose pile of hay and slipped under the covers.

The warmth of his body acted as a magnet. Lenora rolled herself toward his inviting heat. She wiggled against the hard length of his body and he groaned under his breath. Regretting his decision, he battled his primal urges. He had known lust and controlled it before. With Lenora, he challenged an emotion much more powerful and, for him, much more dangerous. It took a mustering of all of his notorious iron will to keep his hands from roaming the soft mounds pressed against his chest.

The battle shifted unexpectedly. An attack came from a surprising source—Lenora. She nestled the tip of her cold nose under his chin and slipped her arm around his chest. He could feel the warm, rhythmic caress of her breath on his neck. Hot, impatient urges taunted him to explore the riches of her body. Roen's eyes closed as his hand cupped one breast and his fingers gently kneaded its softness.

The leather laces, untied from Lenora's tossing, worked to loosen the binding overtunic. With delight, he discovered his fingers could fit through the laces and touch the soft delicate skin of her velvet-soft mound. His fingers leapt forward, eager to explore. Lenora stiffened in her sleep and he heard a breathy gasp.

With painstaking slowness, Roen moved his anxious fingers toward his prize. He allowed Lenora's sleep-drugged mind to grow familiar with his touch. Her breath became more regular, but more rapid. Gooseflesh rose on the sensitive breast. Roen moved to claim his goal; the stiff peak of her bosom vanquished all his willpower.

"Nora." He buried his lips in her hair. The scent of hay and clover filled his nostrils. Lenora moaned in her sleep and he silenced her with his lips. A ravenous hunger drove at him to devour her with his mouth, but his kisses lit on Lenora's lips like butterfly wings. Fluttery kisses that caused her to taste her lips tentatively with the tip of her tongue and sigh. Carnal lust and desire exploded in his loins.

Creak. Roen halted. The protest of wood against wood sounded again. Suppressed footsteps echoed on the hay-covered wooden floor. Roen cloaked himself and Lenora with the blankets. Through a tear in the cover, he saw a black shadow shuffle past. Lenora, her body still awake from his lips and touches, squirmed against him. In an attempt to pacify her, Roen stroked back the hair near her temples.

The dark apparition moved with caution to the stall with Lenora's horses. Roen watched as it paused outside the gate. Shadowy beams of moonlight reflected off a sword hilt. A jewel in the hilt gleamed with malice. No apparition but a man, a knight in a dark cloak. The intruder threw back one corner of his mantle. The moonlight revealed the cloak's torn corner. Lightning hot outrage caused Roen to grit his teeth. Here was the man who had nearly killed Lenora at the scaffold.

Outraged, Roen reached for his sword, but his fingers closed on emptiness. Desperate to find his weapon yet not awaken Lenora, he inched his fingers through the layers of hay. He froze when he heard the dark shadow speak.

"Well, a foal. Silver, your mistress has a talent of undermining my plans." The intruder's voice rang out in the empty stable. Silver looked up but did not move. She sniffed the air, then lowered her head again to sleep.

The would-be assassin resumed his sermon. "Aye, but this night her work will be for naught. Drink well, 'twill be your last." The stranger sprinkled a powder into the water bucket in the stall and over the grain.

Lenora grew restless beside Roen. "Geoffrey," she moaned softly. Roen cursed both her timing and the name of her dream lover. The hooded man stilled. Roen placed his fingers gently over her lips and prayed the moon would stay behind the clouds.

The intruder took a few hesitant steps toward their hiding place, then waited and listened. To Roen, every breath he and Lenora took sounded like a loud wind in the silence of the dark stable. The need to attack ate at him, but he dampened the emotion. The safety of Lenora and her horses must be the priority.

Blending into the shadows, the intruder disappeared. Roen strained to hear the creak of wood, a sign the traitor had left.

When the slap of wood against wood vibrated in the air, Roen eased himself from Lenora's side. A pout formed on her lips when the night air invaded her warm cocoon. He tucked the ragged edges of blanket around the sleeping girl. Her breathing had returned to normal.

Roen strode to the horse's stall. The mare woke and took up watch over the form of her offspring. From outside the stall, he heaved the bucket over the gate and poured the water out. He touched the muddy puddle of contaminated water, sniffed his fingers, then brought them to his lips. The water tasted oddly sweet and smelled of strong herbs.

He returned to the stall and scraped out the grain from the trough. The same "green" smell emitted from the oats. Roen took the grain outside and emptied it into a refuse heap.

The knight reentered the stable and gave the ever watchful mare fresh water and grain. The animal made no move to approach him, but stomped her feet. Roen would have to forgo a physical examination of the horse. The mare was too upset by the birth and the night's activity to allow it.

For some unknown reason, the horse's behavior intrigued him. His senses tingled but his brain couldn't piece together the information. He moved to the back of the barn to search for the means of the intruder's escape. Crouching, he methodically tested each plank. Creak. A firm push and one wooden board swung clear. He squeezed his shoulders through the restrictive opening. When he cleared the secret door, he stood in a dark, narrow tunnel. Faint beams of the almost full moon wafted down between the tangled branches of wisteria overhead. The cold stone of the inner curtain wall and the back walls of the inner bailey structures formed the sides of the tunnel. Then the parts snapped into place, as did his decision. With every turn Lenora's peril grew. He returned to her side.

Oblivious to the night's danger, Lenora slept. Roen knelt on one knee. He felt the hard bite of steel against it. His fingers dug deep into the hay, clasped the hilt of his sword and pulled it free. "Ah, Nora. There's no more time for games. 'Tis time to lay this fellow out. He's one of your father's men, all right. If your temperamental horse knows him, then you must, also. What man knows the secrets of Woodshadow's escape routes save a knight of this keep? Does he act alone, or do others conspire against you?" He reached to stroke the coppery locks.

"Lady Lenora!" a gasping voice hailed from outside. "Lady Lenora, wake up!" Tyrus ran breathless into the stable. Lenora's eyelashes fluttered. Her cinnamon eyes showed confusion. The boy gave her a vigorous shake. "Wake up, Lady. 'Tis Sir Edmund."

Lenora's eyes cleared. She gazed at Roen, a panicked look on her face. "What's wrong, Galliard? What's wrong with my father?"

Tyrus saved Roen from a lengthy explanation of his presence. "Come quick, Lady Lenora. Everyone's a-lookin' for ya. Sir Edmund is callin' for ya." Tyrus looked at the ground, and his voice caught in his throat. "I think he's a-dyin'."

Guilt and fear colored Lenora's face. She jumped from her pallet and ran to the keep. The boy followed close at her heels. Roen stood alone in the darkness of the stable. The night's visitor had struck once more. He started back toward the castle, mindful that his next step must be orchestrated with care. The dark shape could be anyone and have access to all parts of the castle.

He hesitated before he entered the castle proper. As a warrior, he knew what his next decision must be. As a man, he questioned whether he could live the rest of his life with it. Lenora's reaction to his lovemaking showed she was well schooled, and he knew the name of her instructor. Geoffrey. The name left a sour taste in his mouth. She was no different than his mother or any other woman he had come across.

Roen rubbed his chest with his fingertips, aware of a dull ache that had formed near his heart. Lenora doubted that he even had a heart. Roen was painfully aware just now of its presence.

Chapter Ten

"Father!" Lenora rushed to her father's bedside. The pale golden hair of the older man formed a halo on the pillow.

"Calm yourself, girl." Sir Edmund placed his hand over his chest and wheezed, "I'm not gone yet." The ladies of the keep hovered behind her, shaking their heads and dabbing their eyes with sweet-smelling handkerchiefs.

The physician sucked on his teeth and poured an elixir into a chipped mug. "Drink this." He gave his patient no time to quibble over the smell or the taste of the medicine. His fingers pinched Sir Edmund's nose and he poured the contents down the sick man's throat.

The white-haired doctor took Lenora's arm and pulled her to her feet. "His heart has become very weak of late. Another attack like this and..." He scrunched his bushy eyebrows together and sucked his teeth again.

"Can you do nothing for him?" Lenora implored.

"Rest and no worries. 'Tis the only thing I know to prolong his life. He must not strain himself." The medical man shook his wild mane of white hair.

A creak of the door and a shaft of light marked Roen's entrance into the room. She did not pull her eyes from her father's face but she knew the knight waited like a vulture for its prey to gasp its last breath.

Sir Edmund lifted his feeble hand to her face. "The knight will care for you, child. Look to him after I'm gone."

"Nay, Father, do not leave me. Not you, too. I need you with me." Lenora gripped her father's hand with her own, as though to keep his soul in the world of the living.

Her father's eyes focused on Roen near the door. "Come here, son. I give you a rare gift, my daughter. In return, I have a boon to ask." Roen knelt at the foot of the bed. "Leave us, all of you. I need to speak with my son-in-law alone."

Dismissed like a servant, Lenora fought back her tears. She thought that the recent months had brought her and her father closer. Yet he turned her away and brought Galliard into his confidence. Her hand lingered on the latch of the door.

"Come, Lenora," Matilda's high voice called. "Leave these men to plan our futures, and pray your father is generous to us both." She pulled Lenora from the room and closed the heavy-timbered oak door.

"I have always been a man of action. I did not think to end my days such as this." Sir Edmund gave Roen a meaningful gaze. "I had thought to die in battle as befits a knight, not in a room of tearful women." A dry cough caused him some discomfort. After it passed, he fought to push himself upright. His eyes conveyed the trust he bestowed on the younger man.

Roen nodded his accordance. "What would you have me do, sire?"

The older man smiled, tension visibly shaken from him. "When I am sure my daughter is safe, Tom will bring Jupiter around. I wish not to be stopped by any of your men as I ride from here, and do not search for my body when Jupiter returns riderless. I would have it said I died astride, not cosseted in a feather bed."

"Are you sure of this? 'Twill be hard on Lenora." Roen knew the man's answer even before Sir Edmund responded.

"Aye, 'twill be best. I would have her remember me as the man I was, not as an invalid. Lenora must be protected. Whoever has done this to me will not stop until he has Woodshadow. The only way to attain that goal is through Lenora." Sir Edmund's face became flushed.

Roen could read the man's anxiety and fear. "Your daughter will be dealt with." His voice carried affirmation and the undertone of a threat.

"The marriage . . ."

"I have already decided that the only way to protect Woodshadow is to marry her." Why did a part of Roen feel like purring with contentment while another part felt like roaring with frustration?

"You must make her agree, and soon. I cannot leave this world for the next until I am sure she will be looked after."

"She'll agree." Roen started to rise but Sir Edmund's hand on his sword hilt stopped him.

"When may Tom bring Jupiter to me?"

Roen clenched his jaw. He would see the dying man's last request granted. "Tell your man to come the first morning after we are wed. Lenora will be kept at bay until you depart." He turned to leave.

Sir Edmund eyed him shrewdly. "This last escapade of mine will not sit well with Lenora. She will know you had a hand in it. 'Twill not go well with you."

Roen snorted a laugh. "'Tis no matter that. Nothing I do goes well with her."

Laughter gave the older knight a healthy glow. "Aye, Lenora is so like her mother. Now that was a woman who could serve a fatal wound with her tongue." Sir Edmund sighed, a nostalgic smile on his lips. "Would that I could hear one sweet insult from those dear lips again."

Roen shook his head. "I do not understand. Why should you wish for a shrew as a wife?"

"A shrew? Nay, Anor was no shrew. My wife was intelligent and beautiful. There was a fire that ran through her veins. Aye, she may have had a hot temper, but that was because she was a passionate woman. I gladly suffered a barb in the day to feel the fire of her passion at night."

Roen replied coldly, "And what of your pride? To let a woman speak to you in disrespect."

Sir Edmund chuckled. The conversation rejuvenated him. He lost many of his sickly mannerisms as he spoke. "Pride. Anor did not speak from disrespect. She voiced her opinions when she thought me wrong. Which, though 'tis hard for another man to believe, I sometimes was. If I was too thickheaded to recognize the fact, my loving wife put it in a way that I was sure to understand."

The older knight laughed again and gave Roen a sage look. "Mark you, I'm as prideful as the next man, but pride does not keep a man warm at night. Some advice to take to heart, young man, it does no harm to admit a mistake now and again. And a wife is more than happy to compensate for a loss of pride."

Roen gave an indignant sniff. A small part of him wondered what it would be like to be consumed in Lenora's blazing passion. He had tasted its intensity in battle. What would it be like in the marriage bed?

"My daughter is like a flame, Galliard. Feed it gently and do not suffocate it, and the flame will serve you well. But if neglected or provoked, the same flame can burn or more sadly be extinguished. Can you cherish the flame that is my daughter?" Sir Edmund waited for a response.

Roen rose stiffly and moved toward the door. He answered as he gave the thick door a tug. "I'll do my duty, Sir Edmund. 'Tis all that can be expected." The door crashed shut, the sound echoed on the cold stone walls.

Tom approached his liege. Sir Edmund's eyes showed skepticism. "You have seen them together more than I. Are they a match? Must I unfold my plan to its fullest?"

Tom grinned. "Oh, aye, they're a match. Put 'em together and you got a regular bonfire of temper and willfulness." Dragging himself to the foot of his lord's bed, he gave the elder man a wink. "There's something else a-burnin' also. I sees them eyein' the other when they think none's a-lookin'."

Hope colored the weak man's face. "Then I should carry my plan to fruition?"

"Well, if'n ya ever wants the sound of your grandchild in these halls, it's gotta be done. Lord knows, neither of those two will be able to accomplish much on their own."

Grinning, Sir Edmund waved his servant off. "Then let us proceed. The morning of Lenora's wedding, bring Jupiter in full tack. But I must somehow save Lenora from her tongue and Galliard from his temper. She can try a man's soul, and if Galliard should strike her, all would be lost. May the saints bless me and have all go as I plan. And if it works, I pray my daughter does not hate me afterward."

Lenora could not believe the morning sun just barely showed above the treetops of the forest. Between last night and the dawn she felt that a lifetime had transpired. Matilda clucked with false sympathy to the ladies-in-waiting. Beatrice hung in the shadows like a living ghost, unseen and silent. Lenora knew death frightened her cousin. 'Twas a mark of Beatrice's quiet strength that she was here at all.

Her eyes were transfixed on the closed door of her father's solarium. Servants, roused from sleep to attend to the nobles, moved in hushed silence. She waited, an alloy of fear and dread melding her emotions. The massive door cracked open and she leapt to go to her father's side. Roen's broad chest blocked her way.

"We need to talk." He pressed the door shut and prevented her entrance.

"My father is well near death. I have no time to waste with you. Let me pass." Lenora did not ask, she commanded. The audacity of the man. Her father needed her now. Long hours of tutelage came to bear, and she drew on them now. She was the lady of this keep and her orders would be obeyed.

Instead of moving aside, as a gentleman would have, Lenora felt Roen's viselike grip on her arm. "We will talk, and now. Your father desires solitude and peace of mind at the moment, which you will give him." The grip on her arm tightened and Roen led her toward an alcove in the far wall, away from the bug eyes and donkey ears of her aunt.

Shoved onto the stone pew, Lenora turned away from her persecutor. He was a rude, illiterate, uncouth lout. Not even her father's illness caused him to soften.

"We will marry in a fortnight." Roen's voice sounded hollow.

Lenora stared at him in wonder. The statement held no surprise for her. "So, you think to marry me before my father dies. Are you afraid that if he dies, as my vassals' liege, I will order you driven from this castle? Nay, I will not marry you. My father has recovered from such spells many times. When he does, he will see the error his illness has caused."

She paused to gather strength, then threatened, "But if he does die, then my father's vassals will lay their swords at my feet. I will be the liege, and no longer under the will of my father's words."

Roen stood in granitelike silence. Her words tumbled off him like a child's blows against a mountain.

Lenora asked in bewilderment, "How have you lived so long without a heart? How does your body move with no heart within your chest? Do you think to gain my agreement when I am sick with worry over my father? I am not so weak as that. Begone from my sight, and do not keep me from my father's side." Repulsed, she gave Roen a contemptuous stare and rose from her seat.

His foot stamped on the edge of the pew to bar Lenora's escape. She halted and gave him an icy glare. His face took on a look of cruelty as he loomed in front of her. "We marry in a fortnight, or I marry your cousin. 'Tis one or the other, but Woodshadow will be mine."

Words stuck in Lenora's throat but she persevered. "You have seen Beatrice. She cannot marry you. Just the hint of such a union has her near frightened to death. She would take her own life rather than wed you." Lenora felt her tight control slip from her grasp.

Roen shrugged his shoulders, unconcerned. "I will keep her alive long enough to beget an heir. Then what she does is of no interest to me." His lips twisted into a sardonic smile. "When I leave here I will order the servants to prepare my wedding feast. Your vassals will be ordered to appear to pledge their oaths of loyalty to me. The wedding will take place in a fortnight. Who do I say the bride is, you or Beatrice?"

Rage streaked through Lenora's body. How dare this man blackmail her! She was not some weak-kneed coward. Her father and brother had taught her to fight. Yet how could she fight a living statue with no emotions, no feelings?

"You win, Galliard." Defeat did not come easily to her lips.

"Your word on this. You cannot back out at the last moment and naysay me at a later date." Roen's words stung an already tender wound.

Lenora hesitated; to give her word was to condemn herself to this marriage. Pride in her family name and honor would prevent her from casting aside her promise.

Trapped, she faced Roen, her eyes narrowed. "My word, Galliard. I will not break the agreement." Lenora sought deep within her emotional reserves and replenished her aloof facade. "I would go to my father now and tell him of your plans for our nuptials. At least he will draw some small comfort in the misguided belief that you will guard the treasures of Wood-shadow with love and care. I would not trouble him now with the truth, that 'tis naught but greed that drives you." She shoved Roen's leg aside and moved away, her jaw tightening.

She walked with stiff dignity back to her father's room. The wish for quiet conversation vanished as Lenora entered. The eyes of her aunt and cousin studied her face. Matilda's shrewd eyes searched for a weakness, Beatrice's searched for strength.

"Lenora?" Sir Edmund's voice questioned.

"Father, you need to rest." She sat at the foot of his bed. "Everything is fine."

"I can't rest. I need to know if you will be protected." Sir Edmund's voice grew thin.

"Woodshadow will be safe." Lenora could not include herself in the statement. She would not lie to her father.

"Along with all of those within its walls," Roen continued when he entered the room. Lenora purposely snubbed the knight and kept her gaze fixed on her father.

Sir Edmund sighed with relief. "Then you concur, Lenora. You will marry Roen de Galliard?"

"I have agreed to marry him, Father." She hesitated before asking, "Is this what you truly want, Father? Does this set you at ease?"

Her father's eyes glided closed, a peaceful smile on his lips. "Aye, daughter, to know Woodshadow is safe and you are well married does much to mitigate the worries in my heart. But still I sense you are not sure. Sir Roen, come to my side."

Lenora felt dismay at the prospect of being near the bulking knight. Her father shoved her hand into Roen's and proclaimed, "Lenora has a fear of you, Sir Roen."

"I have no such thing," Lenora contradicted.

Sir Edmund smiled. "Then let us quell these reservations. Lenora feels you are a man of bad temper."

"Father."

"This is not true, then? I thought my information most credible." Lenora and Roen turned peeved looks to the innocent face of the old stablekeeper. Tom clasped his hands behind his back and gave them an innocent look.

"Sir Edmund, I assure you I have control of my temper at all times," Roen stated through clenched teeth.

Lenora almost choked. Her father's voice sounded livelier with a touch of amusement. "Well, I am sure that is true, but—"

"But nothing. Since I stepped foot in this castle I have been nothing but insulted." A dangerous red color began to spread up his neck.

"Sir Galliard, rest easy." Sir Edmund tried to smooth the knight's ruffled temper. "I only say my daughter has these fears, not that they are warranted. So, you say you have a well-controlled manner."

"Of course."

"And you would never strike out in anger at a defenseless soul?"

"Of course not."

"And you would swear to this, no doubt."

"Of course," Roen growled.

Sir Edmund patted his daughter's hand, so small on top of the larger callused hand of the warrior. "There, my dear, does that not calm your nerves? The man has sworn not to strike you in anger. All is settled."

Lenora saw the results of her father's verbal victory. Color washed his face, his eyes regained some of their old merriment. Perhaps there was a chance her father would recover as he had before. Somehow she needed to stall for more time.

Her mind raced while she created and discarded plans. The vow stood in the way. No matter the outcome, she had promised to marry Galliard and could see no way around it. She couldn't break her bond.

Suddenly, a dazzling smile spread across her full lips. "Aye, Father, you are right, Sir Galliard is a strong man. It comforts me to know I have his word not to strike me in anger, but what of the other ladies?"

"I have not ever nor do I plan to hit a woman. A man who loses his temper so does not deserve any graces of God." Roen eyed Lenora with forewarning. "Though a spanking might be in order for some."

"So, 'tis your word, which you lay at my ailing father's bed, that should you strike me in anger, you deserve no reward."

"Aye," Roen answered with hesitation.

A plan so deliciously simple unfolded in Lenora's head as Roen uttered his agreement. 'Twas sure to buy her enough time for her father to improve in health and keep Galliard from her bed. A voice of self-preservation cautioned in her head, *May the saints help me if my father or Galliard discovers my plans.* Somehow Lenora knew Galliard's anger would be the worse of the two.

Chapter Eleven

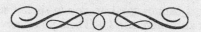

"Where is she?" Roen's voice thundered down the long halls of the keep. He emerged from his room, his skin wet and bright red, wrapped in nothing but a ragged strip of linen. The soaked material molded the knight's anatomy like a second skin. "By all the holy saints above, I will throttle the girl," he promised as he scraped back the heavy wet hair from his eyes.

Servants squeezed themselves against the wall of the foyer to elude Roen's frantic search. Feminine laughter tittered from behind a door on the left. He threw open the oak door with such force it banged against the wall and bounced back on the hinges. A tremendous echo added to the mayhem already in the hall.

"Saints be praised!" Matilda gasped when Roen's nearly bare body intruded into the sewing room. "Sir Galliard, a bit of decorum if you will. There are impressionable ladies in this room. Beatrice and Charmain, avert your eyes." Beatrice needed no warning; she already hid her face behind the shirt she was sewing. Not as shy, Charmain's turquoise eyes roved down the slick, powerful body. Her gaze lingered on the deeply sculpted thighs that emerged from beneath Roen's wrap. She gave him a seductive smile. By the look in her eye, Roen could tell the numerous battle scars on his body were not distasteful to her. Why hadn't this girl assisted him with his bath instead of that half-blind old nag?

"Roen! What has come over you?" Hamlin came up behind his friend. With swords drawn, the men of Roen's elite group stood ready to defend him. Hamlin hunted for an enemy. "By the noise you were making we thought you must be under attack." He caught the sultry smile Charmain gave Roen, then added, "Or perchance 'tis an attack you're looking for. Though I think you could be a bit more discreet. Interesting skin color, Roen. Is this a new bit of camouflage?"

"Your skin would be red, too, if you had nearly been boiled alive. Where is your niece?" Roen demanded of Matilda, ignoring Hamlin. The flustered woman fanned herself with her hand vigorously.

"Please, sir, I cannot speak to you in such a state. Kindly complete your attire and then I will hear your grievance." Matilda bent her head and brought her needlework very close to her face. Her fingers shook, and she was unable to make a stitch.

"Come, Roen, you are disturbing the ladies' sewing," Hamlin coaxed from the doorway.

"Damn women and their pettiness." Roen tightened the towel around his hips and exited. He trod on Hamlin's toes as he slammed the door shut. "Women. Were there but a way to obtain an heir without them, I would do so readily. The day that God created Eve was the last day of man's peace of mind," Roen declared on his way back to his chambers.

Hamlin followed his friend with his hand over his mouth. A small chuckle escaped his lips when they entered their chamber. The smack of a wet towel across his face silenced his amusement.

"Heaven's sake, Roen. Did you intend to bathe the entire room?" Hamlin scanned the puddles of soapy water littering the floor. Two wooden pails lay tipped on their sides near the large wooden tub. Roen splashed barefoot across the puddles, sending sprays of water onto Hamlin's leather boots.

"I swear when I get my hands on her I'm going to shake the very life from that long-legged body." Roen tied on his braes and reached for his leather garters.

"Who? And why are you so angry?" Hamlin tossed aside the wet towel and sought a dry place to stand.

"Who? Why?" Roen finished cross-binding his hose. Hamlin tossed him the unadorned brown woolen tunic, which lay across the back of Roen's clothing chest. The rounded neckline muffled his reply. The still-damp head emerged with a stupefied expression. "Nora, that's who and why. The witch tried to boil me in my bath. I'm surprised I don't have blisters on my behind from the scalding she gave me." Roen rolled up the sleeves of his tunic past his elbows, then tied a leather belt around his waist.

"I see no blisters, and aside from your bright color, no damage. Besides, 'twas not she I saw enter our room with the pails. The hag made a simple mistake."

"Bah. I'd wager my fortune that Nora had something to do with that mistake." Roen slid a golden-handled dagger into his belt.

"Perhaps you are just feeling guilty."

Roen turned on Hamlin. "Me, guilty? For what? I'm sacrificing my entire future to save the woman. What thanks do I get except to be cooked like some shellfish?"

"I suppose your constant snide remarks and blackmail are no excuse. Besides, I heard you swear to Sir Edmund you would never beat the girl in anger," Hamlin pointed out.

Roen placed his hand on the iron door pull. "I'll give your words some leave, Hamlin. I won't throttle her, but a spanking is still not out of the question."

Lenora leaned against the oak tree by the stables holding her aching sides. Peals of laughter rang from her lips while she bundled up the patched kirtle and apron. Galliard was certainly red-hot when she had left him. He never even suspected 'twas she behind the rags and dirt.

A lively tune bubbled from her lips. She pulled the scarf from her head and nodded merrily to the stableboy at the doorway of the barn. After she stashed the old clothes in the corner of Silver's stall, she cupped some water from the pail to splash over her face. It felt cool and refreshing and left her skin clean of the ashes she had rubbed onto her face.

A self-satisfied smirk emerged on her lips. She contrasted the wonderful cool temperature of the water in the barn with the steaming heat of the water she had prepared for Roen's bath. Of all her schemes, this one was the most devious. 'Twas going to be painfully easy to drive Galliard to strike her in anger. Like stealing a sweet from an infant. Lenora collapsed backward into the soft hay, her arms and legs akimbo.

The image of Galliard's cardinal red skin made her tingle with merriment. Her thoughts twisted from mischief to curiosity. She'd only managed a glance at the knight's broad back and powerful chest. The mystery of what lay beneath the soap-filmed water turned the tingle of her skin to a deep ember of heat. If she had just waited before pouring the hot water she might have really seen for the first time what a naked man looked like.

"Lenora." Beatrice flew into the stable. "You must hide. Sir Galliard is in a terrible temper and I fear 'tis you he's angry with." Her cousin peeked over the stall door. "Lenora, please. You must take this seriously. He burst into the sewing room practically—" Beatrice's eyes widened and she choked out the rest "—naked, and demanded Mother tell him where you were."

"Naked!" Lenora sputtered from her laughter. "My, that must have been a sight."

"Lenora, what have you done? 'Tis not good to make a man like him angry," Beatrice warned in a grave voice.

"'Tis more important not to make a woman like me angry. That pompous knight needs to learn that lesson, also." Lenora rolled around in the hay like a puppy. Silver and the colt observed their mistress's strange behavior. The mare plodded over and nudged Lenora with her nose as though to tell the young lady to control herself. Lenora's response was delighted laughter.

Tyrus ran into the stable so quickly he careered into Beatrice before he could stop. "Sorry, Lady Beatrice, but ye told me to come 'n fetch ye if'n he was a-headin' this a-way. An' he's a-headin' this-a-way." Tyrus spoke so fast Lenora could barely make out the words. The lad craned his head to look behind him. "He's a-comin' fast, Lady Lenora. Ye best be disappearin' cause—"

Roen strode into the barn, past the boy and Beatrice. Hamlin followed right behind him.

"He's here," Tyrus finished his sentence in a whisper.

Roen surveyed the guilty looks of Beatrice and the boy. "Where is she? Don't even think about lying for her. I want the truth," his voice blasted in anger.

"Lying? You accuse them of a crime before they utter a breath." Lenora rose from the hay in one languid motion and gave Silver a pat on the muzzle. Just to irritate the man even more, she sauntered over to the gate. She placed her arms on the top rail, leaned her chin on her hands and gave the furious knight a beguiling smile. "Why should they lie to you? Whom do you seek in such a fit of temper?"

"Nora, I am tired of your endless prattle. 'Twill cease now." His voice would have singed her eyebrows if it had been a flame.

The shouts issuing from the barn began to draw a crowd. Alric, Landrick and several others from Roen's group gathered near the barn to hear the exchange. The men buffeted one another about to hear their leader chastise Lenora.

"That's tellin' her, Roen." Alric urged his commander on. "Put the wench where she belongs."

"In a bed and on her back," another of Roen's men added. The male laughter grated on Lenora's ears.

She slipped through the wooden poles of the stall gate and noted Roen's face, his clamped jaw and fixed eyes. He teetered on the edge of control. One little push and he would fall into her plan.

"My name is not Nora and my prattle, as you call it, will never cease." Lenora made her voice as insolent as possible and arched her brow in a knowing way. "If 'tis a silent woman you want, you'll not find it in me. I am most vocal about your shortcomings, of which there are many. Though 'tis no surprise. Just to be a man means you've a shortcoming."

She took in her audience and struck where it would do the most harm. Men always had one weakness and she intended to capitalize on it. Although she hadn't been able to see exactly what endowments Roen possessed, men were usually sensitive on the subject of their virility. "Aye, there's some that say— mind you, 'tis only servant women—that you've a mighty short shortcoming."

The crowd silenced and stared at the warrior and girl. Lenora tilted her chin to an arrogant angle. Roen's hands worked open and closed. They settled into two deadly fists. One blow might kill her but she would risk it for the possibility of freedom. If Roen left in disgrace or in anger, both she and Beatrice would be safe from the greedy knave.

"Come, brave knight," she harassed. "Have you something you wish to say? Nay! It surprises me when you are usually so outspoken. Though even then 'tis not much said of real importance. But then every man cannot be an intelligent speaker. Faith, 'tis a miracle that most can even speak at all."

"Woman, get you from me if you value your life." Roen's fist lifted. He would silence that dagger tongue once and for all. What had he said about a spanking? She needed a good beating. He took a menacing step forward. Lenora stood her ground, a pleased smile on her lips. Roen drew back his fist.

"Nay, Roen, do not do it," Hamlin warned.

Still Lenora did not flinch. Roen could see her body tense for the blow. He looked into her eyes. Instead of liquid gold, they glowed deep amber. Roen faltered. 'Twas not anger that lit her eyes but satisfaction. He lowered his fist and narrowed his eyes to study his adversary. His will took over and he regained his self-control. "Lady Beatrice, I pray, please escort your lady to some other part of the bailey. If you care for her at all, do it now."

The glint in Lenora's eyes sharpened like hard flint. An insulting smile tugged at the corners of her deep red lips. He sensed she was well pleased with herself.

Lenora's crooked smile made her look more childlike. She called, "Come, Beatrice, I've no need to stay longer. I am finished, for now, with the knight." Lenora tossed back her tangled braid and left the group of stunned men. Beatrice gave Hamlin and Roen an apologetic look then ran after her surely demented cousin.

Hamlin stared in shocked confusion. He turned to Roen's thunderous face. "I had thought you too hard on the girl, but nay, 'tis the other way around. She is rude and deserves a good beating. I cannot think you will really marry this shrew." Hamlin shuddered. "Life with her would be a sorrowful institution for sure. Come, let us leave this place. You have not given your word on this marriage. The king can send some other man, one who deserves punishment instead of reward."

Roen's angry white face stilled. The clenched fist slowly untightened. The bulging vein in his neck began to return to normal. His men watched their leader with puzzlement. Roen leaned over and began to laugh. The puzzlement changed to wonder, then concern for his sanity.

Great bursts of gut-tightening laughter erupted from Roen. Tears formed in his eyes from the strength of his amusement. "Oh, Hamlin, I must watch that girl more. I believe she could even teach me."

"Teach you what? How to tear a man in two with words? Has she wounded you so that you are driven mad? I have known you almost all your life and have never seen you act so. What has the girl done?"

Roen wiped the tears from his eyes. "My friend, she warned us at Tintagel that she was intelligent." Hamlin's face showed no comprehension. "Think, man, what did you just say?"

"That we should be away from here as soon as the horses can be prepared."

"And what does the sharp-tongued Lady of Woodshadow wish more than anything?" Roen inquired.

"Right now, I believe she would like to see you cooked slowly over the kitchen spit," Hamlin answered truthfully.

"Aye, that is true enough. But first, she wants me gone. I have her word that she cannot back out of our marriage. Yet I gave no word to her or her father on the marriage. The only vow I swore was not to strike her. To naysay this marriage I must break my word to her father. Then she and her cousin could renounce me and I could not honorably marry either of them."

The fog cleared in Hamlin's mind. "Ah, now I see." He watched Lenora's bouncing red hair as the two girls climbed the forebuilding steps of the castle. "You're right, she did warn us. You came close to succumbing to her plan only moments ago. What stopped you?"

"Her eyes." Roen shrugged uncomfortably under Hamlin's scrutiny. "She can lie with her lips, but not with her eyes. They tell too much if one knows how to read them."

Roen started toward the castle after waving his men back to their duties. Hamlin walked at his side and gave him an irksome look. "'Tis good that you will be able to read your wife so well since she obviously can read you, as well."

"Christ's blood, is my own man to vex me now? The woman has no insight on me," Roen denied.

"Oh, she does, Roen. How else does she know those words that will drive you near mad with anger? I'm afraid that the Lady Lenora reads you like a monk does a book, a huntsman the trail of a boar, like a field man the sky, like a—"

"Will you cease this endless drivel! I liked our conversation before when you thought the woman a harpy," Roen answered, disgruntled. "Now I must hunt the chit down and expose her plan. I'm tired of this foolishness. She must learn that I can't be gotten around so easily."

Roen marched up the steps to the castle, determined to find Lenora. She would marry him and that was it. Her childish behavior would cease, now. She should count herself lucky that a celebrated knight such as he would consider wedding her. He could protect the people and land of Woodshadow better than any other man he knew. There was absolutely no reason why Lenora shouldn't marry him. No reason at all.

Mystified, Roen felt the dull bruise in his heart begin to pain him again. Damn, the woman was giving him indigestion as well as a headache.

Lenora left Beatrice in the great hall with instructions to keep Matilda away. She rushed down the stairs to the kitchen on the ground floor. Alyse strutted around her domain as regal as any queen. She spied Tyrus, who had returned breathless from the bailey and plopped down on the trestle table.

Alyse pointed to the boy with her spoon. "Tyrus, get yourself to the storeroom an' fetch me some greens for the noon meal." The boy snapped up from his lounging position and quickly ran to one of the small rooms built into the walls of the castle. Alyse nodded her satisfaction at the boy's speed. She carried the oversize wooden spoon in her hand as a warning to those whose actions did not meet her strict specifications.

"My lady, I've a need of a word with you." The wooden spoon waved in Lenora's direction. "Where are all my kitchen girls? I seen Mirabella out making candles and I hear Charmain is sewing. Ya know I can't get a decent meal on without enough help."

Lenora gave a tiny jump and sat on the wooden table, littered with preparations for the midday meal. A wooden bowl filled with batter tempted her palate with the aroma of sweetened nut bread.

Alyse never stopped speaking, only paused long enough to fill her lungs with air. "And speakin' of the meal. Ya told the butler for me to prepare the fish. That fish is the bottom of the barrel. 'Tis so salty it'd take a year of soakin' to make it edible." Alyse prepared to continue her tirade but stopped. She watched Lenora scoop a fingerful of buttery nut batter then smacked her lady's knee sharply with the wooden scepter. "What are ya a mind to be doin', young lady? Ya tryin' your darnedest to unravel this keep. Ya got girls who can't make a stitch in the sewing room and—"

"Ouch!" The tall, grizzled man at the fireplace sucked his finger noisily while he tried to baste several chickens cooking on the spit. Most of the birds were covered in ashes from the fireplace. The man kept a steady flow of obscenities flowing while he worked, oblivious that the blackened appearance of the birds signaled their doneness.

Alyse tossed her heavy black-and-gray braid in the clumsy man's direction. "Faith be with me, ya got farmhands in 'ere to turn the meat."

Lenora licked the batter from her finger and gave her a prudent look. "Patience, Alyse. The girls grow bored with the same routine. 'Tis only a chance to give them a change. And Clarence, he sprained his ankle and thus cannot work the demesne these next few days. I thought his strong back could serve in the kitchen and save you the heavy task of turning the spit." Alyse waited, her mighty arms folded across her ample chest. The spoon twitched a steady staccato beat. "I will soon wed and must run this vast keep. Is it not best for me to ease my way in now?"

Alyse snuffled a retort. "Ya've been a-runnin' this keep since ya come home. Oh, you let that harpy of an aunt think she's a-runnin' things but there's not a serf or freeman in Woodshadow don't know the truth. Every time that woman makes a mistake or would put our stores in short supply, ya manage to come up with a way to go around her. 'Tis no secret ya been seein' after poor Sir Hywel. But, love, the man's mind is goin' just like

his father afore 'im. Ya can't keep a-goin' like this forever.''
Alyse began to twirl the wooden spoon in her beefy hand.

Lenora cracked walnuts and deposited the meats into the
batter. "This bread will be wonderful. Will it be ready for tonight's meal?'' She slipped several dark, shriveled nuts into the
batter. The tough meats would give the bread a bitter taste.
Alyse continued on, unaware of the sabotage.

"Ya given that man, Sir Galliard, the wrong impression, girl.
The way ya been carryin' on he'll think ya don't know the first
thing about bein' a lady. 'Tis a wonder he's still thinkin' on
marryin' ya.'' Alyse opened her mouth to continue, but the
nuances of her last sentence sank in.

The cook pursed her lips and sat down heavily on the bench
near the table where Lenora sat. She eyed the girl seriously and
placed her wooden spoon on the timeworn table. "Lady Lenora, ya don't know watch ya doin'. The knight's a fine man.
He's right easy on the eyes, as any of the kitchen girls can tell
ya. Faith, I feel me old bones a-buzzin' when I gets a look at 'im
and it's been a spell since I've felt that.'' Alyse gave her lady's
hand a sympathetic pat. "Ya've got to face the facts. You're
noble-born, not like the rest of us. Ya must marry who your
father chooses and he's chosen Sir Galliard. Don't make it
harder on yourself, lass.''

Lenora's discontent marked her words. "Father promised me
I could choose. And when I do, it shan't be a dull-witted clod.
'Twill be someone gentle and caring. Someone like Father.''

Alyse shook her head in disagreement. "Your father's a man
of high temper. He and your mother had their share of squab-
bles.''

"I know that. But Father loved and respected Mother. I'm
no fool to wish for love, Alyse. But I do think I can expect my
husband to respect his wife. Galliard does not respect any
woman.'' Lenora rose slowly from the table and faced her
concerned kitchen woman. "Don't worry, Alyse, I can take
care of myself. Galliard will realize the folly this marriage
would be. He will go his way and I will be free to marry who I
wish. I'm much too clever for his like.''

She gave Alyse a bright smile and skipped from the kitchen
into the dazzling sunlight of midmorning. Alyse's disapprov-
ing *tsk* sounded behind her back. The sound did not sway her

from her plan. If anyone could make Galliard change his mind it was her. He did not stand a chance.

Roen waited on the top step, just out of sight of the people below, listening to Lenora and the serving woman. A chuckle rumbled in his throat and threatened to erupt into an uncontrolled burst of laughter. The conversation explained much. A tiny trickle of esteem meandered through him for his betrothed. She'd not break her word, but that didn't stop her from seeking another way out of her predicament. Her plan had come close to succeeding outside. The wench knew just the right things to rile him.

Lenora's last statement wiped the smile from his lips. Guilt caused him a pang of remorse. The truth of her speech stabbed an old wound. Love, Roen did not need or want, but he could understand the need for respect. Determined to make amends, he returned to the great hall. He only hoped he could call a truce before Lenora began her poisonous stings. 'Twould be hard to explain his change of attitude if his hands were on her throat.

Chapter Twelve

"I cannot believe your foolishness," Beatrice railed. "The man could have killed you with one blow. What possessed you to purposely vex him so?"

Lenora shrugged her shoulders. "That is between Galliard and myself. Don't worry. I'll take care of things."

Beatrice stopped and whirled around to face her cousin. "Don't worry? Lenora, that is what you always say. I am worried. I cannot help but think that this situation you are in is somehow connected to me."

"Nay, this has nothing to do with you. Galliard is seizing an opportunity to profit from my father's illness."

"I hope you are not sacrificing your happiness because of me, for I think it is of no use." Beatrice's eyes misted.

"You know me better, Cousin. I am most selfish and would never think such a deed," Lenora joked, yet the melancholy did not leave her cousin's face. "Pray, tell me what wears at you."

The overwrought girl hid her eyes behind her slender fingers and contained sobs racked her body. Lenora led her cousin outside the inner wall to a crumbling grape arbor in the garden. The peaceful spot offered a small piece of privacy in the crowded castle.

"I received this from Geoffrey yestermorn." From a pocket at her waist, Beatrice pulled a folded piece of paper. "He is leaving his father's keep as soon as you marry."

"Leaving, but what of you?"

Beatrice's eyes watered freely. "Geoffrey does not believe Woodshadow's new lord will ever condone our union. Lenora, he told me to forget him. That he will never see me again after your wedding.''

Add another sin to Galliard's list, Lenora thought. In saving her cousin from marriage to Galliard, she had lost the young woman her only chance at marital bliss.

Beatrice delicately wiped the tears from her eyes with a linen handkerchief. ''I am sorry to burden you with my problems when you have so many. Excuse me, I would like to meditate in prayer within the chapel.''

Lenora started to follow. ''I will come with you.''

''Nay. I know you mean well but you have never been one for quiet deliberations in the chapel.'' Beatrice spoke in a quiet, tired voice. ''Go and walk in the woods. It has always calmed you in the past. Perhaps there you will find some answers to the problems that smite us now.'' She did not reprove Lenora, only sent a plea for her to understand her need for solitude.

''Aye, 'tis a good idea. I won't be gone long.'' Lenora gave the woman a quick hug and turned to leave the confines of Woodshadow.

The green canopy of the forest cooled the force of the afternoon sun. She waited at the edge and allowed her eyes to adjust to the green wash of the woods. Spring songbirds called to their mates from the high branches overhead. The wind stirred the branches, which added a fairylike quality to the song of nature.

Though many in the village believed the woods were the playground of little people and demons, Lenora plunged into the forest unafraid. The woods offered the privacy that was so hard to achieve at the keep. She kept to the heavily trafficked path and made a mental note of her location. With the turmoil in her mind 'twould be easy to lose her way. No adventuring today, she would head for the clearing that Geoffrey had shown her.

She found the oasis of long silky grass easily. The tranquil spot beckoned. Lenora skipped into the semicircle and breathed deeply. The refreshing scent of crushed grass and the faint perfume of spring flowers glided on the air. She lay down in the middle of the clearing, clasped her fingers behind her head and closed her eyes. The peacefulness of her surroundings sifted into her mind and calmed her worries.

"I see this is one of your favorite spots, also. I suppose the tales of witches and spirits do not scare you?"

Lenora bolted upright then relaxed. "Geoffrey, you are forever sneaking up on me. If I hear a voice in these woods, 'twould more likely be you than a specter."

Geoffrey laughed but it did not reach his eyes. "A recent talent. I remember when we were children, you always found me at hangman."

"Would that we could once again be children." Lenora took the loose ribbon that held her braid from her hair. She shook her head to free the strands and finger-combed the tangles from her hair.

"But we are not children and can never be again. And soon, it may well be that you will bear your own children." Geoffrey sat down near her, his fingers inches from her auburn strands of hair. "Lenora, how can you marry Galliard? You with your words of freedom and quest for knowledge? The man will drink his fill of your vitality and leave you drained, an empty vessel."

Lenora stopped her combing. "I must do as my father wishes."

"Why have you chosen now to become the biddable daughter? I did not see you so easily succumb in the past. Perhaps you are a hypocrite, your feisty words forgotten at the touch of Galliard's lips."

Peeved by his remark, Lenora retaliated. "And who are you to speak of passivity? I have never seen you stand up to your father. At least my father's illness explains my submission. You have no excuse."

His face closed from the humiliation of her words. Immediately, Lenora felt remorse. "I'm sorry, Geoffrey. I know well the mettle of your father. You and Daphne have told me often enough of the perfidy he commits. Pray, accept my apology and forgive me."

"I cannot long be angry with you. How many times did you hide my sister and me from our father when he was in a drunken rage? I owe you much. I love you." Geoffrey passed his fingers through the ends of her hair. "Like a sister."

Lenora separated her coppery locks into three strands and began to rebraid her plaits. "Then as a sister I ask you, do not give up on Beatrice. There still might be hope for the two of you. Your letter broke her heart."

" 'Tis better now than later." The words were said with little emotion. "Now is not the time to worry over Beatrice. You are the one in danger."

"Danger? I would not put it as danger." Lenora tied the ribbon to the end of her braid and began to plait the other side.

"There is more here than just a marriage." Geoffrey's eyes widened. "Wealth, land, justice are at stake. Too many plans have been laid. There must be a way to stop your marriage to Galliard. I never wanted to see you hurt."

Lenora began to feel uneasy under her friend's intense stare. The village talk of evil spirits and demons returned. Could such a thing exist? Could such a thing invade Geoffrey?

"There is nothing that you can do." She inched away from the dark stare.

"I could take you from here, back to my father's." Geoffrey's voice grew more hopeful.

"I'd have more to fear from your father and brothers than Galliard. Besides, Woodshadow is too wealthy a keep for Galliard just to give up. He'll not stop until Woodshadow is his. If I disappeared, 'twould not take long for him to discover my location. Would you bring his wrath to your father's door?"

"Aye, that's true. I think perhaps he and I are much alike. To give up is not in our blood." His eyes took on a maniacal gleam. "We could go from this place to the abbey. I could have a friar marry us, and thus keep Galliard from you."

"Nay, Geoffrey, in your quest to save me you forget Beatrice." Lenora's fingers trembled as she finished her last braid.

"Aye, Beatrice. What to do? What to do?" His voice became like a child's chanting a verse. He picked up a stick from the ground and stabbed it into the dark, loamy soil. Each blow became harder and deeper.

Lenora noticed his left eye twitch in time with his action. She jumped up and the ribbon fell from her hand. "Geoffrey, your distress over Beatrice and me has muddled your brain. Pray, drive this worry from you."

"But I can't." He threw away the stick and gave her a forlorn look. His face shifted to a more sinister expression. "You don't understand. I can't let you marry Galliard." Geoffrey rose from his position like a wolf stalking prey. His hands shot out and latched onto her wrist.

"Let me go," she commanded, and struggled to free herself. His mercurial moods had always been a little unsettling. Today they were frightening.

He smiled. It reminded her of a snake, cold and lethal. His foot on her hem tripped her and she tumbled to the ground, the breath knocked out of her. Her lungs cried for air.

Geoffrey fell with her, his weight preventing her breathless lungs from filling. Her mind a hurricane of emotions and thoughts, Lenora reverted to survival instincts. She kicked with her free leg and bit into his arm.

"Damn you to hell!" Geoffrey shouted. "I only wanted to help you up. You never could take teasing."

Lenora rolled away and reached her feet. She felt foolish for falling into Geoffrey's prank, yet a deep, inner instinct warned her to keep her distance. "I do not think your antics amusing. Sometimes you go too far."

Geoffrey's eyes showed no glimmer of remorse or recognition. He spat out a mouthful of blood and wiped his mouth on the back of his sleeve. He moved toward her, his face in a snarl. "I owed you for your talk about my father. Sometimes I do not go far enough."

"Lenora!" Roen de Galliard reached the clearing and took in the scene and made his conclusions. Coppery locks careened down Lenora's back and cascaded across her shoulders. Her swollen mouth and heaving chest told him all he needed to know. He had interfered with her clandestine meeting with her lover. She played the game of innocent so well, but she was no different from his mother.

Her brown eyes widened and became unreadable for the first time since they had met. She rushed to Roen's side and stood behind him with her hand on the hilt of his dagger.

"Nay, Lenora," the handsome young man implored.

An instant dislike for the fop intensified Roen's anger. Lenora's lover gave Roen a cursory look, then his face turned smooth and treacherous. "You are right. I was momentarily deranged and carried my jest too far. But let us kiss and be friends again—" his eyebrows arched "—for I do so covet your goodwill.'' The knight came toward them, his hands out-stretched.

"Nay, your apology is accepted. There is no need for more.'' Roen felt Lenora begin to slip the dagger from the sheath. He put his hand on hers. Her eyes fought his, but she relented.

"Who are you?'' Roen wanted to yank the answer from the man's throat.

"Sir Geoffrey Champlain. I am a friend of the lady and her cousin. Lenora and I have played—'' Geoffrey paused and accented the last word ''—together since we were children.''

A blaze of emotion engulfed Roen. Geoffrey. The name Lenora had murmured in her sleep when he held her. There must be some truth to the man's insinuations. Anger and betrayal settled like a stone in his gut. Disappointment lingered in his heart. He foolishly believed Lenora could be different from his mother. Instead, she proved his father right, women were vain, faithless creatures.

"Geoffrey, I swear, if you don't stop this I'll kick you again,'' Lenora fumed.

Roen watched the flash of anger move across Geoffrey's aristocratic features. "Then I'll stop. I'm only trying to help, you know.'' He turned to Roen, a challenge in his eyes. "Lady Lenora and Lady Beatrice are dear friends of mine. I do not wish to see either of them hurt, but I fear there is danger nearby for both of them.'' Geoffrey rubbed his arms. "I leave you, Lady Lenora. The air grows cool and I have misplaced my mantle. I will speak with you soon.''

"You may speak with me and my betrothed at the castle on our wedding,'' Roen interjected. "'Tis but three days away.''

"Three days.'' Lenora squeaked out the words as if they were her gallows sentence.

"Aye, your father's wishes. Two of your father's vassals arrive in two days to witness the ceremony. Lord Ranulf and Lord Baldric are your father's strongest allies and will pledge their fidelity to me as their lord. The rest of your knights may do so as they arrive, but the marriage will not wait.''

Geoffrey's smile left his face. "Then I will see you in three days.'' When he turned to Lenora, his gaze grew somber. "I beg your pardon for any offense I caused you. But 'tis my nature to feel your words more than most.''

Lenora did not leave her position at Roen's side. She gave her friend a regal nod. "I know, you have always been more sensitive than most. Let us put this behind us. Do not lose heart, Geoffrey. Things will turn out right."

"Oh, I'm sure they will." Geoffrey melted into the darkness of the forest. Roen watched him until he could no longer discern any movement in the shadows.

"Roen, I am so glad..." Lenora turned to him, her face bright with false sincerity.

"You are never to leave the castle unescorted again." Roen gripped her hand in his and started to drag her down the path to the castle.

"What? I know these woods like I know my own room. I won't get lost."

"Do you hear me? Never again. There is no discussion." Roen pulled her close to him. Her hair smelled of the forest, wild and free. He saw her eyes ignite as he uttered his command. She opened her mouth to speak but he claimed it. His lips roved over hers, exploring and memorizing their contours. The line of her jaw and the delicate skin behind her ears became a path for his lips to explore. His tongue outlined the delicate swirls of her ear. He heard her breathy refusal but did not heed it. The heat of his lips would dissolve away the memories of her lover's touch.

Lenora tried to escape his lips and hands but her attempts were futile against his embrace. "Please, Roen."

Roen lifted his head. "Aye, that I will, Nora. I'll make you forget that pup of a boy. You'll feel a man between your legs this time."

"Nay, Roen. Geoffrey only jested. We have not..." She lowered her golden eyes and he saw a flood of red color her face.

In answer, Roen cupped her buttocks with his hands and jerked her up into his swollen member. "Was he too gentlemanly for this?" He laughed when her color deepened. "Have you only played love games like Queen Eleanor taught you at court? I take what I want and now I want you." He lifted her up into his arms and brought her to eye level. "You are mine," he declared, and lowered her to the soft grass at his feet.

Lenora had no time or energy to fight. His body fell on hers, but he softened the blow by putting the full force of his weight on his elbows. She thought he meant to ravish her lips again, but instead he lowered his kiss to touch the valley between her breasts. He channeled his tongue into the deep cleft.

She wanted to fight him off but she couldn't keep track of his tongue and hands. The muscles in his chest flexed across her breasts. A stab of desire leapt from the point of impact to the pit of her stomach. Control and reason fled from the overwhelming strength of her hunger for Roen.

Her fingers tangled in the long hair at the base of his neck and pulled Roen to her of their own accord. She kissed him with a passion newly erupted and discovered. His callused hands tweaked the sensitive nipples of her breasts and she felt them rise to meet him. He held each like a precious jewel and then his lips moved to taste them.

Her back arched from the incredible joy of his tongue on her breasts. He played her nipple, then nibbled the skin beneath her breasts. She heard a purr like a cat and realized it came from her. Through heavy-lidded eyes she watched Roen flip her gown up and move between her legs.

"Now there will be no more question of you marrying me. You'll have to marry me." Roen reached and tore away her braes.

Reality started to filter into Lenora's passion drugged brain. It wasn't her he wanted, only Woodshadow. The stupor drained away; she regained possession of her body and began to fight. "Nay, I will not be taken like a strumpet on the march!"

Roen brought his knee in between her legs and she felt his fingers close on the triangle of hair between her legs. He said nothing as he stared at the entrance to her virginity. With one hand, he clutched her breast and held her down. His hand came forward and he slowly slid one finger into the gate of her maidenhood.

Confused at the turmoil Roen's actions caused, Lenora let fear overtake her. Although she did not believe her aunt's horror tales about men and women, all the stories and warnings came back. His finger eased inside her, and a thousand bolts of lightning shot through her body. He groaned as her body released a flood of warmth to ease his entrance.

"Do not do this." Lenora could fight no longer. Her body and mind warred. She both cursed and marveled at the passion that compelled her.

"I'm sorry, Nora. I wanted to wait. But 'tis the only way. I've got to keep you safe."

She opened her eyes to see he had lost his braes, also. Power pulsated from the thick shaft between her legs. Lenora wanted to cry in fear but her body cried for fulfillment.

"Do not give me idle words. You take what you want, so then take it and be done." She wanted to sound hard, but her words came out breathy and seductive. The yearnings of her body screamed for her to admit the truth. She wanted him to take her, she wanted him.

Roen lowered himself to her. His hard tip pressed at the edge of her womanhood. The long staff heated the skin of her inner thighs and created currents of ecstasy churning in her core. She squeezed her eyes shut, afraid of what her body felt, afraid of what it demanded to feel. Her natural curiosity got the best of her and she opened them again. Roen's face loomed above hers, locked in concentration. Perspiration beaded his brow. His silver eyes captured hers.

"Nora." He did not look away from her as he gently entered her. She stiffened when the red-hot shaft filled her. Her eyes started to close again, embarrassed that he might see the fervor of her desire. "Nay, Nora. Look at me."

Her eyes flew open. He stopped, suspended above her, and brushed her mouth with his. A new wash of warmth flooded her and the pain subsided. Roen's face transformed, the stern edges softened. He moved deeper and hesitated at the barrier of her maidenhood. Lost in her body's cravings, Lenora gripped his arms and rocked toward him.

"Wait, Nora. Not yet." He pushed her hips down, a look of surprise on his face. "I can't do this right if you keep that up."

Lenora didn't care if he did it right or wrong. Her body exploded with new, wonderful feelings and she wanted more. She increased the rotation of her hips. Gone were any thoughts of anger or hatred. Her body didn't acknowledge those emotions. The spine-tingling bolts of desire were all she wanted to concentrate on. "Roen . . ." The name rumbled in her throat. "I want this. Now."

With a roar like a lion, Roen shook his blond mane and plunged into her core. His lips covered hers to muffle her short cry. Deep inside her, he did not stir, letting her body mold itself around him. Lenora felt full, yet ravenous for more of him. She curled her legs around him and Roen whispered in her hair, "Aye, that's the way of it. You're a fast learner."

A rock of her hips, and she heard Roen gasp. His face became transfixed as she tilted her pelvis toward then away from him. She gave him a saucy look and reminded him, "Are you never to listen to me? I warned you I'm intelligent."

In retaliation, Roen lifted himself up onto his elbows and began moving his hips in a slow gyrating dance that took her breath away. Her gaze flew to his as the hurricane of emotions in her began a crescendo. His body consumed her with the fire of his lovemaking. She wanted to meld with him as deeply and forcefully as possible. Her fingers dug into his back and then raked down his sides to the deeply muscled contours of his buttocks. He plunged deeper. The storm within her reached its maximum force. The tempest cried for more and she delivered. With all her strength, Lenora pushed herself up to meet Roen's thrust. His hands cradled her and lifted her to him.

The surge of ecstasy carried both lovers in the eddies of passion. Lenora's body jerked with each hot stream of seed Roen emptied into the warmth of her womb. Spent, he lowered himself and rested his head on her breasts. The heavy thudding of her heart pounded in his ear. He hoped his obsession would diminished now that he had lain with her, but 'twas the opposite. The sound of her breath stirred his want again. Her milky white breasts teased him to taste their nectar. Roen was full but famished when it came to his Nora.

Lifting his gaze to hers, he lost himself in the warm cider depths. Her eyes glowed with the still-present embers of passion. Withdrawing himself from her, he lowered her skirt. "You are mine, Nora." The words came out soft and tender, yet he told himself he felt none of those emotions. This act consummated his duty to his king, nothing more. Yet as he gathered her warm, pliant body close, his thoughts were on the pleasures his body had just experienced and the joy he felt when he discovered her maidenhead intact. His fingers trailed through Lenora's hair and pushed it from her eyes.

Lenora hid her face, ashamed that she possessed such a sinful nature. The fading wisps of euphoria drained from her body, leaving her bruised and empty on the ground. The act had stripped her of her independence. Now she was like any other woman, an object of ownership, a device to gain wealth.

"You are mine." His crow of victory shamed her even more. He pushed back her hair so that she could see the satisfaction the remark gave him. His hands loosened their hold, and she grabbed the opportunity to escape his clutches. She rolled the opposite way and scrambled to her feet. Her rumpled gown fell down to its proper location. With her body once again modestly covered, she regained some composure.

"Nora, wait, I'll walk you back." Roen moved to collect his clothing.

"Nay, I'll not enter Woodshadow with you. All will know what's occurred."

"All will know soon enough." He began to retie his braes.

"I'm sure of that. No doubt you'll want to hear all the cheers and boasts in your favor at the news you've turned me into a whore." Lenora's anger and disgrace made her throw caution to the wind. "You bastard. You took from me that which was only mine to give. How did such a baseborn man as yourself become a knight?" Lenora did not wait for an answer. She ran back down the path to the castle and the comfort of her own room.

Roen did not follow. The heat and truth of Lenora's words stung deep. So, his father's prophecy finally came true. He stared at the spot where his worst fears had materialized. A blemish of white caught his eye. Lenora's braes lay crumpled, a brilliant red stain marked her innocence. He picked up the proof of his vileness. He shoved the panties into the inner folds of his tunic.

His long legs ate away the distance between him and Lenora. Deep in thought, he shadowed her until after they passed the bailey walls. Both had missed the evening meal. His men would think nothing of it, but what of Lenora's people? He needed to think of a story to spare her inquisitive questions.

"Nora, we must talk."

She whipped around. Hatred burned in her eyes. "Can you not leave me in peace for a moment?"

"Nay, Nora. I spoke wrong. No one need know what happened."

"Why keep silent about your victory, *Sir Galliard?*" She mocked his title. "Will you paint me the harlot on our wedding night when I have no proof of my innocence?" She slapped his cheek.

He felt the stinging imprint on his face. Roen reached out to take her hand but she backed away and ran into the keep.

"Nora, damn you, wait." He pulled up next to her and cursed again. His private guard of men stood together by the central fireplace downing ale. They quickly took in Lenora's disheveled appearance and the mark on his face. A few snickers started and then they all wore sophomoric grins. Lenora cringed and ran up the stairs. Helpless, Roen watched.

"Did you teach the shrew a lesson?" Alric laughed while he gulped his tankard of ale. He let out a loud belch.

Roen's black look quenched Alric's humor. Hamlin stayed quiet and gave the knights a silent hand signal as Roen headed for the jug of spirits on the trestle table. The men faded from the room, leaving Hamlin alone with his friend.

In one swift motion, Roen poured a goblet of strong brew and downed it. He poured a second and brought it to his lips.

"What have you done?" Hamlin's voice sounded no reproach.

As a response, Roen threw back the contents of the cup and poured again. "What had to be done." He drank down his third drink.

"Tell me that you did not rape her," Hamlin pleaded. He noted the speed at which his friend consumed the ale; a few more and he would be headed for trouble.

Roen remained mute and shot back another cup of ale. He refilled the cup. Hamlin swept the bottle from the table, the crash sending slivers of pottery in all directions.

"I thought you meant to make peace with the girl. What demon possessed you? How could you do such a thing?"

" 'Twas a waste of good ale, Hamlin. How could I do such a thing, you ask?" Roen laughed bitterly and drained the cup. He stumbled to his feet and threw his goblet against the wall. With his head resting in his hands, he spoke in a resigned tone. "She was in the woods with Geoffrey Champlain. They are...acquaintances." He slammed his fist against the wall. "I heard her call Champlain's name in her sleep, after I had—" Roen paused "—kissed her."

"Is that why you claimed her, you were jealous?"

"Nay." Roen rubbed his eyes with the palms of his hands. "I lost reason. I—" he floundered for words then gave an acerbic laugh "—had hoped she was different from my mother."

"She is. You must stop allowing your mother's actions to prejudice you against all women."

Guilt painted Roen's face ashen. "You're right. Because of my anger at my mother, I wronged Nora deeply. She and Champlain are not lovers, yet. She was still a maiden when he left her. The same cannot be said for when she left me."

Pity for his friend softened Hamlin's anger. "Go to her, explain the truth about your mother."

Roen rose and leaned against the wall for support. "'Tis no need, she knows the truth, if not by my words then by my deeds. I am a bastard to take advantage of an innocent."

Hamlin guided his inebriated lord up the stairs to the room they shared. He let Roen fall onto the straw pallets on the floor and began to remove his boots. Roen cursed himself and his parents under his breath. Hamlin halted as he pulled a boot from Roen's foot. The bare limb hit the floor with a thump. The impact jolted the drunken man back to coherence.

"When you knew you were wrong, why didn't you stop?" Hamlin asked.

Roen squirmed uncomfortably. "Stop? What kind of man do you think I am? I had gone too far to stop."

"I think you're the kind of man who can outwit any lord in a siege. The kind of man that has the utmost patience. When he desires it."

"'Twas for the best. There will be no more of this nonsense about the wedding. Nora . . . Woodshadow . . . will be safe."

"But if she does have a paramour, then would not marriage to him suffice the king?"

His friend rolled over and kicked Hamlin away. "I grow tired of your mouth, Hamlin. 'Tis time to sleep." Roen closed his eyes and soon the sound of his deep breathing filled the room.

Hamlin studied his lord, then a smile cracked his face. "Roen, you have never known a woman's tender caress, yet I think you desire it more than you will admit." He plopped down on his pallet. "And Lady Lenora of Woodshadow is the woman you desire it from. As your friend, I am honor-bound to get you what you want, even if you're not aware you want it." Hamlin gave a sly smile. "And I know just the person to aid me. Oh, Roen, you don't know how fortunate you are to have me as a friend."

Chapter Thirteen

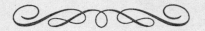

Hamlin looked up as yet another guest entered the crowded hall. The noise level caused his ears to ring. He tried to catch Roen's attention.

The groom sat on the raised dais at the back wall dressed in his wedding finery. Roen kept some part of his body in constant movement. His hand nudged the circlet of rough hammered gold holding back his hair. He dropped his hands to the wide sash that belted his gold-and-forest-green tunic and surveyed the room. Hamlin noted that his friend had never appeared so princely.

Nor had he ever looked so miserable.

Roen's gaze returned to the steps that led to the upper dormitories. The stairs remained vacant; no bride descended. The groom tightened his belt again, then he gave a quick jerk of his head toward the stairs. Hamlin knew the gesture's meaning. He threaded his way across the floor and placed his foot on the first step.

A slender figure moved in front of the narrow slit window in front of him. A plan formulated in his mind. He pulled back his foot and pivoted closer to the shy woman.

Beatrice sat on the floor nearby. Hamlin stood transfixed at the ethereal beauty before him. She reminded him of a pet bird in a cage, only the bars of her prison were made of her fears. As she watched the boisterous approach of more guests, her usually timid blue eyes sparkled with curiosity and elation. He could see her desire to fly free of her cage and her dread of what lay beyond her cell.

A crash behind him made her turn. When she spied him so near, the happiness in her eyes faded.

"What do you want?" She scooted against the wall and drew her knees up.

"I want to talk with you about Lenora." Hamlin smoothed the effects of her beauty from his voice.

"Leave me. Your friend has done enough already to my cousin." The anguish in her eyes mixed with anger. The tilt of her chin mimicked that of her cousin's.

"What did Lenora tell you happened?" Inside, Hamlin felt a longing tenderness to ease away her fears and teach her the gentleness that could exist between a man and woman. Between them, if he could reach beyond her nightmares.

"She told me nothing, but I heard the servants gossiping." Beatrice's eyes began to gleam. "I saw what those men did when they took my father's castle. I know the atrocity that man forced on Lenora. He has no right to her."

Understanding filled Hamlin with compassion, and a flower of hope bloomed. Now that he knew the root of her ailment, he could search for a cure. She needed to see that lovemaking did not always involve pain and humiliation. Unfortunately, today's wedding did not help his case. More than ever he needed his friend's marriage to be peaceful and loving. If not for Roen's sake, then for his own.

"You're right, Lady Beatrice. Roen knows he has hurt Lady Lenora. He would like to make amends."

"How do you make amends for something like that? He has driven a dagger of shame into her heart. Does the man even know the depth of the pain he has caused her?"

"For three days he has known nothing else. She will not look at him or at anyone. He knows she walks these halls like a ghost, not venturing outside or speaking to anyone. We need your help."

"Why should I help you, or him?" Beatrice asked righteously.

"Oh, I do not ask for me. I ask for Lady Lenora." Hamlin smiled to himself when Beatrice gave him her full attention. "This wedding will take place. There is naught that can be done to naysay it now. Thus, as Lenora's friend and I as Roen's, we must work together to see this union is as it should be."

"What can I do?" Beatrice knit her graceful brows together.

"Much, I think." Hamlin ventured to draw nearer. His heart beat a trifle faster when she did not pull away but instead leaned closer. "Think, Beatrice. When Lenora was not overly irritated with Roen, did she ever speak of him or look at him in a gentle way?"

Beatrice glanced about and licked her lower lip. "There were times. Lenora would often steal a look at him at dinner. Sometimes, when he was in the exercise yard, she would tarry a bit longer than necessary. I know she likes his horse," Beatrice added hopefully. "What of Galliard?"

Hamlin's smile grew confident. "I assure you, Lady Beatrice, Roen is attracted to Lenora." He saw Beatrice begin to retreat. "Nay, I mean he cares. He admires her fire and wit."

"Then why does he not tell her? Lenora is forever lamenting that men do not appreciate a woman's thoughts and ideas."

"I wish that he could, but long ago a woman hardened his heart."

Beatrice sighed and turned her gaze to study the tip of her toes. "Then 'tis hopeless. Lenora is too stubborn to admit her feelings and Galliard refuses."

Hamlin chuckled and tilted her chin so that her downcast eyes met his own. "Aye, 'twould be hopeless if there were not the two of us. We must be the words and actions for our friends and find a way for them to find the happiness they deserve. Do you agree to help in this plot?"

Beatrice nodded eagerly. "For Lenora. What must I do?"

Hamlin removed his hand reluctantly. He forced himself not to push the fragile beauty too far too quickly. "Lenora has not put in an appearance at her own wedding. Roen has told no one of what transpired in the wood, but as you said, there is gossip. She must come down and put a stop to the rumors. Not so much for Roen, but for her own sake."

"She told me she plans to come down only for the ceremony, not before. When the cleric finishes the vows, she will return to her room."

"Her room? Sir Edmund vacated his solar for the wedding couple."

"Aye, Roen's things have already been moved in, but Lenora has moved none of her belongings. She said *her* room."

Urgency made Hamlin rush to disclose his plan. "This will only add fat to the fire and make our job more difficult. You must make her see there is nothing to fear."

"Lenora is not afraid of anyone or anything," Beatrice boasted.

"Nay, dove. She fears what Roen fears. To love someone, to care. Roen has never known any affection, so he mistrusts it. For Lenora 'tis the opposite. Her brother, her father and her home, she opened her heart to. All she has lost or will soon lose. She fears to love and lose again."

The girl before him grew quiet. Her sapphire eyes looked at him with a new fortitude of spirit. "Aye, I see what you speak is true. But I have never been the one to give courage. 'Tis always been the other way around with us. Lenora is the one who gives me comfort with her bravery."

Hamlin spoke quietly. "Then 'tis time you return the boon, time for Lenora to draw wisdom and strength from you."

Lenora stared at nothing and everything from the wide balcony window of her room. The brilliant silk banners of her father's vassals passed beneath her, barely noticed. Gay melodies drifted on the air. Her wedding celebration sounded like a wonderful, exciting affair. As a little girl, fantasies of her wedding day had filled her make-believe world. As a real bride, the day brought her only despair.

"You're not even dressed?" Beatrice exclaimed when she entered the room. "Your guests are waiting for you to make an appearance."

Lenora kept her unfocused gaze on the scene outside. "I'm in no hurry."

Beatrice moved to the balcony. "Lenora, come downstairs. As 'tis, we will scarcely have time to ready you by the ceremony."

"There will be time. I've laid my dress out. 'Twill only take a moment to pull it on and lace it."

Her cousin glanced at the bed and horror filled her eyes. "Nay, you cannot mean to wear that. Why, only a fortnight ago I saw you wearing it to do garden work." She crossed to the bed and grabbed the end of the skirt. "See, the hem is pulled and grass-stained."

Lenora tugged her gaze from the parade below and felt a splinter of stubbornness return. "Do you think I will give those people down there the impression this union is something I want? Do you think I do not know what they say about me? Let them think what they want. I will not pretend that this day is joyful to me. Today is the first day of my prison sentence, with Galliard as my jailer."

An ember of anger thawed the ice in her soul. She crossed to the chest that held her clothes and removed an intricately inlaid wooden box. The cold, smooth feel of the lacquered object sickened her. She couldn't bear to touch it any longer.

She thrust the coffer into the other woman's hands. "Look at the penance Galliard does me."

Beatrice opened the hinged box and gasped. Inside lay a chain-link necklace of gold. Coarsely cut beads of emeralds and amber studded the chain. "'Tis beautiful." Her eyes rose and she smiled. Her lips moved in a whisper. "He's right."

"Who's right?" Lenora didn't understand the reaction the jewelry elicited in her cousin.

"Lenora, this necklace is you." Beatrice lifted the chain from the box and held her arm high to let the light dance off the gems. "See, the rope, 'tis delicate but strong. The warm amber stones are like your eyes and the emeralds go with your hair."

"You are a romantic. Galliard is trying to buy my forgiveness. He thinks a trinket will wipe the memory of this day from my mind." Lenora gripped the box and threw it across the room.

"Then show him he did not break you and that petty jewels will not buy you. Let everyone see that Galliard's crime only blackens his name and not yours. Come downstairs with your head high."

Lenora stared at the box on the floor. Completely intact, it showed no damage from the impact with the wall. Beatrice followed her gaze and retrieved it. "See, Lenora, the beauty is still there despite the punishment it received. No scratches or scars mar its beauty."

The highly varnished finish reflected Lenora's blurred image. She took the box from her cousin and rubbed her hands along the sleek lines.

"Lenora, there are many of your father's vassals in attendance." Beatrice added, "As are many of your father's enemies. If they see unrest today, they are sure to store it away for use later on."

"How can so much power be held in my actions, yet leave me powerless?" She tossed the box on the bed and reached for her kirtle.

"Wait, not that gown. Don't make Galliard out to be a martyr."

Lenora paused. "What do you mean?"

"Do not meet your father's underlords dressed poorly. 'Tis Galliard that will reap their sympathy to marry such a woman. They will cluck like old women and give their backing to Galliard that he must marry an uncomely bride." Beatrice grabbed the work gown and tossed it on the floor. "Lenora, I have seen you when your face is lit with life and a cause. You outshine any boring beauty. That is the face you must present, for then any man will see that Galliard is a knave for trying to besmirch your name."

Lenora stood silent then slowly nodded. "How have you suddenly grown so wise, Cousin?"

Beatrice took the brush and positioned Lenora on the side of the bed. The brush moved through the amber tresses with a purpose. "I've had an excellent teacher, Cousin. I am glad to finally be able to return the kindness."

Roen paced across the dais again. His father-in-law sat in a huge chair at the center of the table. He did not speak, only stared at Roen with silent accusation. Hamlin, stationed at the stairs, offered no respite to Roen's discomfort. His friend glanced up toward the gallery, looked away, then turned and looked up the stairs again. A smile, then an open grin split his face. He turned and signaled that Lenora had finally decided to make an appearance. Roen stood ready to meet his bride.

The din of the room silenced as the two females descended the stairs. The hush spread like a flame on a grassland, slow at first, then all-consuming. Roen wiped his palms on the sides of his tunic. He waited, and wondered where all his famed patience had fled to.

Beatrice reached the bottom step and paused near Hamlin. She moved aside to let Lenora pass. Roen moved to claim his betrothed but stopped when she entered the sunlit room. He had pictured the ghost that walked the castle for the last three days; instead a princess entered the hall. Relief and joy pumped into his heart. He feared Lenora dead in spirit but she arose like a phoenix, more beautiful than ever before. His Nora had returned.

She walked gracefully to join him, her red gold hair in two braids that reached well below her waist. Encased in twisted gold ribbons, they shone like copper ropes. His favorite curl did not strain against the confines of her ear but bounced free and saucy. A foliated coronet set with sapphires held a stormy blue gauze veil in place. The fine pleats of her matching bliaut trailed the floor. As she walked, the azure of her veil and gown shimmered in the light.

Long wide sleeves puffed at the upper arm were highlighted with ties of gold ribbon. The spotless white of her silk undergown peeked at the neck and wrist. Over her bliaut she wore a gold honeycomb corselet. A blue-and-gold embroidered girdle wound twice around her body and tied low on her hip.

Like a queen among her subjects, his intended held her head high. She met the eyes of everyone she addressed, her gaze steady and unyielding. Roen waited breathless; the ache to feel the curve of her body at his side became insistent. Lenora filled his vision and he did not wish to break the spell. His hand moved forward and he slid his fingers between hers. The hunger for her deepened and he restrained himself from jerking her into his arms.

Her eyes met his and he felt a part of his heart freeze. No warmth kindled in the two topaz orbs. Like the gem, the beauty glowed, but coldly, with no emotion. Roen noticed she wore no amber-and-emerald jewelry. She wore not even the color green. As her eyes traveled down his emerald tunic, they grew colder.

"Just like a woman to keep us waiting." Sir Edmund motioned his daughter closer. "But the wait was well worth it." His voice grew emotional. "I'm glad I lived to see this day. You've made me a proud father." His voice became louder as he stated the last. He narrowed his eyes to thin slits and stabbed several guests with his stare.

"You do me an honor, Sir Edmund." Roen's voice matched the elder's. The low tittering in the room silenced when he pierced the crowd with his gaze.

Lenora turned her attention from her father to Roen. "Where is the cleric? All documents have been signed and approved. Let this ceremony be done with."

Roen knew that few would take her statement as that of an eager bride. Those of the castle knew her true feelings.

Musicians strummed lyres and played pipes as she and Roen entered the chapel. Her father, helped to his pew in the front, watched with misted eyes. Drawing strength from his steadfastness, Lenora proceeded with Galliard to the cleric. The young monk, nervous in front of the large crowd of nobles, stuttered as he spoke the vows that would bind her forever to the man next to her.

Roen lifted her woodlike hand. She tried to mentally separate herself as he repeated his vows and placed the symbol of her imprisonment on her finger. The silver-and-gold ring gleamed against the whiteness of her skin and made her hand feel heavy.

"Milady? Your vows?" The cleric cleared his throat and rubbed his neck. "Do you need me to repeat them again?"

She looked at the cleric and realized she had missed her cue to speak. "Nay, I know them." In a flat, distant voice she spoke the words that sealed her fate.

The cleric began to conclude the ceremony. The mangled words provoked a final thawing flame. A vow of her own making formed. The specter of shame disappeared and she regained her soul. She would not allow Galliard to suck her dry as Geoffrey had warned.

The placement of the marriage pall startled her from her vengeful thoughts. Beneath the cloth, she turned to her husband. "So, have you any bastards to legitimize, Galliard?" Her voice carried no farther than Roen's ears.

"Nay, I've no bastards. Nor will I ever." His face, like a granite cliff, caused her to feel a moment's regret for the circumstances of her marriage. A life sentence in a loveless relationship could be no one's hope.

The pall removed, the monk passed a thick slice of bread to Roen. He broke off a piece and held it out to her. When she reached for it, he pulled it back. She questioned him with her eyes. In response, he moved forward and held out his hand for her to eat from it. A few of the more expressive terms she had heard Tom and her father use came to mind.

She opened her mouth to deliver a few but Roen stuffed it full of bread. Gagging, she chewed the mouthful down to a wad she managed to swallow. Roen sipped his wine and then held the cup to her mouth. The angle of the goblet caused the liquid to pour down her throat so quickly she had to gulp to keep it from dribbling all over her. He removed the cup and with his tongue licked the excess wine from her lips. Her knees buckled and she sought his arm for support.

Roen placed his hand on her elbow and turned her around to face the assembled witnesses. Shouts of congratulations and good wishes rang from the guests. The sounds of resounding slaps and blows marked the air as each of her father's vassals impressed this day on their mind with a strike to their neighbor's face or back.

Her husband's steady pull on her elbow led them down the aisle. Seeds, to represent a hope for fertility and harmony, showered her head and shoulders. She stared at the joyful faces of the assembled crowd as they offered what she considered wasted wishes. They arrived outside the chapel and were surrounded by even more well-wishers. The hypocrisy of the moment threatened to make her physically ill.

Her father, assisted by several squires, held out his hand and gripped both his daughter's and Roen's hands. "Today, Woodshadow's future is secure. From this union, the next generation of heirs will spring forth." He motioned to the nobles. "Come, swear your fealty to Sir Roen de Galliard, Lord of Woodshadow."

The music hushed and the crowd ringed the hall. One at a time, each of Sir Edmund's men stepped forward and presented himself to his liege. Each knelt at Roen's feet and took the hem of the emerald green tunic in his hands. With clear voices, the vassals swore to bear their faith in life and member for their lord. In Roen's name, they would fight against all men who live and can die, save for King Henry II of England and his heirs. To seal the oath, each kissed the hem of Roen's tunic, rose to his feet and presented his sword to the new Lord of Woodshadow.

Visiting lords and their families stood in hushed silence around the ring of her father's, nay, her husband's vassals. These lords bore homage not to Woodshadow but directly to the king. Lenora spotted Geoffrey standing beside his brothers and father. Her friend gnawed the inside of his cheek and his eye twitched erratically.

When the last man pledged and stood, a cry resounded through the hall. Men took up the chant of Roen's name. He turned to face her. She expected triumph and gloating. Instead, she saw him humbled by the acceptance the knights revealed. Looking at the room of satisfied people crystallized for her the reason her father had pushed her so hard to wed.

Although her marriage cost her much, it provided a stable transfer of power. Roen represented a strong defender against those that would steal or plot against Woodshadow and its many properties. No castle could survive for long without a capable leader.

Lenora did not doubt Roen's ability to protect Woodshadow in war, but her father did more than keep bandits at bay. He governed and led his men in times of peace, as well. Did Roen possess that ability? The full extent of her responsibilities materialized. Besides her duties of before, now she must watch her husband and see to it Woodshadow fared as well under his leadership as it had under her father's.

Roen placed her hand atop his and led her to the floor of the great hall. The musicians struck up a lively tune and the guests joined in the dance. A group of acrobats somersaulted around the couple, then between them. A tumbling wall of bodies soon separated the bride from the groom. Lenora took the opportunity to escape the compelling eyes of her husband.

The crowd, spellbound by the contortions of the performers, allowed her to slip away to a secluded spot along the back wall. She swiped a skin of wine, a loaf of bread and a chunk of cheese from a platter. Secure in her out-of-the-way hidey-hole, Lenora munched and observed.

She brushed off the remains of her meal and stood to shake away any lingering crumbs. The food acted like flint and steel to kindle a spark of vitality in her. Her feet tapped to the gay beat of the music and she moved to the edge of the assembled group. Half-singing the tune played by the musicians, she swayed back and forth. The merriment of the crowd and well-wishers enabled her to forget, for a moment, the disaster her life had become.

"I'm glad you're enjoying yourself."

Lenora started. "Geoffrey." Happiness and worry mixed in her heart. His jest had instigated Roen's actions against her. But it had been her rudeness and insensitivity that pushed her friend to play the trick. When would she learn to watch her tongue?

"Ah, I caught you unaware again." An irksome smile played on his lips. "I came to wish you good tidings on your marriage." He moved closer. "And to extend my deepest regrets about my actions. My only defense is that my frustration got the best of me."

She turned to go, but he held her by the shoulder. "Geoffrey, your actions were unforgivable. Do you know what your words cost me?"

"What, Lenora? I've heard rumors. Tell me."

"It does not matter. Suffice it to say, my life with my husband will not be a peaceful one."

"Oh, but it does matter to me." He released her shoulder and gave her hand a light squeeze. "Dear, sweet friend, please say I am forgiven. Understand my turmoil and futile love for your cousin drove me to madness." He batted his eyes like a flirtatious ingenue.

Lenora laughed. "You are incorrigible."

Geoffrey winked and laughed. "Nay, Lenora, that title is reserved for you. You need only ask that old war-horse Matilda."

The festivities of the day thawed Lenora's demeanor. Her laughter bubbled out. "Aye, you are forgiven. But what of Beatrice? Will you not reconsider?"

"'Tis better this way. Your husband is sure to promise her to one of his own men."

Drawn by their shared unhappiness, she gave him a gentle hug. "Geoffrey, I wish things could be different. Do not give up all hope. Your dreams may still come true."

He pursed his lips and nodded, a disturbing smile on his lips. "Perhaps you are correct. I will not promise anything, but tell Beatrice I will try to contact her when I can." Geoffrey's face lost all amusement.

She tilted her head and wrinkled her brow. "What ails you?"

Suddenly, Lenora found herself spun around to face Galliard. The scowl on his face advertised his temperament.

"I told you that if you wish to speak to Lenora, do so when we are both present." His voice rumbled like an ominous storm.

"Galliard, please. Geoffrey is a friend."

"Then he would do well not to compromise that relationship." Roen placed his arm possessively around her waist and pulled her to his side. She managed to stomp heavily on his instep in the process. A twinge of satisfaction branched through her at his pained grimace.

The two men faced each other. Roen did not hide his displeasure and Geoffrey displayed a look of haughty disdain. Lenora viewed her husband's pounding neck vein and searched for a way to defuse the situation.

"Congratulations, Sir Galliard." Geoffrey's father slapped his son and Roen on their shoulders. Shorter than both men, his blow still bent the younger knights forward.

Sir Champlain stroked his dark, greasy beard. His foul breath nearly knocked Lenora from her feet. He ran his tongue over rotting teeth. "You've done well, Galliard. Woodshadow is a fine keep. There's not much a man would not do for a place as rich as this." He eyed Geoffrey and snickered. "Oh, there's been many that's schemed for it. Witty young men have plotted to win this keep for a long time." The lecherous old man cackled while Geoffrey's face hardened to stone.

"There will be few attempts to rob Woodshadow now that Roen is lord. I would think our problems with your poachers in our wood will soon be settled." She spoke with deliberate firmness. Sir Champlain must not discern any strife in her marriage or he would use it against Woodshadow.

The old man laughed again, the aroma from his unclean body causing her to stumble away. Roen's arms slipped around her waist. She rested her hands on the protective belt of his arms.

"All your talk about not marrying was talk after all." Sir Champlain winked at Roen. "Some said she wouldn't marry. They wagered that cousin of hers would inherit all of this. I knew she wouldn't give it all up to join some nunnery. Just needed some young stag to make her fall into line."

Geoffrey brushed his father's hand from his shoulder and stalked off. His son's action did not anger Sir Champlain. The man threw back his head and laughed uproariously.

"Excuse me, Lord Champlain. We have other guests we must not ignore." Lenora tried to extricate herself from the horrid man's presence. She tilted her face upward to Roen's and gave a tiny wave of her head away from Sir Champlain. A silent plea moved on her lips.

Roen looked down at her and she lost herself in the wonderful blue-gray, almost teal shade of his eyes. His full lips tilted in a tired smile. For once, he followed her lead. She locked her arm in his and guided them away from their unsavory company.

"I noticed none of your people came to the ceremony, Sir Galliard."

Sir Champlain's remark halted Roen's retreat. "My family was unable to attend."

"Really, that's too bad. You know your father and I are related. Cousins in a roundabout way. I spent a lot of my youth carousing with him."

Roen turned to face the old man, and so did Lenora. Sir Champlain stood with his fists on his hips, a sly sneer on his face. "'Tis a pity the elder Galliard could not witness this whole event. He'd be sure to claim you as his own, especially when he learned how you managed to secure this union. There'd be no question of your parentage then."

Lenora felt Roen's body straighten as though from a javelin thrust. A snarl quivered on his lips. The grip on her arm tightened, the large knuckles white. Sir Champlain's verbal arrow had hit its target. Lenora did not understand the barb but knew its wound sank deep into the soul of her husband.

"Sir Galliard has the trust of my father. Something not easily attained, as you well know, Sir Champlain." Lenora let her tongue return wound for wound. When someone attacked Roen, he attacked Woodshadow. Honor demanded retaliation. "My father is very astute in his judgment of men. If he ascertains that Galliard is the man for Woodshadow, not a knight here would venture to doubt him."

Both men stared at her. Roen with surprised gratitude, Champlain with unmasked irritation that she turned his remark back on him. The old knave courted her father's favor, only to be rejected each time. Roen had accomplished what Champlain had tried for years. Jealousy was eating the old man alive.

Seething, the putrid lord growled low under his breath and stalked off. Lenora noticed his departure immediately. She could finally take a breath without the danger of retching.

Roen placed his hand under her chin and gently guided her face upward. The gold circlet on his brow reflected a halo around his head. His breath, tinged with mint, danced across her ear and sent impulses ringing in her head.

"Thank you for your defense, wife." He spoke in a whisper but his last word grated on Lenora.

She pulled away from him, careful to draw no unwanted attention, and warned under her breath, "Take care, Galliard. Do not think things are different between us. 'Tis just my knowledge of the man. He has long wanted Woodshadow land and would have it, if not for my father's battle arm. What he could not win in honest battle he tries to steal in underhandedness. To keep my home safe, we must show a united front."

She gathered the side of her gown in her hand and added, "You should not let Champlain's remarks upset you so. 'Tis only his attempt to rattle you. You fell with ease into his trap." Her features set in serene composure, she turned with a flounce of her dress and left her newly married husband alone in the great hall.

"Was that wise, daughter?" Sir Edmund asked softly as Lenora passed. She immediately went to his side and sat at his feet. With her index finger, she traced the design of the family crest engraved on the side of his chair and avoided his eyes.

"He jumped at Champlain's bait. The new Lord of Woodshadow needs to show more presence of mind."

Sir Edmund shook his head. "Nay, 'tis something more there. He's not the type of man to show his feelings so blatantly.'' He pointed his finger at her. ''You must ferret out this mystery.''

''Why do you not just ask him yourself?'' Lenora asked, a pout on her lips.

'' 'Twill take time, and time is one thing I do not have.''

''Father, do not speak so.'' Lenora stood and embraced him. Her face showed panicked determination. Sir Edmund let out a low sigh. The magnitude of his decision burdened him.

''Child, you know that I love you.'' He placed her hand back on the design embedded in the wood. ''Do you remember when I carved this?''

She nodded, tears formed in the corners of her eyes.

''Let those memories cushion the sorrow when I leave. My going is easier now that I know you are safe with Galliard. Despite what has happened between you, his actions were rooted in your protection. Give him a chance. He's a good man.''

Her father clutched her hand.

''Smile for me, so that I can leave this hall with a vision of your beauty and not your sorrow.'' Dutifully, she smiled, though it did not reach her eyes. ''Go now, daughter, and seek out your husband.'' He sank back into the chair, his shoulders sagged and he placed one hand over his heart.

Two servants materialized from the shadows with Tom in the lead. They lifted the chair and removed Sir Edmund from the hall, leaving Lenora alone in the midst of the crowd.

Solitude. Lenora despaired of ever finding it. Her tiny alcove of privacy swarmed with activity. Ladies-in-waiting circled around her like vultures. They giggled and relayed snappy remarks about the night that awaited her. Matilda, her eyes hard as flint, prepared to give her niece a lecture on what to expect.

Lenora silenced her with a glance. ''No need for the speech, Aunt. I do not intend to sleep anywhere other than my dormitory bed.''

Aghast, the women hushed, gossip already forming on their lips. 'Twould be a short time before everyone, Galliard included, knew she did not intend to sleep in the marriage bed.

Beatrice, in an aggressive manner, shooed the ladies from the area, even her mother. Her cousin radiated with confidence.

Lenora supposed that now that the threat of marriage to Roen had dissipated, Beatrice could afford to be more forceful.

"This cannot be."

"This can and will be," Lenora replied with a determined set to her chin. She prepared to dig in for a battle.

"The marriage must be consummated."

"It already has been. 'Tis no matter 'twas done before the cleric said his words."

"Aye, it does matter. What if a child grows within you?"

Lenora gasped. The thought had not occurred to her. She placed her hand on her abdomen.

Beatrice nodded sagely. "Would you label your child a bastard? You must be with him tonight to protect yourself."

The pout returned to Lenora's lips. Her mind raced like a stallion freed of its reins. "Very well, the man will be in the room with me, but I will not allow him to touch me again, ever."

Searing flames of recalled passion ignited her blood. Her face grew hot, her hands moist as she remembered the intimate way Roen had explored her body. She could not be alone with him again. Her mind did not rule her body as well as she wanted.

"If that is how you truly wish it." Beatrice relented. "But how will you keep him from you? You are his wife and he has the right."

"I'll find a way not to let him touch me again." She had lost herself in the heat of their lovemaking. The all-consuming emotions frightened her. Too much bedding with her husband and Lenora feared she would begin to care, to want more from Galliard than she knew he could or would give. She already had a loveless marriage; she didn't want a broken heart, also.

Lenora climbed the stairs, Matilda and several women following behind. Catcalls and lewd laughter drifted from below. Her mind concentrated on the echo of her footsteps on the cold stone steps. With each hollow tone she repeated her promise not to let Galliard win. Her husband would soon learn she still had her wits about her.

Hamlin reached out and pulled Beatrice away from the queue of women behind Lenora. "Does she go to her chambers or the wedding bed?"

Beatrice's face bloomed crimson. "To her wedding bed, but she does not intend to share it with her husband."

Hamlin smiled and gave Beatrice a cavalier wink. "We've done our part, dove. She's wedded to him and waiting in their bed. Roen can't expect us to do all the work for him."

"Aye, but if I know my cousin, he's in for no light duty." Beatrice resumed her climb upstairs.

"Roen enjoys a good challenge."

Lenora's voice issuing commands sounded from the gallery. The protests of the attending women were silenced with the sound of a crash. Beatrice gave Hamlin a look of disbelief. "If what you say is true, then I daresay, Sir Hamlin, your friend may look ahead to a most enjoyable wedding night."

Chapter Fourteen

"I shan't do it, do you hear?" Lenora threw off the arms of her attending women. Making herself a dead weight, she plopped down in the chair, folded her arms and blotted out the scandalized whispers from her ladies.

"Lenora, stop this foolishness. You are a married woman now who must do service to her husband," Matilda's reedy voice droned.

"Service? I might as well be a brood mare."

"'Tis a woman's lot for her sins in the Garden of Eden." Matilda reached to untie her niece's laces. Lenora pulled away and tightened her crossed arms.

"I'll not lie there naked in that bed like a pagan sacrifice. I have much to discuss with Galliard, and I want to be on equal footing."

Matilda tugged at the ribbon laces of Lenora's dress despite the barrier of her arms. The older woman's eyes sharpened and her lips set in a tight, thin line. She reached into the brocade pocket tied at her side and pulled out a pair of sewing scissors. With a quick snip, Lenora felt her gown loosen.

Outraged, she stood and the kirtle crumpled to her hips, held in place by her corselet and girdle. Her aunt snipped the air for effect and closed in on her. "Nay, Aunt, do not. This girdle belonged to my mother, your sister," Lenora protested.

"Then remove it now or you'll own two instead of one."

Lenora grumbled while her fingers moved quickly to untie the knot. The gown collapsed to the ground. Attending ladies bent swiftly to collect the garment. Lenora did not step away.

Her cousin came forth. "Do not let more damage take place to your wedding garb. You must wear it for your purification after each birthing."

Birthing! The idea gave Lenora shivers of apprehension and an odd feeling of maternal longing. She tossed her braids across her shoulders and stepped stiffly from the folds of the dress. Beatrice swept down and retrieved it. She herded the women from the room and left. The door remained ajar for her mother's exit.

"Now the chemise," Matilda demanded.

Lenora responded instantly, her voice resounding across the room with authority. "I am lady of this keep and will make the demands. Do not think to touch me again and leave with no repercussions."

Matilda drew back. Her dark eyebrows flew up in surprise at the venom in her niece's words. "That woman in Aquitaine has completely ruined you. She taught you nothing of real life."

"And what would you have taught me, Aunt?"

Matilda put away her scissors and faced her. "I would have taught you to learn acceptance. You are a woman, Lenora, not a man. Your lot is to lie in yon bed night after night and bear the attentions of your husband until his seed takes fruit. To suffer the pain of birthing and then to repeat the process until, God willing, he grows bored of you and finds a mistress."

The shock of her aunt's confession left Lenora immobile. "Has your life really been so miserable?"

"My life has been that of a good Christian woman."

"And mine has not?" Lenora replied ruefully.

"'Tis no secret there will be no virgin mark upon this bed's sheets."

Lenora stiffened at her aunt's affront. Icicles of shame began to dampen her rediscovered self-esteem.

"Get out!" Roen shouted the order from the opened door. His fury almost choked him. He lowered his voice to a menacing snarl. "Woman, leave my sight."

Matilda sniffed arrogantly and gave him a haughty nod of her head as she passed. Hamlin and Beatrice waited in the foyer.

"Hamlin, see the lady has her things packed and ready to leave by morning."

The comment stopped Matilda cold. "You cannot mean to throw Beatrice and me out. This is my home by rights."

"I am lord here and my wife is the lady. An insult to her is an insult to me. You will move to the keep at Bridgeton. Sir Hywel will escort you on the morrow." Roen's tone left no room for discussion.

"I will go to the king."

"Go to Henry, but this night is the last you spend here."

"Do not think your fiendishness will go unavenged," Matilda vowed. "Come, Beatrice, let us pack."

Roen clarified his order. "Your daughter stays. She will be one of my wife's ladies-in-waiting."

The mottled red of Matilda's face faded to white. "Nay, you cannot mean to separate us. Beatrice must be with me. She is too frightened to stay alone, here, with all these men."

"She stays." He turned to Hamlin. "My commands stand as we discussed. See they are carried out." Roen closed the door on the ugly scene and entered the chamber. Sir Edmund's room looked unchanged except that now it belonged to him and his wife.

Lenora sat on the chair, dressed only in her chemise. The untied drawstring at the throat of her underslip caused the neck of the silk wrap to slide down her shoulders. One milky white shoulder peeked from the confines of the material.

"Nora?" Roen knelt at her feet and stared into her eyes. He hoped the old hag's words had not smothered the flames of her spirit he had witnessed downstairs.

"You bastard." Lenora kicked her foot out and slammed it into his belly.

He fell back, relieved her foot had not met its lower, intended mark. Her words accomplished what her foot had not. The phrase revealed the truth of his parentage and made bile come to his throat.

Lenora rose from her chair and stood over him. "It did not take you long to fall into the role of lord, did it? In one command you remove my father's relatives and his steward. 'Tis surprising you did not throw them out immediately after that stuttering friar pronounced us wed."

From the floor, Roen looked up and stared at her golden eyes. The copper ropes of her hair hung down her chest. Rising to one knee, he tugged at the ribbon ties that imprisoned her auburn tresses. Lenora pulled away and her braids loosened. A recalcitrant shake of her head and the seductive mantle of red gold locks cascaded uninhibited. She glided across the room and waited, her eyes never leaving his.

Ready to teach the hotheaded she-demon a lesson in humility, Roen prepared to lecture his wife on protocol. The sooner she learned her place, the better. He was lord here and he did not need to discuss his decision with a woman. As he opened his mouth to shout her name, the window behind his wife flooded with moonlight. The bellow was squelched to a choked whisper.

Silvery beams formed a halo around her. His eyes must have betrayed him, because she moved forward, a confused look on her face. He sucked in a breath and she stopped. White-hot blasts of passion sent tremors through his body as the thin chemise and the shimmering moonlight provided a dusky picture of Lenora's attributes. The heavy outline of her bosom and the gentle swell of her hips were contours his eyes could not resist. His throat grew dry when his gaze took in the dark velvet shadow between her legs. Passion consumed him.

Like a lion, he rose to stalk his quarry. The desire for Lenora gnawed at him. He wanted to sate the thirst his body felt on the sweetness of her lips, the ecstasy of her body. This breach of his defenses chewed at his gut. His lust should have abated, but it raged even hotter. The situation and his own emotions needed to be brought back under control. To do that, he needed her to want him as much, if not more, than he desired her.

A battle plan formulated in his mind, the faults and strengths quickly analyzed. Stealth, patience and determination, the qualities of a good skirmish, all belonged to him. Roen prepared to lay siege to his wife's passion.

Lenora took one step back when Roen began to rise. She took several more when she could not decipher the strange emotions that flickered over his face. Anger she had read immediately when he hit the floor. That emotion she liked; she knew how to handle it. Unfortunately, it came and went, replaced by a predatory look. His eyes became the color of the sea on a hot summery day. The color of passion. She did not care for his intense gaze fixed upon her face. Yet she could not pull away. He stood in front of her, too close.

"I have no intention of allowing you to heave my aunt and my father's loyal man out of their home. Matilda and Hywel stay." Lenora crossed her arms and stuck her chin at a jaunty angle.

Roen chuckled but made no move to touch her. "Do you really want me to believe that you want that shrew here in your home? Especially after what she said to you?"

"My feelings aren't important. Beatrice needs her mother."

"Beatrice needs to be allowed to stand on her own feet. To make her own mistakes. Everyone is always trying to protect her."

"You don't understand. She's very sensitive. She's seen terrible things in her life."

"And some wonderful things. But she needs to discover these wonders on her own. She needs to learn that the world offers much, that she can open her arms and embrace it."

Lenora bit her lip and racked her mind for further arguments. There were none. Liberating Beatrice from Matilda's pessimistic attitude could only help her. Away from her mother, Beatrice would be able to build the confidence she so badly needed. With Matilda no longer a barrier, Geoffrey might reconsider his decision.

But Lenora did not want to give up the argument so easily. Roen needed to learn that she should be consulted before he made decisions about Woodshadow.

"Sir Hywel is steward here. He cannot be trotted off to Bridgeton like some old nag," Lenora argued.

Roen sat on the chair and began to pull off his boots. He kept his head down to hide his satisfied grin. Her indomitable sensibility forced her to see his reason. Lenora's ruffled feathers over Sir Hywel would be smoothed, then he would have no more nonsense. He did not intend to spend his wedding night in verbal activities.

The heavy boots hit the floor with a thud. He exercised his cramped toes and loosened his belt. "Nora, we both know Sir Hywel is a good man, but he can no longer be steward."

"Will you stop calling me that ridiculous name. I refuse to answer to it." Lenora turned from him, her face flushed with anger but far from quiet. "He's served my father in an excellent fashion."

"I know, and that is why I send him away now." Roen rolled his hose down and threw them on the floor. The cool night air felt good on his naked legs and feet. He gave Lenora a direct look. "The added duties of seneschal only task his already weary brain." Roen put up his hand to halt her protest. "Anyone in this castle with an open eye can see 'tis you who guides the man's hand. Do not think that Sir Hywel does not know it himself. A man as proud as he would not wish for all his friends to witness his decline. Let him go in the guise of seeing Matilda to her new home. There, without the stress of managing a large and strategic keep, he may hold on to his mind for a little longer. At least, he will not suffer the pity of those whom once he commanded."

Reminded of Sir Edmund's plan, Roen tried to be gentle. "Your father would wish this. He is a man who understands pride."

Her stiff shoulders drooped. Her voice, thick with defeat, admitted the truth of his observation. "Aye, my father has always had a cup too much pride than was good for him."

"Like father, like daughter."

"What is that supposed to mean?" she shot back. "If hubris is a crime, husband, then surely you would be at the gallows now."

Roen chuckled out loud this time. He could not contain his happiness. The word *husband* on her lips sounded natural and pleasant. It pleased him she saw the reason of his actions. Guilt had dogged him about the old man. Sir Hywel had been a strong and devoted man. To force his retirement bothered him. Now, with Lenora's blessing, the guilt abated. He felt more confident and at ease with his decision.

He also felt more confident about his wife. The spark that contained Lenora's soul sparkled with renewed vigor. With every exchange, the embers built until the flame of life in her burned bright and hot. He glanced at the bed; she saw his look and her face went white. Roen cursed himself again. His own lust threatened to extinguish the flame. Patience, he reminded himself. This time, he wanted her willing. This night, he craved her acceptance.

So many days and nights he had sat at siege waiting for the long, stress-filled hours to pass. Roen called to mind the games and activities he and Hamlin had enjoyed. Anything to break the boredom. Roen crossed the room to give both himself and Lenora breathing space. He rested the palms of his hands on the oak table with his back to Lenora.

Roen pointed to the deep rows cut into the tabletop. "By Heavens. Nine Man Morris." A smug smile tugged at his lips. "I'm quite good at this."

"Really?" Lenora's cinnamon eyes widened and she pushed a panel of wood on the side of the table and a drawer popped open. Inside, black-and-white marble stones lay displayed on a velvet cloth. "My father taught me to play. Would you care to play a game?"

Roen started to decline but thought better of it. The game depended on strategy and maneuvering, two qualities of a good commander. He had no doubt he could beat her soundly, yet perhaps it would help to ease her fright and his impatience.

"Aye, I will move the table next to the chest and use it as a seat. You may use the chair." Roen lifted the table and grunted.

"Be careful with that."

He dropped the piece in front of the chest. "Careful? The thing weighs a hundred stone. I could not break it if I dropped it from the window of the watchman's tower."

She started toward the chair. Roen got there first. He lifted it and placed it across from the chest with one swift arch of his arm.

"I said be careful."

"Are all sticks of wood important to you or just a selected few?" He critiqued the craftsmanship then added, "You know, neither piece is all that well made."

"They're wonderful. At least they stand up to your abuse."

Roen picked up the chair and held it upside down. He grabbed the legs and pulled them back and forth. "Look here, the joints are not square."

Lenora swept down on him like a hawk. "Stop that. Father did a wonderful job on them."

Roen immediately stopped his inspection. "Your father made this?" He pointed to the table. "And this, also?"

She nodded, pulled the chair from him and took her seat. From the drawer of the table she pulled the white stones and placed them on the board. Roen grabbed the black and listened to her explanation while he placed his stones.

"Father has always been a man with a lot of energy. During times of war, he could burn off most of it, but in the winter, or in between battles, he needed something to exercise his mind as well as his body. This table and chair were his first projects. He carved the game into the top when he finished and taught me to play."

The words communicated volumes about her relationship with her father. Old resentment stirred in Roen's breast. He closed his eyes and forced his anger to dissipate. "I see. Did he make many other things?"

"A few. They're scattered about the castle."

"Well, I'm sure his craftsmanship improved with practice."

Lenora placed her finger on her mouth to stifle a smile. A delightful laugh escaped her full lips. "Nay, it did not. Louis and I would marvel at how the man could work so hard and never get better. But it kept him happy and that was the purpose. Whatever he made, I saw the beauty in it."

Roen halted in the placement of his stones. His heart ached for lost relationships. He could have given his true father that kind of love and devotion, if his mother had told him the man's name.

"Are you ready? Do you still wish to play?"

Roen pulled the familiar armor he wore around his heart back into place. The pain fought its customary imprisonment but he held strong and refused to allow the torturous boyhood hurts to escape. He looked across at Lenora's face, guarded now as she saw his face reflect the emotions in his heart. Christ's blood, this woman was his wife. What did he care if she came to his bed willing or not? By the vows of marriage, he had the right to take her, use her as he wished.

A low growl escaped his lips. Lenora did not rise or look frightened. Instead a devilish grin brightened her face. "So, you've seen your mistake. Too late." She moved one of her stones forward.

Roen slapped his forehead when he saw her capture one of his game pieces. In one swoop, she had managed to take a lead in the game. The spirit of competition defeated the pain of his childhood abuse. His vigilance returned to the game.

"Care for a small wager on the outcome?"

"Nay, hush, woman." Roen studied the board. Three concentric squares marked the boundaries. The object of the game was to sandwich the opponent's men on either side with one's own stones, thereby capturing them. The winner was the one who seized all of the stones.

"Are you sure? Perhaps something small. I wouldn't want to take all of your belongings."

"Will you hush?" Roen saw her strategy quickly. She baited him with the hope he'd make another blunder. Two could play that game. "Aye, I'll wager. If you win, I'll give you a pretty bauble."

"I don't want pretty baubles."

"Then what is it you wish?"

She paused, then the words raced out. "If I win, you will not sleep with me this night. You will stay in the room, but not touch me."

Roen sucked in air. Her eyes showed her fright; his crime had marked her more than he knew. But he needed to show her that lovemaking could be satisfying between a man and a woman. If he didn't, she would wind up like Beatrice, afraid of every man who passed.

"Agreed. But if I win, you must join me in bed, a willing partner."

"You cannot bet a person's feelings."

"I did not say you need to want me, just that you're willing." Roen counted on his expertise in the game, as well as the bed, to make the wager prove fruitful for him.

He could see her mull over the choices. "Agreed." His eyebrows shot up at her quick concordance. "I've few choices at the moment." She stuck out her hand.

He wrapped his strong fingers around her long, slender ones and gave them a slightly intimidating squeeze while he shook her hand vigorously. "I agree to your conditions."

"If you wish, we may begin again," Lenora offered. She tried to pull her hand from his, but he did not release it.

Roen's pride in his wife swelled. "Nay, we will continue with this game." His thumb caressed her hand, then with reluctance he broke the physical link with her. She lowered her eyes and studied the board.

He turned his attention to the game, as well. Each square had space for three stones. Of the nine stones he began with, only eight remained. Lenora still possessed all nine. Roen dragged a stone to a new position. Without removing his contact from the stone, he reevaluated his location.

"How long is this going to take you?" Lenora queried.

Roen removed his finger, hesitated, then settled back. "Your turn."

She moved her stone with no deliberation. "Now, 'tis yours."

He eyed the board with more care. Desperate to understand her motives, he scrutinized every possible move. None would attain a badly needed capture. He began to move but stopped when she hid her grin with her hand. Again he looked over the board, blind to the mistake he must be making. He decided to move another man to his second-choice position.

Her hand slid the white stone without hesitation. The move showed forethought. One more turn and she would have yet another of his black stones.

Roen began to sweat. She had bluffed him into a mistake. To win, he needed to play offense instead of defense. Forced to concentrate on the board, he tried to keep his eyes from the innocent-looking deceiver seated across from him. He made a bold move, although it would mean the loss of a black stone. *Take the bait,* he prayed.

"You lose another." She swept up the black stone with a gleeful chuckle.

He moved his piece and captured his first white stone. "There, at least I have one."

Lenora did not fold quickly. "You've still a long way to catch me." She moved her piece, then realized the trap he had laid.

Another white stone vanished from the board. With her elbows resting on the table, she placed her chin in her hand. Her glorious hair formed a veil over her shoulders. She wrapped and unwrapped a curl around her finger. The loose neckline of her chemise dropped a fraction lower. Roen scanned the milky flesh and experienced renewed determination to win. The prize across the table tempted him too much to consider a loss.

Minutes dragged by as each played their turn and the number of stones dwindled. Finally, each was left with only three stones.

"Ready to give up?" he asked as he moved his man to a mark.

"Nay, I should ask that of you." Cagey, she retreated from him.

"I'm surprised, most women I know are ready to run from a fight." A black stone moved.

"But I'm not like most women," Lenora warned, and took her turn.

"I pray not," Roen whispered under his breath. His move ended the game. He picked up the white stone, warm from her touch. The game was over, Lenora could not win.

She conceded with a silent nod of her head, no tears or pleas. Instead, she rose and took determined steps toward the bed. Lenora stretched out stiffly on the bed, her face a mask of fortitude. Her arms tight at her sides, eyes screwed shut, she waited for him, willing to endure his attentions but not wanting them. Roen had won the game but the prize still eluded him.

"Nora, open your eyes," Roen chided gently, then sat on the bed at her side. His fingers trailed up and down her arm in a light, teasing caress.

"Nay, I will not. Be done with this. And my name is Lenora."

"Have it your way, but I would think you would like to know what is going to happen to you."

"I already know. What!" Her eyes flew open and Roen chuckled. His thumb continued its slow, complete massage of her nipple. Its stiff peak jutted from beneath the silky folds of her chemise.

"Do you know, Nora? Our first union did not leave time for me to enjoy all the curves and parts of your body fully. Tonight, I have a soft bed, hours of time—" he looked deep into her eyes "—and a willing woman. Nay, wife, there is still much to teach you." His hand stretched the flimsy material tight across her aroused breast. His mouth enveloped the mound, his tongue swirled around and across the hardened nipple. Shivers raced up her arm and her fingers dug into the blankets.

"I do not think this is . . . is . . . is proper."

Roen chuckled. "Nay, 'tis not." He moved his lips from her bosom to the hollow of her throat. Her skin smelled of roses. The sweetness of her body beckoned him to devour; instead he savored. His mouth sucked gently on her jawline and moved to her lips.

Her eyes wide open now, Lenora looked straight at the ceiling. Roen's face blotted the view, and his gray blue eyes met hers. Her heart pounded and a frustrating ache began to take root. His long body covered hers. The warmth of his chest and the tight fit of his hips against her legs made thinking difficult. She took in air but her body hungered for more.

Roen drew her lower lip in his mouth and softly tugged on it. She pushed herself down deep into the plush coverlets to avoid the onslaught of his lips. He captured hers easily, his tongue entered her mouth and skated across her teeth. It teased her tongue. When she tried to force him from the interior of her mouth, his tongue jousted with hers. Her arms rose to encircle him, but she fought to bring them back, tight to her sides.

Her husband's head lifted, a crooked smile on his lips, the rare dimples transforming his face to an expression of boyish pleasure. "Go ahead, Nora, give in. Your body remembers the pleasures I gave it. There's more, much more." His hand moved down her side, across the swell of her hips, and splayed out across her thigh. His fingers left hot trails of passion and a desire to have Roen's lips retrace his movements.

"Nay, I cannot." Lenora shook her head.

His lips burrowed into her hair and his breath tickled the fine hair that framed her face. "Let yourself go, Nora, you're allowed to enjoy this. I can make it so that this act between us is filled with pleasure. There'll be no pain now, I promise."

Tears came to her eyes, she shook her head again and scrunched up the red velvet coverlet in her hands. No pain, more pleasure... The last time she had joined with this man, merged her soul with his. If he gave her more, could she ever regain it back?

"Galliard, I cannot. This act, it leaves me adrift, like a boat with no mooring. I need something to hold on to."

Roen's lips stopped their sensuous path across her face. Warm teal eyes bored into hers. "The past is gone, our future lies ahead. We are married now, wife. Let us put aside our differences and start anew." He kissed away a tear from Lenora's face. His voice became tight with emotion. "And if you feel the need of support, I will be here for you, as you were for me this night. If the need arises, hold on to me, Nora."

Her fingers uncurled. Unsure of her decision, she lifted them and placed her hands on his sides. He took her hand and brought it to his lips. Each finger felt the suction of his full mouth, then her palm. The knot of her chemise gave way, baring her breasts. Her husband did not touch her, only stared at her body.

"Is something amiss?"

Roen smiled and shook his head. "Nay, they are perfect." His hand slid down her breastbone to the flatness of her abdomen. She gasped when his hand rested on the soft curls between her legs. Then arched as he reached inside. She felt her body's eagerness to welcome him. Warmth flooded over her and the aching need for more inflamed her.

Roen poised above her, his weight on his arms. "Now we are truly wed, Nora." He entered the cavity and felt the tightness of her womb surround the sheath of his manhood. Surges of hot, wet fluid bathed him and nearly ripped all conscious thought from him.

He fought his baser instincts to ram into her until his need was spent. Instead, he began a slow, rhythmic dance, allowing her to grow accustomed to his size and presence. He felt her tension lessen when she realized there would be no virginal pain.

Soft, throaty whimpers filled his ears when he moved inside of her. His pace quickened. Her whimpers changed to moans as her body's passion erupted. She arched her back. He kissed the aroused nipples of her breasts. Her fingernails dug into his back and her long, slender legs tightened around his waist. With a primal roar he plunged into her. Falling. Joining. Interweaving his self with hers. Bursts of soaring elation poured into him as he gave forth his seed into his wife's womb.

Shudders of excruciating release coursed through Lenora. Roen held her tightly as she felt both of them reach the summit of their passion. She could not stop herself from clinging to him. The smoky smell of his hair, the sharp, salty taste of his skin, the reassuring weight of his body on her own comforted her. His hands cradled her as though she might break if squeezed too hard.

She did not speak, could find no words. Emptiness invaded her as he eased from her. Rolling to his side, Roen slipped his arm beneath her head and drew her close.

"Nora, are you well?" His concerned eyes searched her face.

"Aye, I'm well, very well." She yawned and snuggled up close to his side. Suddenly, she opened her eyes and stared at him somberly. "Roen, is this what it's like between a man and a woman?"

Roen chuckled. "Nay, wife. I would wager there's not many a man or woman who has experienced mating like we have."

"This is not the usual way a man and woman join?"

"Oh, the act is common enough, but the passion our bodies feel for each other, that is unique."

"Then, if we were to do this again, it might not be the same?" Her voice sounded wistful.

Grinning, Roen looked down at Lenora's swollen lips, her face radiant from his lovemaking, and responded, "I venture 'tis only one way to find out?"

"How is that?"

Roen began to stroke her back. "We'll just have to try it again and see."

Her eyes widened in surprise, then creased into laughter. "Well then, husband, proceed with your experiment. I am most curious to discover the answer."

Roen's lips slanted over hers and he marveled that he could want her again so quickly. Tonight he would have her again and again. He would preserve this capsule of time for as long as possible. On the morrow, the desire that filled her eyes now would turn to hate. For some reason, this thought caused his desire to flare even more intensely, as though his body realized what it stood to lose, even if his heart was afraid to admit it.

Chapter Fifteen

Lenora struggled to open her sleep-heavy eyes. Her mind registered several conflicting sensations. Gooseflesh prickled along her arm and neck, yet parts of her body glowed with warm, almost uncomfortable heat. She lifted her head to survey the problem and became disoriented. The furniture belonged in her father's room, but the objects were all rearranged. The explanation for her fuzziness became apparent when she craned her neck for a look around the room.

She lay intertwined with Roen's body. Her head rested on his shoulder, his arm under her head and across her chest. His large hand entrapped her breast possessively. Except for his muscular thigh draped across her hips, she wore no covering. Every blanket, pillow and coverlet had been stripped from the bed during the night of lovemaking. Their heads were at the foot of the bed, which explained her feeling of misplacement. She was out of place, not the furniture.

Her eyes closed. She prayed that the scene was just a horrible dream. Memories of the intimate touches of her husband played across her mind's stage. Tentatively, she peered at Roen through heavy lids. His eyes were closed, his breathing natural.

Asleep, minus the hardened sneer and granite eyes, he looked younger. Lenora wondered what had turned him into such a heartless individual. Years of battles and wars, no doubt. His hair fell over his eyes, and she moved to brush it away, stopped, then gave in to her fancy. The white blond strands felt silky and soft, like Silver's mane. She placed her hand on his chest and felt the light sprinkle of crisp curls that covered his chest.

His lips twitched as her finger meandered down the line of curls. Her breath stopped, her finger ceased its motion. The steady up-and-down pattern of his chest resumed. He did not awaken. An alarm blared in her head, warning her to quit her exploration, but curiosity consumed her. Twice she had been with him and never able to really see what a naked man looked like. She would remain ignorant no longer.

Easing away from the tangle of their limbs, she tried to get a full look. Old scars crisscrossed his arms and torso. His legs and knees showed signs of battles, old and new. The object of her quest remained hidden from her view. Still too close, she scooted farther away. His arm released her and he rolled over to his stomach.

"Drat," she whispered loudly. Her fingernail tapped impatiently on his back. He shrugged it off and readjusted himself on the bumps in the mattress. An inspired plan caused her to smile. She scratched her fingernails lightly down his back toward his buttocks. Roen squirmed and began to turn over. Lenora waited, her eyes riveted to his lower abdomen. He scrunched up his knees in a fetal position, obscuring her vision once more.

"Damn." Her hand clapped over her mouth so tight she could barely breathe. This whim did not constitute a wish to spend the rest of her immortal life suffering in Hades. A hasty sign of the cross and a fervent prayer of penance absolved her of the small sin. Bending her elbow, she propped her head up with her hand. Sunlight flooded the room, the beams straining to reach every corner. "By the Blessed Virgin!" Lenora hopped up, vaulted over Roen's sleeping form and ran to the window.

Sounds from the bailey floated up to her through the arched opening. She could make out the tiny dots of sheep in the far meadow, the serfs working in the fields. The steady blow of the blacksmith's hammer clanged in her head. Mortified, she rested her head against the rough stone arch.

"Are you always so energetic in the morning?"

She turned back toward the bed. Roen's eyes rested on her and lingered down her body. The heat of his gaze made her aware of her naked state.

Lenora grabbed one of the discarded sheets from the floor and wrapped it around her. "Do you have any idea of the hour?

The sun is high in the sky. Everyone is already up and about. We've missed the morning meal and the nooning break must be soon." She stooped and began to pick up the pillows and blankets from the floor.

"So? Come back to bed, or did you get a chance to see everything you wanted?"

"You were awake! Oh, you are the most devious man alive." She flung a pillow at him.

He caught it and pitched the cushion back in one smooth swing. It hit Lenora on the top of the head. In retaliation, she threw a pillow back and wadded the blankets up to toss at him, also. Laughing, Roen spilled from the bed and pounded her with one of the down-filled bolsters. She pelted him across the side and face with another. The sound of tearing cloth came from both cushions, and feathers exploded, covering the floor, Lenora and Roen.

Weak from laughter, she sank to the floor with a hand clutching the bed sheet to her chest. Roen stood above her, naked except for the coating of goose feathers. She paused when she saw his organ. The length of his manhood terrified and thrilled her. She tore her gaze away and met her husband's dark aquamarine eyes. Passion flared in the depth of his gaze.

"Nay, we cannot. 'Tis the middle of the day."

His answer was to drop to her side and tear the sheet from her bosom. The torridness of his gaze caused her breasts to tighten, and her body rejoiced at the anticipated pleasure. A blush covered her face and traveled down her chest.

They lay amidst the rumpled coverings and the soft, snow-like down. He blew gently on her face and brushed away a feather caught on her lashes.

"Roen, to satisfy one's lust in the middle of the day is not proper."

"I know." His lips began to nibble her ear.

"Then I will probably like this very much." Lenora sighed and succumbed to her body's and her husband's desires.

Roen heard the commotion outside the door. He had expected this moment since early morn. His hand pulled a velvet cover across Lenora's nakedness. She frowned in her sleep when he moved from her embrace. He tucked the cover around her and gave her a light kiss.

Her hair tumbled about her head, a delightful tangle of curls and feathers. Her skin glowed from his lovemaking like a golden statue come to life. Last night had been magnificent; they had coupled three fiery times. 'Twould be enough for any man, yet this morning when she touched him, the fire of his lust rekindled. His arousal was just as strong the last time as it had been the first. The heady night of passion made what must come even more difficult.

He rose from the floor and pulled on his tunic and hose. Heedless of the haste required, Roen etched the image of his sleeping wife in his mind. This picture and the memories of last night would have to satisfy him for the rest of the lonely nights ahead. From his pocket he pulled a scrap of stained white cloth. With reverence he placed it among the coverlets on the bed.

Roen opened the door to his bedchamber and gentled the sound of the closing door. His wife needed her rest to face the sorrow that would soon come her way.

"Get your hands off of me. I am a noble-born lady. I'll have you flogged for this," Matilda screeched at the man stationed outside the newlyweds' door. She turned her wrath on Roen as he stepped into the hall. "You murdered my brother-in-law."

Roen gripped the hysterical woman's upper arm and propelled her down the stairs, away from Lenora's hearing. He motioned for his man to remain on guard. "Tell me when my wife wakes. Bring her straight to me."

"Aye, bring her to him so he can fill her ears with lies. Don't think you'll get away with this. The king will hear of this atrocity." Matilda continued to rant, her voice rising and falling in pitch.

"Tell him what you want, but leave this castle now." They reached the bottom step and found Beatrice and Hamlin waiting by the hearth. His men stood uneasily around them. The knights of Sir Hywel mingled about the room. They eyed him and his guardsmen with suspicion.

"Hamlin, were my orders carried out?"

"Aye, Roen, to the letter. Sir Edmund's stallion returned a few minutes ago." Hamlin hesitated, then added, "The horse was riderless. I've sent no men to look for him as you directed." Hamlin lowered his voice. "Are you sure this is what you want?"

Roen shook his head, "'Twas never a question of my wants, but of Sir Edmund's. I promised the old man he would die in the saddle, not wasting away as an invalid."

"Do you see? He admits his treachery! Sir Hywel, I command you to slay this man and avenge your lord." Matilda swept her arm out and pointed her long bony finger at Roen.

Sir Hywel instead looked at the stairs behind her. The room hushed. Roen knew without turning who stood upon the steps. His guard rushed ahead, an apologetic look on his face. "My lord, your lady."

"What goes on here?" Lenora demanded. Roen turned to answer. He could see the confusion in her eyes and hear the fear in her voice. She tied and retied the belt of her robe.

"You've been fornicating with your father's murderer." Matilda's shrill voice caused Roen to squint his eyes. "He kept you entertained on your back while he arranged to rid himself of Sir Edmund." His wife's eyes widened.

"What has happened to my father?" She raced down the steps and stood in front of him. He wanted to lie and tell her everything was fine. To sweep her up in his arms and return to the sanctuary of their bedroom. Instead, he answered, "He's dead."

Roen caught her in his arms as her knees gave way. Tears streamed from her grief-filled eyes.

"Nay, how could this be?"

"Because your husband had him murdered," Matilda proclaimed. Her obvious joy at Lenora's pain bordered on obscene. For the first time in his life, Roen seriously considered striking a woman.

"Lenora, sit down. I'll explain." He settled her on a bench and held her hands in his. "Your father begged me to allow him to die with dignity. He wanted you to remember him as a strong, healthy man, not an invalid. The night you agreed to marry me, he told me of his plans. He rode out on Jupiter early this morning and died like a warrior."

Lenora stared at him in shock. She recoiled from the touch of his hands. "You agreed to this? Why didn't you tell me? Sir Hywel, order a search party."

"Nay." Roen spoke with a gentle but firm tone. "Your father rode deep into the wood and requested his death be a private affair. I gave him my word his last orders would be fulfilled.

"But I could have stopped him!"

"Perhaps this time, but what of the next, or the time after? The man had pride—you yourself told me. Do you think he really wanted to waste away in front of your eyes? To have you see him die a little every day?"

"Pretty lies. I tell you he planned it," Matilda screeched at her niece and the knights. "Now there is no question as to who is lord here. Everything has fallen into his lap quite well, even the daughter of the keep."

She grabbed Beatrice's hand and pulled her to stand in front of Lenora. "Why do you think he insists on keeping my daughter here? To be your lady-in-waiting? Aye, he has her waiting, to fill his bed when you're swollen with child. Look at her and tell me he would want you when Beatrice is around. If she had been next in line to inherit, suffer no doubt, 'twould be Beatrice he kept in bed till the noon sun rose, not you."

Lenora didn't answer. The hall waited in silence, even Matilda. A childhood memory flashed. She had climbed the big oak, dared by her brother. Determined to reach the top, she ventured out onto a weak branch. The sharp crack of it breaking, the vision of the fast-approaching ground, her scream all resounded in her mind. Then her father's arms caught her, saved her. He simultaneously scolded her and hugged her, meted out a punishment for her foolish act and thanked God for sparing her. Last night, she could have repaid the debt to her father, saved him from an unwise decision.

Her eyes met Roen's. He had promised to be like the lifesaving arms of her father; instead he proved to be the weak branch, catapulting her into misery.

"Lady Lenora?" Sir Hywel stood near her. Sharp, focused eyes asked a silent question. His hand moved to the hilt of his sword. In unison, all her knights assembled widened their stances in preparation for battle.

Neither Roen nor his men moved. Weaponless, her husband waited. Hamlin gently pushed Beatrice toward the stairs. Matilda scurried away from her position near Roen and Lenora.

Lenora wanted to scream, to cry, to strike the giant in front of her hard enough to bring him to his knees. He stood there, impassive, uncaring that he had just helped to deprive her of her father. Yet she must put aside her wants. Woodshadow must come first. Destroy Roen now, and she left the keep vulnerable to a takeover by another, perhaps worse tyrant. Nor could she doubt his orders. Either action would put Woodshadow in a vulnerable position.

"Roen de Galliard is my husband, Lord of Woodshadow." The statement answered her seneschal's question. Still, he kept his hand on the pommel of his weapon. "All his orders are to be carried out as directed. Now leave us." Lenora's voice echoed in the silence.

"My lady, I do not think that is wise," Sir Hywel cautioned.

"Leave us."

The elder knight gave her a curt nod and marched from the hall, followed by his men. Roen's guard stood their ground. Their leader did not remove his gaze from his wife's face but waved them off with his hand. The knights retreated, escorting Beatrice and Matilda from the hall. The servants melted from the room like a morning fog, disappearing into the recesses of the castle.

Lenora could not remember the room ever being so empty, so devoid of life. No dogs searched for scraps, Tyrus did not try to hide under a table or behind a pillar to catch a nap. Even the hearth fire burned silently. The great hall echoed with the absence of life, but overflowed with betrayal.

She rose and sought to find the man of last night. No laugh wrinkles creased his eyes, he made no movement to touch or to comfort her. Worse, he showed no remorse.

The grief in her heart made her speak plainly. "If I had the strength I would call you out myself and thrust a sword through your heartless chest. Alas, I do not possess it and your death would only lead to more suffering for my people."

"'Tis not as she says." Roen's quiet voice cut through her threat. "Matilda is wrong."

"Not as she said?" Lenora accused. "Do not make your crime greater by lying. You took me in the woods so that I had to marry you and you would thereby gain Woodshadow. Can you stand before me and deny it?''

"Nay, that I do not deny, nor do I apologize for. You needed to wed to be protected."

"Protected from what, from whom?"

"I do not know."

Her sarcastic laugh bounced around the empty room. "So you shame me to protect me from an unknown danger. I can name it, 'tis you."

Roen reached out and grabbed her wrist. She tried to twist from his grasp. He held it firmly but not painfully. When she stopped her struggles, he turned her hand over and stared at her palm. With the finger of his free hand he traced her life line. "What she said about Beatrice, 'tis not true."

"Then let her accompany her mother to Bridgeton."

"I can't."

"You won't." She tore her hand from the shackle of his grip. "You've taken my virtue, my father and my home from me. I beg you, spare my cousin this shame you have planned. Let her leave."

"Nay, I cannot, Nora."

"Then may God curse you for this crime you commit." Tears no longer in check, she ran out the door and down the steps of the castle.

Roen once received a blow that would have killed another man. The icy breath of death had blown against his soul with excruciating pain. Yet that pain paled against the hurt he felt now while he watched Lenora retreat from his touch and presence.

She didn't understand why he must keep Beatrice here. If Matilda was the traitor, Beatrice served as hostage. A safeguard against any more attempts to control the keep through Lenora's death. In the depth of his soul, he knew the real reason he would not let the girl leave, he wanted to prove Matilda wrong. If he sent Beatrice away, his wife would always wonder if the stinging words were true. Only by keeping her cousin here could he show Lenora he did not desire the timid beauty. That, in truth, the only woman he wanted could not stand the sight of him.

Chapter Sixteen

"We're going for a ride." Roen pushed Hamlin's feet from the table edge, nearly sending the knight crashing to the floor.

The servants retreated quickly, and Hamlin wished he could do the same. Roen's attitude had deteriorated from rude to mean in the last few weeks since Sir Edmund's disappearance. A ride in the woods with Roen, in his black temper, would not be restful.

"Are you coming?"

A self-sacrificing sigh passed Hamlin's lips. "Do I have a choice?"

Roen did not respond, but strode out of the hall. On the step of the forebuilding he paused and surveyed the keep. The crops grew green in the fields, the cattle and sheep grazed contentedly. His villeins labored at their work.

"Who are you looking for?" Hamlin needled.

"No one. I want to make sure none of my people are shirking their duties."

"Ah." Hamlin nodded and started down the stairs. Roen continued to scrutinize the inner bailey. "I thought perhaps you were looking for your wife. But I see I was mistaken. If you were, I could inform you of her whereabouts. But since you aren't...."

Roen closed the gap between him and his friend with two strides. "How is she? The few times I've seen her, she looks pale, sad."

"How would you know how she looks?" Hamlin replied at the entrance to the stable. "You've been absent from every meal, away most of the day. She is pale. She is sad. By the heavens, the girl has lost her father. Your wife feels alone and deserted. Most of all, I think she feels betrayed, by you."

Roen remained silent, his jaw clenched. He stepped into the barn and grabbed his saddle.

Hamlin finished his tack and waited while his friend rechecked his horse's girth. They led the animals out to a groom who held them while they mounted. The smell of the mares sent Destrier into a nervous prance. Roen worked to keep his horse under control.

"Seems your horse has better sense than you do," Hamlin quipped. "He'd rather stay here than go traipsing off into the woods."

The dark scowl across his commander's face silenced Hamlin's banter. The ride would be sullen enough without adding to his comrade's bad mood. Outside the bailey walls, they broke into a hard canter. Roen kneed his mount into a full gallop. Hamlin ate dust until the forest caused Roen to slow Destrier's gait down to a fast walk.

The cool shade of the trees provided a welcome respite from summer heat. The green canopy of leaves allowed only scattered beams of sunlight to pierce the perpetual darkness of its interior. An accumulation of dead leaves and pine straw cushioned the hooves of the horses and muffled their sound. The men rode silently, each deep in his own thoughts.

At midday, Roen pulled up near a stream. He dismounted and loosened his animal's girth to allow Destrier to graze. Hamlin followed his friend's lead. Before releasing his mount, he pulled a loaf of dark bread from a bag tied on his saddle.

He broke the slightly stale loaf in two and tossed part to Roen. Hamlin munched on his repast and slaked his thirst from the spring-fed water of the stream.

Roen brushed away the crumbs from his tunic. "I have been checking on her, you know."

Hamlin gave him a questioning look. "What?"

"Nora." Roen threw the last bit of bread to a couple of mourning doves pecking at the forest floor. "After she retires, I go into our room. I stay until morning and leave before she wakes."

"Roen, why not go to her? Talk with her?"

"And say what? I'm guilty, I let her father die?"

"How about, 'I'm sorry'?"

"Don't you think I've tried? I sent her expensive brocades and jewelry. She sent it all back."

"Roen, tell her." Hamlin spoke like a frustrated parent. "Speak the words."

The blond knight stood and broke a twig from the overhead tree. "Hamlin, I don't know the words. I don't know what she's feeling. I never had a father, at least one that would claim me."

Hamlin gripped his friend's shoulder. Sympathy showed in his eyes. "Then tell her that much at least. If you're going to be cruel, at least tell her why." He released Roen and moved into the brush for some privacy.

Roen cursed under his breath at the truth in Hamlin's words. His childhood had not been nurturing or loving. His mother had emotionally separated him from the man whose name he bore, and from everyone else, as well.

"Roen, come here, quick."

Pulled from his melancholy, Roen grabbed his sword and ran toward Hamlin's voice. He found him crouched on the ground near a fallen tree.

"Look at this."

He resheathed his sword and drew near. The skeleton of a large animal lay at Hamlin's feet. A weathered leather collar with metal studs encircled the neck.

"The poor beast was staked out to die." Hamlin lifted a heavy chain attached from the collar to a stake near the tree. "I wonder who would do something like that to an animal? Better to strike it down with an arrow than to let it starve to death."

Pins of suspicion pricked Roen's mind. He pushed Hamlin out of the way and lifted the collar. The skeleton broke apart and clattered to the ground. The rain-worn leather felt stiff. He worked the rusted buckle several times before it released. Roen held the leather strip open and his heart sank. Inside, scratched in childish letters, was Lenora's name.

Snippets of his conversation with Tom returned. The remains of his wife's favorite hound lay at his feet. "So, Gladymer, the traitor got you, too." Roen squeezed the collar tightly. Anger stoked the fires of vengeance in his heart. The man responsible for this would pay with his life.

"Roen? How is it you know the name of this unfortunate animal?"

He opened the collar and pointed out Lenora's scrawl. "'Tis her animal, no doubt. By Tom's description of the hound, 'twould not be easily led off."

"Unless whoever took it was well-known to the animal." Hamlin finished the thought. "'Tis as you said. Whoever planned this lives in the castle. It must be Matilda. She's hired a man to do her work for her."

"Aye. Even with her gone, the man may still remain. We must find him."

"Roen, Lenora is safe now that she is wed to you."

"But not avenged. And they will pay for the pain they have caused her." Roen slipped the leather collar into his pocket and headed back for his horse.

Lenora stiffened her back and climbed the steps from the kitchen to the main hall. She readjusted the heavy wooden bowl on her hip and pushed the door open. The servants looked up, then away quickly. Her proud stance weakened a small amount. Woodshadow resounded with the noise of a tomb. No one talked above a whisper, and when she appeared, conversation stopped. The groups of people scattered without making eye contact, whispering behind her back.

It galled her to think Roen had tried to cover up his crime of rape. Her pantalets, with the virgin stain, dispelled the belief in Roen's offense. Now, her people eyed her with caution and unvoiced questions.

She slammed the bowl onto the table, and the assorted fresh greens spewed out. "Ow!" A dirty blond head peeked from beneath the table linen. "Have care there, Lady Lenora."

"Tyrus. Catching a nap, I see." Lenora laughed. It felt good to have an unstilted conversation with someone.

He put his finger to his lips. "Sh. Alyse will be up from the kitchen with that spoon of hers if'n she knows I'm 'ere. I'm a growin' boy. I needs my rest, ye know."

She sat back on her heels to be at eye level with him. Merriment danced in the boy's eyes, despite his serious composure. "With the amount of rest you take, you should be nigh as tall as the castle's drawbridge gate by now," Lenora noted.

Tyrus took on an affronted look. "'Ere now, Lady, I was up all night a-lookin' after your mare and colt."

"Is something wrong with Silver?" Lenora demanded.

"Nay, not that I could see. But milord, he give me orders and a gold piece to sleep out in the barn with them every night since the mare gave birth."

"Roen did that?" Lenora wondered out loud. "Whatever for?"

Tyrus shrugged, reached his grubby hand up and rummaged a carrot from the table. He chewed the end of the unwashed vegetable. "Don't know, Lady Lenora. He just says to tell 'im if'n they act funny. I'm to remember who feeds and waters 'em and I report it to 'im every day."

Worry roiled in her gut. Why would Roen care about her horses? Why hadn't he spoken to her about it? Every night she retired alone and each night she dreamed her husband came to her, whispered soft words, held her in his arms. The rising sun burned away her dreams like a winter frost. She would look about her large, empty bed and feel the depth of her loneliness.

"Don't be frettin' none, Lady." Tyrus paused in his chomping. "The animals are fine."

She replaced the table linen across his head and smiled. "I think I'll pay them a visit all the same. Thank you for being so diligent in your duties." Standing, Lenora grabbed a couple of carrots as a treat for her animals and headed for the barn.

The noonday sun blazed and caused her to squint when she exited the shadows of the castle. The heat felt good on her face and arms. In the weeks since her father's memorial and Roen's betrayal, the spring had merged with the early days of summer. The leafy limbs of the ancient oak near the stable beckoned to her like a Druid priestess. Lenora ran to its comforting shade and live smell.

"I told you it weren't the right thing to do," Tom's voice scolded.

A deep voice murmured back, "Give it time."

Lenora leaned around the trunk and spotted Tom. Another man, his back to her, stabbed the ground with a polished cane. Curious, she drew closer. The man with the stablekeeper looked familiar, but she couldn't place him.

"Tom?" She craned her neck to get a glimpse of the stranger. He quickly pulled his cap down low over his face and slipped into the stable.

"'Ere now, what are ye doin' down 'ere?" Tom blocked her way into the barn.

"I've come to check on Silver and the colt. Who was that?"

"Who was what?" Tom's eyes grew large with confusion. "Oh, 'im? That bent-up old man that was just 'ere?" A snort sounded from the barn. "Ain't nobody to worry yourself over. 'E's me cousin, Cervin." A look of relief passed over the old groom's wrinkled face. "Took a turn to liviin' in the city and found 'e didn't like it. A freeman, mind you, like meself. Seein' how I'm so close to the lord and lady 'ere, 'e thought 'twould be an easy fit for 'im."

"Oh." Lenora tried to look past the elder man's shoulder into the interior of the barn. Tom swayed to block her view. "Does he intend to work with you in the stable or does he have another trade?"

Tom scratched his head. "Well, I reckon he could do that."

"'Tis a carpenter I am, Lady Lenora," a hoarse voice called from the barn. Tom shook his head and rolled his eyes.

"Well then, carpenter, come out so that I can meet you." Lenora waited impatiently. The man's voice and carriage were vaguely familiar. She wanted to place the face.

"Well, now there's the jinx of it. See, me cousin is, well—" Tom's voice grew hushed "—'e's ugly. Plain ol' ugly. Scars all over 'is face from the pox. No eyelashes or eyebrows. Terrible sight. 'Tis what's sent 'im from the city. People shyin' away from 'im and callin' 'im names and all." Tom drew her away from the stable. "'E don't like people a-lookin' at 'im. Give 'im time and 'e'll start to show 'imself."

Lenora nodded sagely. "I understand. But his voice... Outside the barn I had a feeling I had heard it before."

"Oh. Nay." The stablekeeper shook his head from side to side. "'Twas the fever that changed it. It comes and goes. Mostly 'tis gone." Tom's voice rose in volume. "He don't do much talkin' anymore."

Her heart went out to Cervin and his troubles. "Tell your cousin he's welcome as long as he works his fair share. I'll tell Sir Hamlin he's here."

"What about the Lord Roen? Shouldn't he know?" Tom's cousin asked from the shadows of the barn.

"Sir Hamlin will tell him, no doubt. He's more likely to see and speak to Lord Roen than I am." She turned to Tom. "I intend to check on my horses. If your cousin does not wish to be seen, I suggest he find another refuge."

Tom gamboled into the stable and reappeared moments later. " 'Ere ye go, Lady Lenora. 'E's gone now."

Lenora could not contain her worry. She ran into the stall, causing the mare to shy. Contrite, Lenora began a thorough examination of the two horses. Nothing looked out of place. "Tom, I don't understand why Roen wants Tyrus to sit up with them every night. I don't see anything wrong with them."

No answer came. He must be off with Cervin. She plumped up a pile of fresh hay in front of the stall and sat. After the animals finished their oats, she would look them over once more.

Roen and Hamlin rode into the bailey eyeing every man they met. Each searched for the possible hired hand of Matilda. The footmen gave cursory salutes, their eyes showing their distrust. Matilda had planted a seed of discontent among the men. He would not find his culprit now.

He and Hamlin dismounted. A snap of his fingers brought a lad to take their horses. "Rub them down good, then put them in the pasture to graze." Roen ordered. The boy nodded vigorously and took off at a slow run with the two animals.

"I'm wagering the man's still here. Matilda will want a spy," Hamlin noted.

"I think so, too." Roen motioned Hamlin to join him in a slow walk toward the fish pond. "It could be any one of them. I could question every man here, but I doubt they would tell me anything. I'm not a popular person right now."

Hamlin snorted his agreement. They neared the pond and spotted a man clutching a coarse sack, kneeling near the water. He grabbed a large stone and dropped it into the bag. The serf nodded to his lord reverently and stepped away from the knights' path.

"Beg pardon, milord." The bag jerked back and forth in the man's hand. An angry yelp sounded from it.

"What's that you have?" Roen questioned.

"I'm the kennel master. This 'ere's a runt. He won't make it for long with the bigger pups pushin' 'im away. I plan to drown 'im. Better a quick death than starvin'."

"Let me see that." Roen untied the bag, and shoved his large hand inside. "Ouch!" He jerked his hand back and sucked his index finger. Drops of blood seeped from two puncture wounds.

"'E may be small, but 'e's a mean' un. I'll take care of 'im."

"Nay, never mind the pup. I'll take him." Roen removed the rock from the bag. His hand emerged with a series of staccato teeth imprints. The kennel master retreated with raised eyebrows and a look of disbelief.

"What do you plan on doing with that?" Hamlin asked.

Roen shrugged. "If the pup is strong enough to take me on, he's strong enough to live." He headed to the stable. "I'll put him in there for now."

The wooden bowls of food and water remained on sentry duty under the loft stairs. Gladymer would never again use them; the pup might as well get some use from Lenora's diligence. Roen tilted the bag upside down and a black gray bundle tumbled out. A tiny thing, barely a handful of fur and teeth. The pup sat for a moment stunned, then jumped to all fours. The hair on its back bristled and it started barking at the cobwebs between the stairs.

"What's that you have there?"

Lenora's voice startled Roen so badly he jerked his head up and knocked it against the stairs. He rubbed the back of his head with his hand and stepped from the alcove.

"A pup." Roen pointed to the fur ball attacking the remnants of the torn blanket. His eyes met hers. The sight of his wife intoxicated him with her beauty. Her dark gold overtunic accented the golden highlights of her eyes. A slight darkness under them marked her sorrow. Her crown of red gold hair, tied back with a thong of leather, haloed her face. His favorite curl, determined to remain free of checks, cascaded across the corner of one eye.

He wanted her. Night after night as he lay beside her, holding her in his arms, he feared she would awaken and order him from her sight. She had every right. The one night and morning they had shared haunted his dreams at night and thoughts during the day. The knowledge that she reviled him cut him deeply.

"I'll leave the dog here. There's food for him." Roen turned to leave but the light touch of her hand on his arm stopped him.

"You can't just leave him here. He can't eat this." She pointed to the table scraps. "He's not old enough to digest it."

At a loss, both from her question and touch, Roen answered, "Then what will you do with it?"

"Me? 'Tis not my animal, 'tis yours."

Roen shook his head and hands emphatically. "Nay, I just brought the pup here for you. I don't claim it as mine."

"I don't want anything from you."

He shook off her hand and stormed from the stable. Outside, at the trunk of the oak, he stopped. He ordered his breath to stop its erratic pattern, but it did not obey. The spot on his arm Lenora had touched still radiated with her warmth. Would the craving in his loins ever lessen to a bearable level?

Lenora sat under the steps with her knees bent and rested her elbows on them. Then she cried. It felt good to release the pent-up frustration of the past few weeks. 'Twas plain Roen did not want her company. Matilda's stinging insults resounded. Beatrice remained at Woodshadow; 'twas only a matter of time before Roen carried out her aunt's prediction.

"Ouch!" Lenora pulled away the hem of her gown to find Roen's pup tugging at her big toe. She wiggled her toes and the dog froze, then began to frantically bark at them.

She pestered the animal again with her foot. The pup executed a series of lunge attacks and yapped louder. "Such a fighter for one so little. You just don't give up."

Tired of the game, she stopped teasing the dog. Confident with its victory, the puppy sauntered over to the folds of her dress. After winding round and round, the tiny bit of fur settled its jaws on the tip of its tail.

"Nora?" Roen's voice questioned as he entered the barn. He moved toward her resting place and braced his head against the beam he had struck earlier. The red rims of her eyes caused his heart to lurch. He cursed himself for being the instrument of her sorrow. Outside he had fought his body's desires, prayed to suppress them. His prayers remained unanswered, and the need had only grown, becoming so strong that he ventured back, just to see her once more.

"What do you want?" Lenora sniffed and wiped tears on the sleeve of her dress.

"I...I...I..." He sought some excuse for his return. "I came for the pup. If you don't want him, I'll give him back to the kennel master."

"He's not here."

"Where did he go?" Roen began to search the area, lifting the blankets and finally the bowls.

Despite her tears, Lenora laughed. "I know he's a bit of a dog, but, Roen, he could not hide beneath the bowl."

Her laugh, however gentle and halfhearted, rang like music to his ears. His gaze rested softly on her tear-streaked face. Her bereavement echoed in his own soul. He dropped his gaze to the floor.

"You've no idea where it may have gone?" Roen questioned.

"Nay, I am not partial to your gifts."

Roen sat down beside her. The tip of a furiously wagging tail lay exposed beyond the hem of Lenora's dress. "Aye, I know. You sent back the cloth and jewels. You never wear the wedding gift I gave you."

"Wedding gift?"

"The amber-and-emerald necklace."

She turned, and he could see her search his face. He felt unsure of what she found because her face screwed up in a horrible grimace. "Lenora, what is wrong?"

"Nothing." Her voice rose in pitch and she bit her lips.

He tried to take her in his arms, and his heart clamored against his chest. "Are you ill?" She grabbed her knees and squeezed her eyes closed. "What's wrong?"

"Get that hound!" Lenora pulled her dress up over her knees and revealed the pup, its teeth tugging at the tender skin near her little toe.

Roen lifted the animal by the scruff of its neck. Lenora lifted her leg with it. Her foot dangled high in the air, and her gown slid up, displaying the sensuous curve of her calf and thigh. He shook the pup to dislodge it.

"Ouch. That hurts."

His finger slipped into the animal's mouth and pressed down. The strong jaws parted and Lenora freed herself. He placed the little beast on the hay and plopped one of the empty wooden feed bowls over it.

"There. See? The mongrel could fit under a bowl."

Lenora massaged her injured toe. "Where did you get that little hellion?"

A full belly laugh erupted from Roen. Tears came to the corners of his eyes, and every time he thought he would gain his composure, another laugh blurted out.

"Stop it. 'Twas not that comical." Lenora pinched him, hard.

"That hurt." The statement lost some of its recriminations because he burst out in another attack of laughter.

She pinched him again, harder.

"Peace, wife. I'll stop or be black-and-blue soon." He could not help but notice the smile Lenora tried to keep at bay.

"Well, what are you going to call it?"

Roen's laughter came under control. "I gave the beast to you. 'Tis your place to name it."

She shook her head. "Nay, you name it."

"Call it Dog, for all I care."

"That is precisely the point. When you name something, you claim it as your own. It has your mark upon it. A name shows that you do care. 'Tis the only way I will accept it."

"Nora, 'tis nothing but a scrap of fur and teeth."

"Name it." Lenora lifted the bowl. The pup lay curled up, asleep.

Roen started to protest, then stopped. 'Twas a little thing, and if it made her happy he would do it. He pursed his lips, staring upward as though for heavenly inspiration.

"Goliath. His name is Goliath"

"That little fur ball you name after a giant? I'll sound like a fool calling him that." She crinkled up her brows and scratched the pup behind the ears.

"Nevertheless, 'tis his name. He may not look the part, but he acts it." He smiled at the relaxed stance of his wife. The tension that had lain between them thinned. Could he break through the barrier that separated him from Lenora?

"Why did you give me this animal?" Lenora's somber voice asked.

From his pocket, Roen pulled the worn collar. He handed it to her. She took the strip of leather from his hand and stretched the band open. Her finger traced the letters written on the inside.

"How—" she bit her lower lip "—did you find this?"

"In the woods. I found his body near a green clearing. There were no broken bones. I think he died peacefully. Probably just fell asleep and did not awaken." He spoke the white lies so easily. Why tell her the truth and increase her pain?

"Thank you." She hugged the collar to her chest. "For bringing me this and giving me Goliath." Tears clouded her golden eyes. Without thinking, Roen gathered her up in his arms. She wrapped her arms around his neck and released the tears.

She cried for Gladymer, for her father, even for Roen. It felt wonderful to lie cocooned in Roen's arms and not have to be strong.

Every tear spent, she lifted her face from his shoulder. A huge wet blot darkened his tunic. Her tears caused the red thread on the embroidery at his neck to run. She sniffed and rubbed the stain with her fingers. "Look, I've ruined this. The dye has marked your tunic."

Roen closed his fingers over hers and gave them a gentle squeeze. "'Tis nothing, no need to speak of it."

"That's your answer to everything." She pushed herself from his arms, her resentment knotted up inside her. "But I need to speak. Why? Roen, why did you do this thing to my father, to me, to us?"

"I gave the man my word. I did not know you would take it thus."

A scream of frustration and rage at the back of her throat. "How did you expect me to react? How would you react if 'twas the reverse? If 'twas your parent that had died?"

His mouth grew tight and grim. The heightened pulse of the vein in his neck marked his mood. How dare he get angry with her? She had been wronged, not him. His long body jolted upright and he looked down on her with his fists clenched at his side. He moved from the alcove without answering her questions.

She jumped to her feet and followed him. "Not this time, Galliard. You will answer me. You owe me that much." She ran and, ignoring the danger, planted herself in front of him.

"How can I answer? I have no knowledge of what you ask," he rasped through gritted teeth.

"Just because you are still blessed with your parents is no excuse. Can you not imagine how you would feel at their loss?"

"Nay, 'tis not that." Raw hurt glittered in his stony eyes. " 'Tis I cannot imagine parents." He paused, letting the statement sink into Lenora's brain.

"I don't understand. Roen, you must have parents."

"There's a man whose name I bear, but I'm not his." His jaw tightened. "Lenora, you married a true bastard, in deed as well as birth."

He stepped around her, leaving her stunned and silent. She shook her head to recover her wits and again ran after him. He stood near the oak with his back to her, blotting out the sun with his body.

Her compassion overcame the outrage in her heart. The need for battle ended. This was a time for healing. She slipped her arms around his waist and leaned her head on his arm. In a hushed voice she gave the gentle command, "Tell me."

He tilted her chin up, his eyes wary. " 'Tis no more to tell. I am a bastard with no true name."

"There's more, Roen. Tell me."

Hamlin had said the same thing earlier. Roen gazed down into her eyes. Tenderness softened the golden tones, and the sight melted his last resolve. He cleared his throat and moved from her embrace. The words clung in his throat. After so many years, the hurts, the insults, the injustices still caused him pain.

"The mark of a bastard has been with me since the day I was born. They only had to look at me to see I did not belong. I am one of six brothers and the only light-haired one of them. No one else has my eyes or build."

"But that alone could not mean you were a bastard. Your mother, was she—"

"Nay, she was dark and small, also. There were other things."

"Like what?"

Roen turned his head from her and tried to regain the iron belt of restraint he kept on this part of his life. "I can read."

Lenora's eyes widened in bewilderment. "I don't understand."

"My mother engaged a tutor for me against Galliard's wishes. I was directed to study late, by candlelight. My teacher told me Galliard would be so proud of my fast progress. Then my mother arranged for me to entertain a crowd of visiting noblemen at mealtime. A passage from the Bible had been selected by my tutor. I stood and read those words with so much hope." He pounded his fist on the trunk of the oak then leaned his head against it.

Lenora's quiet voice tore through his anguish. "What happened, Roen?"

"'Twas all a joke on her part, another way to mark me as different." Roen tried to hide the pain from his voice. "They had all tried, every one of my brothers . . . they had all tried to learn but they couldn't. They were just like Galliard. The letters got all jumbled up and backward. None of them could read. None except for me."

"Did your father never ask, never seek more than just these superficial marks?"

Roen closed his eyes, the blackness transforming into red-hot bands. "'Tis easy for you, with your eyes and hair, even your stance so like your sire's. There could be no doubt in your father's mind whose issue you were. I remember the first time I saw you and Sir Edmund together, so alike . . . I wanted the same with my father, whoever he might be."

"My father would have loved me if I were short and darkhaired with green eyes."

"'Tis an easy thing to say, but not so easy to prove."

Her eyes melted into pools of weary wisdom. "Nay, not hard at all. Ask any about my brother, Louis. He bore those colorings, yet Father never doubted his birthright. It wouldn't matter what any of his children looked like—he knew my mother loved him and he her."

Unsettled, Roen blasted back, "Galliard wanted more proof. He pleaded, begged and even beat her for the truth."

Hate laced his every word. "My mother never admitted nor denied it. She would only smile. Lord, how I hated that smile. When I read that passage, I still remember her smiling at me. No matter how many times Galliard dragged me out into the exercise field and struck me over and over again in full view of her, she stood silent and smiled. With every blow he demanded an answer. It fell into a pattern, the sound of the lash, the sting of its blow on my back and the question, 'Is he mine?' I think she took great pleasure out of the man's uncertainty."

"How could she do such a thing? How could he? Why didn't he send you away?"

The laugh that came forth carried no merriment. "And admit his wife had cuckolded him? In front of guests and his vassals, I was his true son. In private, I was his wife's bastard."

"What about your brothers?"

"They sided with my father. My childhood was filled with insults, taunts and fistfights until I was fostered out."

"I'm so sorry, Roen. Your mother must have hated your father very much."

"And me." He picked up Lenora's hand and held it to his chest. "She had many sins on her soul when she died, but the worst was to me. I knelt by her bed, I held her hand when the rest of the family had sequestered her away in a dirty hole of a convent cell. The only thing I begged from her was my father's name, and she would not give it. When I left her room, there was a message from Galliard waiting. 'Twas one question, Are you my son? I sent back a blank paper."

Roen felt the trauma of his youth burst the seams of his emotional armor. The endless attempts for approval from a man who would never accept him. The longing for family that cursed his existence. The child that had wilted from neglect, replaced by a youth dead inside, all tender feelings destroyed.

Her voice tight with emotion, she asked, "That's why you left the pantalets on our wedding bed?"

He looked at the tears in his wife's eyes and pulled her roughly into the circle of his arms. "I know what it is to live with the stigma of another's crime. I would not let you bear the shame for my transgression." He saw her try to hide a sniffle.

His large hand took her face and tilted it upward. "In battle I learned of duty, loyalty and respect. Those I will give to you freely. When you speak of love between your parents, your brother, of that I know nothing."

The scent of her perfume wafted in the air. She stared at him with warm, open eyes, no looks of recrimination because of his birth. "I can teach you, Roen. If you give me the chance." Lenora stroked his cheek.

A bitter sadness lodged in his gut. "Nay, I'm too old and too weary to learn. Wife, you must take me as I am. Will you?"

With her hand, she guided his mouth to her lips. He crushed her to him and pressed his mouth on hers. She gave no resistance, her arms tightening around him. A hunger ravaged in his loins, a hunger for Lenora's body, for the pleasure she could give, and his kiss grew more demanding.

His hands caressed her face, her throat, and slid down her chest to her breasts. She parted her lips and the tip of her tongue teased his upper mouth. A ragged breath escaped his throat and he tore himself from her. His need tempted him to have her on the ground here and now. He gripped her hand in his and pulled her toward the castle.

"Roen. Wait." Lenora dug her heels into the hard packed ground.

The tension in his loins flared. Wait? He couldn't.

She turned to the stable and looked at him through thick, red gold lashes, her face slightly flushed. "There's a loft in the stable."

He stopped pulling on her arm and felt a slow grin spread across his face. A victorious cry on his lips, he swooped his wife up into his arms and carried her inside to the ladder. He climbed the steps, his arms on either side of her, afraid that she might change her mind and try to retreat from his embrace.

When they reached the soft hay-covered upper floor, Roen pounced. Lenora was willing prey. His fingers nimbly untied her laces. With his hands on her naked breasts, his lips nibbling at her ear, he asked, "Mating in the middle of the day and in the barn. Nora, is this proper?"

One slim hand wiggled down his hose and pinched his bare bottom. "Nay," she said, releasing a low, pleased groan when his lips tugged playfully at her breast, "but it makes it all the more enjoyable."

Lenora rested in her husband's arms, still radiant from his touch. The passion of their mating both frightened and thrilled her. Roen's deep, regular breathing comforted her. His arm tightened around her and he lightly slapped her backside. She turned and kissed his neck.

He opened one eye and wrinkled his nose. "I suppose we must dress and go about our business, Nora."

"Aye, but we can lie here for another few moments." Her fingers trailed down his chest in feather-light touches.

Grabbing her wrist, he warned, "Keep that up, and we'll be here for more than just a few moments."

"I suppose you're right. 'Tis only a few hours till dusk anyway. I'd not want to tire you out."

Roen tossed her dress over her head and donned his tunic. "We've plenty of nights ahead to tire each other, Nora." He leaned over and kissed her lips as she emerged from the neck of her gown.

"And plenty of nights to teach you how to love," she vowed under her breath. Her dressing finished, she followed Roen down the ladder, an ingenious assortment of lesson plans formulating in her head. And not one of them could be considered proper!

Chapter Seventeen

"Let go of that." Lenora tugged on the end of the leather rein. Goliath wagged his tail and clamped his jaws down tighter on the opposite end. She gave a hard yank and the strip came free. "Look at what you've done. Tom will have a fit when he sees this." Goliath barked in agreement and scurried about, looking for more mischief to get into. Humming under her breath, she returned the leathers to the tack room. A white slip of paper, stuck between the boards, caught her eye.

The paper unfolded and she read.

Know you will see this. Have her meet me in the woods before the evening meal this Sabbath. Important. G.

Her fingers trembled with relief. Geoffrey wanted to see Beatrice. He had acted so strangely the last few times they had met. Doubt clouded her mind, but she dusted it away. Like a sticky cobweb, her misgivings remained. She concentrated on the many times Geoffrey had demonstrated his friendship. The man was her friend and Beatrice loved him. Her cousin would welcome the chance to rekindle her relationship with him. She stuffed the message inside the tight sleeves of her undertunic.

"Goliath." The pup instantly appeared at her side and bumped along in his customary place near her left leg. The lanky animal had become her shadow these last few weeks since Roen had given him to her. He had also grown to thrice his size.

She heard voices from the loft above. "Tom, is that you? Is your cousin about?"

"Aye, he's here with me." Tom appeared on the steps. A dark shadow moved behind him. "What need have ye of 'im?"

"I need him to build something for Lord Roen."

Tom winced and asked, "What might it be, Lady Lenora?"

"A tub. A large tub." She felt a flush of color burn her cheeks.

"You've a fine tub up to the castle," Tom noted.

"Aye, but Roen is a very large, er, long man and there's no room in it."

"Now, how much room does he need to bathe?"

"More than he has." The rose tint of her cheeks darkened to scarlet at his question. Vivid memories of last night's bath caused her to blush even more. Roen had pulled her into the tub and torn the neck of her chemise to touch her bare skin. Unable to move in the small wooden bath, he stood, naked and dripping wet. Her wet gown clung to her and she reveled in the gleam that came to his eyes. They consummated their passion on the bed, but the tub had been delicious fun while it lasted.

"How large does it need to be?" The question came from above.

"Cervin, can you make one large enough for, um, two people?"

Tom's eyebrow quirked. "I know 'e's a big one, but as large as two people? Ye think that much? I thought 'e wanted to bathe, not swim."

Lenora wrinkled up her nose at him. "I'm discussing this with Cervin, not you. When will it be ready?"

"By next Sabbath day should be plenty of time." A low chuckle followed his prediction. Tom joined in the merriment at her expense. "Just the same as I told Sir Roen when he requested a tub this morning. You nobles must have a powerful need to bathe."

She left the barn with no reply. A pleasant tingle warmed her. Four days would not be long to wait. She decided to search for her husband and remind him she prepared the household orders. She wanted no more repeated requests.

Roen waited until the girl settled in the garden. Her yellow white hair flashed from the morning sun. The pale skin had gained color since Matilda left for Bridgeton. He shifted his weight back and forth from one foot to another. By the Holy Land, he did not know what he would say to her but he needed to milk any information she might have.

His footsteps fell silently on the thick grass. The heavy, sweet smell of jasmine coated the air. He could taste the smell when he breathed. Beatrice took a claret-colored rosebud in her hand and placed it in the straw basket in her lap. Roen's shadow fell across the path. Startled, the young girl tumbled the basket from her lap. Rose petals scattered across his feet.

"Excuse me, Lady Beatrice." He bent to gather up the fallen blossoms. "I would like a word with you."

"Aye, my lord, what do you wish?" Beatrice's fingers gripped the handle of the basket with white knuckles.

"Things have been well for you these last few weeks since your mother left?"

"Aye."

He fished for more information. "I had thought to send a few more knights to Bridgeton on the morrow. Could you suggest a few names that were special to your mother? Did she favor any?"

Beatrice straightened her back and rose to her feet. "My mother is a lady, Sir Roen. She showed no favors to any man."

He rubbed his chin. "I meant no disrespect, I assure you. I only thought your mother might welcome the company of some old friends. What of the servants?"

"How dare you speak of my mother in such a manner?" The tone of her voice surprised him as well as her. A trace of his wife's temper showed in the usually timid girl's words. Her brilliant azure eyes widened in shock. "I am sorry, Lord Roen. I forget my position here."

"Nay, forgive me. I am afraid my questions gave the wrong impression. I wanted to ease your mother's banishment by sending a trusted friend or companion to her." He chuckled low. "'Tis good to hear you speak to me without fear. There's a touch of my Nora in your words."

The tight line of her jaw relaxed, the rigidness in her shoulders eased. "Mother always said Lenora influenced me too much."

"But for the better." Roen relaxed, also. The girl knew nothing about her mother's scheme. Hamlin had been right, despite his emotional attachment to the girl.

"Will Sir Hamlin be going to Bridgeton?" Her voice wavered.

"Nay, I need him here." Roen watched her. Did she sigh with relief at his words? How many times had he seen Hamlin's eyes focused on her as she moved across the hall? That his friend had a keen interest in the girl he did not doubt, but what of Beatrice's fear? Could she return Hamlin's feelings? He decided to ferret out the girl's emotions. "But mayhap 'twould be good to send him at that."

"Oh, nay. I believe you are right in your first assessment. Sir Hamlin is a great help here as your seneschal. 'Twould not do to have him absent for long." The lines between her brows deepened. The pitch of her voice rose slightly.

"Beatrice—" he forced himself to continue "—I'll ask you simply, do you have feelings for my friend? If you do, I know 'twould please him. If you don't, then tell him, so he'll not follow you with puppy-dog eyes."

Beatrice quieted like a frightened rabbit. Roen thought he might have ruined Hamlin's chances with the shy creature. She took in a great gulp of air and exhaled it slowly. The palm of his hand rose and rested on her shoulder. He spoke from the depths of his friendship. "Pray, be honest with him. Do not lead him on if he stands no chance with you, if you cannot be with him as a wife."

She did not flinch from his touch and placed her hand over his. "I feel for you as a brother, Roen. You don't frighten me anymore. 'Tis plain to see there is no woman for you save my cousin. I don't know if I can have the kind of relationship you two share, but watching you has taught me that marriage is not an evil thing." Patting his hand, she gave him a level look. "I will take your advice into consideration. There are things I must attend to before I speak to him."

Lenora rounded the garden arbor, her eyes searching for Roen. She saw him, the sunlight a halo around his blond head. Her steps faltered when she saw him place his hand on Beatrice's shoulder. Her cousin did not run or faint. Instead, she placed her hand over his. Ugly streams of jealousy coursed through her. The thin, screeching voice of her aunt mocked her. "Look at her and tell me he would want you with Beatrice around." A knife of pain and uncertainty sliced through her chest. She trusted Roen and Beatrice. Matilda had to be wrong.

When her husband left, a sense of deep loss filled her. A desire to touch him, kiss his lips, make love to him wrapped around her heart. As soon as she delivered Geoffrey's note, she would find him and do just that.

Goliath at her heels, she rushed to her cousin. "Beatrice, I need to give you this." She slipped the note from her sleeve and placed it in the younger woman's hand.

Beatrice read the note, and Lenora's heart sank. Her cousin's face paled. Never good at hiding her emotions, Beatrice gave away her answer before she spoke. "I can't meet him, Lenora. I just can't." She stuffed the message under the roses in her basket.

"Why? I know he's sorry that he broke it off. He wants to see you. Now that your mother is gone, perhaps he can ask for your hand." A pang of remorse tore at Lenora's heart. Deep inside, she wanted Beatrice and Geoffrey together so that her cousin would no longer provide a temptation to her husband.

"Nay." Beatrice's eyes opened in alarm. She looked at Lenora with eyes that begged her to understand. "I don't feel the same about him. I've grown up these last few months. I don't think I ever really loved him. He just sheltered me from all my fears. He made me feel safe. That's not love."

The fear returned. How did she know unless someone had taught her? Lenora refused to surrender to her jealousy. Trust, she would trust Roen and Beatrice. "I'll speak to Geoffrey for you, if that's what you want."

"Thank you, I would appreciate it, Cousin. Tell him—" she rubbed her lips with her hand "—I'm sorry." The words came out choked with tears. Beatrice grabbed her basket and left Lenora alone. Crushed rose petals littered the garden walk. Their bruised aroma reminded her of the concern in her heart.

Life without Roen's love she could survive, but if she could not trust him, what life could they have together? Roen promised her loyalty; she had to put her faith in his word. She would push these terrible thoughts from her mind and think of the sunset. Then she could wrap herself in her husband's arms and dispel all her questions.

No matter what move she made, victory eluded her. Another loss stared her in the face. Roen's cheerful whistling from the opposite side of the table caused her to fume. "Stop that infernal racket. I can't concentrate."

The glow of success lit his face. He reminded her of a boy who had managed to hit the quintain for the first time, full of bluster and arrogance. She ought to be used to that look; she had seen it every time they played. This night would be no different.

A pout came to Lenora's lips and she threw up her hands. "I lose again." Roen hooted and slapped his thigh. Goliath lifted his head from Lenora's feet and peered about with one sleepy eye. He chomped his jowls loudly, then fell over into a deep sleep.

A crooked smile, which caused Roen's dimples to appear, crossed his full lips. "I win again. Nine Man Morris is a game I don't ever intend to lose. The prize is too great to lose." A naughty wink accompanied his last remark.

Lenora felt a tingle of excitement in her body. Despite the wonderful surrender she gave to Roen each night and the bliss she found in their lovemaking, she would like to win this game just once. She came so close, so many times, but never a win. 'Twould do her husband well to deflate his vanity a bit.

Beatrice, seated near the hearth, looked up from her needlework and tried to console her. "Perhaps next time."

Hamlin draped his arms along the rim of her cousin's chair and chimed in, "You've got to get the upper hand."

"Of course she does, but she can't." Roen crowed with satisfaction. He laced his fingers together and stretched out his arms and long legs.

Hamlin moved to sit against the arm of Beatrice's chair. "Don't be so certain, my friend. There's always a weakness."

Roen shrugged his wide shoulders in a roguish manner. Lenora bit her lip. Just once she'd like to ruin that arrogant armor.

Her giant of a husband rose and unexpectedly brushed his lips across her cheek. He didn't make tender gestures often, especially in front of others. "I need to speak with the night guard. I'll be up soon." His eyes darkened to an indigo gray. Lenora understood his message. He expected her to be in their room when he returned; he meant to collect his winnings. His eyes twinkled with conquest yet burned with lust.

Her gaze followed his long, powerful strides across the hall to the door. She could close her eyes and picture every line and contour of his body. The way his hair tumbled down around his back, the scars that marked his battles and beatings from his father; all were as familiar to her as the paths in the woods near her home.

"I wonder just what he wins each night that makes him so happy?" Hamlin gave Beatrice a wink.

"Don't tease," Beatrice warned. She threatened the knight with the tip of her sewing needle. Hamlin threw up his hands in mock surrender. The two young people laughed, their eyes on each other. Lenora listened to the banter and realized Beatrice exhibited none of her old fears.

Roen was correct. In the last few months, Beatrice had managed to pick her way out of the shell of her fear. She no longer withdrew inside of herself if a man approached. Vitality had returned to her and it made her even more beautiful, even more of a temptation. The cold warning of Matilda's words stabbed through her consciousness. Her conversation earlier in the day with Beatrice replayed in her mind.

"I know how you could win that game." Hamlin's voice sounded cocky.

Lenora shook her head and cast off the dread she felt. "How is that? Drug him?"

"In a way, you could call it that." Hamlin raised his eyebrows and looked around as if he were about to impart a great secret. "'Tis his concentration. You've got to break it."

Lenora shrugged her shoulders and waved her hands in dismissal. "Don't you think I've tried? It doesn't work. I've teased him, ridiculed him, nothing."

"Those are the ways a man might do it, but you're a woman. Use the talents of a woman to best him."

Lenora looked to Beatrice for clarification. Beatrice's cheeks tinted dark rose. "I think Sir Hamlin means to say..." Beatrice dropped her needlework and took Lenora's hand. "Look at your husband as you do, when you think he can't see you. As you were just doing."

"Exactly." Hamlin nodded. "Rest your gaze on him like that and I guarantee he'll lose all thoughts."

Lenora bolted up from the chair and hit the edge of the table. The bag of stones fell and its contents spilled across the floor. Her fingers trembling, she tried to replace them.

Beatrice knelt beside her and attempted to put her arms around Lenora. "We've upset you. I just thought if you told him how you really feel..."

"Nay." Lenora stood and shook off her cousin's help. "I'm not upset. I've lost the stones is all." Did Beatrice's words mean to warn her about Roen, that he might be drifting from his wife to her cousin? "Roen and I have discussed this. We've pledged our loyalty, respect and trust. 'Tis all he wants." She hesitated before adding, "All we want."

A painful lump caught in her throat. She passed the bag to Beatrice and nearly ran from the room. Like a little shadow, Goliath trotted at her heels.

It hurt that others could see her caring, yet Roen did not. The more painful wound stung from the fact that she did care, deeply, for her husband, and he did not return those feelings. Despite the fact that she had been warned, it did not lessen her injury. To tell him her tender feelings would only embarrass him and topple their newfound happiness. Better to go on as they were and live with what emotions Roen consented to express.

The stones fell into the velvet bag from Hamlin's hand. Beatrice pulled the gold-cord drawstring. "Did we do the right thing?" Her voice shook with emotion.

"Aye. We've got to make one of them crack that stubborn shell. How are they ever going to know they're in love unless one of them breaks down and tells the other?" Hamlin took Beatrice's hand and led her to a chair. He knelt at her feet and leaned back against the arm of the chair.

Beatrice watched the dark brown head move. She reached out her hand and held it suspended just above the curls. With a feather touch, she felt the silky smoothness of his hair. "Speaking from your heart is always difficult. It leaves one vulnerable."

His head turned, and she jerked her hand back to her chest. "Are you regretting your part in my scheme?" Hamlin's eyes met hers.

"Nay, 'tis only the entanglements I regret."

He nodded sagely. "There is always a spiderweb of complications when one plays Eros."

Beatrice picked up her needlework and whispered under her breath, "I pray 'tis not I that is caught up in the web."

Chapter Eighteen

Water trickled through the slats of the gigantic wooden tub in the middle of the floor. Lenora sat cross-legged on the bed, her skirts pulled across her knees. "This is useless," she complained. "'Twill never fill."

The shoddy workmanship was her own fault. Tom had warned her Cervin needed more time, but she had insisted on delivery as promised. She stared at the wet floor and moped.

"The wood's lookin' like it's finally goin' to swell tight, Lady Lenora," the servant commented while he poured in another heavy bucket of steaming water. "We'll have it full for ye soon."

"Thank you, Darrot." Lenora skipped to her trunk and extracted a soft cloth and a bar of her favorite scented soap. She grabbed the cloth and soap and laid them on the table her father had made. The game board reminded her of her conversation with Beatrice and Hamlin. How could she tell Roen how she felt? How could she tell him she loved him when he didn't even understand the emotion? Without sound she mouthed the words, *Roen, I love you.* Nay, 'twas not right. She continued her silent practice. *Roen, my husband, I need to say this. I love you.* She shuddered. Definitely not right. Out of the corner of her eye, she caught the confused look of her servant.

"I'm memorizing a new passage from the Scriptures."

"Uh huh." He nodded and raised his eyebrows. Darrot dumped the last pail of hot water into the tub.

"'Tis all filled for ye, milady." He scooped up the rope handles of several empty buckets and excused himself from her presence.

She rolled up her sleeves and tested the water with her elbow. Steam rose from the surface of the water like a cloud. The moisture clung to her face and throat. She reached for a towel and groaned. Roen would arrive at any moment and she had forgotten to pull a towel from the linen press. Hoping to return before her husband, she made a dash for the press.

The squire had just managed to pull off Roen's tunic when Lenora rushed into the room. Color washed her face and she bit her lower lip. She tossed the towel onto the bed and grabbed the cloth and soap. Kneeling by the wooden tub filled with hot water, she urged him to enter his bath. "I'm sorry I wasn't here to assist you, but I forgot a towel. Hurry, or the water will grow cold."

Roen waved his squire off and finished undressing. His skin protested the temperature of the water. With his back to his wife, he sat on the stool and soaked in the hot water. The smell of honey drifted to him from the soap in Lenora's hand. Her strong fingers massaged his shoulders and arms. He couldn't see her face, but he felt the gentle rise and fall of her chest against his back.

"This tub is much more to my liking." The slap of the cloth stung his back. He stretched out his legs and pointed his toes, then sprawled out using as much room as possible. "There's more than enough room for two." He waited to see if she took the hint. "Nora?" He cricked his neck to see her behind him.

"Hmm?" She shook her head and tucked back a curl behind her ear. "I'm sorry, I did not hear you."

"Nothing," he grumbled. For the past several days he had sensed an internal conflict in his wife. She daydreamed and had silent conversations with herself. Each time he broached the subject, she only smiled and told him 'twas nothing.

"You're quiet tonight, wife. 'Tis not usual."

"Relish it." Firm pressure from her hand eased his head off the tub ring and forward. The cloth moved in large circles down his back.

So she didn't want to speak about it. He would respect her wishes, for that had been his promise to her. Yet he ached to share her worries. She moved to sit at the side and he leaned back. The honey-scented soap in her hand lathered his chest with bubbles. Lenora did not meet his eyes while she washed his neck and chest.

Intent on breaking her melancholy, Roen scooped up a handful of suds and threw them at her. Her eyes flew open wide. "Roen! What are you doing?"

"Paying you back for an earlier bath. You almost blistered me."

The nagging look of worry eased from her face. The familiar glint of mischief returned to her eyes. A gentle warmth spread through his chest. "I don't know what you mean, sir."

"You sent that old hag to boil me alive."

A secretive smile slanted across her lips. "I sent no hag to you."

"You're lying."

The smile evaporated from her lips. "Nay, husband, there is one thing you can be sure of, I do not lie." The smile returned. "I sent no hag, because—" Lenora changed her voice to a reedy waver like an old woman "—I was the hag. A scrap of old clothes and some dirt and you didn't even recognize me."

"Then I must repay you for the temperature and the conversation of that bath." He made a grab for her and the soap dropped into the foamy water. His fingers wrapped around her wrist and plunged her hand into the water. His voice husky, he commanded, "Find it."

Her full lips parted in surprise, and he heard a tiny gasp. Pulling her closer, he trailed his finger down the side of her face. He had her full attention, all distractions forgotten. She slid her arm gently under the water and made contact with the inside of his upper thigh. Instantly, he could feel the heat seep into his groin. When her fingers danced down his leg, he halted them and moved them in the opposite direction.

Tentatively, her arm glided through the steamy water along his leg. He closed his eyes and allowed the hot licks of passion to devour him. A deep groan of pleasure shuddered from him when her hand touched his organ. Soapy fingers slid up and down the hardened shaft. Slowly, so achingly slowly, they encircled him, tugged at him, then withdrew.

"I found the soap."

Roen opened his eyes. He watched, mesmerized, while she rolled the bar in her hand, over and over again, building up a huge lather. The soap slipped from her hand again and disappeared between his legs. Her hand followed, brushing the tip of his manhood then gliding down its heated length. Like a child playing with fire, she teased the flames of his passion.

"Nora." The need grew too great, the heat too intense. He wanted to taste her, to feel the soft skin of her breasts against him, see her nipples harden from his touch. Her touch left ripples of desire across his skin and stoked the yearnings in his groin.

"My name's Lenora."

A robust laugh shook him. He had her back with him now and he intended to make the most of it. A tug and a lift, and she tumbled over the edge of the tub.

"Roen, what are you—"

He drowned her words with his lips. It could not be plainer what he intended. His hands tore at her chemise to expose the rosy circles of her breasts. His lips covered them and he suckled the essence from each milk white orb.

"Isn't this what you had in mind when you ordered such a monstrosity built?" He chuckled in her ear. His tongue darted across the tender skin to punctuate his intent.

"Nay." Breathless, she nipped his neck with her sharp teeth. "I thought 'twas you who ordered it."

"Aye, so 'twas." He held her face in the palm of his hand. His gaze dropped from her eyes to her shoulders to her bare breasts. "'Tis well our thoughts are so much in tandem." He touched each perfect globe, marveling at its softness.

"Roen, I . . ." She stopped midsentence.

He looked up from his passionate explorations and waited. "What is it, Nora?"

"You're pleased with our marriage, are you not?"

"Aye." His thumbs massaged the tiny, erect peaks of her breasts. "I am well pleased with our marriage." He couldn't help grinning at her solemn expression. So this was her dilemma. He should have known she needed more sweet words, more compliments. Women needed that sort of thing.

"You don't feel anything is lacking, then, in our union?" Her dark eyes wavered.

"I'll let you be the judge of that." He brought his lips to hers and let her feel all of the passion he held in check. She tasted like the smell of the soap, clean and sweet. She clung to him. Her beautiful hair spilled across her shoulders and floated in the water like copper-colored water lilies.

Water splashed over the tub in deep swells. His hand moved beneath the swimming folds of her gown to her braes. The handful of cloth gave way to his insistent pull and freed delicate curls for his fingers to explore. Her head thrown back, the graceful arch of her neck exposed, Lenora guided him to her.

Her grip on him tightened. He gritted his teeth and pulled her to him. Using his knees as a brace, he cleared away the yards of material from her gown and had her straddle him. With a push, he plunged his engorged shaft into her. He buried his face into the deep valley of her breasts, his hands cupped the cheeks of her derriere. She moaned, a sound filled with pleasure and desire.

Roen floated in the ecstasy of the feel of her wrapped around him. He kissed a path from one milky white breast to the other. The low purrs from Lenora heightened his yearnings. He shifted his weight and could not control the outcry of erotic gratification when he eased even deeper into her.

She began to rock. The waves of water moved in time with her. Surges of fevered heat enveloped him. He moved with the flow of the tide Lenora created. Her pelvis ground against him, causing a storm of golden passion to rip through him. He could feel the involuntary tremors of arousal pulsating through him, through her.

Lenora's rocking lost its gentle meter and became more insistent, more demanding. A hot tide of excitement raged through him. His body craved release from its enchanting torture. Lightning streams of passion poured into her womb. Her fingernails bit into his shoulders while a desire-rich groan spilled from her lips. Spent, she leaned against him, her head on his shoulder.

The tepid water swirled, soapy lather covered the floor. Roen held her to him tightly, afraid somehow she would melt away in the water and leave him alone once more. His voice wavered with awe. "I believe that's the best prize ever."

Lenora lifted her head, an impish grin on her lips. "I know what I'll ask for when I win our game."

"Pray, tell me."

"I'm going to make you look for the soap."

The involuntary tremors of their lovemaking still coursed through her body while she rested in his arms. She sucked the skin on his neck and giggled when gooseflesh prickled along his skin. He tasted soapy and slightly salty. The long locks of his blond hair were plastered to his face and head. As always when he smiled, years drifted away from his face and manner. He looked like a carefree young man, not the lord of an important keep. Not a man haunted by the mistakes of his parents.

She traced the line of his lips with her fingers. His blue gray eyes darkened to aquamarine. He had never had the opportunity to be young, to be a child. 'Twould only add to his burdens if she confessed her love to him now. They needed more time to discover each other's feelings, more time for Roen to learn how to care as deeply as she did. She kissed him on his lips, chin and the tip of his nose. His fingers fiddled with her laces.

"Roen, you can't mean to."

The laces came free, and his hands ran up her naked ribs and pulled off her netgown.

She protested, "The water is too cold."

A stab of heat in her loins told her otherwise.

Lenora pulled a dry gown from the trunk and wiggled into it. She didn't even bother to put on a chemise, just her tunics. The sun had long ago reached its zenith in the summer sky; the evening meal preparations had already begun. She would be late for her meeting with Geoffrey. Roen had already dressed and left to attend to business. 'Twas time she did likewise.

She ran down the steps to the main hall, still adjusting her girdle and hair. With impatient hands, she braided her wet and tangled tresses. 'Twould take all night to dry and tomorrow her hair would be a frizzy mess. A small price to pay for the afternoon's lovemaking. A delicious flood of tenderness filled her.

Absorbed in her thoughts, Lenora collided with a side table. A basket of rose petals skidded across the top. She captured the basket in midair. Petals fell like a gentle winter snowfall. With her foot, she hurriedly scraped the flowers back against the wall and made her way beyond the keep.

Roen tried to flag down his wife but she was too far away. Forgot something, no doubt. He smiled at her retreating figure. Of course, he had distracted her all afternoon, so he should bear some of the blame. He knew he was smiling but he couldn't help himself. He felt . . . good. Everything he had ever wanted was his. An important keep, good comrades . . . and a wife. Despite his reaction the first time he had met her, Lenora had turned out to be more than acceptable. A relaxing fatigue from their lovemaking still remained. He couldn't wait for the evening meal to be over and their nightly game to begin. Although he no longer need win to gain his wife's willingness, victory did make their mating sweeter, more intoxicating.

He moved through the hall envisioning Lenora's red gold locks floating in the water. The overpowering smell of roses assaulted him. An off-center basket of roses lay amid a light scattering of petals. The skewness bothered him. He pushed the basket to a central position. After another appraisal, he moved it a bit to the left. His hand on his chin, he gave it another look.

A pale white corner of paper jutted up from the dried flowers. He removed and unfolded it. The words hit him like a boulder of despair. *Have her meet me in the woods before the evening meal this Sabbath.* The basket belonged to Beatrice; he recognized it from the garden. She was to give this note to "her." Bile rose in his throat, and the contentment he had gloried in only moments before bubbled away in the heat of his anger. He knew who this letter was intended for. Hadn't he seen "her" racing off to meet her former love? Lenora was with Geoffrey. Now that she no longer need fear the loss of her maidenhead, Lenora was free to couple with her paramour with no repercussions.

He threw the basket and table across the room. The crash created a shuffle of servants' feet and hushed, frightened whispers. His fury carried up the stairs to his broadsword. Yanking it from the wall, he belted it to his waist. The armor that he had encased his heart in returned, tarnished and confining, but protective. This matter with Sir Geoffrey would be settled once and for all, his way. Then he would settle with his wife. Of the two, Lenora would suffer the most. Only vengeance would salve the wound created by her betrayal.

Chapter Nineteen

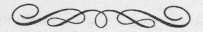

"Damn him. Now he's to have everything, Beatrice included." Geoffrey's face turned a mottled red. His upper lip twisted into an angry sneer.

"Nay, 'tis not as you think. Beatrice has changed these last few months. She's grown stronger, her fears have lessened." Lenora tried to explain again but the spurned lover would not listen. Goliath's ears perked up, his lip curled back. She put her hand on the dog's collar and gave the silent command to sit.

"And, pray tell me, what man has she dared to let touch her?" Geoffrey's words dripped with bitterness.

His words burned even deeper Lenora's memory of Roen's hand on Beatrice's shoulder, of Beatrice's hand on his. Her heart thudded against her chest.

"Aha!" Geoffrey pointed his finger at her. "I can see it in your face. Beatrice and your husband are at each other like dogs in heat."

"Nay!" How could he be so cruel? "'Tis not so, Geoffrey. Roen is blameless. Nothing exists between them, save friendship."

"Oh, Lenora, for someone who professes a pride in her wits, you put yourself to shame. I can see it in your eyes. You've seen them together, haven't you?" He grabbed her shoulders and shook her. Goliath sprang to attack, his sharp teeth sinking into Geoffrey's arm. He threw off the pup and Lenora in one shove.

She stumbled back, then fell across a piece of rotten wood. Beetles and grubs scattered across her skirt and leggings, trying to retreat from the unaccustomed light. Her dog stood over her, teeth bared, prepared to protect her. Lenora scrambled to her feet and pushed her hair back from her eyes. Geoffrey stood in the center of the clearing, his eyes wild with fury. She kept her arm on Goliath, for her protection as well as Geoffrey's.

"Curse him and everyone in that castle," Geoffrey muttered. "He wins everything, the keep, the wealth, the women." He turned toward her, the snarl now a childish pout. "Do you know how long I've dreamed of living at Woodshadow, the things I've done to be a part of it?" He sank to the ground and wept.

Dreams, Geoffrey always lived in dreams. She contemplated how alike he and Roen were. Two children caught up in households devoid of love. Fathers who used their children for their own gain. Roen's youth had made him hard, a warrior. The same circumstances had turned Geoffrey into a poet, a composer of verse and wild tales of adventure.

She wanted to put her arms around him, but didn't. Pity wouldn't help. Woodshadow and Beatrice could no longer play a part in Geoffrey's life. He must see that, and as his friend, she must help him see the truth. "I believe neither Roen nor Beatrice would betray me in that way. I trust them as I would you."

Geoffrey's tears evaporated and a crazed laughter came from him. "Lenora, you are a fool." The laughter faded and the snarl returned. "You want to believe your husband and cousin aren't sharing a bed, because you love him. I thought you were wiser than that."

She felt the sting of tears in her eyes. The steady thud of her heart against her chest pounded in her ears. "Aye, I love him and I trust him."

"Then I offer my sympathies, for your future will be bleaker than any childhood terror I experienced." He rose and dusted off the seat of his pants.

Geoffrey's mood swings were like a wild pendulum, one minute a sensitive friend, the next a hurt child, driven to tantrums; she could not be sure what reaction he would have next. "How can you say such a thing?"

"Because you give too much and get too little in return. You give your love and trust, and what does he give you? Does he profess his love and trust to you?"

"I have his trust and respect."

"And his love?"

She stiffened her backbone and held her head high. "'Twill come, in time." She patted her dog's head for reassurance.

"Lenora—" his voice softened, the anger gone like an afternoon thunderstorm "—if you or Beatrice have need of me, I am still your friend. Always know that I am here and ready to help." He turned to go, then stopped. She could read the pity in his eyes. "Don't let your feelings blind you. When the time comes, send for me. I will be your refuge.'

The sound of heavy hooves drummed in the air. They turned toward the noise. Goliath howled a welcoming call. A charging shadow appeared in the woods. Geoffrey ran for the cover of the trees but the figure burst into the clearing and cut him off. Lenora rushed forward to save her friend, then stumbled to a stop. Roen, dressed in his hauberk, sat astride the warhorse. In his hand, the heavy broadsword gleamed. He flicked his wrist and the steel weapon sliced through the air. Geoffrey grabbed his face, blood seeping between his fingers.

"Roen, stop!" Lenora could not believe she had witnessed the violent act. The dog sat back on his haunches and yipped, as though completely in accord with Roen's action.

From the height of the horse's back, his face like a thundercloud, Roen's voice boomed with anger. "Why, wife? Do you value your lover's pretty face so much?" With his knees, Roen guided the horse closer to the stunned Geoffrey. As Destrier gave him a push with his nose, the sharp points of the animal's armor made Geoffrey cry out in pain.

Lenora rushed to Roen's side and pounded on his leg with her fists. "Stop it, stop it! Have you gone insane?"

Roen kicked her away. She stumbled back and fell, her head hitting the ground. The dog whined, and his head whipped from master to mistress, but he kept his sitting position. Lenora tried to clear her eyes and stop the spinning in her head.

"Aye, I was insane." Roen slid from his saddle and stalked her. He lifted her from the ground with a jerk of his powerful hand. His grip on her arm bit into her skin. "I was insane to believe you could be different. At least a whore is honest in her profession." He dragged her over to Geoffrey.

"Geoffrey, I'm so sorry." The wound would scar his face, a mark of her husband's anger. Her temper turned to Roen. "You're wrong. Geoffrey and I are just friends."

Roen spat on the ground, and his voice shook with hostility. "Why did your *friend*—" he smeared the word with distaste "—not come to the castle and make his presence known to all? Why this secret meeting in the covering of the forest? Is this the custom here between friends?"

She looked into her husband's eyes and saw a warrior, ready to kill.

"Nay, 'tis not the custom. I am here to speak for another," she stuttered, her mind searching for a way to defuse the situation.

Roen snarled like a wild animal. "Give me the name of this other. Now." He raised his sword for a death blow above Geoffrey's neck.

"Tell me again, what is it you receive from this union?" Geoffrey asked Lenora, taunting her.

The ruby in the hilt of the sword cast a red glow onto Roen's face. He meant to kill her friend. Lenora jumped between Geoffrey and the weapon. "You cannot strike him down, he has no weapon. 'Twould be murder."

A tremor ran down the muscles in Roen's arms from the strain of holding the heavy weapon aloft. "Give me the name of this other if you can, wife, or stand aside and see me rip the head from your lover's neck."

She crossed her hands across her chest and willed herself to be strong. "I'll not move, for to do so would condemn your soul to the tortures of hell for slaying an innocent man. Nor will I speak a name, for you should not need it, my word is good enough." The newly forged foundation of her marriage began to crumble.

Her husband raised the sword. She closed her eyes and felt the push of air, the quiet *swoosh* as he struck. Silence. She opened her eyes, the razor-sharp blade just a hairbreadth from her throat. He had checked his swing at the last moment. Goliath sat between her and her husband, the whining replaced by a confused whimper.

Roen resheathed his sword and his arm encircled her waist. He threw her over the saddle, belly down, then jumped up behind her. Unable to see his face, she heard his words to Geoffrey. "The next time we meet, I will kill you." Then he bounded away, his hand pressing down on the small of her back, holding her over the horse's back for several minutes before he pulled up and halted at the edge of the forest. The distant sound of Goliath's barking signaled her pet's safety. The sun dipped below the treetops, the heat of the day still lingered.

He dropped her to the ground like a sack of grain. Her legs tingled from lost circulation. The physical pain did not compare to the pain in her heart.

His voice matched the icy glare from his eyes. "Give me the name. Prove your innocence."

"Do not ask it and prove your trust in me," she countered. *God*, she prayed, *make him understand how much she needed this from him.*

"You play with words, yet give me no answer." He pulled on the rein and the horse kicked up dust. "Or perhaps it does show me the way. You stall, for you have no name and thus fear to show your guilt."

She wanted to scream at him to open his heart and trust her as she had him. Instead, she met his wintry gaze. "I do not fear, for I have no guilt. But no name will come from my lips, and you may believe what you like. Think me guilty, I do not doubt you will, for 'tis the easy thing to do." She stomped off toward her home. Goliath, winded from his run, trotted up to her side. After only a dozen steps she heard the thunder of hooves behind her. She kept her eyes ahead and did not move from the road. Roen brushed by her, leaving her covered in the dust of the road and the pain of his mistrust.

Beatrice snapped the stem of a lavender plant and declared, "I will tell him the truth. I won't let you be punished because of me." She placed the flower in her basket and scratched Goliath between the ears. The dog wiggled deeper into the cool dirt of the garden.

"You'll do no such thing," Lenora ordered. She pushed back a tendril of hair from her eyes and put her hands on her back. The backache eased and she returned to tending the herb garden. With each tug she thought of Roen, alternating between imagining the weed as his neck or his stubbornness.

"But, Lenora, he won't let you out of the bailey. I know how much your freedom means to you...." Beatrice's voice trailed off. The shadow of a guardsman fell over them. "Must you stand so close?" Beatrice demanded.

The guard moved off, only to resume his surveillance just out of earshot.

"This is all my fault." Beatrice sank to the ground next to Lenora.

"Cousin, do not hold yourself to this. Roen must learn to trust me as I do him. My trust was tested when my father died. I believed him about my father's wishes, now he must believe in me." She broke off stems from a nearby mint bush. The sharp, cool smell of the plant drifted in the air.

"But it has been weeks and still I see no change. Hamlin has spoken to him and he threatened to send him to Bridgeton if he broached the subject again. The servants are frightened of him. Has he said anything to you?"

Lenora shook her head and plucked a leaf from the mint. She took a deep breath of the crisp smell hoping to clear her head and her heart. "Nay, he does not speak to me except to demand a name or my confession. I am guilty in his eyes yet I hold some hope."

Beatrice's frown eased. "Why is that?"

Lenora twirled a stem between her fingers. "He refuses to allow me to sleep anywhere else but at his side. I know he holds me to him each night. I feel his arms around me in my sleep. Each morning he is gone, yet I can feel the spot next to me and find the warmth his body left. I put my faith in those emotions and pray Roen will allow his feelings for me to cool the heat of his temper."

"And how long do you intend to wait for that to happen?" Beatrice asked.

"As long as I must. I have no choice." Lenora rose and shook the dirt from her dress. "You and Hamlin were right. I've made the dreadful mistake of falling in love with my husband."

Beatrice rose and gripped her cousin's hand. "Promise me that you will think with your head and not your heart. If Roen is not what you hope, do not sacrifice your happiness. You said Geoffrey would help us, despite what I've done to him."

She patted Beatrice's hand and smiled. "Aye, I believe he would, though I don't know what he could do." Odd, but Beatrice had grown stronger, more confident in Lenora's eyes, and Geoffrey weaker, less trustful.

"Promise me you'll seek out Geoffrey's help should you need it."

"Roen would murder him."

"Not if you could reach sanctuary with Sir Ranulf or the king. Promise me, Lenora."

"Very well, I promise. Does that make you feel better?"

"Aye, because I intend to make you keep your promise," Beatrice vowed. The two women rose and headed for the castle, trailed by Goliath and the reluctant guard.

Chapter Twenty

"Lady Lenora." Alyse tapped the end of her wooden spoon against her crossed arms. "Something's got to be done with that animal." She pointed her spoon at Goliath's sleeping form by the hearth. "He's eaten two of my birds right off the spit."

Goliath continued to snore, then licked his chops and belched in his sleep. Lenora sighed and called to her pet. "Goliath, come here." He opened one sleepy eye, saw Alyse with the spoon and quickly shut it. His snoring grew louder.

"Goliath." Lenora made her voice sterner and bit her lip to keep from laughing. Laughter. It felt strange to have a merry thought after so many months; Roen's accusation had stripped her life of merriment and laughter.

"Goliath." She snapped her fingers to get her dog's attention. This time the animal rose, his big head nearly trailing the ground, his tail low. A true picture of canine remorse. He fell like dead weight on her toes and rolled over to show his belly. By the stars, he had certainly grown into his name these last few months.

Alyse recrossed her arms under her ample chest and continued with her list of the dog's transgressions. "Yesterday, he got on my worktable and spilt two pitchers of milk. Last week he chased my laying hens, and we had no eggs for three days. The day before that, he ate the centers out of three pies I had left to cool. Just the centers, mind ye."

"I'll see to him, Alyse. I promise." Lenora tried to rise, but the heavy weight on her feet pinned her in the chair. She put down her sewing and wiggled her toes out from under the animal.

"Well, see that ye do, Lady Lenora, or—" the kitchen cook addressed the dog on the floor "—you'll wind up on the spit instead of stealing from it." In a huff, she left the room to return to her realm downstairs.

When the woman exited, Goliath padded over to the hearth to retrieve a slimy piece of rawhide. He dropped it at Lenora's feet and sat upright, an expectant look on his face.

"Nay, I'll not toss your toy for you," Lenora rebuked him. The dog picked up the rawhide and set it in her lap.

"You may as well throw it. He won't let up until you do," Beatrice advised. She put aside her sewing, also, and walked to her cousin's side. "He needs to stay in the kennel or the barn."

"I know, but he would be miserable after sleeping near me all this time." Lenora threw the strip of leather. "I would miss him, too. He keeps me from being too lonely." Goliath leapt after it, captured the strip with his front paws and began to tug and chew his toy.

"When are you going to allow me to tell Roen the truth about your meeting with Geoffrey?" Beatrice placed her hand on Lenora's shoulder. "'Tis been months now. You can't keep living like this. The strain is making you ill."

Lenora lowered her head and closed her eyes. 'Twas not her estrangement from her husband that caused her nausea. She had kept her secret for three months now; soon she would be able to hide it no longer.

"Beatrice, you must not tell. There is more to this than you think." Her cousin moved to sit at her side. Lenora glanced around to see if anyone was in earshot. The guard sat across the room, cleaning his weapons. The servants moved about, concerned with their duties. "I am with child. I believe three months."

Beatrice's eyes widened, and a smile graced her lips. "Oh, Lenora, how wonderful!" She gave Lenora a hug.

"Sh. I do not wish it known to all just yet."

"Why?" Beatrice's smile faded. Then realization dawned. "He won't believe 'tis his, will he?"

"'Twould be the time when he saw me with Geoffrey. I fear 'tis his past that haunts him and will cause him to reject our child."

"Then let me go to him and clear his mind of these evil thoughts."

Lenora shook her head and crossed the room to stare at the embers in the hearth. Beatrice went to her side, and Lenora spoke to the dying flames. "And what will it prove? If he doubts my word, why would he believe you? In his mind I am guilty. It really matters little what anyone says. If we are to have a life together, he must break down this wall he has put between us himself. No one else can help him."

"What if he does not make amends before you can no longer hide the babe from him?" Beatrice kept her voice low and glanced over her shoulder at the guard. He no longer cleaned his sword but stared at them.

"Then there is no future for us. I'll not have my child grow up in a home such as this one is now. I'll leave, perhaps return to Aquitaine."

Beatrice laced her arm through Lenora's and drew her away from the fire. In a hushed whisper she said, "Come, let us retire to your chambers. There we will have more privacy to discuss this matter. Besides, you will need to start your layette soon or the heir to Woodshadow will lie naked in his crib for his first months."

Arm in arm, they climbed the stairs to the seclusion of the master chamber. Goliath followed in their shadow. Roen intercepted the guard as he started for the stairs.

"Raymond, what went on between the two?" he inquired.

The guard shrugged his shoulders. "I do not know, Lord Roen. They share a secret but I was not close enough to hear."

Roen nodded and dismissed the man. He sat in the chair his wife had vacated and propped his elbows on the arms. With his hands folded, he rested his chin on his extended index fingers while he studied the brocade edge of his tunic.

Hamlin leaned against the warm stones of the hearth. Familiar with his commander's mood, he demanded, "What do you know, Roen?"

He dropped his arms to hang loose. His head tilted to rest on the back of the chair. "I believe my wife is expecting a child."

Hamlin's mouth dropped open. With his foot, he pushed himself off the wall of rock. "Are you certain? Has she told you this?"

"She has said nothing to me. But she cannot hide the changes in her body."

Hamlin whacked his friend on the back and gave him a jubilant grin. "Congratulations, old man, and when is the blessed event to occur?"

Roen slanted his head and gave his companion a sideways glance. "I would suspect sometime after the New Year." He paused to let the date sink in.

"What a wonderful way to begin a year. We must plan a special celebration for the occasion." Hamlin started waving his hands. "A huge feast, dancing, jugglers. I love jugglers...." His hands froze in midair and the gaiety left his voice, replaced with dread. His hands dropped and he asked, "You don't believe the babe is yours, do you?"

"There's that possibility. It could be her lover's child." The words ripped from him, the pain unconcealable.

"Roen, you are my commander. In battle, I would not hesitate to carry out your orders." Hamlin stood over him. "But more than that, I consider you and I friends. Loyal friends."

"Aye, 'tis true." He waited for the point of Hamlin's speech.

"I tell this in that vein, as a friend." Hamlin sucked in a breath, and the words rushed out. "You are a fool, Roen. I know Lenora tells the truth."

"How?" Roen looked up, desperate for some shred of proof to nullify his charges.

"Because she loves you. Even after all the hurt you've caused her, she still loves you." Hamlin snorted when Roen rose and turned from him. "You can walk away from me, but you can't walk away from your wife and child. What are you going to do?"

His shoulders sank, and defeat caught in his throat like a bitter ale. "I will do what I must for the child's sake and uphold the marital agreement I made with Sir Edmund. Lenora's firstborn son is heir to Woodshadow, regardless of who fathered him."

"The woman believed you about her father. Can you not see it in yourself to put the same trust in her?" Hamlin asked as Roen walked away.

The truth of the question haunted him. Why had she believed in him then, when by all rights she should have allowed her men to kill him on the spot? When he told his side, she listened to him, eventually, then placed her faith in him. Why had she done that? Could Hamlin be right? Did she love him?

Roen groaned at the idea. It would only lace the situation with more guilt. For if she did love him, could that elusive emotion be sustained in her heart after the way he treated her? Nay, if she had not hated him before, she would now.

He left the keep and wandered to the old oak. Bright red and orange leaves floated in the air. A daydream of his wife materialized in the autumn light. The image spoke of how proud she was of him, how much she respected him. He would murmur back how pleased he was with her. The image leaned toward him, her full lips ready to meet his own.

A voice in his conscience chastised him. Pleased. Respected. Those weren't the words he wanted spoken. How would it sound on her lips, "I love you?" How would it sound on his own?

A child's cry broke his thoughts. A brown-haired little boy ran toward the tree, his finger held close to his chest. "Halt, boy, stop that racket," Roen yelled.

The wail stopped, but the boy's lower lip trembled. He started to hiccup and cry at the same time. He cradled one hand in the other.

Roen looked down at the dirty, tear-streaked face. Brown eyes looked up at him. "Why all the blubbering? You're too old to be crying like a baby."

On chubby legs, the child reviewed him. Finally, he extended his finger, the hiccups in control. Roen knelt down and examined the appendage. A long, nasty sliver of wood pierced the skin and lay under the flesh. The edge, too small to grasp with his large fingers, extruded from beneath the surface. Roen grimaced. It looked painful even to him.

"Come here, boy." He motioned to the tree. "Sit, and I'll see if I can help you."

The lad obeyed, his tears drying. He stuck his thumb into his mouth and waited. Roen crossed his legs and sat next to him. The splinter lay just under the surface of the skin, so he tried to massage it out. The lad turned his face away and started to cry again.

"Hush," Roen ordered. The big brown eyes widened at the tone of his voice. "Hush," he ordered again, but this time his voice softened.

"Hurts," the lad informed him. He stuck his finger right under Roen's nose. "Fix it."

With a smile, he answered, "Aye, I'll fix it, but 'twill hurt some."

The boy plopped down into Roen's lap and put his small finger into the large calloused hand of his benefactor. "Fix," he ordered, then returned his thumb to his mouth. The brown eyes looked at him without fear.

Roen removed his sharp dagger and showed it to his patient. The boy's eyes rounded. "Don't worry, I'll be as gentle as I can." Roen kept his voice quiet. "'Twill only take a minute if you keep your hand very still. Can you do that?"

The little head nodded up and down slowly. Roen felt the arm he held grow stiff, and the small body leaned against his chest. Quick, before his patient changed his mind, he took the needlelike tip of his dagger and made a shallow incision. With a gentle squeeze, the splinter came free.

"Good boy, you were certainly brave through that," he praised the child. The little head nodded up and down in agreement. A shudder ran along the child's body, and Roen rubbed the gooseflesh from the baby-soft arm.

"Marvin, what are you doing?" A haggard-looking woman raced up to them. She bobbed a clumsy curtsy to him and swept the child from his lap.

"Ah, so Marvin is the name of my brave patient." Roen felt the loss of the small body. His arms and lap were suddenly empty. To escape the feeling, he rose and stretched his legs. "He had a splinter, so I cut it out. He's a most capable lad. You might wrap his finger with a cloth to stanch the blood." Marvin's mother nodded while she pulled her son farther from him.

Marvin showed his mother the still slightly bleeding finger and ordered, "Kiss." A maternal smile softened the woman's face. Dutifully, she leaned over and gave her son's injury a loud smack. Marvin giggled. "Better."

"Thank you, my lord, for your concern." The mother scooped up her son and rested him on her hip. "The second year is such a trying time. They're always into some mischief."

"He's only two. I thought him older." Roen looked at the boy, contentedly sucking his thumb in his mother's arms.

"You'll learn to size 'em better after you've a few of your own." Her chin nuzzled the top of her child's head. She moved off patting Marvin's back and humming a lullaby.

Roen watched the brown head rest on the woman's shoulder. Children of his own. When would that time come? He never really considered the prospect except in terms of producing an heir. Brown hair and brown eyes. Lenora's child might look very similar to Marvin if Geoffrey was the father. Would her child ever look at him with trust and order him to "fix" some hurt? Would he be able to look at the child with tenderness? He kicked at the piles of dead leaves around the trunk of the oak, unsure of the answers in his heart.

"Here, we can cut this down." Beatrice held up a linen dress. "We can make several gowns for your baby from this."

Lenora nodded, finally giving in to her excitement. Despite her relationship with the father, she wanted this baby. She couldn't wait to be able to count all the little toes and fingers. She dreamed of holding her child in her arms and feeling it nurse at her breast.

"The child must have a mantle for the winter." Beatrice started to make a verbal list of all the things a newborn would need. "Some warm woolen gowns..." She threw open one of the chests in Lenora's room and withdrew a pale undertunic. "Let's take the silk from this old dress and sew some strips onto the baby's blankets. I've a bit of ermine left from the gown I made. Let's put that on the baby's cloak. And a hat, he'll need a hat, also."

Lenora laughed. "Beatrice, you'll have the babe dressed better than the crown prince." She knelt near the chest, also, and withdrew a bolt of soft blue wool. The color reminded her of Roen's eyes when he was happy, a blue gray. She wondered if their child would have the same shade of eyes. If it did, would that be enough for Roen to claim it as his own?

Beatrice took the cloth from her hand. "Let's get started right away." She looked around the chamber for somewhere to lay the bolt out. "Here, this table will do." A sharp flick of her wrist and the wool snapped out of its folds and draped across the game table. Pulling out a piece of chalk from her pocket, Beatrice drew the simple shape of a baby's gown on the fabric.

Lenora rose slowly, her fingertips resting on the table. The Nine Man Morris game had not been used for some time now. She placed her hand on her barely protruding abdomen. "Aye, Beatrice, let's begin." She had a baby to think of and worry over now. As much as she wanted Roen to share this joy, she couldn't let his attitude toward her ruin these next few months. She fished about in her pocket, searching for her scissors.

"Heavens, I forgot my scissors downstairs. But I've an old pair stashed in the drawer of the table." She pulled on the drawer but it would not budge. The long disuse and humidity had made the drawer stick. She braced one hand against the tabletop, leaned in and yanked. The drawer catapulted out and flew across the room. Lenora landed flat on her backside, stones and the scissors raining down. Goliath woke from his dream and started barking. Lenora sputtered into a giggle, then a chuckle, and finally erupted into gut-aching laughter. Weak from her humorous release, she crawled on all fours and began to pick up the mess she had created.

Beatrice moved to get the drawer. "Have you given any thought to a name yet?"

"Nay, not really. Perhaps Edmund or Louis if a boy, after my father or brother. I think Anor, after my mother, if 'tis a daughter." Lenora paused in her work. Names somehow made the life within her more real.

"What about Roen? Won't he want to have something to do with the child's naming?" Beatrice lifted the drawer from the floor.

"Nay." She patted her dog's head. "Roen would not want to name a child he did not claim. I had to force him to even name Goliath. I thought it a silly name when first he said it, but he chose well, didn't he?"

"By the saints." Beatrice's voice sounded hollow and frightened. In her trembling fingers, she held a thick fold of paper. She dropped the heavy wooden drawer at her feet and sat on the edge of the bed.

"Beatrice, what's wrong?" Lenora went to her side.

Her cousin passed the paper to her. "'Twas stuck on the back of the drawer." She placed her hands over her mouth and began to rock back and forth.

Dread flooded Lenora's body. This paper held some terrible message. She took a deep breath before she allowed her eyes to focus on the letter. Halfway down the page she realized what it meant. All the blood siphoned from her face and she felt screams of anger and confusion at the back of her throat, but she couldn't make a sound.

Beatrice lowered her hands and held them palms together. Her lips moved in a silent appeal for divine help. "He lied to us all. This is your marriage contract, isn't it?"

"Aye, my father's signature is at the bottom as well as Roen's." She felt distant, like an observer in her own body.

"How could this happen?"

"Father must have been too ill to notice the changes and signed a counterfeit agreement after Roen hid the original." She carefully folded the paper and wrapped it in the leather binding.

"Do you think he was alone in this treachery?" Beatrice asked.

Lenora's shoulders sank. "Nay, how could he be? He needed help to procure the counterfeit."

Large tears rolled down Beatrice's cheeks. "Hamlin?"

"He is his second in command, privy to all his secrets."

The blond girl rolled over on the bed and released the dam of tears and sorrow. After a few moments, more in control, she wiped her face with the edge of her apron. "What are we going to do?"

Lenora rose and grabbed the drawer from the floor. "First, we are going to put this back where it was. I don't want any of them to know we've found their secret."

Beatrice helped her to stuff the letter and drawer back into its proper position. "Now what, Lenora? We need help."

"Patience, Cousin," Lenora advised. "I need time to think. 'Tis not just us to worry about, there's my child, also."

"He wouldn't dare harm your baby."

"I don't know." Torn by conflicting emotion, she suddenly realized that she really didn't know her husband at all, or what he was capable of. "Beatrice, the true contract would enable my child to inherit everything, regardless of the father. His accusations about Geoffrey 'tis just a way for him to use his false contract to steal Woodshadow from my child." She clenched her fists at her side and began to pace the floor.

"But your child is to inherit in both contracts." Beatrice looked confused at her cousin's fear.

"The false document gives Woodshadow to Roen's—" she stressed her husband's name "—and my child. By putting a shadow of doubt over the baby's parentage, he can use his contract to nullify the child's rightful inheritance."

"Then 'tis useless for me to ever go to him and tell the truth about you and Geoffrey. He would still discount my story." Beatrice rose from the bed to stand near her. "We must get a message to the king. Expose Roen for the criminal he is."

Lenora tapped her foot and threw up her arms. "If we expose his duplicity, my baby may still be in jeopardy, for then we would become the wards of the king. As his wards, he would have control over us completely. Henry and Roen are very close. I'm a woman with a child, Roen is a tested warrior to whom the king owes much. How do I know he won't side with Roen?"

She took up her pacing again, thinking aloud. "If I choose to keep silent, pretend not to know the true nature of my father's contract, then Roen may let me and my baby leave. Neither Henry nor Roen could touch me at Eleanor's court in Aquitaine. I am in favor with the queen and she could protect me."

"You would give up your home and child's birthright?" her cousin asked.

Lenora straightened her back and took a breath. "Aye, if it means my child will be safe. Beatrice, you must keep silent of this. Tell no one, understand?"

The other girl protested, "You can't do this alone. You need help."

"I'll figure something out." She turned from her cousin. What didn't make sense was why Roen had kept the original contract, or had her father suspected the act and hidden it himself? If that was the case, maybe Roen had more to do with her father's disappearance than he claimed. Icy fear twisted around her heart, freezing the embers of her love. Was Roen guilty? Could he be a murderer? Her love told her nay, yet the facts pointed otherwise. She steeled herself to be strong and prayed she wouldn't break down and cry.

Beatrice nodded to reassure her cousin, but for once, she didn't think Lenora's wits were enough. Nay, they needed help immediately and she knew where to look for it. She only prayed he would listen to her regardless of how he felt about her.

Chapter Twenty-One

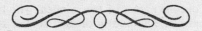

Men rushed past her on the steps, weapons in hand. Lenora leaned over the wooden railing to better hear the exchange between the assembled knights below her. Only bits of dialogue could be heard over the clanging of swords and shields, but the message became clear. The men were going to battle and all were eager to see action.

With her eyes, she hunted through the mob of warriors for Roen. Her husband, surrounded by knights, leaned over a map-covered table in the middle of the great hall. She studied him as she had for the past seven nights. This morning the truth became no clearer. His duplicity about the contracts remained a mystery. Why the heartless deception?

"How many men did you see, Winton?" Roen interrogated a stranger in the middle of the great hall.

"I counted about fifty, Lord Roen," Winton answered, and squirmed in his infantryman's uniform. The hauberk stifled the soldier's movements across his shoulders and cut into his mid-section. With distaste, Lenora noted its poor condition. Between the rust and rips, it offered little protection in battle.

"Only fifty? We'll have short work today," Hamlin boasted.

The men cheered their agreement. Roen silenced them with a wave of his hand. "Aye, but if we don't move fast and decisively, a small band could ruin Lord Cyril's harvest and thus starve his people for the winter."

Lenora placed her hand over her heart. Her vassal, Lord Cyril, under siege! That paragon of readiness and perfection? He was the most meticulous individual she had ever met. He drove her and her father daft with his preciseness. His men stood for inspection every week. Lord Cyril looked at every weapon and battle instrument and demanded it be in perfect order. Her vassal might be in trouble, but this man "Winton" could not be from his troops.

The soldier turned toward her, his droopy mustache glistening from perfumed wax and grease. His smile showed a large gap where his front tooth should have been. Lenora tried to shake off her uneasiness but couldn't.

Roen called out the names of several men, who began to assemble their patrols. The poorly dressed soldier stood transfixed, staring at her.

Her husband looked at Winton and followed his gaze to her. "Winton, fill these men in on the details." His shoulder knocked the messenger aside when he brushed past. She watched Roen approach her, his eyes never leaving her own.

Her guard skipped down the stairs to meet him. "Lord Roen, may I accompany them?"

"Nay, Raymond, your duty is here," Roen answered.

The young boy's face fell. Her heart went out to him. "Roen, let the boy have his first taste of battle. It should be a small skirmish and not last long." Raymond's face lit with excitement. He nodded like a puppet on a string.

"He's here to protect you," Roen countered.

Her anger got the best of her good intentions. "For my protection? I did not know I needed protection in my own demesne. Do you fear Alyse will do me in with her spoon?"

She saw Raymond's smile invert to a frown while he slunk past the couple and down the stairs. He took up his station at the bottom amid the eagerly waiting knights.

Roen felt hard-pressed not to discipline his wife's rudeness in front of his men, but more important matters commanded his attention now. A vassal had sent a request for help, and honor demanded he answer. "I have to leave, immediately," he informed her, and wondered how she took the news. With worry or joy?

"I know." She licked her lips and tilted her chin up. "When will you be back?"

Her moist red lips commanded his attention now. A longing to feel her mouth on his own consumed him. The musky smell of her body called to him like an ancient Greek siren. He looked at the fullness of her breasts, the rounding of her hips and abdomen. Her face radiated a Madonna-like serenity. The rush of desire filled him as always. No matter what he suspected, he still needed her, still wanted to feel her body against his. He couldn't sleep if his arms weren't filled with her lovely curves. Last night while she slept, he had felt the stirring of life in her womb. How much longer would she try to hide it from him? More important, why? He feared he knew the answer.

"When will you be back?" she asked again.

"I don't know."

"Oh." She glanced at the soldier from Lord Cyril's keep. Her fingers drummed on the stair railing and she gnawed her lower lip. "Roen, I don't trust that man, Winton. Are you sure that—"

"First you're rude, and now you doubt my abilities to protect my vassals." Roen could not believe her audacity. If she didn't even respect his ability to protect his vassals, how could she love him? Through clenched teeth he informed her, "Winton brought a missive with him sealed with the Lord Cyril's insignia. Does he look the type to be able to read or write? Nay, he does not."

"Still, there are things that do not feel right."

"Blast you, woman, stick to your kitchen and garden. Leave the battles to me." Roen did an abrupt about-face and left his wife on the stairs. He noticed Winton glance once more toward his wife. "Raymond," he bellowed.

The boy rushed to his side, his eyebrows raised, eyes wide. "You have changed your mind, my lord?"

"Take my wife upstairs, see that she stays there until we leave." The shuffle of Lenora's steps retreated up the stairs, away from him. Despite the noise below, his ears listened until he heard her footsteps on the floor above. He rejoined his men in the hall.

"You should let the boy go." Winton scratched his scruffy chin. "He'll miss all the excitement."

"His duty is here, to guard his mistress," Roen growled, warning the man away from any further interference.

"And what kind of guard is he to be if he never sees battle?" Winton's eyes narrowed. "If he's never wetted his sword on anything but a quintain, how do you know he'll have the nerve when the time comes to really protect your lady?"

"He's a point there, Roen." Hamlin joined in. "Come on, let the boy go. There will be plenty of men left behind to protect the castle."

Roen slammed his fist onto the table. The maps and goblets shook from the tremor. He didn't want to admit in front of this stranger that he didn't trust his own wife or that a traitor might still be within the walls of Woodshadow. Nor did he want the information to get back to Lord Cyril. The vassal might interpret that his wife needed rescue from her own husband. Perhaps a more seasoned knight would be a better choice.

"Fine, he can go. Crandall," he called to a knight seated near the hearth with a bandage wrapped around his leg. "You will stay behind?"

The knight nodded and slapped his thigh. "'Tis on the mend, though stiff. I doubt I could sit a horse for long."

"Then stay in the castle and oversee the guards left behind. Pay careful attention to your lady." The elder knight nodded and eased his body off the hearth, being careful not to put weight on his injured leg.

Roen pointed to his squire. "Run up and tell Raymond to prepare." The squire rushed up the stairs. Moments later, a loud war whoop echoed from the gallery above. Half running, half falling, the boy came down the steps. At the bottom, he pulled himself up short and tried to look dignified. The ear-to-ear grin foiled the attempt. Roen asked his friend, "Are you satisfied now?"

Hamlin gave him a toothy grin. "Aye, and so, I warrant, is Raymond."

"Let's go then, unless you have any more suggestions?" The men turned to the doors.

Hamlin's smile faded. "Just one, though I don't suppose you'll like it."

"What's that?"

"You could climb those stairs and kiss your wife goodbye." Hamlin snaked through the crowd of men to escape any comment Roen might make.

Beatrice entered the hall and nearly ran into Hamlin. He stopped and opened his mouth to speak. The girl turned away and refused to acknowledge him. It gave Roen a secret glee to know that despite all of Hamlin's ready advice, his relationship fared no better. He wondered what his friend had done to cause the girl so much anger.

Roen stopped by the foot of the stairs and considered Hamlin's suggestion. Any battle carried the potential for danger. Not that Roen expected much resistance; still, an unlucky blow and he might never see her again. His foot rested on the first step, his hand on the rail.

"Lord Roen, your charger is chewing up the stableboy." An ugly black-and-blue mark colored the groom's forearm. "We cannot hold him much longer."

Roen sighed. Once Destrier bore the armaments for battle, he demanded action. His charger could easily kill one of the grooms if he didn't calm the beast. Lenora would have to wait. He would have plenty of time to deal with her when he returned.

The sun turned a brilliant shade of orange as it began its slow descent below the treetops of the forest. Lenora watched it until only a tiny arc of light showed. Cool autumn air slipped through the loose weave of her chemise and caused her to shiver. The smell of burning leaves still lingered from the harvest bonfire earlier.

"Lenora, come in from the balcony," Beatrice cajoled. "You'll catch a chill."

She lingered, her eyes focused on the most distant mark beyond the castle gate. Jittery impulses tingled in her fingers. Her intuition warned her Winton was not what he seemed. Deep inside, she knew Roen was in danger.

Her cousin joined her in the tiny space and wrapped a woolen blanket around Lenora's shoulders. "He did not say he would return tonight," her voice warned.

"Aye, he told me nothing, nor would he listen to my qualms." Lenora clutched the ends of the blanket with her hand. The other rested on the balcony rail.

"How can you still care for him?" Beatrice asked.

Lenora tilted back her head and observed the faint light of the night's first star. "I cannot order my heart to undo what it already feels. Love is not an emotion that can be blown out as quickly as a candlewick." She turned to her cousin. "When I look at Roen I see two people. One, the man I love, who I believe, in time, will come to care for me." She paused before continuing. "And the other, the man I fear is guilty of heinous crimes against me and my father."

Goliath leaned the weight of his body against her leg and whined. She scratched his head and murmured, "You miss him, too, don't you?"

Her cousin took her hand and led her from the open air. "I'll stay here with you tonight."

Lenora jumped to sit on the edge of the bed. She crawled on her hands and feet to the pillow bolsters and pulled down the velvet coverlet. "Nay, Cousin. I am very tired and will no doubt fall asleep as soon as I close my eyes."

"Are you sure there is nothing I can do for you?"

Lenora yawned and stretched her arms wide. "Check the kitchen for me. Just before I retired, I ordered the embers kept warm and a leg of meat wrapped, in case they return tonight or early on the morrow."

"I will check again for you." Beatrice paused. "Are you sure you will be all right alone tonight?"

"Of course." Lenora rubbed her sleep-heavy eyes. "If I have need of anything, all I must do is open the door. Servants will be sleeping in the hall and foyer. Tyrus will be at my door."

"Crandall is not pleased with that situation."

Lenora shrugged. "'Tis all that can be done. We've too few knights guarding the keep to remove one just to please this obsession of Roen's. 'Twas bad luck Crandall fell after supper. He cannot be expected to climb the stairs over and over now that he has further damaged his leg. Tyrus is a bright lad. He will see that Crandall is informed of my whereabouts at all times."

A butterflylike movement in her womb caused her to laugh. She waved her hand to Beatrice, who ran to her side. Lenora placed her cousin's hand on her abdomen.

"Ah, 'tis the babe." Beatrice's face lit with surprise and pleasure. Then her smile dimmed. "Does Roen know yet?"

Lenora's glimmer of joy evaporated. "Nay, I've not told him and he has not questioned me. He pays so little attention to me, he does not see the thickening of my body.'' Lenora leaned back on the bed.

"Perhaps a solution to our problem will come soon," Beatrice prophesied. She took the edge of the fur-trimmed cover and tucked it under her cousin's chin.

"Leave the candle." Lenora felt like a child afraid of the dark. She pulled the blankets closer to her.

Beatrice nodded and opened the door. She stepped over the sleeping body of the young servant and closed the door. Lenora sighed deeply and snuggled into the soft mattress of her bed.

Fatigue coated her like heavy dust. Her eyes itched and her head nodded. Eager for the comfort of sleep, she closed her eyes and waited. But the welcome relief of slumber did not come. Tonight, the softness of her bed offered no comfort; it suffocated her.

She kicked the pillows and covers off and sat up in bed. Goliath dragged himself from his position against the wall, then collapsed on top of the pillows.

Lenora drummed her fingers on the mattress and watched the shadows the candlelight cast around the room. Her mind kept replaying scenes of her husband, bloody and wounded, and still not knowing that his child grew in her body. The pounding in her head quickened and she rubbed her temple.

The sound of footsteps reached her. "Roen, is that you?"

She vaulted over the sleeping dog and walked to the door. It only opened a crack when she heard a sleepy voice ask, "Do ye have a need with me, Lady Lenora?"

Tyrus fought to keep a yawn at bay. He looked at her with heavy lids, just thin slices of his eyes showing beneath his lashes. He rubbed his eyes with his fists and sat up on his pallet.

Lenora looked down the hall. No footsteps heralded her husband's return. "Nay, Tyrus, I thought I heard the lord return. I'm having trouble sleeping tonight is all."

The boy nodded. "Tea. I'll get ye a cup of chamomile tea. That should do the trick." He rose and trudged away, leaning on the wall to support his sleepy body.

Lenora dragged a woolen blanket from the bed, trailed it behind her and headed for the balcony. The moon hung low in the night sky. Its softer glow illuminated dark shapes moving about the keep. Torches burned in isolated spots. Crickets chimed a natural lullaby. She wrapped her blanket around her and folded her legs under her. Goliath sauntered over from his pillows to lie beside her, his head in her lap.

The fresh air muffled the pounding of her head; the evening concert erased the scenes in her mind. She leaned against the wall, hard and stiff against her back. Her eyelids drifted up and down, like the surf of the sea. Finally, the heavy weight of her lids forced her to shut her eyes.

Lenora jerked herself from sleep. Something had struck her! Her eyes flew open. She couldn't see, everything looked gray. Her hands reached out and touched coarse fur.

"Goliath!" She pushed him away with her hand. He sprang forward, growled deep in his throat and crouched for an attack. "Goliath, what is it?"

She heard the rustle of the rushes on the floor of the bedroom. Goliath leapt into the air and stalked the sound. His growling changed into a snarl. Lenora called him back. "Goliath, come here." He chose this time not to listen.

She crept forward into the room, toward the glow of the low fire in the hearth. Goliath's protective growl came from the far wall, the one the bed rested against. She could make out his shape and heard his nails scraping down the wall, digging at the corner.

"Come here, boy." The animal jumped up and placed his front feet on the wall. He whined, then growled and sniffed the wall. Dropping to all fours, he inspected the corner with his nose. After a few reluctant steps, the dog looked back at the wall. He continued to watch behind him until he reached his mistress.

"What is it? What has you so upset?" She could feel the tension in the dog's body. His square head rotated back and forth, his ears perked for any sound. His nervousness flared in her. What had him so upset? Her heart pounded in her chest. Every shadow appeared to be a demon or specter. Then the image melted into harmless darkness. Goliath positioned himself between her and the far corner of the room.

A tiny push came from her womb. The baby flip-flopped around then quieted. Her panic had affected the baby; she must calm herself. The mug on the table reminded her of her request. Tyrus must have brought in the tea while she slept on the balcony. She raised the cup to her lips. Goliath whipped his head around and snarled. His sharp canine teeth bared, he came toward her.

Uncertain of the madness that possessed her pet, she froze, afraid to move. He sprang at her, knocking her aside, and then she saw it. Gleaming red eyes shone from under the table. She threw the cup at the shining eyes and heard it thud against the black body. The rat opened its mouth, displaying long, yellow teeth.

Larger than most cats, it slunk out from under the table. She gripped her dog's collar and yanked him away. Rat bites always caused infection and she didn't want to risk Goliath's health. The rodent scurried along the wall, and she could still see the hellish glow of its eyes when it paused to look at her. It disappeared into the shadows beneath her bed. From a safe distance, she strained to make out its shape under the bed. Nothing. No eyes gleamed back, no shadow moved.

She gave her bodyguard a squeeze. Goliath licked her face with his wet tongue. "Good boy. Good boy." She wondered where the rodent had come from. Rats that size were usually found only in the cesspools or in the most unused parts of the castle.

"I don't think I would rest easy in my bed knowing that creature lies beneath it," she said to Goliath, scratching his ears. "If we don't disturb it, then perhaps it will not move." She gripped the collar and led her dog back to the balcony. "'Twill only be a few hours until the household begins to awaken. Come, Goliath, we will watch the sunrise, and in the morning we will request a cat. A very large cat to run off our unwelcome visitor." She frowned with regret. The empty tea mug lay on its side, the contents in a puddle that leached down into the rushes. "Too bad about the tea. 'Twould help calm my nerves." She'd not disturb Tyrus again. In a few hours she'd sneak down to the kitchen and get her own cup.

Roen tossed and turned on the ground. He rolled over on his side and felt a rock jut into his hip. His fingers dug beneath him and he fished out the stone. That idiot of a squire must have laid his bed on a field of rocks. Another jab in the leg and Roen rested on his elbow, ready to move to another part of the camp.

The moonlight softened the shapes of the men around him into dark, indiscernible mounds. A thick stand of forest encircled the camp. From it came the sounds of the night—the call of an owl, the occasional rustle of a deer. One of his night watchmen stood away from the fire, not allowing its brightness to blind him in the dark.

Roen looked at the moon and judged hours still stood between night and the first break of day. The silver light of the moon gleamed through the bramble surrounding the camp. His eye caught a flash of silver amid the darkness. A cloud passed over the moon and blotted out its light. When the shadow passed, the glint of steel returned. Someone waited in the woods, someone with weapons drawn.

If he approached the sentry, it might warn off the attackers and Roen wanted to know who plotted against him. He threw the stone in his hand at the mound of blankets next to him. Hamlin's curly head peeked from beneath the folds. Roen placed his finger to his lips, commanding silence. With gestures, he pointed out the danger. His friend nodded. Both men reached for their daggers and rolled away from their pallets. They traveled in opposite directions.

On bent knees, Roen ran to a bush and hid in its shadow. He waited until a hunched-over form materialized from the woods. The assailant darted from tree to tree, heading for the back of the watchman. A flick of the wrist and the dagger in Roen's hand plunged into the man's back. He fell, without a cry, to the ground.

Hamlin caught Roen's attention with a wave. The second in command cocked his head to one side and pointed to his ear. Roen listened, then made out the sounds of movement in the woods encircling them.

Across the camp, Hamlin belly-crawled to the mound of blankets nearest him and whispered to the man within. Roen motioned the night guard to lie down and pretend to be wounded. Hamlin traveled to the next mound, and then the next. Roen crept back to his blankets and withdrew his broadsword. Soon, his knights waited in their blankets, their swords at their sides, for his call.

Figures loomed from behind the trees. Dressed in old leather tunics and frayed woolens, the bandits entered the camp confident of victory. Too confident, as if they knew there would be no guard. Roen recalled Lenora's suspicion of Winton. Saints' blood, he should have listened to her. What had she seen that he hadn't? The coming battle took on new connotations; he had more to lose than just his life. The thought of never seeing his wife again made him grip the handle of his sword with vengeance.

Hamlin waited on the opposite side of the camp for his signal. Like a spider awaiting his prey, Roen let the would-be ambushers enter his camp.

"To arms!" Roen stepped forward and slashed at the torso of one of the bandits. Blood sprayed across his face and tunic. His knights responded immediately, and within seconds Roen heard the sounds of clashing steel. The cries of dying men and the acrid smell of blood assaulted his senses.

The advantage of surprise lost to them, the assailants tried to make for the safety of the darkness. Roen's knights chased them down, their training and weapons making short work of their adversaries. "I want one alive," Roen ordered. His men raced to capture the disappearing men.

Roen reached over to the dead man at his feet and examined the body. From the corpse's belt he pulled a heavy bag, and poured its contents onto the chest of its owner. Ten gold coins landed like decorations down the man's tunic. "Check the other bodies." Roen moved to the next mangled body on the ground.

This one had a bag hidden under his shirt, and the next had one dangling from a belt. He returned to Hamlin and asked, "These all have heavy purses, what of yours?"

Hamlin nodded. "Aye, the same. A large piece of coin for such a motley crew. Life as a bandit must be better than I was led to believe."

His men began to reappear from the woods. Roen resheathed his sword and called out, "Earnst, did you get one alive?"

The knight shook his dark beard and laughed. "Nay, not I, but Raymond managed to have a good hunt."

Near the fire, Raymond held the tip of his sword against the spine of Lord Cyril's messenger. Shed of his hauberk, he wore the leather tunic and woolens of the bandits. Self-recrimination stabbed at his conscience. Lenora had seen through his disguise.

"Who hired you?" Roen demanded. He faced Winton and controlled the desire to close his fists around the man's throat.

Winton spread his hands wide in supplication. "The boy here's made a mistake, Lord Roen." The man smiled. "These young ones are just too eager. I was a-chasin' those men and the boy mistook me for the wrong side."

Roen grabbed the leather pouch that weighed down one side of his prisoner's belt. He ripped open the drawstring with his dagger and let the coins fall to the ground. Twelve coins shone in the firelight. "I take it you took more for yourself since you had the harder job of luring us here for the ambush." His fist clenched the man's neckline and he ordered, "Tell me who paid you."

Raymond pressed his sword into the base of Winton's neck, until blood trickled down and seeped under his leathers. Still, Winton wore a cocky smile. "Ye won't kill me. I'm the only one with the answers ye want, and for a price I'll tell ye."

Roen's dagger slashed down Winton's face. He jerked his head back but not before Roen held half of the man's mustache in his hand. "I won't kill you." He dropped the clump of hair and wiped his hand of the grease on his prisoner's sleeve. "But that doesn't mean I won't make it so you wished you were dead." The needlelike tip of the dagger traced lightly around the base of the man's ear. "I could chop you up into pieces. Little ones first, an ear, a few fingers at a time. Maybe an eye or—" he lowered the tip to circle the man's genitalia "—other parts. When I run out of small pieces, I'll start with bigger ones, like your arms and legs."

Winton started to sweat. He moved his fingers and shuffled his feet back and forth. "Mind ye, 'twas nothing personal. Just a job, and I was paid well for it. This'll go bad on my reputation."

"I think I'll start with your nose first." Roen advanced and squeezed Winton's nose between two knuckles.

"Wait, wait, I'll tell ye." Roen withdrew his crushing grip on the man. Winton rubbed the tip of his nose. "Don't know 'is name." He clamped his hand over his nose when Roen growled. "In me business, I don't ask names. 'E were a lord, had rich clothes, but not like your'n. They was like they had been fine once, but were worn out now. An' 'is cloak—" Winton withdrew his hand "—the corner were torn off."

Roen's heart stopped beating. White points of anger appeared in his vision. He found Hamlin's face in the crowd of men. Sir Edmund's demon haunted them still, but why? That danger should have been dispelled with Lenora's marriage. Why did the villain reappear now, after so many months of peace?

"Did you really think to kill a band of knights?" Raymond asked, his voice showing how incredible he thought the act.

"Nay, not all. We were to sneak in and kill only the lord here and that one." He pointed to Hamlin.

Roen narrowed his eyes. "Why then draw out so many men with us?"

"I got paid extra if I could pull out a troop of men from your castle. And 'im especially." This time he threw back his thumb and pointed at Raymond. "I was to get three extra coins if I kept the lot of ye away from the castle for the night."

Roen looked at the sky. The darkness of night had lessened into the lighter shades of morning. He ran for his horse, Hamlin at his side. "Earnst, drop our prisoner at Bridgeton. Raymond, you stay with Winton and guard him well. The rest, follow when you can." He vaulted onto the bare back of his charger.

"Roen, you can't ride all the way back to Woodshadow bareback!" Hamlin shouted. "Wait for us."

"I can't." He dug his heels into the animal's belly and set off at a gallop. "Lenora." The wind tore the name from his lips and whipped it away. He prayed that when he arrived home her spirit would not be the same, torn and whipped from her lifeless body.

Chapter Twenty-Two

Grays and pinks feathered the early dawn sky when Roen ordered the castle gate opened. Each clink of the chain represented time lost in reaching his wife. The gate creaked up foot by foot. He didn't wait for the men to tie it off before he spurred his horse forward, through clutches of nesting chickens and sleeping serfs.

Destrier skidded to a stop in front of the forebuilding. Roen jumped from his back and entered the keep. Servants, still hazy from sleep, blinked their eyes and started to rush to their morning duties. On a bench near the table, Crandall scratched himself in sleep.

"What are you doing here?" Roen bellowed as he towered over the wounded man.

"Fell down the stairs," Crandall began.

Not waiting for the knight's excuses, Roen bolted for the stairs and climbed three steps at a time. Outside his door, he nearly tripped over the sleeping body of Tyrus as he entered his chamber.

The light of morning streamed in. Roen raced to the bed and threw back the covers. Empty! His heart ached with despair. Next to the bed, a dark crimson pool stained the floor. He knelt and reached out a trembling hand to touch it. It came back red, and the smell of blood tainted his fingers.

A stab of anguish buried itself in his heart. Nora, what have I done? Raw, primitive grief overwhelmed him. He sat back on his heels, his fist clenched at his chest, and lowered his head. A shudder ran along his body and lodged in his heart. Something brushed his arm, and he lifted his head. Tyrus stood at his side.

"Milord, she's asleep on the balcony." The boy pointed to a bundle of cloth reclining against the outside rail. "And I needs to tell ye . . ."

Roen staggered to his feet and forgot the boy. He drew closer, and the mound started to writhe. Goliath's head sprang up from under the blanket. The dog's ears swiveled toward him and he could hear the steady thump of the animal's tail on the floor.

"Come, Goliath," Roen coaxed. The dog didn't move, but whined. Fear spread through his body like a fever. He flexed his hand several times before he could bring himself to pull back the blankets. Had her pain been brief? It made no matter to him. He vowed that her killers would suffer hours for every minute of pain his wife had endured.

The blankets unfolded like a spring rosebud. Lenora lay in her cocoon, enveloped by her red gold hair. Remorse clawed at the pit of his gut and he longed to kiss the sprinkle of freckles across her pale skin. With a tenderness he should have showed her in life, Roen knelt to kiss her cold cheek.

His eyes rested on her chest. It rose and fell. She lived. He combed back her silky tresses and delighted in the warmth of her cheek. The dark fringe of her lashes fluttered but she did not wake. Roen heard his own release of air. He had not realized he held his breath until now. Goliath tried to rise, whined, then replaced his head in his mistress's lap.

"Are you injured?" Roen's hand moved down the dog's head. His hand came in contact with Lenora's, her fingers firmly clamped on her pet's collar. Gingerly, he released each of her fingers and freed the animal. Goliath licked his master's hand and walked forward, extending a leg with every step. The dog's bones popped and cracked into place as he headed for the other side of the room.

"Goliath?" Lenora yawned and reached out her hand. She caught hold of Roen's wrist and patted it. "Good boy, lie still." She snuggled back into the covers.

The sound of her voice brought a lump to his chest. He gathered her up in his arms and rubbed his chin on the top of her hair. Her arms slipped around his neck and she nuzzled his throat. A kittenlike yawn, and then she resumed her sleep.

His thumb stroked the side of her cheek. "Nora, what am I to do with you?" he asked under his breath. The rest of the world ceased to exist for him; he wanted to hold on to this moment and his wife forever. He kissed her face and eyelids, the tip of her nose and the spot where one curl tumbled over her eyes.

"Roen?" Her voice sounded wispy, like a summer breeze.

"Aye, love." The word formed on his lips so effortlessly. He both rejoiced and ached from the release. His Nora lived, breathed and spoke. The long dark ride had ended at last.

"I wasn't waiting up for you, you know." She yawned again.

"Nay, I would not think so." His throat constricted with emotion and he wrapped his arms around her tighter. Rocking her like a baby in his arms, he tried to lull her back to sleep.

"'Twas the bed, I could not sleep." Her nose snuggled beneath his chin. "Too big and empty." She yawned while she spoke. He could barely make out her words. "And soft, 'twas much too soft. Not anything like you." Her cheek rubbed against his chest and her head nodded forward. He heard the deep breaths of slumber.

Roen carried his precious bundle to their bed, where she rolled from his arms. A frown creased Lenora's moist lips, but one gentle kiss smoothed it away. Sitting next to his wife while she rested, he reached out his hand then stopped several times before he could place it on her womb. The life within remained, a fortress wall to separate them. As unbreachable as the bailey wall that surrounded Woodshadow. With a slow, deliberate action, he removed his hand. It traveled to her hip, across the seductive arc of her backside and down her thigh.

"She is well?" Hamlin whispered from the door.

Roen rubbed his fingers together. Heat still radiated in them, Lenora's heat. Making a loose fist, he brought it to his lips. After a silent prayer of thanks, Roen joined Hamlin at the door. Goliath scratched the wall at the corner of the room.

"Aye, it seems so. Though I don't know why she slept on the balcony." He led his friend to the stain on the floor. "And this is here."

Hamlin bent down on one knee. "'Tis blood." The dog sat and faced the wall. His whine increased to a bark.

"Quiet, dog," Roen commanded, "You'll wake your mistress."

Goliath did not comply. Roen stretched out his long arms and grabbed the dog's muzzle. Soft murmuring came from the bed, then returned to the gentle sound of restful sleep. The animal broke free and scratched at the corner again.

"I think I see what has distressed your pet." Hamlin peered under the bed. Roen joined his friend and peeked under the bed. The bark diminished to a low whine.

A gigantic rat lay in a pool of coagulated blood. The beast's mouth was parted in a hideous death grin. Blood seeped from its mouth and ears. A cup, its contents mixed with the rat's blood, lay next to it. The two knights pulled the rushes forward, drawing the dead rodent closer.

A long, plaintive howl came from the corner of the room. His master stormed over to quiet the animal. "Stars, I'll silence you for good if you're not quiet!" Lenora rolled over in the bed, obviously exhausted.

"I wonder what killed it so horribly?" Hamlin nudged the body of the rat with the toe of his boot.

"God's wound, Hamlin." Roen pointed to the mug on the floor. "Don't touch that, and keep the dog from it. I suspect 'tis poison. Look here at what's lodged in the wall."

His friend kicked the mug over toward the carcass. He joined Roen in the corner of the room and helped to push back the muscular dog from the wall. A dark strip of woolen material stuck out from between the wall and floor. The edge frayed into threads by Goliath's claws.

"Help me." Pushing against the stones near the cloth, Roen tested his theory. Nothing happened. "My first audience with Sir Edmund was in this room. He mentioned that a secret passage led into the chamber." Each block bore the knights' inspection until a sharp click broke the quiet of their concentration. The sound of a rope swinging with a heavy load groaned from behind the stone bricks, then a section of wall popped forward.

"Our quarry knows this place better than we do." The thought shrouded Roen with dread. Would his sword arm be strong enough to guard Lenora from the traitor's knowledge of Woodshadow's secrets?

Dust and a musty smell permeated the darkness. Taking a few steps forward, he heard the scurry of feet all around him. The dim light that filtered in illuminated a multitude of gleaming red eyes.

A dark cloak draped across the floor. He picked it up and shook it violently. Roaches and millipedes spilled out. Withdrawing from the foul-smelling passage with the cloak, he and Hamlin resealed the bedchamber.

The two knights moved with utmost silence into the hall, filled now with servants, their ears glued to the stone wall outside the master's chamber. For one long minute no one moved. The snooping serfs jumped and resumed their work when the Lord of Woodshadow cast them an angry scowl. All of them bustled about but leaned their heads toward him, anxious to hear a snippet of gossip.

Wrapping the cloak around his arm, Roen led his second in command to the wardrobe. The boy, Tyrus, pulled at his arm. "Milord, I have a need to speak with ye."

"Not now, boy." Yanking his arm free, Roen ordered, "This door stays open. Do you hear me?" The lad nodded. "You stay here in the doorway. Your mistress is to sleep until she wakes. No one goes in that room. And it will be quiet."

"Aye, milord, but I still—"

The lad's words fell on thick wood as Hamlin followed Roen into the small, adjoining wardrobe and shut the door. Roen dropped the cloak onto the back of a chair to assess it.

A rich dark wool made up the garment. Several rips and tears, mended with neat, fine stitches, showed long use. Two gold serpents with small garnet eyes form the garment's clasp. It hung at a tilted angle, the sharp pin in the back bent and twisted.

Roen took the edge of the cloak and ran the material through his hands. The frayed corner showed a rip where it had caught in the passage door. The other end had the corner ripped away. From his pocket he pulled the bit of cloth found on the scaffolding. It fit the cloak and the garment fit the description of the man who had hired the thugs to waylay him.

"'Tis the same." Hamlin sat in a chair and rested his chin on his elbow. "Why? Why has the man returned, and what good would it do to kill your wife now?"

Stuffing the cloak into his private chest, Roen speculated, "Perhaps he did not intend to kill her." His companion's eyebrows wrinkled together. Logic dictated Roen's words. "The rat died of the drink, but 'tis a much smaller creature. I think our man wanted another result, for Lenora's baby to be aborted."

"But who would stand to gain from such a loss?"

Roen bit the tip of his tongue to keep from blasting out the obvious answer.

Hamlin rose from the chair. "Nay, Roen, I cannot believe it. Beatrice is Lenora's friend. She'd not conspire in a crime like this."

"She's one of the few that know my wife has conceived. If Lenora dies with no heir, she'd stand to gain."

"But you forget, no one, save us, knows that. Everyone thinks you get all in your marriage. Beatrice could not know the truth. Even you do not know the location of the real contract," Hamlin countered.

Roen started to pace up and down the room, his hands clasped behind his back. "What piece of this puzzle do I not possess?" He strode from one side of the room to the other. Finally, he stopped, his fists on his hips. "Get Sir Edmund's man. I think Tom needs to be advised of these new complications."

"Aye, I'll bring him here straightaway." Hamlin exited the room.

Yelling down the hall, Roen barked a command. "Find me the person who brought Lenora tea last night and send up an able-bodied man and a chambermaid."

He traveled back down the hall to his chamber. Tyrus leaned on the doorway, his back against the frame. He stood at attention when Roen crossed the threshold.

"Milord, now can I talk with ye?" The boy's voice sounded tired and slightly irritated.

"Later." A quick glance at his wife put him at ease. She rested, unaware of the danger the night had brought to her.

"Need a cat," her voice mumbled on. "Red eyes...big cat."

So the rat had been the reason for the restless night on the cold floor. A smile creased his lips and he kissed her cheek, his thumb massaging the kiss into her skin. When had this woman woven herself into his heart? His fingers played through her coppery tresses. Roen lifted his hand and let the strands of hair fall through his fingers. Whatever riches he might gain in his lifetime, none could compare to the wealth that lay in his bed now.

Tyrus nudged his shoulder. "Lord Hamlin's in the hall with Tom," the boy whispered in his ear. "And when you've time, I need . . ."

Lenora's life hinged on the end of this mystery. Without hesitation, he led the men back to the wardrobe. A beefy man stood outside the door with a large woman.

"You." He pointed to the maid. "After my wife is moved to another room, all the rushes in my bedchamber are to be changed, today. Burn the old ones. Don't give them to anyone else to use, understand?" The woman nodded, grabbed a bucket on the floor next to her and exited in the direction of his room.

"My wife's trunks are to be moved to another room. I'll tell you which one later. Right now, get them out of my room." The man's chin dropped, and he made a *tsking* noise with his lips. Roen paid it no heed. "And one more thing, get me the stonemason." He opened the door and beckoned Hamlin and the stablekeeper in.

"Eh, now. What's a-goin' on 'ere?" Tom looked from one man to the other.

"I need to know where the original marriage contract is." Roen did not request, he ordered.

"Why, 'tis safe enough, I know for a fact."

"How? Have you seen it recently?"

The man crowed. "That I have. Now tell me what's goin' on?"

Roen sighed. "There's been an attempt on Lenora's life."

"As well as my own and Roen's," Hamlin chimed in.

The grizzled face paled beneath the stubble. Tom's eyes lost their lively gleam. "Can't be. It just can't be."

"Well, 'tis. Last night someone used a secret passage to sneak into our room and tried to poison her. Only by God's intervention, certainly not mine, was she spared.'' Roen combed his fingers through his hair. "No one, save we three, knows the truth of my marriage contract. Who else might know?''

Tom shook his head, his shoulders sagging. "Nay, the secret is kept. But how would anyone know about that passageway? Even your lady is not aware of it. Only Sir Edmund, I and his seneschal used it."

"Sir Hywel knew of it." Hamlin clamped his hand to his forehead. "The man is daft. He could have told anyone about it and not remembered doing so."

Roen gritted his teeth to keep from screaming out his frustration. A knock came at the door. He answered it and Tyrus stepped in.

"Is my wife awake yet?"

"Aye, Lord Roen. That talk I said I was needin'—" Tyrus began.

"Later. I must speak with my wife." He turned to the men. "Both of you, find me the person who brought Lenora her tea last night. Maybe we can get some answers from him."

"But, sire, that was me." Tyrus's words stopped Roen dead in his tracks. "Well, it were supposed to be me, but it weren't." The lad scratched his head and grew thoughtful.

"Make sense, boy." Roen heard the strain of the night in his voice.

Tyrus pulled out two apples from his pocket and held them out to Roen. "Lady Lenora, she asked me for some tea. When I ran to the kitchen, I remember I ain't checked her horses like you asked me to. I found these in the bottom of the hay bag. 'Tis what I been tryin' to show ye since ye arrived."

The shiny red objects appeared normal; Roen waited for the boy to explain.

"Smell 'em." Tyrus pushed the apples up toward his lord's face. The pungent odor made Roen grimace.

"They're bad, but they don't look bad. Somethin's in 'em, and if'n it makes 'em stink like that, they can't be good for the horses."

"You're right, Tyrus, but what of the tea?" Roen tossed the apples to Tom, who dropped them into a leather pouch at his waist.

"By the time I got back, I peeked into the room, and thought she was a-sleepin' in the bed. I didn't see no cause to wake her for tea to help her to sleep when she was already a-sleepin'." The boy looked at him, clearly expecting him to agree with his logic.

"Aye, but you saw no drink at the table?"

"I did not notice."

Roen sighed and waved the boy off. "Thank you, Tyrus. Go tell your mistress I'll be with her shortly." The boy ran off to do his bidding.

Roen looked at Hamlin. "When will the rest of our men be here?"

"Anytime now. I told them to travel in groups of ten and to take a different way home."

"Good. When they arrive, I want three men at Lenora's door at all times. None of hers. We don't know which of them we can trust." He turned to the stablekeeper. "Tom, which room here is the most secure? No secret way to enter or leave."

"There are several, but I'd say the small inner room across from your chamber 'twould be best. The hall runs straight. Your men would have a clear view of the foyer and can see below by walking a few steps to the upper walk."

"Then that's where I intend to move Lenora until we unravel this." He sighed and rubbed his temple. "That room's more like a cell than a bedchamber. I suppose she's not going to take the move well."

"Will you tell her the truth of the problem?" Tom asked.

Roen shook his head. "Nay, even if she would believe me, my Nora is not one to run and hide. Right now, my first priority is to keep her safe. Tom, find Fenton and have Lenora's things transferred to the sewing room."

He left to seek out his wife and prayed somehow he would be able to sort out all the clues. Today he had discovered he cared more deeply than he would like for his wife, and how that had happened still remained a mystery to him. He had a lifetime to discover how, but only if he found out the identity of Lenora's attacker.

Tom climbed the steps to the loft above the stable. "Are ye here, Cousin?"

"Aye, here I am, Tom," a voice called from the shadows.

Tom sat down in the hay next to Cervin. "We've got trouble. Your plan ain't a-workin'."

"What's happened?"

" 'E's back again, only this time 'e's after both the lord and the mistress."

"Is Lenora all right?"

"Aye, this time, but it were just luck that saved her. We got to go and tell them the truth." Tom tugged on Cervin's sleeve.

The man rose, and the cloth around his head fell to his shoulders. Red gold hair shone in the light. He started for the steps, then stopped and put his hand to his heart. His breath came out in tight gasps. "Confound it, another attack."

Tom supported the weaker man. "Sir Edmund, ye have to relax. 'Twill make it pass all the sooner and then ye'll be yer old self once again."

Clutching Tom's elbow, he took a deep breath. The seizure passed, leaving him drained. Sir Edmund cursed again the poison that had so weakened his heart.

Tom ran and retrieved an old horse blanket and laid it on the straw for his lord. "Rest a bit, milord. Your girl is safe enough and that husband you picked for her will see she don't move for now."

Tom patted the resting man's hand. His bones ached and his feet hurt, sure signs that things were to get much worse before they got better.

Chapter Twenty-Three

"Fenton, what are you doing?" Lenora demanded. Her foggy mind tussled to regain her senses. The insides of her eyelids scratched her eyes and she felt drowsy, despite the night's sleep.

The burly man hefted her trunk onto his shoulder and grunted. "Not my doin', Lady Lenora, 'tis the lord's orders. I'm to move your things to the room across the hall."

"Which room?" She twisted her hair into a more manageable braid and used a bit of lace to tie it back.

Fenton gulped several times, his adam's apple bobbing up and down. "The little one, across from the solarium." He backed out of the room quickly. "Remember now, I had nothin' to do with it."

Heavens, how many hours had she suffered in the tiny room under her aunt's tutelage? Why would Roen order her moved there? She pulled a thin blanket around her and peeked down the hall. Goliath greeted her with a cheerful bark, placed his front paws on her shoulders and washed her face with his wet tongue.

"Down, Goliath." The dog trotted from the room in search of breakfast. Nay, by the light of day, that hour had passed some time ago. Heavens, how long had she slept? When had Roen returned to the keep? She took a step out in the hall.

"Back inside, Lady Lenora. You're not to leave your room," Crandall warned. The knight dragged his wounded leg and posted himself just outside her door. His voice sounded raspy and dry. "And leave the door open."

Her hand covered her mouth and bile rose in her throat. This morning she did not blame her condition for the nausea. The fullness of her body had finally betrayed her to Roen. He intended to make her a prisoner. She wanted to collapse on the floor and cry but fought the weakness. Think. There must be some way to spare her child and herself.

Fenton returned and hefted another trunk onto his back. He gave her an apologetic shrug, then shuffled out the door. Beatrice paused to let the servant leave before she entered.

Lenora rushed into her cousin's arms and whispered in her ear. "I am in sore need of a friend now." They walked to the balcony to escape the eavesdroppers in the hall.

"He knows about the baby." Lenora spoke low and kept her eyes on the doorway. Crandall's back rested on the open door of her room but he did not appear to be interested in her conversation. She whispered to her cousin, "Roen intends to move me to the sewing room. He cannot even abide sleeping in the same room with me any longer." The flicker of love in her heart dampened. The thought that Roen might one day accept her and their child evaporated.

"Have faith, Cousin. I have found us help." Beatrice smiled through the tears in her eyes.

"How? Who?" Lenora asked.

The blond girl drew close, her voice barely able to suppress her hope. "Geoffrey." She put a finger to Lenora's opened mouth. "Sh, I got word to him of your peril." From her sleeve she pulled a bit of paper. "I found this in the rose garden last night before I retired."

Lenora put her back to the door and unfolded the missive. Remorse stabbed at her heart. "He writes he has the proof I seek about Roen. All I need do is reach the woods and he will find me." Lifting her face to meet her cousin's gaze, she asked, "But, proof of his guilt or innocence? He does not say."

"Can you still dream of a life with this man, even now as he orders you from his sight?" Beatrice shook her head in dismay. "Have you forgotten his treachery? Lenora, he's probably responsible for your father's death. If you won't think of yourself, then think of your child. Can you risk your baby's life on a hope?"

Lenora pressed both hands to her eyes. "Nay, I must put aside my heart's foolish wishes." Her hands lowered. "But how can I escape this room? There's a guard outside my door. I wish I could crawl back in bed and sleep till this whole episode was resolved." Her fist dropped and an idea blossomed. She grabbed Beatrice's hand and rushed to the bed.

"Watch the door. Make sure Crandall does not look in." Lenora grabbed the silk pillows from the floor and formed a long bolster. She flipped the heavy blankets back over and chopped at the pillows until satisfied with the shape. Racing over to the last of her chests, she threw open the top. "Listen, there's not much time. All must be prepared before Fenton returns."

"There is a visitor to see you, Lord Roen," the ewerer informed him.

"Later." Roen strode down the hall to his room.

Crandall stood at attention by the door. He favored his left leg. "She's with the other one, Lady Beatrice."

Roen entered, the dog at his heels. The animal headed for the bed, then veered off to sniff at a trunk. The rushes remained unchanged and the brown red stain near the bed caused his heart to miss a beat.

Beatrice snapped the curtains around the bed closed and met him halfway. "Lord Roen." She stopped him before he could reach Lenora. "Your wife is ill. She's taken to her bed."

"Ill? She's not lost the child, has she?" An icy fear gripped him. Maybe she had sipped the tea after all.

"Nay, not that you would care," Beatrice taunted. She kept her voice low and steered him back to the door. "But Lenora didn't sleep well last night, and the turmoil this morning has her worn out."

Fenton grunted as he lifted the last trunk. The man strained to place the large trunk on his shoulder.

"That one is to go to the lower storage room," Beatrice instructed. She gave Roen a haughty look, reminiscent of her mother. "The small room you have committed her to won't accommodate all her belongings." Fenton nodded, and the sweat on his brow stood out in large droplets. He hefted the trunk to a better location and took a hard breath. Goliath jumped up and down around the man's feet. The dog left, chasing the weary man's heels.

"I'll just check on my wife, then be on my way." Roen started for the bed.

"I do not think the sight of the man who brings her so much grief will soothe her troubled nerves." Beatrice intercepted him and clutched the sleeve of his shirt. "Your wife will succumb to the stresses around her if you do not give her time to regain her strength."

The impulse to push the woman aside tempted him, but Lenora and her condition must be the priority. Pregnancy endangered a woman's life, and he'd not risk upsetting Lenora now in her weakened state. "Very well, but this door stays open. After the midday meal I'll speak with her and she'll move to her new room." Roen stormed out of the room and yelled, "Crandall, send me word as soon as she stirs. I'll send up a replacement when my troops arrive."

"Lord Roen." The ewerer met him on the stairs.

"What?" How well he understood how Lenora must feel; his nerves were raw, also.

"The guests are waiting."

"See they are fed and given wine. I've much to attend to now." Roen brushed the disgruntled ewerer off. Probably another group of hungry pilgrims. "Let them sleep in the hall tonight, not upstairs."

"But, my lord, they have come to see you."

Roen gave the man his attention. "Do they have some message for me?"

"I do not know, Lord Roen. I believe they have just come to visit."

"Who are they?" He expected no one. If they weren't messengers, why did they need to see him? "See to it that a heavy guard is placed on them."

"'Tis done, milord. Five knights do not ride into this keep unwatched. We've three men to their one." His ewerer gave him a pinched look and sniffed. "Even if the man claims to be your cousin, we still know to watch our backs."

Sounds grew muffled, his ears rang. Roen's chest constricted and he fought to breathe. After years of ostracism, they ventured to reach out to him. Now that he owned a rich fief, the vultures intended to claim him as their own. Perhaps they thought to strip the lands from Lenora if he should die? He'd soon put them straight. They had not claimed him as a Galliard when a child, they'd not reap benefits from him as a man.

He leaned over the gallery and studied the five men below. The tallest, a fair-haired young man, had his back to him. A dark-complected older man with a sarcastic sneer across his lips brought back visions of Roen's father. Even the stranger's height, the shortest in the room, marked him as a Galliard.

The others were young but nondescript. Roen's stomach churned with indignation.

His steps dragged down the stairs. Confrontation was not what he wanted now. Not today, when more important matters needed his attention. Yet, a morbid curiosity compelled him to see what this man wanted. The child inside him still craved to belong.

"Let's be gone from here, Falke. This man is most rude to his guests," the black-haired one complained to his compatriots. Lifting his full goblet of wine, he drank it down. A maid rushed forward and filled it again.

"'Tis not so bad." The blond laughed and buried his face in the hair of a young servant girl. She giggled and whispered in the young man's ear. He responded by patting her backside with his hand.

Roen called to the dark man, "So, you claim me as your cousin. I see the blood of my father's people in your features."

The black-haired man nearly choked on his wine. Snickers rippled across the room. Raising his head from the wench's neck, the tall, fair-haired knight winked at Roen. "Nay, 'tis not Ozbern that lays that claim, 'tis I. Your mother and mine are sisters. And I see the blood of the Chevarases in your features."

Icicles crystallized in Roen's blood. His mother's people. In all the long years in Normandy, his parents had never spoken of his mother's family. Nor had any member ever visited or sent a letter that he knew of. "'Tis you who are wrong. My mother had dark hair and her eyes were not light."

"Aye, the only dark-haired girl in a sea of fair-haired children. Her father called her Evening Star. A beauty that cast a shadow over her blond sisters. What was it the minstrel said of her? 'An exotic flower that blossomed in the sunlight of her father's pride and love.'"

A sympathetic pout on his lips, the man continued, "Sadly, we have not inherited that beauty. 'Twould please my mother to know you look like the rest of us common Chevarases."

Roen's heart began to pound. He looked like his mother's people. Why hadn't she told him? Why had his father insisted he was a bastard? Surely he had met his mother's family at some time.

Roen eyed his cousin again. From the hair to the color of his eyes, the man looked enough like Roen to be his brother. But this man, years younger than himself, smiled readily and seemed to be enjoying a private jest.

"I am Falke de Chretien." His cousin made a courtly bow, his head swaggering with an irritating cockiness. He paused and looked at Roen with raised eyebrows. "One of the many younger sons of Bernard de Chretien." The man straightened and waited, an expectant smile on his face.

"My name and parentage you know, or you would not be here," Roen replied. He did not like the man's attitude, too *laissez faire.* "What is it you want?"

Falke's smile wavered, his chin came in just a little and his eyebrows furrowed together. "My uncle intends to name me his heir. I and my friends—" his hands pointed to his group "—are traveling north to his fief. I heard your name mentioned at our last abode and knew it immediately as that branch of our family from Normandy. I thought that since we are kin, you might offer us the hospitality of your fine home." The arrogant smile returned.

There was no time to entertain guests. Yet a yearning to have information about this mysterious side of his family gnawed at Roen's soul. He wanted answers and he would have them. Lenora slept upstairs guarded by Crandall. As soon as she woke, he'd move her to the secure chamber and have the stonemason wall up the secret door. Besides, before he investigated further, he needed his private guardsmen to return.

"Aye, you may stay," Roen relented.

Falke's men clapped each other on the back and returned to their drinking. Falke's gaze followed the swaying hips of a serving wench who went to fetch more wine.

The wench rounded the corner and his cousin's attention returned to Roen. "Perhaps a walk in the orchard would be pleasant. We could talk of family and such." He turned to the one called Ozbern who stood near his drinking comrades. "Stay here and watch those two. I don't want them so far into their cups they can't sit a horse tomorrow."

Ozbern snorted. "What does it matter? They can't sit a horse even when they're sober." Nevertheless, he pulled over a vacant chair, turned it around backward and straddled it. He rested his elbow on the back and propped his cheek against it.

A comfortable smile came to Falke's face. "The man gripes continually. A real bore at times." He laughed and waved for Roen to follow. "Come, let us take that walk."

His cousin's manner irked him more and more. The too quick smile, the casual ambience of the man rubbed him like salt in a wound. But he craved answers about his mother, answers this obnoxious man might be able to provide. The idea that this supposed cousin might also be involved in Lenora's danger also entered his mind. Roen decided to talk and listen. Listen for anything that might show the group of men were more than they seemed.

A crisp breeze swirled the fallen autumn leaves into whirlwinds along the path. Roen took a deep breath of the cleansing air. He walked along the cobblestones and waited for the other man to speak.

They reached a wooden bench and Falke stopped. He placed his foot on the bench seat and leaned his elbow on his knee. The young knight rubbed his chin, then asked with a trace of wonderment, "Your mother, Maeve, she never spoke of my father, did she?"

Roen chose his words carefully. "Why do you say that?"

"Because if she had, I doubt you would have opened your doors to me so readily."

"Your father treated my mother in a dishonorable way?"

The younger man gave him a small smile and shook his head. "Nay, my father is and has always acted with honor. His duties to his father, his lord and his king have priority in all matters.''

"As it should be with any knight," Roen countered.

"Perhaps." The crooked smile returned. He motioned for Roen to sit and warned, "Mind you, the story I tell does not paint your father in a favorable light, nor my father, for that matter."

Roen sat, his body tense. "Go on, and I will judge for myself." He prayed this cousin would at last reveal the truth of his parentage. Was Bernard de Chretien his father? Could Falke be his half brother?

"Very well." The knight sat with his knees akimbo and slapped his thighs. He leaned on the back of the bench and clasped his hands behind his head. "My father, Bernard, and your mother, Maeve, were betrothed to marry when both were but infants. The match, at first to seal two strong families together, soon turned into a union of love." Falke scratched his cheek. "My mother said her sister's beauty could overshadow the sun's light. Minstrels compared Maeve's skin to moonlight and her eyes to ebony. Her voice to that of bird song. Sir Chevaras doted on the dark-haired child and lavished her with attention. Through her union with the Chretiens, he hoped to forge great power and wealth." He waved his hand at Roen. "Of course, all this you already know as you have seen and lived with the woman."

Roen nodded, but his mind tried to relate the visions of the cold, pale woman he knew with the portrait his cousin painted. Perhaps, if he allowed his imagination to run, he could picture his mother as a maiden, but he could put no life into the shell. To him, his mother had always been a breathing ghost, her spirit lost and forgotten.

"When she reached the age of fourteen, the marriage ceremony was arranged. Hundreds came for the gala. They traveled from all over England to feast with such a powerful group of people. A message came from one of my father's vassals. The man was under siege and requested help. I suppose one of Stephen's robber barons decided that with so many men away, 'twould be a good time to attack. My father, ever bound by honor, left his beloved and went to assist his vassal."

"As he should. The woman could wait, not the promise of feudality." Roen did not care for the way the man ridiculed the importance of honor. Chivalry demanded nothing less from its knights.

"Of course." Falke dropped his hands from behind his head. His eyes narrowed, then he continued, "And so, Bernard left with a promise he would return shortly and marry his bride. At the festivities, Galliard became enamored with the bride's beauty. He followed her and tried in his own crude way to woo her. Maeve would have none of him and she laughed at his attempts at poetry and song. She humiliated him in front of the guests by mocking his ill-chosen phrases and uncouth lyrics."

His cousin paused again. Roen sensed that he hesitated to go on with the story. "Rest assured," Roen informed his guest, "that whatever you may say of my father, your berth is set for the night. I'll not throw you out for an insult to the man's character."

Falke's smile widened. "Very well, I'll continue. Galliard was so incensed by Maeve's public rebuff that he waited for the girl. Waited till he could find her alone." He paused and the smile disappeared from his face. "When he had her alone, he gagged and raped her."

Roen shot from his chair and gripped the hilt of his dagger. "By the saints, not even my father would be so base as to take a woman against her will on the day of her wedding!"

"I'm afraid 'tis so. Maeve was able to point out her rapist. Her father wanted to kill Galliard on the spot but Maeve's mother stayed his hand."

"Why?" Roen cried. "I'd torture the fiend until he begged to die, then I'd deny him even that mercy." The blood in Roen's veins screamed for revenge against the monster. Then the scream strangled itself on his own crime. Hadn't he done the same thing to Lenora? Hadn't he taken from her that which was hers to give?

For her own protection, his conscience answered, yet deep in his loins he feared he stood with his father. Lord Champlain's taunts on his wedding day came back. Roen had thought the insults referred to his parentage. Now he understood; Champlain had compared him with Galliard.

"Her mother feared Maeve might be with child from the rape. What would the family do with such a bastard? What if Bernard would not have her now that she was no longer unspoiled? A message was sent to Bernard on the battlefield. The explanation of the affair was brief. The families awaited his answer. If he did not want Maeve, another Chevaras daughter would fulfill the betrothal. After all, much negotiation and power were at stake."

"Your father rejected her." Roen supplied the ending.

"Nay, not exactly. Bernard thought over the proposal. What would honor dictate he do? Meanwhile, while he contemplated the most honorable decision, the Chevarases panicked. They took no answer as a rejection. Since Maeve had now become an embarrassment instead of a profitable commodity, they must get rid of her. In respectable fashion, of course."

Falke spread his hands wide. "And so a wedding took place, Galliard and Maeve's. I mean, after all, they did have the cleric and guests and all that food prepared. Your mother and father were married and sent on their way with the express wishes of everyone concerned that if either decided to once again visit England, they'd never live to touch its shores."

The puzzle pieces of Roen's life fell into place. No wonder his parents hated him. His fair coloring only haunted them both. He personified the family that had kept Galliard from important contacts in England and had abandoned his mother.

"And so," Falke continued, "my father returned and the next sister was offered, Niccolete, my mother. And, as ever honor-bound, he married her, though he cared nothing for her, scarcely knew her name. And as honor dictates, he sired her many children. Thus did I see the light of birth as the seventh son, born in the seventh month and on the seventh day." Falke stood and stretched out his arms and cracked his knuckles.

Roen felt the breath knocked out of him. The fog that surrounded his mother lifted and revealed the bareness of her life. Through him, his mother exacted retribution for the crime committed against her. And that heinous act must have been a raw wound on Galliard's soul. Far easier for his father to accuse Maeve of adultery than to see in his son the family he had wronged. The parallel between his own marriage and his parents became clear. He did not bear the scorn of a bastard, for

Galliard was truly his father. Crime for crime he matched the man. Brutality for brutality, he superseded his sire. Rape to win what he wanted, torment to punish the woman for his own crimes. Did he really believe Lenora carried another man's child?

Nay, 'twas but a pretext to keep a wedge between them because he feared his wife. Feared the way his heart sang when she smiled. Feared the deep feelings she awakened with her soft touch. Feared the power she had over him. He loved his wife without barriers, and no emotional wall would separate him from her again. Nor from their child. The reality of it caused him to smile. Falke's image blurred through the tears in Roen's eyes.

"I know what you say is true." Roen swallowed and took a deep breath. "Now, tell me, why are you here?"

His cousin lost his arrogant composure. "What do you mean? I just thought to visit a kinsman."

"Nay." Roen shook his head. "No man would enter a keep dragging such a history with him."

A crooked smile crossed Falke's lips. "A mutual friend sent me. As I said, at my last abode, 'twas suggested that I come. My host thought that perhaps with your time in battle and your lack of ties in England, you may not know the circumstances of your parents' marriage."

"And who is this friend we share?"

"King Henry. A man who does what he can for those he considers a friend." Falke spoke the words with pride.

Gratitude overwhelmed Roen. The king had offered Roen a wife in payment for years in battle. In reality, his liege had given him a priceless gift, a woman who could teach Roen to love.

"I must speak with my wife. 'Tis most urgent." Rising from the bench, Roen gave his cousin a grateful nod and turned back toward the castle.

"Pray, do not let me keep you." Falke started to walk into the garden then turned. "Do not think me rude, but after the story I just told, I would think you would have questions, or accusations at the least. What must you discuss with your wife that is so urgent?"

"A name." Roen's steps lengthened with each stride he took. "I have to choose a name for my child." The walk broke to a jog, then a run. He rushed up the stairs just as the midday meal horn sounded. Crandall remained on guard outside the open door of Roen's chamber.

Beatrice no longer hovered nearby, nor did Goliath jump at him in greeting. He approached the bed and sensed something amiss. Even before he stripped the blankets from the bed he knew what he would find. *"Nora!"* His bellow rang down the hall and ricocheted off the walls. A confusion of voices and bodies rushed into the room.

He stared at the empty bed and the pillows that impersonated his wife's form. Too late. He sank to his knees, unable to stop the flow of tears down his face and heedless of who saw them.

Chapter Twenty-Four

"Tell me where she's gone to!" Roen roared at Beatrice.

The woman sat on a stool in the middle of the great hall. Her lower lip trembled and her eyes rained tears but she refused to speak.

"You'll get no information from her by shouting," Hamlin chided. He knelt at her side and made his voice gentle. "The dog led us to her empty trunk downstairs, you must have helped her to steal away. Lenora's in grave danger, Beatrice, pray tell us where she's gone."

Her eyes narrowed and tears spiked her lashes, but her voice gained strength as she spoke. "Aye, there's danger and we know from whence it comes." She pointed a trembling finger at Roen. "From her husband. We found the true marriage contract and know of your deception."

Apprehension slashed through Roen's anger. "Who else did you tell?"

"A friend." Beatrice rose and faced her interrogators. "One who is helping Lenora to reach safety."

Roen fought the impulse to shake the name from her. His voice deceptively calm, he asked, "Who is this friend?" From a burlap bag on the floor, Roen pulled out the dark mantle with the serpent clasp. "Do you recognize this cloak? Does it belong to your *friend?*" Goliath leapt at it and sank teeth into the garment.

Beatrice drew back, her blue eyes wide. She placed one hand over her mouth. The look on her face answered Roen's question. This friend had tried to kill his wife; he would have his name.

"Whose is it?" Hamlin tried to coax the answer from the startled girl.

"Nay, why give you the name when you must already hold him captive? What have you done with him?" Beatrice demanded. "This is all a game. 'Tis you that expose Lenora to peril." She tried to rush past them to the door of the barbican.

Falke and his companions blocked the girl's exit. Beatrice fought to break free of the barricade of men.

"Tell him the name, Beatrice." A hollow voice issued the command from behind the wall of men.

The knights stood aside and Tom approached, supporting a slumped man with his arm around his waist. A collective gasp echoed in the hall when the weaker man lifted his head. Beatrice shrank back from the man's outstretched arm. Servants and noblemen alike looked at one another in fear. Several made the sign of the cross to ward off an evil spirit.

Roen swore under his breath, then repeated the curse out loud. Used. Both he and Lenora had been deceived. A bitter taste coated his mouth. The accusations flung at him, the tension between him and his wife, all a waste.

Ozbern rushed forward to relieve Tom of his burden. "The deception was mine," Sir Edmund admitted in a tired sigh. "I planned my demise to force out the knave who was trying to poison me. The person who tried to drive my daughter away. Tell him the name he seeks or Lenora's life is forfeit. I fear your friend is Woodshadow's traitor."

"Nay, Geoffrey would not do such a thing!" Beatrice wailed.

"Champlain. I should have known. Come. I know where they are." Roen rushed past the quaking girl. Falke and his men fell in step behind.

Roen passed his father-in-law and paused. Sir Edmund took a long, wheezing breath. "I did not think it in the boy to do such evil. I never suspected him."

"There is much you did not suspect. Did you suspect your death would be an easy trial for your daughter to bear? Do you know what pain she endured?"

The older man nodded. "I knew. And if you do not rescue her, that pain will have been for naught." His hand gripped Roen's forearm with surprising strength.

The man still possessed a fierce thread of vitality, a will to survive. If Roen found Lenora dead, would that slender thread break? Would he himself break? Roen returned the elder knight's handshake and roused the knights of the keep.

A call to arms sounded and the inner bailey surged with life. Horses and men filled the area below the barbican steps. Destrier paced back and forth, not winded from the morning ride. Goliath increased the bedlam by running in between the horses' and men's legs.

"Goliath, heel." Roen mounted his charger and spotted his second in command on a chestnut stallion. Goliath obeyed the command. At the zenith of its path across the sky, the sun issued a warning. Autumn days left little time for afternoon light. The canopy of the woods would shorten that light even more. He had wasted too much time with Beatrice.

Falke and his knights, mounted on their horses, formed the core of the troop. Roen extended his hand to his cousin. "My thanks for your aid."

"Lenora is my cousin, also, now that she has married into the family."

The doors of the inner and outer baileys creaked open and framed the road and woods beyond. Today a pall hung over the green. Death hovered over the treetops, grinning at Roen.

Destrier's hooves touched the hard dirt of the road. Roen squeezed his knees and the horse broke into a gallop. The thunder of hooves pounded behind him. He looked ahead to the dark gloom of the forest. Death would not go away empty-handed this day.

"Just a bit further, Lenora," Geoffrey called from around a curve on the trail.

Her side ached from running. Perspiration stung her eyes. She wiped her face with the end of her chemise. A ring of dust along the edge of the undergown marked every step she had taken from her home. Even with her familiarity with the forest, Geoffrey had managed to twist and turn down so many paths that she couldn't be sure of exactly where they were. The knowledge offered her some comfort. If she couldn't have found them, neither could Roen.

"Are you coming?" Geoffrey poked his head out from behind a birch tree at the bend in the trail.

"Aye." Lenora started off at a slow trot down the path. She couldn't see Geoffrey, but she sensed his motion. The sound of his footsteps and the scrape of branches snapping back in place told her he didn't outdistance her by much.

Around one more turn and she saw her friend cupping water with his hand from a clear brook. The dryness of her throat made her close the gap between them and drop next to him. Leaning on her side, she sank her hand deep into the cool water. Each sip gave her strength to continue. Her thirst slaked, she rolled over to sit on the stream's bank.

"I know you're tired, Lenora." Geoffrey gave her a weak smile. "But just a few steps more and then you'll have the proof you seek."

She smiled back. "Thank you, Geoffrey. You've been a true friend to me."

"I have tried." Geoffrey's voice cracked as he helped her rise from the brook. His hand felt cold and icy. A chill of disquiet rushed through her and she longed to stay at the stream. She hesitated before following.

"You cannot postpone the inevitable," he said, and moved into the brush.

No matter the heartache, the truth about her husband must be revealed. Lenora gathered what was left of her stamina and mirrored her rescuer's steps.

Geoffrey stood near a fallen tree and stared at his feet. Lenora looked down and her heart missed a beat. Broken bones littered the leaf-covered ground. A centipede crawled through the eye sockets of an animal skull. Geoffrey bent and picked it up.

"Geoffrey, put that disgusting thing down." Lenora backed away from him.

He looked up at her, his mouth turned down in a pout. His eyes chastised her. "Is that any way to greet an old friend?" He bent and began to rearrange the bones like a puzzle.

"Come, let's be gone from this place." She gritted her teeth and forced herself to sound unafraid.

"In a moment, but first, come closer and see what I've done." Geoffrey stood and waved his hand at his creation.

She took the smallest steps possible to approach the macabre object. Geoffrey had opened the skull to show the mouth wide in agony. Curved ribs were stuck in the moist, fertile soil to stand upright. A long tail wrapped around the body. He had filled in missing bones with small rocks.

"Doesn't it remind you of something?" Geoffrey's voice teased. His smile looked like that of a little boy who had been caught being naughty. He pushed her in front of him for a closer look.

The skeleton screamed at her in death. The long body cried out to her in silent recrimination. She looked away and then, in horror, looked back. Fleshed out, with dark black fur, the bones formed the shape of... "Gladymer." She choked out the beloved name.

"Aye, that's it." Geoffrey danced in a circle. He captured her hands with his and forced her to join in the jig.

She lost control of her anger and struggled to free herself. "Stop. Stop it. This is too cruel."

He froze, one knee bent in the air. The expression on his face melted from one of childlike joy to sorrow. "Nay, Lenora, do not call me cruel." He dropped her hands and a tear trickled down his cheek. The upraised leg lowered slowly, and his breathing became loud and heavy. "I thought you would welcome seeing your old and true friend once again. Through his death, you can trace the person responsible for all your grief."

Geoffrey's sympathetic demeanor confused her. How could he think to show her such a tragic sight, now, when they were running for their very lives? This could have no relevance to Roen's guilt or innocence. Or could it? She left Geoffrey and returned to the whitened bones of her dog.

Kneeling at the remains of her pet, she forced her fingers to probe through the moldy leaves and dirt. They closed on the hard, cold touch of steel. She tugged hard, and the rusty but still strong length of chain popped through the layers of composting debris and snapped in her hand when it reached the tree trunk.

"Geoffrey, look. Someone chained Gladymer out here. Do you know what this means?" She rose and faced her friend. The chain dropped from her hand and she rushed to embrace him. "Roen could not have done this. He was in Tintagel when Gladymer disappeared."

"Aye, that he was." With his hand at her elbow, he led her back toward the tree trunk. "Does it make you happy to know your husband is not guilty of the crime you suspected?"

"A heavy weight has lifted from my shoulders," Lenora said. "Yet, still I do not understand his actions. You say that whoever is responsible for Gladymer's death is the cause of my troubles. But 'tis Roen who tricked my father and lied to me."

Geoffrey rested his hands on her shoulders. "I think perhaps he was trying to protect you." His hands trailed down her arms and encircled her wrists. "I wish he had been more successful." Sobs caught in his throat as he twisted her arms behind her back. Startled, Lenora tried to bolt, but Geoffrey yanked her arms upward. Pain lanced up her arms and shoulders, stopping her flight. Holding her wrists with one hand, Geoffrey grabbed the heavy chain and wrapped the links around her wrists. Tears fell freely down his handsome face as he spoke. "I was always gentle with you. I never wanted to kill you. I begged you to leave. You know that!" She felt hard leather and chain bite into her flesh. The snap of a lock clarified her danger. He helped her to the ground. Her arms tingled at her shoulders from the tension he exerted on her leash. He yanked the chain. A desperate need for her agreement flashed across his face. "You know that, right?"

"Aye." Terror raced through her. Geoffrey's eyes burned with a strange inner light. She struggled to her knees.

A flash of irritation quirked Geoffrey's lips. "Why didn't you leave when you had the chance?" He shook his head to chastise her.

Lenora forced herself to think and remain calm. She coached her voice to a soothing tone. "Then let me go, Geoffrey. I'll do as you say. I'll return to Aquitaine if that's what you want."

A sad smile creased his lips, and once again he was her old friend Geoffrey. With gentle hands, he caressed her cheek. "You could have been my salvation, my refuge from my father's torments, from Daphne's shame." Accusation hardened his voice. "But you fell in love with him instead of me."

She pulled away, startled at his confession.

With his hand, he recaptured her chin. "Aye, 'tis true. I loved every quip and insult you flung at my father. Your words stirred me to such passion." His lips lowered, and Lenora twisted to avoid them. Like a vise, his hand forced her to meet them. He lifted his mouth from hers, and she spat the taste of him from her mouth.

"But, there is the problem. You're too strong for me." He released her and sat against the trunk of a tree. "You only saw me as a friend, not as a mate. Which meant I had to settle for Beatrice and get rid of you. But I didn't want to hurt you." He sighed with frustration. "I worked so hard, Lenora, to think of ways to drive you away." His tone implied an insult at her inconsideration. "First your dog, then your horse. And of course, I killed your father. And it was all to protect you."

"Nay, Geoffrey, my father died of illness and his own pride."

He crowed with glee. "Nay, dear friend, 'twas me." The mad gleam in his eye flared. "I found the secret passage to his room and poisoned him. And I was so clever about it. Just a little at a time. That was his illness." He snapped his fingers together.

"Why did you do this?" Her fingers tried to work the leather band around her wrists. Anger and fear spread through her body. Murder meant nothing to this man. Insanity had purged the compassionate soul of her friend.

"For Woodshadow, of course. 'Tis my home. A haven from the blows of my father." He looked at her so innocently she found it hard to believe he had caused her so much pain. "You think you know the level of his depravity, but you do not."

"You would always be welcomed at Woodshadow."

He jumped to his feet. She stopped the frantic movement of her fingers and held her breath.

"Welcomed." He pounded his chest with his fist. "I don't want to be welcomed. I need to be in control." His fist dropped and so did the volume of his voice. "I need a place where I am safe and so is Daphne. Father can't touch her at Woodshadow. And he touches her, touches her where a father should never place his hand." Geoffrey's eye twitched and he massaged his temple. His eyes grew misty.

Lenora's heart ached at the pain reflected there. Poor, wretched Geoffrey, his father's evil had driven him mad. "'Tis all right, my friend." She tried to reach a kernel of the boy she had grown up with. "Bring Daphne to Woodshadow and she'll be protected. Roen and I will protect you both."

"Roen and you?" Geoffrey snorted in disgust. "He'd be the same as Father. He'd touch her, too, just like he did Beatrice." He wiped the palms of his hands on his tunic. They left sweaty prints on the worn material.

"Woodshadow has to be mine. 'Tis the only way Daphne and I can truly escape Father. Beatrice's request for aid explained the true contract. Since Beatrice believes Roen is a deceiver 'twill be easy enough to convince her to marry me. Then I will be Lord of Woodshadow." Standing rigid, he jutted his chin out in a defiant manner. Then his stance softened and he gave her an apologetic look. "But to be lord now, I have to kill you. And your child. 'Tis the only way." His hands reached out and closed around her neck.

"Fan out." Roen swept through the clearing, beating the tall grass with his broadsword. They must be here! Where else would she meet him? He listened for a call, some signal from one of the men that his wife had been found. None came.

Goliath bounded through the long blades of grass. He chased at Roen's heels then raced away. The dog brought him a stick and laid it at his feet.

"Not now, Dog." Roen pushed him away. Goliath ran off, then brought him a bigger stick.

Hamlin called from across the clearing. "No luck. They're not here."

Roen raked his fingers through his hair. "Where? Where would the coward go to do his fiendish deeds?" Goliath barked and picked up the stick again. His tail wagged back and forth. Heaven, he could do without the beast's commotion. He needed to think. To think like Geoffrey. Goliath's barks increased in volume and pitch.

"Heavens, that's it!" Roen resheathed his sword and raced toward Hamlin and Destrier. "The dog, Hamlin! Remember the dog? He must have her there." Roen leaped onto Destrier's back. His spurs dug into the stallion's withers.

The white charger's front legs climbed into the air. Roen felt the thud when all four feet hit the ground. Air whistled in his ears. He gave the horse free rein to pick the way through the woodlands. With gentle pressure, he guided the direction. How many times had his mount's excellent training saved him in battle? This battle could be won or lost in a hoofbeat.

The stream flowed between the banks of soft, wet grass. An idyllic picture to mask the treachery nearby. He pulled the charger to a halt and dropped the reins. The stallion was winded, Destrier's belly rose and fell in deep breaths. Three hard runs in less than a day; the horse could give no more.

Roen pulled his broadsword from the scabbard and melted into the brush. Gladymer's bones should be just ahead. Darkness began to overtake the afternoon light. The shadows of the trees grew fat and blended into one another. He kept to the darkness and circled closer to the area where the bones lay.

With the tip of his sword, he parted the brambles of a berry bush. Thorns scratched his face and stuck to his leather jerkin. The log lay to the left of his vision. Out of the corner of his eye, he saw movement. Red gold color flashed across the top. His Nora lived.

Every nerve burned to hold his wife, to hear her voice. He took a step forward. Stopped. Watched. Listened. The crown of Lenora's head thrashed back and forth. Only the sad song of a bird broke the silence. Had Champlain staked her out like the dog, to die of exposure and starvation?

From shadow to shadow he scrambled nearer. Close enough to hear his wife's muffled cries and her attempts to break the bonds holding her. He slid from the darkness. No challenge rang from the oppressive gloom around him.

Drawing near to Lenora's shaking form, he saw that half of her face lay in the compost of the woods' floor. Staked to the ground like a Druid sacrifice, she tried to sit up but the short chain prevented her.

"Nora." He tried to warn her of his approach. Her head swiveled around. Dark gold eyes darted from side to side. The agitated sounds from the gag amplified. She kicked out her legs wildly. Kneeling to remove her gag, he noticed her eyes focus behind him.

The explosion of his battle instincts warned him of motion. Roen leaned over Lenora's body and a flash of steel cut the air. Pain ripped through his sword arm and across his hand. His weapon fell from his grip. Warm blood ran down his arm and dripped on his wife's face. His fighting arm swung uselessly at his side. Geoffrey kicked the long blade out of his reach. With his good arm, Roen pushed himself off the ground. He must maneuver the fight away from Lenora. He retreated and Geoffrey lunged.

A deep chuckle came from the man's lips, then his voice changed to a youthful chant. "Galliard's goin' to die. Galliard's goin' to die." At each stanza, Geoffrey's eye twitched and he slashed his blade at Roen's chest.

The truth hit him hard. Insanity lit his foe's eyes with a demoniac gleam. The eerie contrast between the satanic features and childish voice sent a shiver up Roen's spine. To be vanquished now would mean death not only for himself but also for Lenora. He reached for his belt and retrieved his own dagger.

"I heard you coming," Geoffrey taunted. His eye twitched and distorted his features. "I was going to kill her right away, but I decided to wait. To use her as bait." The rhyme caused him to laugh. "Ah, Lenora always did enjoy my prose." He turned to look at the woman twisting on the ground.

Roen utilized his opponent's distraction. He swept his dagger in an arc and aimed at Geoffrey's torso. The blade bounced off the thick leather belt around his waist. Like a mad bull, Roen charged and wrapped his arm around Geoffrey's waist.

Geoffrey's fist slammed into Roen's wound. Pain burned inside his damaged arm. It sucked the air from his lungs. Geoffrey scrambled to his feet, his laughter turned victorious.

"What a predicament you find yourself in." The insane man advanced on Roen with slow, deliberate steps. "You can't run or I'll kill your wife. But if you stay, you'll die and I'll kill her anyway."

"Nay!" Roen's roar silenced the birds and insects. He rushed to tackle the killer.

Geoffrey scrambled to Lenora and seized a mass of her hair. He pulled hard on the leash and she arched her neck upward. Roen stumbled back, his mind searching for a rescue plan.

His blade high in the air, Geoffrey let a crazed smile touch his lips. "'Tis time to die."

A blur of dark gray hurtled itself from behind the log that served as Lenora's stake. Goliath's growl matched Roen's.

Sharp fangs clamped down on the wrist that dared to threaten the lady.

Roen used the chance to smash his clenched fist into Geoffrey's face. Blood spurted from the sadist's nose. The hard contact of Roen's hand against teeth and bone caused him to rejoice. He brought his fist down again and again. Vengeance possessed him.

The man's cries for mercy drove him to extinguish all life from the vile creature. His enemy's body folded to the ground. Still, Roen kept the steady beat of his fist on the blood-covered face.

Lenora! The fire of concern merged with and overtook the heat of revenge. Geoffrey's moans showed life maintained its hold on the beaten body. Roen dropped the mangled face and, summoning a reserve of inner fortitude, dragged himself to Lenora. Goliath curled up next to her and whined. Her blue lips shivered and her body trembled. Sinking to the ground, Roen wrapped his body around her cold, shaking form and willed his warmth to flow into her.

Darkness blanketed them. The night sounds began their concert, accompanied by Geoffrey's rasping breaths and the dog's sorrowful howl. A distant pounding echoed in his ears. The ground seemed to shake from his own shivering.

"I love you." Roen used the last of his strength to whisper the words to his unconscious wife. His eyes closed and sound ceased.

Chapter Twenty-Five

A shiver ran to the very marrow of her bones. Lenora tried to wrap herself in the comforting warmth around her but streamers of pain shot through her arms. Her upper back felt tight and her muscles protested any movement on her part.

"Lenora? Are you awake?"

A woman's voice from far away called her name. Weariness held her captive. She struggled to open her eyes. Sunlight pierced through the window and caused multicolored specks to jump across her vision.

The mattress sank on one side as someone sat on the bed and took her hand. A man's voice rumbled in the background. Panic erased the weariness. Geoffrey! Tortured memories drowned out her pain. Lenora pulled her hand free and began to fight. Fear for her child made her strong.

"'Tis me, Cousin. Beatrice."

The soft tone wove around Lenora's panic. Gentle hands stopped her wildly thrusting fists. A cool, damp cloth wiped the fever from her brow. Consciousness returned with agonizing slowness, and she opened her eyes.

Beatrice sat on the edge of the bed. Dark circles rimmed her red eyes. "Lenora? Are you really awake? Do you know me?"

"Aye. I know you, dear cousin." The words came out raspy and dry.

Retrieving a mug, Beatrice held it to Lenora's lips. "You've been asleep for two days. I feared you would never awaken."

Hot, rose-flavored tea quenched her thirst and loosened her throat. She sipped again and inhaled the aromatic vapor. Her mind cleared and she looked around her. The sight filled her with joy. Her fingers dug into the familiar soft coverings of her bed. Roen's musky scent lingered on the linen sheets and pillows.

Her last memory was of blood. The look of it, the smell of it, the taste of it. Blood had drenched her face from Roen's arm. She remembered him weak from the loss of it and Geoffrey's blade against her neck. Lenora struggled to rise. "Roen? What did Geoffrey do to him?"

"He lives. 'Twas his voice that set you off just now. I ordered him from the room." Beatrice tried to keep her cousin lying down. It proved a futile attempt.

Lenora pushed herself up into a sitting position. Her arms and shoulders campaigned against it. "He lives," she repeated under her breath. Just two words, but they lifted the yoke of dread from around her heart.

Tears streaked her cousin's face. She hugged Lenora as she choked out her words. "I'm so sorry, Lenora. This is all my fault. All along 'twas Geoffrey causing you so much heartache. Can you forgive me?"

"Nay, Cousin. 'Twas not your fault at all. Geoffrey's soul was mangled." Lenora's tears joined with Beatrice's. "The corruption of Sir Champlain drove his son to a darkness no light could pierce."

The thought of that darkness reminded her of Roen. Geoffrey had been too weak to withstand day after day of ridicule from his father. Her husband had survived similar circumstances. He possessed no sense of family or tender feelings, yet that absence had probably saved him from Geoffrey's fate.

"What happened to Geoffrey?"

Wiping her face with her hands, Beatrice released her cousin. Her voice shook with anguish and sorrow. "Dead. He cannot hurt you ever again."

"Blessed saints, did Roen kill him?" Lenora vaguely remembered the fight.

"Nay." Beatrice took a deep breath. "Geoffrey still lived when Hamlin and Roen's kinsman arrived. Roen had lost a great deal of blood and 'twas plain to see you needed immediate attention. It took Falke and two of his men to lift Roen to horseback. In their haste to see to you, Geoffrey managed to crawl away. Your husband had left his charger in the bushes.

Geoffrey tried to mount the beast and..." She pressed her hand against her mouth, her jaw quivering.

"Say no more. I know Destrier's temperament. Geoffrey was never much of a horseman." Lenora could picture the results.

"The animal trampled him to death. His body was returned to his father in a bag. Falke went with Roen's men to speak with Sir Champlain and the old man just shrugged his shoulders when they explained what happened. He didn't even care his own son was dead." Beatrice's body shook with anger.

"At last Geoffrey has peace. I pray God judges his soul with compassion." Lenora felt real sorrow at her friend's death.

Beatrice stood and began to fiddle with the cloth on the table. Her eyes darted from the door to Lenora.

"What more is there?" she questioned. Her voice sounded so tired to her ears.

"I'm afraid to tell you. You're still not strong yet."

"Only some bruises that will heal in time. I swear I can bear no more secrets. Tell me what more I should know."

Her cousin wrung her hands in the folds of her apron. "God preserve me, let this be the right thing to do." She looked to the heavens. "You'll know soon enough. Lenora, your father lives. He planned this whole deception to ferret out the one who was trying to kill him."

Lenora's heart skipped a beat. Her ears rang. A deep, cutting hurt opened in her heart. Her father would not do such a thing. "It cannot be true."

"Aye, but it is." Beatrice rushed on. "Sir Edmund devised the plan with Tom's help. Everything was a ruse, his death, the marriage contract, your wedding."

"My marriage?" The wound widened and deepened.

"Roen was sent by King Henry to investigate your father's suspicions. Sir Edmund convinced Roen the only way to protect you was to marry you."

Lenora couldn't speak, couldn't move. Poor Roen. Saddled with a wife he didn't want or need. The insults she had hurled at him stung her conscience. He endured her temper and sharp tongue all for his king. Now the danger had ceased, but Roen still must bear the harness of his marriage. With her father alive, he could not even be called the lord of the keep. He must hate her family. He must hate her.

Only one solution came to mind. Lenora swung her legs over the edge of the bed and tried to tame the dizziness in her head. She had to get this over with now, before she lost heart. Lost heart? Her heart no longer existed; it had been broken into tiny pieces.

"Lenora, you can't mean to get up. You're not well enough yet!"

"Stay your hand." Her voice came out curt and rough. Her cousin faltered and drew away. Lenora stood on shaky legs and pointed to an overtunic lying on the chest. Inside, she felt washed out and terribly alone. "Help me dress. I will go downstairs and set matters straight." Beatrice bit her lip and nodded, then hurried to comply.

The dress fell down over her chemise, and Lenora added under her breath, "I will see my father and free my husband."

His arm rested in the cradle of a linen sling. Roen poked at the fire in the hearth with an iron. Ashes flew up and were carried on the draft. He wanted to sit alone in his grief and self-pity. All had obeyed the request except for one.

"What are you going to do?" Sir Edmund questioned him from the dais of the high table.

Roen ignored him.

"Damn it, man, speak to me. I'm your father-in-law."

He threw down the iron and shouted back, "Aye, and a penance it is. What could you have been thinking of to marry your daughter to me?"

"Of her." Sir Edmund lifted a tankard to his lips and repeated, "Of her. I wanted her safe, and marriage to you would keep her that way."

"It very nearly didn't. Do you know how close she came to dying out there?" Roen strode across the floor and faced the elder lord.

"I know well enough. I've thought of nothing else since they brought the two of you in."

Pent-up anger exploded. Roen kicked at a bench near the table and sent it crashing to the floor. The poison had weakened Edmund but that didn't give him the right to trick his daughter into marriage. Her father had joined Lenora to a man whose voice sent her into hysterics.

What would she do when she learned the truth about her father? What would she do when she learned the truth about her husband? She had been coerced into marriage and the church might honor a plea for annulment. With Edmund's support, Lenora could leave him and he would never see her or his child again.

"My seed grows within her. Do you hear me, old man? Mine!" Roen thundered.

Edmund took a long swig of ale and refilled his cup. "And why should that concern me?" He poured a second tankard full and handed it to his son-in-law.

Roen took the drink and swallowed the contents. The liquid burned his throat. "Because it makes her mine."

"Really?" His father-in-law took a sip of ale and arched his brow. "And what if Lenora does not wish to be yours? I will support her in whatever decision she makes."

A feminine voice broke through the male standoff. "Father, you look well for a dead man."

Lenora stood with her hand resting on the carved wooden knob at the end of the stairs. Her hair cascaded like a waterfall of autumn color around the paleness of her face. Dark circles under her eyes showed the formidable strain of the last few days. Her eyes, dimmed with fatigue, met Roen's. In their depths, the fire of her courage and determination burned. He realized that his wife stood before him only because of her grit and strength.

"Daughter, 'tis good to see you up. There's much to explain."

"Beatrice has already told me everything I need to know." With slow, deliberate steps, she tore her gaze from her father's and crossed the room.

Roen took a stride toward her but she waved her hand to stop him. He had seen the dark ugly bruises on her arms and across her back. Pain would be with her for a long time yet.

Sir Edmund said nothing but rose from his chair and offered it to his daughter. She seated herself and looked down at her father from the dais. "I pray that someday I will be able to understand your actions."

"I was concerned for you. I needed to protect you."

"But at what cost?" She turned her face to Roen. Her sienna eyes glistened with despair.

Roen found he had everything to say and no voice to speak it.

"Sir Galliard, I wish to thank you for all your help." Lenora addressed him as if he were a guest. He didn't like the sound of it.

"Lenora, you shouldn't be down here. I order you to return to your room." He wanted to sweep her up in his arms and carry her upstairs, away from her father. A stabbing pain in his injured arm brought a curse to his lips.

"I will stay." Lenora arched a golden brow and his father-in-law did the same. A trickle of uneasiness threaded through his self-assurance.

"Daughter, do not tax yourself so soon." Sir Edmund looked as uncomfortable as Roen felt. "You will cause yourself to be ill again."

"Then I will ride out on Jupiter and find the miraculous cure you did. If you could come back from the dead, surely my small weakness will be easily mended." She spoke sweetly, but the words stung. Her father retreated from the dais. Both men looked at her in silence.

"King Henry should be proud he has such loyal men to serve him." Lenora's knuckles turned white on the arms of the chair. Her red lips stood out against the paleness of her skin.

The older lord spread his hands out, palms raised. "I suspected a traitor, but I wasn't sure. I didn't want to worry you needlessly. And then when I did find out, well, things moved too quickly."

She cut him off before he could go on. "I understand perfectly. For all your talk about how proud you are of me, you still didn't trust me enough to tell me the truth. Instead, you plotted behind my back. Forced me to marry someone I didn't choose. Why? Why didn't you just tell me your suspicions?"

"And what would you have done?" Roen blurted out. "Gone to your friends? Gone to Champlain for help? You would have fallen right into his hands."

She brushed back the loose curls around her face several times, her eyes downcast. When she lifted them again, Roen saw commitment in their depths. Commitment to what he did not know.

"Sir Galliard, I apologize for the way my father tricked you into marriage." She took a deep breath, then continued. "And I am sorry for the terrible insults I inflicted on you. I realize now that you suffered through all this out of loyalty to King Henry."

"Lenora, stop this." Who was this cold, collected woman seated across from him? He wanted his Nora, fighting and spitting mad at him. A sharp word or barb from her lips would be considered a cherished endearment.

"Please allow me to finish." Her eyes glistened with tears. "The church allows annullment on the grounds of coercion. My father will talk to the cleric and set the process in motion. Compensation for you and your men will be arranged. I am sure you would like to put this mistake behind you."

Sir Edmund nodded his approval of her statement. Roen roared back, "Mistake? You call our marriage a mistake?"

Her lower lip trembled just a little as she spoke. "Aye. I think mutual freedom is the right choice. And again, I will see you get a proper payment for your work."

"Nay. You are my wife." Roen bellowed across the hall. Servants came running at the noise. The elder lord dismissed them. They withdrew, but Roen knew they were within earshot.

He wished she'd stop trying to make him out to be nothing more than a hired mercenary. Money, lands, what did all that mean without his Nora at his side? The only wealth he ever truly possessed sat across from him. He needed to convince her of that, but how?

"I will have no annullment." Roen strode up the dais and looked down at his wife. His fist rested on his hip and he made his stance erect and formidable.

"Roen." She spoke his name with impatience and frustration. "The marriage contract you showed me is invalid. You won't get Woodshadow if I die."

"Do you think that matters to me? You carry my child, that makes you mine," Roen shouted. "Let Rupert inherit it all."

Her eyebrows wrinkled, as did her father's. Both asked simultaneously, "Who is Rupert?"

Roen threw up his hand at their denseness. "Our son, of course."

"Rupert? You want to name our son Rupert?" Lenora slumped back in the chair and looked up at him with her mouth open.

His face flushed with warmth and he played with the collar of his tunic. "Aye. I had an instructor by that name when I fostered out. He was a good man. 'Tis a strong name."

She closed her mouth and sat up straight in the chair. Her eyes brightened, like a fire on a cold winter day. When she rose, a soft gold light burned deep within them. Her finger poked him in the chest. "Roen de Galliard, are you refusing to free me?"

"By the saints, you are daft!" Roen yelled back. "That's what I've been trying to tell you."

"Why?" Lenora demanded. "A few days ago you accused me of adultery. Why don't you want your freedom? Why now do you claim this child? Do you say these words so that Father may relent and renegotiate our marriage prenuptial? If I lose my babe, will you still lay the claim that I am yours?"

Sir Edmund raised his eyebrows and asked, "Aye, I'd like to know the same myself."

"I'd like to know, too." Hamlin gave him a big grin and nodded toward Beatrice. "She wants to know, too."

Roen stood surrounded by expectant faces. Only one consumed his vision. Her mouth parted and she licked her lips. He wanted to reach out and taste the sweetness and fire they offered. The want warmed to a longing, then flamed to hot desire.

"I realize that our marriage was arranged under somewhat unusual circumstances, but still I think that, all in all, 'tis been an acceptable situation...."

Her mouth screwed up into a disappointed pucker. Her head wagged back and forth. She didn't believe him. Hamlin crossed his arms and shook his head.

A trickle of sweat worked its way down his shoulder blades. No breeze eased the stifling heat of the hall. Lenora began to turn from him. He caught her around the waist with his free hand.

She lifted her head. A curl fell over one amber eye. He released her to comb it back from her face. The palm of his hand cradled her cheek. The rest of the room faded away and he lost himself in the beauty of her features. He didn't feel the stares of the others; only she mattered.

"I'm sorry, Nora. I'm sorry I didn't trust you and believe in you. I'm sorry that I deceived you. Sorry I was afraid of being a father like my own."

A serene smile graced her lips and her stance relaxed. Roen heard his heart crashing through the armor surrounding it. He could not deny his true desires any longer. "But, God forgive me, I'm not sorry we're married. Whatever happens with the child, I can't let you go. I won't let you go."

His lips sealed against hers tenderly. He caressed her mouth with his own, rediscovering its sweet nectar. The tip of her tongue flicked across his lower lip. His body flared with need.

Her arms wound around his neck and he felt her breath against his ear. He buried his head in the gentle crook of her neck and felt tears come to his eyes. A burst of incredible joy overcame him. In this woman's arms, he felt secure and content.

The sounds of people milling about brought him back to reality. He wanted to be alone with his wife. Lifting his head, Roen pulled her toward the stairs. She dug in her heels.

"Nora?" Why was she hesitating? What more did she want?

"Say it." With soft pressure she pulled her hands from his. "You've said you're sorry, now say the rest. I'm not moving from this spot until you do."

The heat returned to Roen's face, though passion did not inspire it. "Lenora . . ." He stretched out her name in controlled frustration.

She tilted her chin, hugged her elbows and began to tap her foot. "You know, you're in sad need of a bath, Galliard." Then she winked!

The heat in his body ignited. Erotic memories of their last steamy bath erased all his trepidation.

"I love you. Don't count on hearing it again. Now stop this foolishness and come to . . ." He couldn't finish because she jumped up and wrapped her arms around his neck. She covered his face in kisses.

"About damn time." Sir Edmund's hand slapped him on the back. A cheer came from Hamlin and the troops. Falke and his group tipped their goblets to him and drained them. When had the room filled with people? Roen realized he didn't care, as long as his wife's soft and loving body nestled in the crook of his arm.

"I've loved you since that day in the loft," Lenora said in a soft voice.

"Then why the hell didn't you tell me? 'Twould have saved a lot of trouble on all our parts." Roen wrapped his favorite curl around his finger.

"Because you were being such an insufferable, uncouth barbarian." She pretended to snap at his hand.

Roen opened his mouth to argue but caressed the nape of her neck instead. "What a little deceiver you are."

Lenora rested her head against his chest. "Me? 'Twas I who was deceived."

He kissed the top of her hair, and the smell of wildflowers scented the air. The silky strands tickled his nose. "Nay, of us all, you are the one who created the greatest deception." She tilted her head and wrinkled her brows together. "'Twas you who tricked this hardened warrior. You pulled the armor from my heart and made me believe in love. I pray this veil of love will never be lifted."

On tiptoe she reached up and pressed her lips to his own. Her voice quivered with emotion when she spoke. "I intend, warrior, to keep you deep within its folds."

Loud cheers and goblets rose in the air to toast Roen and the future. But the words were unnecessary. All of his deepest wishes existed in the beauty and love of the woman he called his wife. He thanked his Creator for the precious gift bestowed on him and vowed that he would never again be part of a deception against his Nora.

Except, perhaps, when it came to Nine Man Morris—the prize was just too good to give up.

Epilogue

Lenora moved her stone to the next square and captured one of Roen's black markers. Her foot moved under the table to her husband's leg. Slipping off her shoe, she walked her toes up the inside of her opponent's calf. She got the desired response. His eyes left the board and gazed into hers. A coy shake of her head, a slow wetting of her lips, and Roen's concentration no longer resided with the game. He made a wrong move. The win would be hers.

"'Tis not fair, wife." Roen shooed her foot from his thigh. She kicked off her other shoe and started the whole process over again.

Hamlin slapped his knee. "So, she wins again."

Beatrice, seated in a chair nearby, called to her husband. "Hamlin, quit teasing the poor man." She rested her hands on her swollen stomach. "Do you think you could reach that pillow for me?"

He jumped to place the pillow behind her back, then rested his hand on his wife's womb. A proud smile came to his face. "I feel Rupert jumping around in there. I know 'twill be a son."

"That's what Roen said, too," Lenora warned.

"More, Grandda. Play more." She turned to see her father on the floor with his two-year-old granddaughter. Maeve's black curls bounced up and down while she squirmed to escape her grandfather's tickling fingers. Goliath stood guard to ensure the roughhousing did not go too far.

"Child, let your grandfather rest," Lenora admonished with a gentle voice. "Father, you should not tax your heart so much playing with her."

"I'm fine." Her father reached for a cup on the table, finished off his drink and smacked his lips. "This tea Alyse has brewed for me from her foxglove plants has eased the pain in my chest considerably."

"Still, I think 'tis enough for tonight. Come, Maeve, 'tis time for bed."

The child's wide blue eyes twinkled with mischief. She turned to run away from her mother's outstretched hand. The rushes parted, her foot lost traction and she fell to the floor. The wail that erupted from her little mouth deafened the entire room.

"Maeve!" Roen called from his seat. "Stop that racket!"

Her father's voice silenced Maeve to a loud sob.

"Come here and let me see." Roen backed his chair from the table and held out his arms. His daughter pulled herself up and hurtled into his protective embrace.

"Show me where it hurts." Roen looked at the tiny hands Maeve displayed to him. He gave Lenora a wink above the tiny ebony-haired girl.

"Here, Papa." She bent her arm back and presented him with her elbow.

Roen examined the joint and brushed it with gentle fingers. Lenora peered over from her seat. Aside from a slight redness, the delicate baby skin showed no injury.

"Hurt." Their daughter looked from one parent to the next for a remedy for her nonexistent ailment.

"I can see that," Roen agreed. "What do you think we should do, Mother?"

He knows his daughter so well, Lenora thought. Playing along, she pursed her lips and looked again. "Well, if 'tis as bad as she made it out, I think Maeve may need to stay in bed for the next few days." Lenora covered her mouth with her hand to hide the grin on her lips.

Her husband nodded his head. "Aye. I agree. 'Tis a shame, too. Spring has finally arrived and I thought to take her out on that new pony tomorrow."

Maeve's eyes turned from joy to disappointment. "You fix me, Papa." She pushed her elbow under her father's nose. "Kiss. Make it all better."

A loving smile slanted across his lips. Roen tapped his finger on her arm. "I think that might work. Should I kiss it right here?"

Her chubby finger moved his just a shade to the left. "Here."

Roen bent and made a loud smack with his lips. Maeve broke into delighted giggles. "All better, Papa." She threw her arms around her father's neck and gave him a big kiss in his ear.

He patted her backside and whisked her to the floor. "Now, off to bed with you, and no dallying." Quick hugs and slobbery kisses for her mother and father were all the stalling the child could accomplish.

Turning her daughter over to the capable hands of the nurse, Lenora promised, "I'll be in to check on you later." The dark head already drooped against the shoulder of her nanny.

Lenora watched them climb the stairs to the nursery above. In a few months, Beatrice's child would add another bed. And by late fall, her second child would join the group.

"Rupert is the name I've chosen. I picked it two years ago. Hamlin, you can't use it," Roen argued.

"But you didn't use it." Hamlin's eyes twinkled but he kept his face stern.

The man loved to tease her too serious husband. For seven months now he had threatened to name his child Rupert just to antagonize Roen.

"Well, you didn't expect me to name a girl Rupert, did you?" Roen countered. "Lenora's expecting another baby in the fall. That one may be a son. We can't have two Ruperts running around. 'Twould be too confusing."

"I've always thought Edmund was a fine name," her father interjected.

Roen's eyes rolled upward, his usual response to his father-in-law. "Aye, so you've told me. Time and time and time again."

"Edward. Edwina. Edmund." Sir Edmund sat near the hearth and ruffled Goliath's ears. "Aye. All fine names for a boy or a girl."

Lenora decided that her husband had endured enough ribbing for one night. She rose and took his hand. "'Tis late, husband. Let us retire for the night."

"But, Lenora, this issue with the name."

"Will wait, Roen. Come, I want to claim my prize for winning." With no more argument, he bade his friends good-night and followed her to their chamber.

She heard the door of the room close and his order to her ladies to leave. The light touch of his fingers lifted her heavy braid. With practiced movements, he removed the strip of lace that held her tresses. His fingers traveled the length of her hair and fanned it out across her shoulders. His touch sent quivers of arousal down her neck. Gooseflesh prickled her skin where his breath touched it.

The tie of her laces came undone and her tunic fell in a heap on the floor. Spring air swirled about her chemise-clad body. A breeze, scented with rain and new green plants, flittered across the room. Roen's lips nibbled at her mouth. The strength of his hands enveloped her.

He broke from the kiss and lifted her from the floor. She embraced his neck and tilted her head to get a better look at him. Years slipped from his face when this gentle smile played across his lips.

She sighed when he headed for the balcony. For some reason, he enjoyed holding her in his lap for hours on their terrace. One more way that he had changed since their declaration of love. He still made her angry, she still lost her temper, but always love softened the words.

Roen settled on a pallet of furs he had placed on the balcony. The soothing circle of his arms, the caress of his fingers through her hair made her whole being glow with happiness and contentment. Faint beams of moonlight glided down from the star-filled night. Her lips brushed against his like the caress of the breeze. "Husband, I don't know why you like this spot so much, but I'm glad you do. 'Tis a place I feel very cherished in."

Roen's lips against her ear sent delicious sensations pouring through her blood. "Aye, wife. This place is special indeed. For 'tis here that first I realized how much I truly treasured you."

The circle of his arms loosened and she turned toward him. Flames of love deepened his eyes to teal. His hand dipped into the opening of her chemise to cup her breast. His lips touched the hollow of her neck like a whisper. Passion flared like the spring, new and exciting time and time again. A moan of pleasure drifted from her lips. The chemise fell from her shoulders. He slid his hand under her and lifted her from his lap. Her covering floated free. Her naked skin tingled from the air and contact with his hard body.

He eased her down onto the furs. With reverence, his fingers traced the features of her face. "'Twas here I held you and prayed you had not died. 'Twas here I thought my heart might break if you did not open your eyes." The words came out choked and strained.

"Hush, love." Lenora kissed the corners of his mouth. "That time is over now. Well put behind us." She guided his hand to her still-flat abdomen. "Soon another sign of our love will be visible to all."

His fingers rested on her stomach, sending flashes of arousal through her. He bent down and kissed her navel, then trailed his tongue lower. Her body arched of its own accord, eager for the pleasure it would soon receive.

"Roen." His name became a caress on her lips. He moved lower still, his fingers exploring her body.

Through eyes drugged with desire, she saw her husband shed his clothes. The length of his naked body covered her. The crisp curls of his chest tickled the aroused peaks of her breasts.

"Nora," he whispered over and over again, his mouth suckling one breast, then the other.

"We should go inside." She made a halfhearted protest.

His tongue danced across the stiffened nipples. She gasped with pleasure and relished the tremors of ecstasy that streamed through her body. An ache for fulfillment pulsated and grew.

"Someone might see . . ." The feel of his fingers at the opening of her womanhood consumed her thoughts. Flames of passion burned within her like a bonfire. Each touch, every caress fed that fire, a fire she wanted to burn forever yet craved to have reach its climax.

"What were you saying?" Roen's low chuckle made her smile.

"I was saying, I don't think making love on the balcony is at all proper." She ran her fingers along his side like a sprite in flight. Her action caused his body to arc.

"Then, wife, you will surely enjoy it." His voice sounded deep and husky with desire.

And she knew he was right. She would. This time and the next and the next. Her warrior deceived her no longer. Love with its infinite magic had wiped away the years of neglect and torment. For love was the ultimate deceiver, making a man believe he did not seek it, when all along it was the only thing he ever really wanted.

"Love me, Roen," she commanded.

"I already do." Then he proceeded to show her.

* * * * *

Coming in April from

By award-winning author

MARGARET MOORE

"A story brimming with vibrant
color and three-dimensional characters...
emotion and power on every page."
—*Romantic Times*

Available wherever Harlequin books are sold.

BIGB96-2

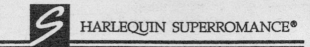

BRIDE'S BAY RESORT

UNLOCK THE DOOR TO GREAT ROMANCE
AT BRIDE'S BAY RESORT

Join Harlequin's new across-the-lines series, set in an exclusive hotel on an island off the coast of South Carolina.

Seven of your favorite authors will bring you exciting stories about fascinating heroes and heroines discovering love at Bride's Bay Resort.

Look for these fabulous stories coming to a store near you beginning in January 1996.

Harlequin American Romance #613 in January
Matchmaking Baby by Cathy Gillen Thacker

Harlequin Presents #1794 in February
Indiscretions by Robyn Donald

Harlequin Intrigue #362 in March
Love and Lies by Dawn Stewardson

Harlequin Romance #3404 in April
Make Believe Engagement by Day Leclaire

Harlequin Temptation #588 in May
Stranger in the Night by Roseanne Williams

Harlequin Superromance #695 in June
Married to a Stranger by Connie Bennett

Harlequin Historicals #324 in July
Dulcie's Gift by Ruth Langan

Visit Bride's Bay Resort each month wherever Harlequin books are sold.

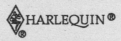

HARLEQUIN ®

BBAYG

Fall in love all over again with

This Time... MARRIAGE

In this collection of original short stories, three brides get a unique chance for a return engagement!

- Being kidnapped from your bridal shower by a one-time love can really put a crimp in your wedding plans! *The Borrowed Bride*— by **Susan Wiggs**, *Romantic Times* Career Achievement Award-winning author.

- After fifteen years a couple reunites for the sake of their child—this time will it end in marriage? *The Forgotten Bride*—by **Janice Kaiser.**

- It's tough to make a good divorce stick—especially when you're thrown together with your ex in a magazine wedding shoot! *The Bygone Bride*— by **Muriel Jensen.**

Don't miss THIS TIME...MARRIAGE, available in April wherever Harlequin books are sold.

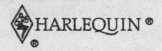

HARLEQUIN ®

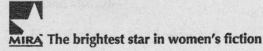

Yo amo novelas con corazón!

Starting this March, Harlequin opens up to a whole new world of readers with two new romance lines in SPANISH!

Harlequin Deseo
- passionate, sensual and exciting stories

Harlequin Bianca
- romances that are fun, fresh and very contemporary

With four titles a month, each line will offer the same wonderfully romantic stories that you've come to love—now available in Spanish.

Look for them at selected retail outlets.

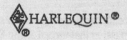